Andersen's Fairy Tales

The Little Mermaid (Sweden, 6 years old)
(STORY PAGE 65)

Fairy Tales

of Hans Christian Andersen

With 25 illustrations in full color
by children of eighteen nations.

The Orion Press / New York
Distributed by Crown Publishers, Inc.

Contents

Andersen's Fairy Tales

Page

List of Illustrations

Note: *Twenty-two of these illustrations have been selected from among entries to a contest sponsored by the International Union for Child Welfare and its affiliate, the Red Barnet of Denmark. Children from forty-eight nations participated in this contest which was held in Copenhagen. Three additional illustrations are the work of three Italian children, students of Federico Moroni of the elementary school of Bornaccino.*

The Tinder Box

A soldier came marching along the highroad. One, two! One, two! He had his knapsack on his back and his sword at his side, for he had been to the wars and now he was on his way home. He met an old witch on the road. She was so ugly that her lower lip hung right down onto her chin.

She said, "Good evening, soldier! What a nice sword you've got, and such a big knapsack. You are a real soldier! You shall have as much money as ever you like."

"Thank you kindly, you old witch," said the soldier.

"Do you see that big tree?" said the witch, pointing to a tree close by. "It is hollow inside. Climb up to the top and you will see a hole into which you can let yourself down, right down under the tree. I will tie a rope round your waist so that I can haul you up again when you call."

"What am I to do down under the tree?" asked the soldier.

"Fetch money," said the witch. "You must know that when you get down to the bottom of the tree you will find yourself in a wide passage. It's quite light there, for there are over a hundred blazing lamps. You will see three doors which you can open, for the keys are there. If you go into the first room you will see a big box in the middle of the floor. A dog is sitting on the top of it and he has eyes as big as saucers, but you needn't mind that. I will give you my blue-checked apron, which you can spread out on the floor. Go quickly forward, take up the dog, and put him on my apron. Then open the box and take out as much money. as you like. It is all copper, but if you like silver better, go into the next room. There you will find a dog with eyes as big as millstones. But never mind that. Put him on my apron and take the money. If you prefer gold you can have it too, and as much as you can carry, if you go into the third room. But the dog sitting on that box has eyes each as big as the Round Tower. He *is* a dog, indeed, as you may imagine. But don't let it trouble you. You only have to put him on my apron. Then he won't hurt you, and you can take as much gold out of the box as you like! "

" That's not so bad," said the soldier. " But what am I to give you, old witch? You'll want something, I'll be bound."

" No," said the witch. " Not a single penny do I want. I only want you to bring me an old tinder box that my grandmother forgot the last time she was down there."

" Well, tie the rope round my waist," said the soldier.

" Here it is," said the witch. " And here is my blue-checked apron."

Then the soldier climbed up the tree, let himself slide down the hollow trunk, and found himself, as the witch had said, in the wide passage where the many hundred lamps were burning.

Now he opened the first door. Ugh! There sat the dog with eyes as big as saucers staring at him.

" You are a nice fellow! " said the soldier, as he put him onto the witch's apron and took out as many pennies as he could cram into his pockets. Then he shut the box, put the dog on the top of it again, and went into the next room. Hallo! There sat the dog with eyes as big as millstones.

" You shouldn't stare at me so hard. You might get a pain in your eyes! " Then he put the dog on the apron, but when he saw all the silver in the box he threw away all the coppers and stuffed his pockets and his knapsack with silver. Then he went into the third room. Oh, how horrible! That dog really had two eyes as big as the Round Tower, and they rolled around and around like wheels.

"Good evening," said the soldier, saluting, for he had never seen such a dog in his life. But after looking at him for a bit he thought, "That will do." And then he lifted him down onto the apron and opened the chest. Heavens! What a lot of gold! He could buy the whole of Copenhagen with it, and all the sugar pigs from the cake-woman, all the tin soldiers, whips, and rocking horses in the world. That was money indeed! Now the soldier threw away all the silver he had filled his pockets and his knapsack with and put gold in its place. Yes, he crammed all his pockets, his knapsack, his cap, and his boots so full that he could hardly walk. Now, he really had got a lot of money. He put the dog back onto the box, shut the door, and shouted up through the tree, "Haul me up, you old witch!"

"Have you got the tinder box?"

"Oh, to be sure!" said the soldier. "I had quite forgotten it." And he went back to fetch it. The witch hauled him up, and there he was standing on the highroad again with his pockets, boots, knapsack, and cap full of gold.

"What do you want the tinder box for?" asked the soldier.

"That's no business of yours," said the witch. "You've got the money. Give me the tinder box!"

"Rubbish!" said the soldier. "Tell me directly what you want with it or I will draw my sword and cut off your head."

"I won't!" said the witch.

Then the soldier cut off her head. There she lay! But he tied all the money up in her apron, slung it on his back like a pack, put the tinder box in his pocket, and marched off to the town.

It was a beautiful town. He went straight to the finest hotel and ordered the grandest rooms and all the food he liked best, because he was a rich man now that he had so much money.

Certainly the servant who had to clean his boots thought they were funny old things for such a rich gentleman, but he had not had time yet to buy any new ones. The next day he bought new boots and fine clothes. The soldier now became a fine gentleman, and the people told him all about the grand things in the town, and about their king, and what a lovely princess his daughter was.

"Where is she to be seen?" asked the soldier.

"You can't see her at all," they all said. "She lives in a great copper castle surrounded with walls and towers. Nobody but the King dares to go in and out, for it has been prophesied that she will marry a common soldier, and the King doesn't like that!"

"I should like to see her well enough," thought the soldier. But there was no way of getting leave for that.

He now led a very merry life. He went to theatres, drove about in the King's Park, and gave away a lot of money to poor people, which was very nice of him. He remembered how disagreeable it used to be not to have a penny in his pocket. Now he was rich, wore fine clothes, and had a great many friends who all said what a nice fellow he was— a thorough gentleman—and he liked to be told that.

But as he went on spending money every day and his store was never renewed, he at last found himself with only two pence left. Then he was obliged to move out of his fine rooms. He had to take a tiny little attic up under the roof, clean his own boots, and mend them himself with a darning needle. None of his friends went to see him because there were far too many stairs.

One dark evening when he had not even enough money to buy a candle with, he suddenly remembered that there was a little bit in the old tinder box he had brought out of the hollow tree, when the witch helped him down. He got out the tinder box with the candle end in it and struck fire. But as the sparks flew out from the flint, the door burst open and the dog with eyes as big as saucers, which he had seen down under the tree, stood before him and said, "What does my lord command?"

"By heaven!" said the soldier, "this is a nice kind of tinder box, if I can get whatever I want like this. Get me some money," he said to the dog, and away it went.

It was back in a twinkling with a bag full of pennies in its mouth.

Now the soldier saw what a treasure he had in the tinder box. If he struck once, the dog which sat on the box of copper came. If he struck twice, the dog on the silver box came. And if he struck three times, the one from the box of gold.

He now moved down to the grand rooms and got his fine clothes again, and then all his friends knew him once more and liked him as much as ever.

Then he suddenly began to think, "After all, it's a curious thing that no man can get a sight of the Princess. Everyone says she is so beautiful! But what is the good of that when she always has to be shut up in that big copper palace with all the towers. Can I not somehow manage to see her? Where is my tinder box?" Then he struck the flint and, whisk! came the dog with eyes as big as saucers.

"It certainly is the middle of the night," said the soldier, "but I am very anxious to see the Princess, if only for a single moment."

The dog was out of the door in an instant, and before the soldier had time to think about it, he was back again with the Princess. There she was, fast asleep on the dog's back, and she was so lovely that anybody could see that she must be a real princess. The soldier could not help it, but he was obliged to kiss her, for he was a true soldier.

Then the dog ran back again with the Princess, but in the

morning, when the King and Queen were having breakfast,
the Princess said that she had such a wonderful dream about
a dog and a soldier. She had ridden on the dog's back and the
soldier had kissed her.

"That's a pretty tale," said the Queen.

After this an old lady-in-waiting had to sit by her bed at
night to see if this was really a dream, or what it could be.

The soldier longed so intensely to see the Princess again
that at night the dog came to fetch her. He took her up
and ran off with her as fast as he could, but the old lady-in-
waiting put on her galoshes and ran just as fast behind them.
When she saw that they disappeared into a large house, she
thought, "Now I know where it is," and made a big cross
with chalk on the gate. Then she went home and lay down,
and presently the dog came back with the Princess. When
he saw that there was a cross on the gate, he took a bit
of chalk, too, and made crosses on all the gates in the town.
Now this was very clever of him, for the lady-in-waiting
could not possibly find the gate when there were crosses on
all the gates.

Early next morning the King, the Queen, the lady-in-
waiting, and all the court officials went to see where the
Princess had been.

"There it is," said the King, when he saw the first door
with the cross on it.

"No, my dear husband, it is there," said the Queen, who
saw another door with a cross on it.

"But there is one! And there is another!" they all cried
out.

They soon saw that it was hopeless to try to find it.

Now the Queen was a very clever woman. She knew more
than how to drive in a chariot. She took her big gold scissors
and cut up a large piece of silk into small pieces, and
made a pretty little bag which she filled with fine grains of
buckwheat. She then tied it onto the back of the Princess.

And when that was done she cut a little hole in the bag, so that the grains could drop out all the way wherever the Princess went.

At night the dog came again, took the Princess on his back, and ran off with her to the soldier, who was so fond of her that he longed to be a prince, so that he might have her for his wife.

The dog never noticed how the grain dropped out all along the road from the palace to the soldier's window, where he ran up the wall with the Princess.

In the morning the King and the Queen easily saw where their daughter had been, and they seized the soldier and threw him into the dungeons.

There he lay. Oh, how dark and tiresome it was! And then one day they said to him, "Tomorrow you are to be hanged." It was not amusing to be told that, especially as he had left his tinder box behind him at the hotel.

In the morning he could see through the bars in the little window that the people were hurrying out of the town to see him hanged. He heard the drums and saw the soldiers marching along. All the world was going. Among them was a shoemaker's boy in his leather apron and slippers. He was in such a hurry that he lost one of his slippers, and it fell close under the soldier's window where he was peeping out through the bars.

"I say, you boy! Don't be in such a hurry," said the soldier to him. "Nothing will happen till I get there. But if you will run to the house where I used to live and fetch me my tinder box, you shall have a penny. You must put your best foot foremost."

The boy was only too glad to have the penny and tore off to get the tinder box. He gave it to the soldier and—yes, now we shall hear.

Outside the town a high scaffold had been raised, and the soldiers were drawn up round about it as well as crowds of the townspeople. The King and the Queen sat upon a beautiful throne exactly opposite the judge and all the councilors.

The soldier mounted the ladder, but when they were about to put the rope round his neck, he said that before undergoing his punishment a criminal was always allowed the gratification of a harmless wish, and he wanted very much to smoke a pipe as it would be his last in this world.

The King would not deny him this, so the soldier took out his tinder box and struck fire, once, twice, three times. And there were all the dogs—the one with eyes like saucers, the one with eyes like millstones, and the one whose eyes were as big as the Round Tower.

" Help me! Save me from being hanged," cried the soldier.

And then the dogs rushed at the soldiers and the councilors. They took one by the legs and another by the nose and threw them up many fathoms into the air, and when they fell down they were broken all to pieces.

" I won't! " cried the King, but the biggest dog took both him and the Queen and threw them after all the others. Then the soldiers became alarmed, and the people shouted, " Oh, good soldier, you shall be our King and marry the beautiful Princess! "

Then they conducted the soldier to the King's chariot, and all three dogs danced along in front of him and shouted " Hurrah! " The boys all put their fingers in their mouths and whistled, and the soldiers presented arms. The Princess came out of the copper palace and became Queen, which pleased her very much. The wedding took place in a week, and the dogs all had seats at the table, where they sat staring with all their eyes.

The Princess on the Pea

There was once a Prince who wanted to marry a Princess; but she was to be a *real* princess. So he traveled about, all through the world, to find a real one, but everywhere there was something in the way. There were princesses enough, but whether they were *real* princesses he could not quite make out: there was always something that did not seem quite right. So he came home again, and was quite sad: for he wished so much to have a real princess.

One evening a terrible storm came on. It lightened and thundered, the rain streamed down; it was quite fearful! Then there was a knocking at the town gate, and the old King went out to open it.

It was a Princess who stood outside the gate. But, mercy! how she looked, from the rain and the rough weather! The water ran down from her hair and her clothes; it ran in at the points of her shoes, and out at the heels; and yet she declared that she was a real princess.

"Yes, we will soon find that out," thought the old Queen. But she said nothing, only went into the bedchamber, took all the bedding off, and put a pea on the flooring of the bedstead; then she took twenty mattresses and laid them upon the pea, and then twenty eider-down beds upon the mattresses. On this the Princess had to lie all night. In the morning she was asked how she slept.

" O, miserably! " said the Princess. " I scarcely closed my eyes all night long. Goodness knows what was in my bed. I lay upon something hard, so that I am black and blue all over. It is quite dreadful! "

Now they saw that she was a real princess, for through the twenty mattresses and the twenty eider-down beds she had felt the pea. No one but a real princess could be so delicate.

So the Prince took her for his wife, for now he knew that he had a true princess; and the pea was put in the museum, and it is there now, unless somebody has carried it off.

Look you, this is a true story.

The Traveling Companion

Poor John was very sad; for his father was very ill, and just dying. There was no one but the two in the little room, and the lamp had nearly burned out; for it was late in the night.

"You have been a good son, John," said the sick father, "and God will help you on in the world." He looked at him, as he spoke, with mild, earnest eyes, drew a deep sigh, and died; yet it appeared as if he still slept.

John wept bitterly. He had no one in the wide world now; neither father, mother, brother, nor sister. Poor John! he knelt down by the bed, kissed his dead father's hand, and wept many, many bitter tears; but at last his eyes closed, and he fell asleep with his head resting against the hard bedpost.

Then he dreamed a strange dream: he thought he saw the sun shining upon him, and his father alive and well, and even heard him laughing as he used to do when he was very happy. A beautiful girl, with a golden crown on her head, and long, shining hair, gave him her hand; and his father said, "See what a bride you have won. She is the loveliest maiden on the whole earth." Then he awoke, and all the beautiful things vanished before his eyes, his father lay dead on the bed, and he was all alone. Poor John!

The week after, the dead man was buried. John walked

behind the coffin which contained his father, whom he so
dearly loved, and would never again see. He heard the earth
fall on the coffin-lid, and watched it till only a corner
remained in sight, and at last also disappeared. He felt as
if his heart would break with its weight of sorrow, till those
who stood round the grave sang a psalm, and the sweet, holy
tones brought tears into his eyes, which relieved him. The
sun shone brightly down on the green trees, as if it would
say, "You must not be so sorrowful, John. Do you see the
beautiful blue sky above you? Your father is up there, and
he prays to the loving Father of all, that you may do well
in the future."

"I will always be good," said John, "and then I shall
go to be with my father in heaven. What joy it will be when
we see each other again! How much I shall have to relate
to him, and how many things he will be able to explain to
me of the delights of heaven, and teach me as he once did
on earth. Oh, what joy it will be! "

John pictured it all so plainly to himself, that he smiled
even while the tears ran down his cheeks.

The little birds in the chestnut trees twittered, "Tweet,
tweet"; they were so happy, although they had seen the
funeral; but they seemed as if they knew that the dead man
was now in heaven, and that he had wings much larger and
more beautiful than their own; that he was happy now,
because he had been good here on earth, and they were glad
of it. John saw them fly away out of the green trees into the
wide world, and he longed to fly with them; but first he
cut out a large wooden cross, to place on his father's grave;
and when he brought it there in the evening, he found the
grave decked out with gravel and flowers. Strangers had
done this—they who had known the good old father who
was now dead, and who had loved him very much.

Early the next morning, John packed up his little bundle
of clothes, and placed all his money, which consisted of

fifty dollars and a few shillings, in his girdle; with this he determined to try his fortune in the world. But first he went into the church yard; and, by his father's grave, he said " Our Father "; and then added: " Farewell, dear father; I will always be a true and good man, and do thou ask the good God to make me good."

And as he passed through the fields, all the flowers looked fresh and beautiful in the warm sunshine, and nodded in the wind, as if they wished to say, " Welcome to the green wood; here all is fresh and bright."

Then John turned to have one more look at the old church, in which he had been christened in his infancy, and where his father had taken him every Sunday to hear the service and join in singing the psalms. As he looked at the old tower, he espied the ringer standing at one of the narrow openings, with his little pointed red cap on his head, and shading his eyes from the sun with his bent arm. John nodded farewell to him; and the little ringer waved his red cap, laid his hand on his heart, and kissed his hand to him a great many times, to show that he felt kindly towards him, and wished him a prosperous journey.

John continued his journey, and thought of all the wonderful things he should see in the large, beautiful world, till he found himself farther away from home than ever he had been before. He did not even know the names of the places he passed through, and could scarcely understand the language of the people he met, for he was far away in a strange land. The first night he slept on a haystack, out in the fields, for there was no other bed for him; but it seemed to him so nice and comfortable that even a king need not wish for a better. The field, the brook, the haystack, with the blue sky above, formed a beautiful bedroom. The green grass, with the little red and white flowers, was the carpet; the elder bushes and the hedges of wild roses looked like garlands on the walls; and for a bath he could have the

clear, fresh water of the brook; while the rushes bowed their
heads to him, to wish him good morning and good evening.
The moon, like a large lamp, hung high up in the blue ceiling,
and he had no fear of its setting fire to his curtains. John
slept here quite safely all night; and when he awoke, the
sun was up, and all the little birds were singing round him,
" Good morning! good morning! Are you not up yet? "

It was Sunday, and the bells were ringing for church.
As the people went in, John followed them; he heard God's
word, joined in singing the psalms, and listened to the
preacher. It seemed to him just as if he were in his own
church, where he had been christened, and had sung the
psalms with his father. Out in the churchyard were several
graves, and on some of them the grass had grown very high.
John thought of his father's grave, which he knew at last
would look like these, as he was not there to weed and
attend to it. Then he set to work, pulled up the high grass,
raised the wooden crosses which had fallen down, and
replaced the wreaths which had been blown away from their
places by the wind, thinking all the time, " Perhaps some
one is doing the same for my father's grave, as I am not
there to do it."

Outside the churchyard door stood an old beggar, leaning
on his crutch. John gave him his silver shillings, and then
he continued his journey, feeling lighter and happier than
ever. Towards evening, the weather became very stormy,
and he hastened on as quickly as he could, to get shelter:
but it was quite dark by the time he reached a little lonely
church which stood on a hill. " I will go in here," he said,
" and sit down in a corner; for I am quite tired, and want
rest."

So he went in, and seated himself; then he folded his hands,
and offered up his evening prayer, and was soon fast asleep
and dreaming, while the thunder rolled and the lightning
flashed without. When he awoke, it was still night; but the

The Princess on the Pea (Uruguay, 8 years old)
(STORY PAGE 11)

storm had ceased, and the moon shone in upon him through the windows. Then he saw an open coffin standing in the center of the church, which contained a dead man, waiting for burial. John was not at all timid; he had a good conscience, and he knew also that the dead can never injure anyone. It is living, wicked men who do harm to others. Two such wicked persons stood now by the dead man, who had been brought to the church to be buried. Their evil intentions were to throw the poor dead body outside the church door, and not leave him to rest in his coffin.

"Why do you do this?" asked John, when he saw what they were going to do; "it is very wicked. Leave him to rest in peace, in Christ's name."

"Bosh!" replied the two dreadful men. "He has cheated us; he owed us money which he could not pay, and now he is dead we shall not get a penny; so we mean to have our revenge, and let him lie like a dog outside the church door."

"I have only fifty dollars," said John; "it is all I own in the world, but I will give it to you if you will promise me faithfully to leave the dead man in peace. I shall be able to get on without the money; I have strong and healthy limbs, and God will always help me."

"Why, of course," said the horrid men, "if you will pay his debt we will both promise not to touch him. You may depend upon that"; and then they took the money he offered them, laughed at him for his good nature, and went their way.

Then he laid the dead body back in the coffin, folded the hands, and took leave of it; and went away contentedly through the great forest. All around him he could see the prettiest little elves dancing in the moonlight, which shone through the trees. They were not disturbed by his appearance, for they knew he was good and harmless among men. They are wicked people only who can never obtain a glimpse of fairies. Some of them were not taller than the breadth of a finger, and they wore golden combs in their long yellow hair. They were rocking themselves two together on the large dewdrops with which the leaves and the high grass were sprinkled. Sometimes the dewdrops would roll away, and then they fell down between the stems of the long grass, and caused a great deal of laughing and noise among the other little people. It was quite charming to watch them at play. Then they sang songs, and John remembered that he had learned those pretty songs when he was a little boy. Large speckled spiders, with silver crowns on their heads, were employed to spin suspension bridges and palaces from one hedge to another, and when the tiny drops fell upon them, they glittered in the moonlight like shining glass. This continued till sunrise. Then the little elves crept into the flower buds, and the wind seized the bridges and palaces, and fluttered them in the air like cobwebs.

As John left the wood, a strong man's voice called after him, " Hallo, comrade, where are you traveling? "

" Into the wide world," he replied; " I am only a poor lad; I have neither father nor mother, but God will help me."

" I am going into the wide world also," replied the Stranger; " shall we keep each other company? "

" With all my heart," said he; and so they went on together. Soon they began to like each other very much, for they were both good; but John found out that the Stranger was much more clever than himself. He had traveled all over the world, and could describe almost everything. The sun was high in the heavens when they seated themselves under a large tree to eat their breakfast, and at the same moment an old woman came toward them.

She was very old and almost bent double. She leaned upon a stick and carried on her back a bundle of firewood, which she had collected in the forest; her apron was tied round it, and John saw three great stems of fern and some willow twigs peeping out. Just as she came close up to them, her foot slipped and she fell to the ground screaming loudly: poor old woman, she had broken her leg! John proposed directly that they should carry the old woman home to her cottage; but the Stranger opened his knapsack and took out a box, in which he said he had a salve that would quickly make her leg well and strong again, so that she would be able to walk home herself, as if her leg had never been broken. And all that he would ask in return was the three fern stems which she carried in her apron.

"That is rather too high a price," said the old woman nodding her head quite strangely. She did not seem at all inclined to part with the fern stems. However, it was not very agreeable to lie there with a broken leg, so she gave them to him; and such was the power of the ointment, that no sooner had he rubbed her leg with it than the old mother rose up and walked even better than she had done before. But then this wonderful ointment could not be bought at an apothecary's.

"What can you want with those three fern rods?" asked John of his fellow-traveler.

"O they will make capital brooms," said he; "and I like them because I am a whimsical fellow." Then they walked on together for a long distance.

"How dark the sky is becoming," said John; "and look at those thick, heavy clouds."

"Those are not clouds," replied his fellow-traveler; "they are mountains—large lofty mountains—on the tops of which we should be above the clouds, in the pure, free air. Believe me, it is delightful to ascend so high; tomorrow we shall be there." But the mountains were not so near as they appeared; they had to travel a whole day before they reached them, and pass through black forests and piles of rock as large as a town. The journey had been so fatiguing that John and his fellow-traveler stopped to rest at a roadside inn, so that

they might gain strength for their journey on the morrow.
In the large public room of the inn a great many persons
were assembled to see a comedy performed by dolls. The
showman had just erected his little theatre, and the people
were sitting round the room to witness the performance.
Right in front, in the very best place, sat a stout butcher,
with a great bulldog by his side who seemed very much
inclined to bite. He sat staring with all his eyes, and so
indeed did every one else in the room. And then the play
began. It was a pretty piece, with a king and queen in it,
who sat on a beautiful throne, and had gold crowns on their
heads. The trains to their dresses were very long, according
to the fashion; while the prettiest of wooden dolls, with
glass eyes and large moustaches, stood at the doors, and
opened and shut them, that the fresh air might come into
the room. It was a very pleasant play, not at all mournful;
but just as the Queen stood up and walked across the stage,
the great bulldog, who should have been held back by his
master, made a spring forward, and caught the Queen in
his teeth by the slender waist, so that it snapped in two.
This was a very dreadful disaster. The poor man, who was
exhibiting the dolls, was much annoyed, and quite sad about
his Queen; she was the prettiest doll he had, and the bulldog
had broken her head and shoulders off. But after all the
people were gone away, the stranger, who came with John,
said that he could soon set her to rights. And then he brought
out his box and rubbed the doll with some of the salve
with which he had cured the old woman when she broke
her leg. As soon as this was done the doll's back became
quite right again; her head and shoulders were fixed on,
and she could even move her limbs herself: there was now
no occasion to pull the wires, for the doll acted just like a
living creature, excepting that she could not speak. The man
to whom the show belonged was quite delighted at having

a doll who could dance by herself without being pulled by the wires; none of the other dolls could do this.

During the night, when all the people at the inn were gone to bed, some one was heard to sigh so deeply and painfully, and the sighing continued for so long a time, that every one got up to see what could be the matter. The Showman went at once to his little theatre and found that it proceeded from the dolls, who all lay on the floor sighing piteously, and staring with their glass eyes; they all wanted to be rubbed with the ointment, so that, like the Queen, they might be able to move by themselves. The Queen threw herself on her kness, took off her beautiful crown, and, holding it in her hand, cried, "Take this from me, but do rub my husband and his courtiers."

The poor man who owned the theatre could scarcely refrain from weeping; he was so sorry that he could not help them. Then he immediately spoke to John's comrade, and promised him all the money he might receive at the next evening's performance, if he would only rub the ointment on four or five of his dolls. But the fellow-traveler said he did not require anything in return, excepting the sword which the Showman wore by his side. As soon as he received the sword he anointed six of the dolls with the ointment, and they were able immediately to dance so gracefully that all the living girls in the room could not help joining in the dance. The coachman danced with the cook, and the waiters with the chambermaids, and all the strangers joined; even the tongs and the fire shovel made an attempt, but they fell down after the first jump. So, after all, it was a very merry night. The next morning John and his companion left the inn to continue their journey through the great pine forests and over the high mountains. They arrived at last at such a great height that towns and villages lay beneath them, and the church steeples looked like little specks between the green trees. They could see for miles around, far away to places they had never visited, and John saw more of the beautiful world than he had ever known before. The sun shone brightly in the blue firmament above, and through the clear mountain air came the sound of the huntsman's horn, and the soft, sweet notes brought tears into his eyes, and he could not help exclaiming, "How good and loving God is to give us all this beauty and loveliness in the world to make us happy! "

His fellow-traveler stood by with folded hands, gazing on the dark woods and the towns bathed in the warm sunshine. At this moment there sounded over their heads sweet music. They looked up, and discovered a large white swan hovering in the air, and singing as never a bird sang before. But the song soon became weaker and weaker, the bird's head drooped, and he sunk slowly down, and lay dead at their feet.

"It is a beautiful bird," said the traveler, "and these large white wings are worth a great deal of money. I will take them with me. You see now that a sword will be very useful."

So he cut off the wings of the dead swan with one blow, and carried them away with him.

They now continued their journey over the mountains for many miles, till they at length reached a large city, containing hundreds of towers, that shone in the sunshine like silver. In the midst of the city stood a splendid marble palace, roofed with pure red gold, in which dwelt the King. John and his companion would not go into the town immediately; so they stopped at an inn outside the town, to change their clothes; for they wished to appear respectable as they walked through the streets. The landlord told them that the King was a very good man, who never injured any one; but as to his daughter, "Heaven defend us! "

She was indeed a wicked Princess. She possessed beauty enough—nobody could be more elegant or prettier than she was; but what of that? for she was a wicked witch; and in consequence of her conduct many noble young princes had lost their lives. Any one was at liberty to make her an offer; were he a prince or a beggar, it mattered not to her. She would ask him to guess three things which she had just thought of, and if he succeeded, he was to marry her, and be king over all the land when her father died; but if he could not guess these three things, then she ordered him to be hanged or to have his head cut off. The old King, her father, was very much grieved at her conduct, but he could not prevent her from being so wicked, because he once said he would have nothing more to do with her lovers; she might do as she pleased. Each prince who came and tried the three guesses, so that he might marry the Princess, had been unable to find them out, and had been hanged or beheaded. They had all been warned in time, and might have left her alone, if they would. The old King became at last so distressed at all these dreadful circumstances, that for a whole day every year he and his soldiers knelt and prayed that the Princess might become good; but she continued as wicked as ever. The old women who drank brandy would color it quite black before they drank it, to show how they mourned; and what more could they do?

"What a horrible princess!" said John; "she ought to be well flogged. If I were the old King, I would have her punished in some way."

Just then they heard the people outside shouting, "Hurrah!" and, looking out, they saw the Princess passing by; and she was really so beautiful that everybody forgot her wickedness, and shouted, "Hurrah!" Twelve lovely maidens in white silk dresses, holding golden tulips in their hands, rode by her side on coal-black horses. The Princess herself had a snow-white steed, decked with diamonds and rubies. Her dress was of cloth of gold, and the whip she held in her hand looked like a sunbeam. The golden crown on her head glittered like the stars of heaven, and her mantle was formed of thousands of butterflies' wings sewn together. Yet she herself was more beautiful than all.

When John saw her, his face became as red as a drop of blood, and he could scarcely utter a word. The Princess looked exactly like the beautiful lady with the golden crown, of whom he had dreamed on the night his father died. She appeared to him so lovely that he could not help loving her.

" It could not be true," he thought, " that she was really a wicked witch, who ordered people to be hanged or beheaded, if they could not guess her thoughts. Every one has permission to go and ask her hand, even the poorest beggar. I shall pay a visit to the palace," he said; " I must go, for I cannot help myself."

Then they all advised him not to attempt it; for he would be sure to share the same fate as the rest. His fellow-traveler also tried to persuade him against it; but John seemed quite sure of success. He brushed his shoes and his coat, washed his face and his hands, combed his soft flaxen hair, and then went out alone into the town, and walked to the palace.

" Come in," said the King, as John knocked at the door. John opened it, and the old King, in a dressing gown and embroidered slippers, came toward him. He had the crown on his head, carried his scepter in one hand, and the orb in the other. " Wait a bit," said he, and he placed the orb under his arm, so that he could offer the other hand to John; but when he found that John was another suitor, he began to weep so violently that both the scepter and the orb fell to the floor, and he was obliged to wipe his eyes with his dressing gown. Poor old King! " Let her alone," he said; " you will fare as badly as all the others. Come, I will show you." Then he led him out into the Princess' pleasure gardens, and there he saw a frightful sight. On every tree hung three or four king's sons who had wooed the Princess, but had not been able to guess the riddles she gave them. Their skeletons rattled in every breeze, so that the terrified birds never dared to venture into the garden. All the flowers were supported by human bones instead of sticks, and human skulls in the flowerpots grinned horribly. It was really a doleful garden for a princess. "Do you see all this?" said the old King; "your fate will be the same as those who are here, therefore do not attempt it. You really make me very unhappy—I take these things to heart so very much."

John kissed the good old King's hand, and said he was sure it would be all right, for he was quite enchanted with the beautiful Princess. Then the Princess herself came riding into the palace yard with all her ladies, and he wished her "Good morning." She looked wonderfully fair and lovely when she offered her hand to John, and he loved her more than ever. How could she be a wicked witch, as all the people asserted? He accompanied her into the hall, and the little pages offered them gingerbread nuts and sweetmeats; but the old King was so unhappy he could eat nothing, and besides, gingerbread nuts were too hard for him. It was decided that John should come to the palace the next day, when the judges and the whole of the counselors would be present, to try if he could guess the first riddle. If he succeeded, he would have to come a second time; but if not, he would lose his life—and no one had ever been able to guess even one. However, John was not at all anxious about the result of his trial; on the contrary, he was very merry. He thought only of the beautiful Princess, and believed that in some way he should have help, but how he knew not, and did not like to think about it; so he danced along the highroad as he went back to the inn, where he had left his fellow-traveler waiting for him. John could not refrain from telling him how gracious the Princess had been, and how beautiful she looked. He longed for the next day so much, that he might go to the palace and try his luck at guessing the riddles. But his comrade shook his head, and looked very mournful. "I do so wish you to do well," said he; "we might

have continued together much longer, and now I am likely
to lose you; you poor dear John! I could shed tears, but I will
not make you unhappy on the last night we may be together.
We will be merry, really merry this evening; tomorrow, after
you are gone, I shall be able to weep undisturbed."

It was very quickly known among the inhabitants of the
town that another suitor had arrived for the Princess, and
there was great sorrow in consequence. The theatre remained
closed, the women who sold sweetmeats tied crape round
the sugar sticks, and the King and the priests were on their
knees in the church. There was a great lamentation, for no
one expected John to succeed better than those who had been
suitors before.

In the evening John's comrade prepared a large bowl of
punch, and said, "Now let us be merry, and drink to the
health of the Princess." But after drinking two glasses, John
became so sleepy, that he could not possibly keep his eyes
open, and fell fast asleep. Then his fellow-traveler lifted him
gently out of his chair, and laid him on the bed; and as
soon as it was quite dark, he took the two large wings which
he had cut from the dead swan, and tied them firmly to his
own shoulders. Then he put into his pocket the largest of the
three rods which he had obtained from the old woman who
had fallen and broken her leg. After this he opened the
window, and flew away over the town, straight towards the
palace, and seated himself in a corner, under the window
which looked into the bedroom of the Princess.

The town was perfectly still when the clocks struck a
quarter to twelve. Presently the window opened, and the
Princess, who had large black wings to her shoulders, and
a long white mantle, flew away over the city towards a
high mountain. The fellow-traveler, who had made himself
invisible, so that she could not possibly see him, flew after
her through the air, and whipped the Princess with his rod,
so that the blood came whenever he struck her. Ah, it was

a strange flight through the air! The wind caught her mantle, so that it spread out on all sides, like the large sail of a ship, and the moon shone through it. "How it hails, to be sure!" said the Princess, at each blow she received from the rod; and it served her right to be whipped.

At last she reached the side of the mountain, and knocked. The mountain opened with a noise like the roll of thunder, and the Princess went in. The traveler followed her; no one could see him, as he had made himself invisible. They went through a long, wide passage. A thousand gleaming spiders ran here and there on the walls, causing them to glitter as if they were illuminated with fire. They next entered a large hall built of silver and gold. Large red and blue flowers shone on the walls, looking like sunflowers in size; but no one could dare to pluck them, for the stems were hideous poisonous snakes, and the flowers were flames of fire, darting out of their jaws. Shining glowworms covered the ceiling, and sky-blue bats flapped their transparent wings. Altogether the place had a frightful appearance. In the middle of the floor stood a throne supported by four skeleton horses, whose harness had been made by fiery-red spiders. The throne itself was made of milk-white glass, and the cushions were little black mice, each biting the other's tail. Over it hung a canopy of rose-colored spider webs, spotted with the prettiest little green flies, which sparkled like precious stones. On the throne sat an old Magician with a crown on his ugly head, and a scepter in his hand. He kissed the Princess on the forehead, seated her by his side on the splendid throne, and then the music commenced. Great black grasshoppers played the mouth organ, and the owl struck herself on the body instead of a drum. It was altogether a ridiculous concert. Little black goblins with false lights in their caps danced about the hall; but no one could see the traveler, and he had placed himself just behind the throne where he could see and hear everything. The courtiers who came in afterwards looked noble and grand; but any one with common sense could see what they really were, only broomsticks, with cabbages for heads. The Magician had given them life, and dressed them in embroidered robes. It answered very well, as they were only wanted for show. After there had been a little dancing, the Princess told the Magician that she had a new suitor, and asked him what she should think of for the suitor to guess when he came to the castle the next morning.

"Listen to what I say," said the Magician; "you must choose something very easy: he is less likely to guess it then. Think of one of your shoes: he will never imagine it is that. Then cut his head off; and mind you do not forget to bring his eyes with you tomorrow night, that I may eat them."

The Princess curtesied low, and said she would not forget the eyes.

The Magician then opened the mountain and she flew home again, but the traveler followed and flogged her so much with the rod, that she sighed quite deeply about the heavy hailstorm, and made as much haste as she could to get back to her bedroom through the window. The traveler then returned to the inn where John still slept, took off his wings and lay down on the bed, for he was very tired. Early in the morning John awoke, and when his fellow-traveler got up, he said that he had had a very wonderful dream about the Princess and her shoe; he therefore advised John to ask her if she had not thought of her shoe. Of course the traveler knew this from what the Magician in the mountain had said.

"I may as well say that as anything else," said John. "Perhaps your dream may come true; still I will say farewell, for if I guess wrong I shall never see you again."

Then they embraced each other, and John went into the town and walked to the palace. The great hall was full of people, and the judges sat in armchairs, with eider-down

cushions to rest their heads upon, because they had so much
to think of. The old King stood near, wiping his eyes with
his white handkerchief. When the Princess entered, she
looked even more beautiful than she had appeared the day
before, and greeted every one present most gracefully; but
to John she gave her hand, and said, " Good morning to you."

Now came the time for John to guess what she was
thinking of; and O, how kindly she looked at him as she
spoke. But when he uttered the single word *shoe*, she turned
as pale as a ghost; all her wisdom could not help her, for
he had guessed rightly. O, how pleased the old King was!
It was quite amusing to see how he capered about. All the
people clapped their hands, both on his account and John's,
who had guessed rightly the first time. His fellow-traveler
was glad also, when he heard how successful John had been.
But John folded his hands, and thanked God, who, he felt
quite sure, would help him again; and he knew he had to
guess twice more. The evening passed pleasantly like the
one preceding. While John slept, his companion flew behind
the Princess to the mountain, and flogged her even harder
than before; this time he had taken two rods with him.
No one saw him go in with her, and he heard all that was
said. The Princess this time was to think of a glove, and he
told John as if he had again heard it in a dream. The next
day, therefore, he was able to guess correctly the second
time, and it caused great rejoicing at the palace. The whole
court jumped about as they had seen the King do the day
before, but the Princess lay on the sofa, and would not say
a single word. All now depended upon John. If he only
guessed rightly the third time, he would marry the Princess,
and reign over the kingdom after the death of the old King;
but if he failed, he would lose his life, and the Magician
would have his beautiful blue eyes. That evening John said
his prayers and went to bed very early, and soon fell asleep
calmly. But his companion tied on his wings to his shoulders,

took three rods, and, with his sword at his side, flew to the palace. It was a very dark night, and so stormy that the tiles flew from the roofs of the houses, and the trees in the garden upon which the skeletons hung bent themselves like reeds before the wind. The lightning flashed, and the thunder rolled in one long-continued peal all night. The window of the castle opened, and the Princess flew out. She was pale as death, but she laughed at the storm as if it were not bad enough. Her white mantle fluttered in the wind like a large sail, and the traveler flogged her with the three rods till the blood trickled down, and at last she could scarcely fly; she contrived, however, to reach the mountain. "What a hailstorm!" she said, as she entered; "I have never been out in such weather as this."

"Yes, there may be too much of a good thing sometimes," said the Magician.

Then the Princess told him that John had guessed rightly the second time, and if he succeeded the next morning, he would win, and she could never come to the mountain again, or practice magic as she had done, and therefore she was quite unhappy.

"I will find out something for you to think of which he will never guess, unless he is a greater conjuror than myself," said the Magician. "But now let us be merry."

Then he took the Princess by both hands, and they danced with all the little goblins and jack-o'-lanterns in the room. The red spiders sprang here and there on the walls quite as merrily, and the flowers of fire appeared as if they were throwing out sparks. The owl beat the drum, the crickets whistled, and the grasshoppers played the mouth organ. It was a very ridiculous ball. After they had danced enough, the Princess was obliged to go home, for fear she should be missed at the palace. The Magician offered to go with her, that they might be company to each other on the way. Then they flew away through the bad weather, and the traveler followed them, and broke his three rods across their shoulders. The Magician had never been out in such a hailstorm as this. Just by the palace the Magician stopped to wish the Princess farewell, and to whisper in her ear, "Tomorrow think of my head."

But the traveler heard it, and just as the Princess slipped through the window into her bedroom, and the Magician turned round to fly back to the mountain, he seized him by the long black beard, and with his saber cut off the wicked conjuror's head just behind his shoulders, so that he could not even see who it was. He threw the body into the sea to the fishes, and, after dipping the head into the water, he tied it up in a silk handkerchief, took it with him to the inn, and then went to bed. The next morning he gave John the handkerchief, and told him not to untie it till the Princess asked him what she was thinking of. There were so many people in the great hall of the palace that they stood as thick as radishes tied together in a bundle. The council sat in their armchairs with the white cushions. The old King wore new robes, and the golden crown and scepter had been polished up so that he looked quite smart. But the Princess was very pale, and wore a black dress as if she were going to a funeral.

"What have I thought of?" asked the Princess, of John. He immediately untied the handkerchief, and was himself quite frightened when he saw the head of the ugly Magician. Every one shuddered, for it was terrible to look at; but the Princess sat like a statue and could not utter a single word. At length she rose and gave John her hand, for he had guessed rightly.

She looked at no one, but sighed deeply, and said, "You are my master now; this evening our marriage must take place."

"I am very much pleased to hear it," said the old King. "It is just what I wish."

Then all the people shouted " Hurrah! " The band played music in the street, the bells rang, and the cake-women took the black crape off the sugar sticks. There was universal joy. Three oxen, stuffed with ducks and chickens, were roasted whole in the market place, where every one might help himself to a slice. The fountains spouted forth the most delicious wine, and whoever bought a penny loaf at the baker's received six large buns, full of raisins, as a present. In the evening the whole town was illuminated. The soldiers fired off cannons, and the boys let off crackers. There was eating and drinking, dancing and jumping everywhere. In the palace, the high-born gentlemen and the beautiful ladies danced with each other, and they could be heard at a great distance singing the following song—

> *Here are maidens, young and fair,*
> *Dancing in the summer air;*
> *Like to spinning wheels at play,*
> *Pretty maidens dance away—*
> *Dance the spring and summer through*
> *Till the sole falls from your shoe.*

But the Princess was still a witch, and she could not love John. His fellow-traveler had thought of that, so he gave John three feathers out of the swan's wings, and a little bottle with a few drops in it. He told him to place a large bath full of water by the Princess's bed, and put the feathers and the drops into it. Then, at the moment she was about to get into bed, he must give her a little push, so that she might fall into the water, and then dip her three times. This would destroy the power of the Magician, and she would love him very much.

John did all that his companion told him to do. The Princess shrieked aloud when he dipped her under the water the first time, and struggled under his hands in the form of a great black swan with fiery eyes. As she rose the second time

Thumbelina (Italy, 11 years old)
(STORY PAGE 45)

from the water, the swan had become white, with a black ring round its neck. John allowed the water to close once more over the bird, and at the same time it changed into a most beautiful Princess. She was more lovely even than before, and thanked him, while her eyes sparkled with tears, for having broken the spell of the Magician.

The next day, the King came with the whole court to offer their congratulations, and stayed till quite late. Last of all came the traveling companion; he had his staff in his hand and his knapsack on his back. John kissed him many times and told him he must not go, he must remain with him, for he was the cause of all his good fortune. But the traveler shook his head, and said gently and kindly, "No: my time is up now; I have only paid my debt to you. Do you remember the dead man whom the bad people wished to throw out of his coffin? You gave all you possessed that he might rest in his grave; I am the dead man." As he said this, he vanished.

The wedding festivities lasted a whole month. John and his Princess loved each other dearly, and the old King lived to see many a happy day, when he took their little children on his knees and let them play with his scepter. And John became king over the whole country.

Little Ida's Flowers

"My poor flowers are dead," said little Ida. "They were so pretty yesterday evening, and now all the leaves are hanging down quite withered. Why do they do that?" she asked of the student who sat on the sofa. She liked him very much; he could tell the most amusing stories and cut out the prettiest pictures—hearts, and ladies dancing, castles with doors that opened, as well as flowers. He was a delightful student. "Why do the flowers look so faded today?" she asked again, and pointed to her nosegay, which was quite withered.

"Don't you know what is the matter with them?" said the student. "The flowers were at a ball last night, and it is no wonder they hang their heads."

"But flowers cannot dance?" cried little Ida.

"Yes, indeed, they can," replied the student. "When it grows dark, and everybody is asleep, they jump about quite merrily. They have a ball almost every night."

"Can children go to these balls?"

"Yes," said the student, "little daisies and lilies of the valley."

"Where do the flowers dance?" asked little Ida.

"Have you not often seen the large castle outside the gates of the town, where the king lives in summer and where the beautiful garden is full of flowers? And have you not fed the swans with bread when they swam towards you in the lake? Well, the flowers have capital balls there, believe me."

" I was in the garden yesterday with my mother," said Ida. " But all the leaves were off the trees and there was not a single flower left. Where are they? I used to see so many in the summer."

" They are in the castle," replied the student. " You must know that as soon as the king and all the court are gone into the town, the flowers run out of the garden into the castle, and you should see how merry they are. The two most beautiful roses seat themselves on the throne, and are called the king and queen. Then all the red cockscombs range themselves on each side and bow. These are the lords-in-waiting. After that the pretty flowers come in and there is a grand ball. The blue violets represent little naval cadets and dance with hyacinths and crocuses, which they call young ladies. The tulips and tiger lilies are the old ladies who sit and watch the dancing, so that everything may be conducted with order and propriety."

" But," said little Ida, " is there no one there to hurt the flowers for dancing in the king's castle? "

" No one knows anything about it," said the student. " The old steward of the castle, who has to watch there at night, sometimes comes in. He carries a great bunch of keys, and as soon as the flowers hear the keys rattle, they run and hide themselves behind the long curtains and stand quite still, just peeping their heads out. Then the steward says, 'I smell flowers here,' but he cannot see them."

" Oh, how capital! " said little Ida, clapping her hands. " Should I be able to see these flowers? "

" Yes," said the student. " Mind you think of it next time you go out. No doubt you will see them if you peep through the window. I did so today, and I saw a long yellow lily lying stretched out on the sofa. She was a court lady."

"Can the flowers from the Botanical Gardens go to these balls?" asked Ida. "It is such a distance!"

"Oh, yes," said the student, "whenever they like, for they can fly. Have you not seen those beautiful red, white, and yellow butterflies that look like flowers? They were flowers once. They have flown off their stalks into the air, and flap their leaves as if they were little wings to make them fly. Then, if they behave well, they obtain permission to fly about during the day, instead of being obliged to sit still on their stems at home. And so in time their leaves become real wings. It may be, however, that the flowers in the Botanical Gardens have never been to the king's palace, and, therefore, they know nothing of the merry doings which take place there at night. I will tell you what to do, and the botanical professor, who lives close by here, will be so surprised. You know him very well, do you not? Well, next time you go into his garden, you must tell one of the flowers that there is going to be a grand ball at the castle. Then that flower will tell all the others and they will fly away to the castle as soon as possible. And when the professor walks into his garden, there will not be a single flower left. How he will wonder what has become of them!"

"But how can one flower tell another? Flowers cannot speak."

"No, certainly not," replied the student, "but they can make signs. Have you not often seen that when the wind blows they nod at one another and rustle all their green leaves?"

"Can the professor understand the signs?" asked Ida.

"Yes, to be sure he can. He went one morning into his garden and saw a stinging nettle making signs with its leaves to a beautiful red carnation. It was saying, 'You are so pretty, I like you very much.' But the professor did not approve of such nonsense, so he clapped his hands on the nettle to stop it. Then the leaves, which are its fingers,

stung him so sharply that he has never ventured to touch
a nettle since."

" Oh, how funny! " said Ida, and she laughed.

" How can anyone put such notions into a child's head? "
said a tiresome lawyer, who had come to pay a visit. He did
not like the student, and would grumble when he saw him
cutting out droll or amusing pictures. Sometimes it would
be a man hanging on a gibbet and holding a heart in his
hand as if he had been stealing hearts. Sometimes it was
an old witch riding through the air on a broom and carrying
her husband on her nose. But the lawyer did not like such
jokes, and he would say as he had just said, " How can
anyone put such nonsense into a child's head? What absurd
fancies they are! "

But to little Ida, all these stories which the student told
her about the flowers seemed very droll, and she thought
over them a great deal. The flowers did hang their heads,
because they had been dancing all night and were very
tired, and most likely they were ill. Then she took them
into the room where a number of toys lay on a pretty little
table, and the whole of the table drawer besides was full of
beautiful things. Her doll Sophy lay in the doll's bed asleep,
and little Ida said to her, " You must really get up, Sophy,
and be content to lie in the drawer tonight. The poor
flowers are ill, and they must lie in your bed. Then perhaps
they will get well again." So she took out the doll, who
looked quite cross and said not a single word, for she was
angry at being turned out of her bed. Ida placed the flowers
in the doll's bed and drew the quilt over them. Then she
told them to lie quite still and be good while she made
some tea for them, so that they might be quite well and
able to get up the next morning. And she drew the curtains
close round the little bed, so that the sun might not shine
in their eyes. During the whole evening she could not help
thinking of what the student had told her. And before she

went to bed herself, she peeped behind the curtains into the garden where all her mother's beautiful flowers grew— hyacinths and tulips, and many others. Then she whispered to them quite softly, "I know you are going to a ball tonight." But the flowers appeared as if they did not understand, and not a leaf moved; still Ida felt quite sure she knew all about it.

She lay awake a long time after she was in bed, thinking how pretty it must be to see all the beautiful flowers dancing in the king's garden. "I wonder if my flowers have really been there?" she said to herself, and then she fell asleep. In the night she awoke; she had been dreaming of the flowers and of the student, as well as of the tiresome lawyer who found fault with him. It was quite still in Ida's bedroom; the night lamp burned on the table and her father and mother were asleep. "I wonder if my flowers are still lying in Sophy's bed?" she thought to herself. "How much I should like to know!" She raised herself a little and glanced at the door of the room where all her flowers and playthings lay. It was partly open, and as she listened, it seemed as if someone in the room was playing the piano, but softly and more prettily than she had ever before heard it. "Now all the flowers are certainly dancing in there," she thought. "Oh, how much I should like to see them!" But she did not dare to move for fear of disturbing her father and mother. "If they would only come in here," she thought, but they did not come. And the music continued to play so beautifully, and was so pretty, that she could resist no longer. She crept out of her little bed, went softly to the door, and looked into the room.

Oh, what a splendid sight there was to be sure! There was no night lamp burning, but the room appeared quite light, for the moon shone through the window upon the floor, and made it almost like day. All the hyacinths and tulips stood in two long rows down the room. Not a single

flower remained in the window, and the flowerpots were all
empty. The flowers were dancing gracefully on the floor,
making turns and holding each other by their long green
leaves as they swung round. At the piano sat a large yellow
lily which little Ida was sure she had seen in the summer,
for she remembered the student saying she was very much
like Miss Lina, one of Ida's friends. They all laughed at
him then, but now it seemed to little Ida as if the tall yellow
flower was really like the young lady. She had just the same
manners while playing, bending her long yellow face from
side to side, and nodding in time to the beautiful music.

Then she saw a large purple crocus jump into the middle
of the table where the playthings stood, go up to the doll's
bedstead and draw back the curtains. There lay the sick
flowers, but they got up directly and nodded to the others
as a sign that they wished to dance with them. The old
rough doll with the broken mouth stood up and bowed to
the pretty flowers. They did not look ill at all now, but
jumped about and were very merry. Yet none of them
noticed little Ida. Presently it seemed as if something fell
from the table. Ida looked that way and saw a slight carnival
rod jumping down among the flowers as if it belonged to
them. It was, however, very smooth and neat, and a little
wax doll with a broad-brimmed hat on her head, like the one
worn by the lawyer, sat upon it. The carnival rod hopped
about among the flowers on its three red stilted feet, and
stamped quite loud when it danced the mazurka. The
flowers could not do this dance—they were too light to stamp
in that manner.

All at once the wax doll on the carnival rod seemed to
grow larger and taller, and it turned around and said to
the flowers, " How can you put such things in a child's head?
They are all foolish fancies." And then the doll was exactly
like the lawyer with the broad-brimmed hat, and looked
as yellow and as cross as he did. But the rough doll struck

him on his thin legs, and he shrunk up again and became quite a little wax doll. This was very amusing, and Ida could not help laughing. The carnival rod went on dancing, and the lawyer was obliged to dance also. It made no difference whether he made himself great and tall, or remained a little wax doll with a large black hat; still he must dance. At last some of the flowers interceded for him, especially those who had lain in the doll's bed, and the carnival rod gave up his dancing. At that moment a loud knocking was heard in the drawer, where Ida's doll Sophy lay with many other toys. Then the rough doll ran to the end of the table, laid himself flat down upon it, and began to pull the drawer out a little way.

Sophy raised herself and looked round quite astonished. "There must be a ball here tonight," she said. "Why did not somebody tell me?"

"Will you dance with me?" said the rough doll.

"You are the right sort to dance with, certainly," said she, turning her back upon him.

Then she seated herself on the edge of the drawer and thought that perhaps one of the flowers would ask her to dance, but none of them did. Then she coughed, "Hem, hem, a-hem"—but for all that no partner came. The shabby doll now danced quite alone, and not very badly, after all. As none of the flowers seemed to notice Sophy, she let herself down from the drawer to the floor, so as to make a very great noise. All the flowers came round her directly and asked if she had hurt herself, especially those who had lain in her bed. But she was not hurt at all, and Ida's flowers thanked her for the use of the nice bed and were very kind to her. They led her into the middle of the room, where the moon shone, and danced with her, while all the other flowers formed a circle round them. Then Sophy was very happy and said they might keep her bed: she did not mind lying in the drawer at all. But the flowers thanked her very much and said, "We cannot live long. Tomorrow morning we shall be dead, and you must tell little Ida to bury us in the garden, near the grave of the canary. In the summer we shall wake up again and be more beautiful than ever."

"No, you must not die," said Sophy, as she kissed the flowers.

Then the door of the room opened and a number of beautiful flowers danced in. Ida could not imagine where they could have come from, unless they were the flowers from the king's garden. First came two lovely roses with little golden crowns on their heads. These were the king and queen. Beautiful stocks and carnations followed, bowing to everyone present. They also had music with them. Large poppies and peonies had pea shells for instruments, and blew into them till they were quite red in the face. The bunches of blue hyacinths and the little white snowdrops jingled their bell-like flowers, as if they were real bells. Then came many more flowers: blue violets, purple heart's-ease, daisies, and lilies of the valley, and they all danced together, and kissed each other. It was very beautiful to behold.

At last the flowers wished each other good night. Then little Ida crept back into bed again, and dreamt of all she had seen. When she arose the next morning, she went quickly to the little table to see if the flowers were still there. She drew aside the curtains of the little bed. There they all lay, but quite faded; much more so than the day before. Sophy was lying in the drawer where Ida had placed her, but she looked very sleepy.

"Do you remember what the flowers told you to say to me?" asked little Ida. But Sophy looked quite stupid and said not a single word.

"You are not kind at all," said Ida. "And yet they all danced with you."

Then she took a little paper box on which were painted beautiful birds, and laid the dead flowers in it.

"This shall be your pretty coffin," she said. "And by and by, when my cousins come to visit me, they shall help me to bury you out in the garden, so that next summer you may grow up again more beautiful than ever."

Her cousins were two good-tempered boys whose names were James and Adolphus. Their father had given them each a bow and arrow, and they had brought them to show Ida. She told them about the poor flowers which were dead, and as soon as they obtained permission they went with her to bury them. The two boys walked first with their crossbows on their shoulders, and little Ida followed, carrying the pretty box containing the dead flowers. They dug a little grave in the garden. Ida kissed her flowers, and then laid them, with the box, in the earth. James and Adolphus then fired their crossbows over the grave, as they had neither guns nor cannons.

Thumbelina

There was once a woman who wished very much to have a child, but she could not obtain her wish. At last she went to a fairy and said, "I should so very much like to have a little child. Can you tell me where I can find one?"

"Oh, that can be easily managed," said the fairy. "Here is a grain of barley different from the kind that grows in the fields and that the chickens eat. Plant it in a flowerpot and see what will happen."

"Thank you," said the woman and gave the fairy twelve pennies, which was the price of the barleycorn. Then she went home and planted it. Immediately there grew up a large handsome flower, something like a tulip in appearance, but with leaves tightly closed as if it were still a bud.

"It is a beautiful flower," said the woman, and she kissed the red and golden colored leaves. While she did so the flower opened and she could see that it was a real tulip. Within the flower, upon the green velvet stamens, sat a very delicate and graceful little maiden. She was scarcely half as long as a thumb, and they gave her the name of Little Thumb, or Thumbelina, because she was so small. A walnut shell, elegantly polished, served her for a cradle. Her bed was formed of blue violet leaves, with a rose leaf for a counterpane. Here she slept at night, but during the day she amused herself on a table, where the woman placed a plate full of water. Round this plate were flowers with their stems in the water, and upon it floated a large tulip petal which served Thumbelina for a boat. Here the little maiden sat and rowed from side to side, with two oars made of white horsehair. It really was a very pretty sight. Thumbelina could sing so softly and sweetly that nothing like her singing had ever before been heard.

One night as she lay in her pretty bed, a large, ugly, wet toad crept through a broken pane of glass in the window, and leaped right upon the table where Thumbelina lay sleeping under her rose leaf quilt. "What a pretty little wife she would make for my son!" said the toad, and she took up the walnut shell in which little Thumbelina lay asleep, and jumped through the window with it into the garden.

In the swampy margin of a broad stream in the garden lived the toad with her son. He was uglier even than his mother! When he saw the pretty little maiden in her elegant bed, he could only cry, "Croak, croak, croak."

"Don't speak so loud or she will awake," said the old toad. "And then she might run away, for she is as light as swan's down. We will place her on one of the water lily leaves out in the stream. It will be like an island to her—she is so light and small—and then she cannot escape. And while she is away we will make haste and prepare the state-room under the marsh, in which you are to live when you are married."

Far out in the stream grew a number of water lilies with broad green leaves, which seemed to float on the top of the water. The largest of these leaves appeared farther off than the rest, and the old toad swam out to it with the walnut shell, in which little Thumbelina lay still asleep. The little creature woke very early in the morning, and began to cry bitterly when she found where she was. She could see nothing but water on every side of the large green leaf and no way of reaching the land. Meanwhile the old toad was very busy under the marsh, decking her room with rushes and wild yellow flowers, to make it look pretty for her new daughter-in-law. Then she swam out with her ugly son to the leaf on which she had placed poor little Thumbelina. She wanted to fetch the pretty bed, that she might put it in the bridal chamber to be ready for her.

The old toad bowed low to her in the water and said, "Here is my son. He will be your husband and you will live happily together in the marsh by the stream."

"Croak, croak, croak," was all her son could say for himself. So the toads took up the elegant little bed and swam away with it, leaving Thumbelina all alone on the green leaf, where she sat and wept. She could not bear to think of living with the old toad and having her ugly son for a husband. The little fishes who swam about in the water beneath her had seen the toad and had heard what she said, so they lifted their heads above the water to look at the little maiden. As soon as they caught sight of her they saw she was very pretty, and it made them sorry to think that she must go and live with the ugly toads. "No, that must never be!" So they assembled together in the water around the green stalk which held the leaf on which the little maiden stood, and gnawed it away at the root with their teeth. Then the leaf floated down the stream, carrying Thumbelina far away, out of reach of land.

She sailed past many towns, and the little birds in the bushes saw her and sang, "What a lovely little creature!" The leaf swam with her farther and farther till it brought her to other lands. A graceful white butterfly constantly fluttered round her, and at last alighted on the leaf. Thumbelina pleased him, and she was glad of it for now the toad could not possibly reach her, and the country through which she sailed was beautiful, and the sun shone upon the water till it glittered like liquid gold. She took off her sash and tied one end of it round the butterfly and fastened the other end to the leaf, which now glided on much faster than ever, taking little Thumbelina with it. Presently a large cockchafer flew by. The moment he caught sight of her, he seized her round her delicate waist with his claws and flew with her into a tree. The green leaf floated away on the brook, and the butterfly flew with it, for he was fastened to it and could not get away.

Oh, how frightened little Thumbelina felt when the cockchafer flew with her to the tree! But especially was she sorry for the beautiful white butterfly which she had fastened to the leaf, for if he could not free himself he would die of hunger. But the cockchafer did not trouble himself at all about the matter. He seated himself by her side on a large green leaf, gave her some honey from the flowers to eat, and told her she was very pretty, though not in the least like a cockchafer. After a time, all the cockchafers who lived in the tree came to visit her. They stared, and then the young lady cockchafers turned up their feelers and said, " She has only two legs. How ugly that looks! "

" She has no feelers," said another.

" Her waist is quite slim. She is just like a human being. Oh, she is ugly! " said all the lady cockchafers, although Thumbelina was very pretty.

The cockchafer who had run away with her believed all the others when they said she was ugly, and would have nothing more to do with her, and told her she might go where she liked. Then he flew down with her from the tree and placed her on a daisy, and she wept at the thought that she was so ugly that even the cockchafers would have nothing to say to her. And all the while she was really the loveliest creature that one could imagine, and as tender and delicate as a beautiful roseleaf.

During the whole summer poor little Thumbelina lived quite alone in the wide forest. She wove herself a bed with blades of grass, and hung it up under a broad leaf to protect

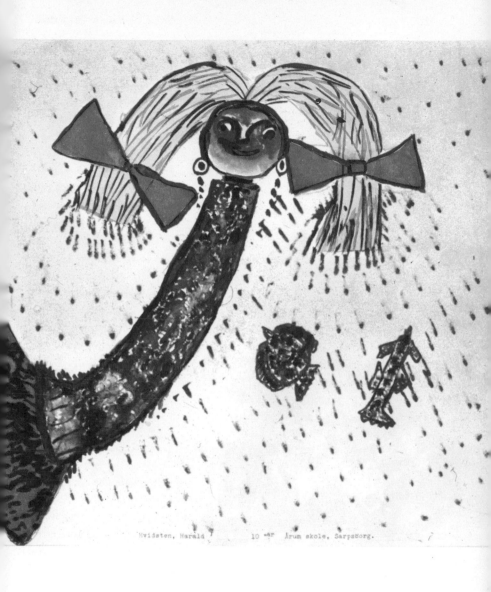

Hvidsten, Harald   10 år   Ärum skole, Sarpsborg.

The Little Mermaid (Norway, 10 years old)
(STORY PAGE 65)

herself from the rain. She sucked the honey from the flowers for food, and drank the dew from their leaves every morning. So passed away the summer and the autumn, and then came the winter—the long, cold winter. All the birds who had sung to her so sweetly had flown away, and the trees and the flowers had withered. The large clover leaf under which she had lived was now rolled together and shriveled up; nothing remained of it but a yellow withered stalk. She felt dreadfully cold, for her clothes were torn and she was herself so frail and delicate that poor Thumbelina was nearly frozen to death. It began to snow too, and the snowflakes, as they fell upon her, were like a whole shovelful falling upon one of us, for we are tall while she was only an inch high. Then she wrapped herself up in a dry leaf, but it cracked in the middle and could not keep her warm, and she shivered with cold.

Near the wood in which she had been living lay a large grain field, but the grain had been cut a long time. Nothing remained but the bare dry stubble standing up out of the frozen ground. It was to her like struggling through a large wood. Oh, how she shivered with the cold! She came at last to the door of a field mouse, who had a little den under the stubble. There dwelt the field mouse in warmth and comfort, with a whole roomful of grain, a kitchen, and a beautiful dining room. Poor little Thumbelina stood before the door just like a little beggar girl, and begged for a handful of barley, for she had been without a morsel to eat for two days.

"You poor little creature," said the field mouse, who was really a good old field mouse. "Come into my warm room and dine with me." She was so pleased with Thumbelina that she said, "You are quite welcome to stay with me all winter, if you like. But you must keep my rooms clean and neat, and tell me stories, for I like to hear them very much."

And Thumbelina did all the field mouse asked her, and found herself very comfortable.

" We shall have a visitor soon," said the field mouse one day. " My neighbor pays me a visit once a week. He is even better off than I am. He has rooms, and wears a beautiful black velvet coat. If you could only have him for a husband, you would be well provided for indeed. But he is blind; so you must tell him some of your prettiest stories."

Thumbelina did not feel at all interested about this neighbor, for he was a mole. However, he came and paid his visit, dressed in his black velvet coat.

" He is very rich and learned, and his house is twenty times larger than mine," said the field mouse.

He was rich and learned, no doubt, but he always spoke slightingly of the sun and the pretty flowers, because he had never seen them. Thumbelina was obliged to sing to him, " Ladybird, ladybird, fly away home," and many other pretty songs. And the mole fell in love with her because she had such a sweet voice, but he said nothing yet, for he was very cautious. A short time before, the mole had dug a long passage under the earth, which led from the dwelling of the field mouse to his own, and here she had permission to walk with Thumbelina whenever she liked. But he warned them not to be alarmed at the sight of a dead bird which lay in the passage. It was a perfect bird, with a beak and feathers, and could not have been dead long, and was lying just where the mole had made his passage.

The mole took a piece of phosphorescent wood in his mouth, and it glittered like fire in the dark. Then he went before them to light them through the long, dark passage. When they came to the spot where lay the dead bird, the mole pushed his broad nose through the ceiling, the earth gave way so that there was a large hole, and the daylight shone into the passage. In the middle of the floor lay a dead swallow, his beautiful wings folded close to his sides, his

feet and his head drawn up under his feathers. The poor
bird had evidently died of the cold. It made little Thumbelina very sad to see it, for she greatly loved the little birds
who had sung and twittered for her so beautifully all the
summer. But the mole pushed it aside with his crooked legs
and said, "He will sing no more now. How miserable it must
be to be born a little bird. I am thankful that none of my
children will ever be birds, who can do nothing but cry,
'Tweet, tweet,' and always die of hunger in the winter."

"Yes, you may well say that, you clever mole," exclaimed
the field mouse. "What is the use of his twittering, for when
winter comes he must either starve or be frozen to death?
Still birds are very highbred, I suppose."

Thumbelina said nothing, but when the two others had
turned their backs on the bird, she stooped down and stroked
aside the soft feathers which covered the head, and kissed
the closed eyelids. "Perhaps this was the one who sang to
me so sweetly in the summer," she said. "And how much
pleasure you gave me, you dear pretty bird."

The mole now stopped up the hole through which the
daylight shone, and then accompanied the ladies home. But
during the night, as Thumbelina could not sleep, she got out
of bed and wove a large beautiful carpet of hay. Then she
carried it to the dead bird and spread it over him, with some
down from the flowers which she had found in the field
mouse's room. It was as soft as wool, and she spread some
of it on each side of the bird so that he might lie warmly
in the cold earth. "Farewell, you pretty little bird," said
she. "Farewell. Thank you for your delightful singing during
the summer, when all the trees were green and the warm
sun shone upon us." Then she laid her head on the bird's
breast, and she was alarmed immediately, for it seemed as
if something inside the bird went thump, thump. It was the
bird's heart. He was not really dead—only benumbed with
the cold—and the warmth had restored him to life.

In autumn, all the swallows fly away into warm countries, but if one happens to linger and the cold seizes it, it becomes frozen and falls down as if dead. It remains where it fell, and the cold snow covers it. Thumbelina trembled very much: she was quite frightened, for the bird was large, a great deal larger than herself—she was only an inch high. But she took courage, laid the wool more thickly over the poor swallow, and then brought a leaf which she had used for her own counterpane and laid it over the head of the poor bird. The next night she again stole out to see him. He was alive but very weak. He could only open his eyes for a moment to look at Thumbelina, who stood holding a piece of decayed wood in her hand, for she had no other lantern.

"Thank you, pretty little maiden," said the sick swallow. "I have been so nicely warmed that I shall soon regain my strength and be able to fly about in the warm sunshine."

"Oh," said she, "it is cold out of doors now. It is snowing and freezing. Stay in your warm bed. I will take care of you."

Then she brought the swallow some water in a flower leaf. And after he had drunk, he told her that he had wounded one of his wings in a thornbush and could not fly as fast as the others, who were soon far away on their journey to warm countries. Then at last he had fallen to the earth and could remember no more. He did not know how he came to where she had found him. The whole winter the swallow remained underground, and Thumbelina nursed him with care and love. Neither the mole nor the field mouse knew anything about it, for they did not like swallows.

Very soon the springtime came and the sun warmed the earth. Then the swallow bade farewell to Thumbelina, and she opened the hole in the ceiling which the mole had made. The sun shone in upon them so beautifully that the swallow asked her if she would go with him. She could sit on his back, he said, and he would fly away with her into the green woods. But Thumbelina knew it would make the field mouse feel very sad if she left her in that manner and said, "No, I cannot."

"Farewell, then. Farewell, you good, pretty little maiden," said the swallow and flew out into the sunshine.

Thumbelina looked after him, and the tears rose in her eyes. She was very fond of the poor swallow.

"Tweet, tweet," sang the bird as he flew out into the green woods, and Thumbelina felt very sad. She was not allowed to go out into the warm sunshine. The corn which had been sown in the field over the house of the field mouse had grown up high into the air, and formed a thick wood to Thumbelina, who was only an inch in height.

"You are going to be married, Thumbelina," said the field mouse. "My neighbor has asked for you. What good fortune for a poor child like you! Now we will prepare your wedding clothes. They must be both woolen and linen. Nothing must be wanting when you are the mole's wife."

Thumbelina had to turn the spindle, and the field mouse hired four spiders who were to weave day and night. Every evening the mole visited her and was continually speaking of the time when the summer would be over. Then he would keep his wedding day with Thumbelina, but now the heat of the sun was so great that it burned the earth and made it quite hard, like a stone. As soon as the summer was over, the wedding should take place, but Thumbelina was not at all pleased, for she did not like the tiresome mole. Every morning when the sun rose, and every evening when it went down, she would creep out at the door. And as the wind blew aside the leaves of the corn so that she could see the blue sky, she thought how beautiful and bright it seemed out there, and wished so much to see her dear swallow again. But he never returned. By this time he had flown far away into the lovely green forest.

When autumn arrived, Thumbelina had her outfit quite

ready, and the field mouse said to her, "In four weeks the wedding must take place."

Then Thumbelina wept, and said she would not marry the disagreeable mole.

"Nonsense," replied the field mouse. "Now don't be obstinate, or I shall bite you with my teeth. He is a very handsome mole. The queen herself does not wear more beautiful velvets and furs. His kitchens and cellars are quite full. You ought to be thankful for such good fortune."

So the wedding day was fixed, on which the mole was to fetch Thumbelina away to live with him deep under the earth, and never again to see the warm sun, because *he* did not like it. The poor child was very unhappy at the thought of saying farewell to the beautiful sun, and as the field mouse had given her permission to stand at the door, she went to look at it once more.

"Farewell, bright sun," she cried, stretching out her arm towards it. And then she walked a short distance from the house. The corn had been cut, and only the dry stubble remained in the fields. "Farewell, farewell," she repeated, twining her arm round a little red flower that grew just by her side. "Greet the little swallow for me, if you should see him again."

"Tweet, tweet," sounded over her head suddenly. She looked up, and there was the swallow himself flying close by. As soon as he spied Thumbelina, he was delighted. And then she told him how unwilling she felt to marry the ugly mole, and to live always beneath the earth and never see the bright sun any more. And as she told him she wept.

"Cold winter is coming," said the swallow, "and I am going to fly away into warmer countries. Will you go with me? You can sit on my back and fasten yourself on with your sash. Then we can fly away from the ugly mole and his gloomy rooms—far away over the mountains into warmer countries, where the sun shines more brightly than here;

where it is always summer and the flowers bloom in greater beauty. Fly now with me, dear little Thumbelina. You saved my life when I lay frozen in that dark dreary passage."

"Yes, I will go with you," said Thumbelina. And she seated herself on the bird's back with her feet on his outstretched wings, and tied her sash to one of his strongest feathers.

Then the swallow rose in the air and flew over forest and over sea, high above the highest mountains, covered with eternal snow. Thumbelina would have been frozen in the cold air, but she crept under the bird's warm feathers, keeping her little head uncovered so that she might admire the beautiful lands over which they passed. At length they reached the warm countries, where the sun shines brightly and the sky seems much higher above the earth. Here on the hedges and by the wayside grew purple, green, and white grapes. Lemons and oranges hung from trees in the woods, and the air was fragrant with myrtles and orange blossoms. Beautiful children ran along the country lanes, playing with large gay butterflies, and as the swallow flew farther and farther, every place appeared still more lovely.

At last they came to a blue lake, and by the side of it, shaded by trees of the deepest green, stood a palace of dazzling white marble, built in the olden times. Vines clustered round its lofty pillars and at the top were many swallows' nests, and one of these was the home of the swallow who carried Thumbelina.

"This is my house," said the swallow, "but it would not do for you to live there. You would not be comfortable. You must choose for yourself one of those lovely flowers, and I will put you down upon it. And then you shall have everything that you can wish to make you happy."

"That will be delightful," she said, and clapped her little hands for joy.

A large marble pillar lay on the ground, which in falling had been broken into three pieces. Between these pieces grew the most beautiful large white flowers. So the swallow flew down with Thumbelina and placed her on one of the broad leaves. How surprised she was to see, in the middle of the flower, a tiny little man, as white and transparent as if he had been made of crystal! He had a gold crown on his head, and delicate wings at his shoulders, and was not much larger than Thumbelina herself. He was the angel of the flower—for a tiny man or a tiny woman dwells in every flower—and this was the king of them all.

"How beautiful he is!" whispered Thumbelina to the swallow.

The little prince was at first quite frightened at the bird, who was like a giant compared to such a delicate little creature as himself. But when he saw Thumbelina, he was delighted and thought her the prettiest little maiden he had ever seen. He took the gold crown from his head, placed it on hers, asked her name, and asked if she would be his wife and the queen over all the flowers.

This certainly was a very different sort of husband from the son of the toad, or the mole with his black velvet and fur. So she said, "Yes," to the handsome prince. Then all the flowers opened and out of each came a little lady or a tiny lord, all so pretty it was quite a pleasure to look at them. Each of them brought Thumbelina a present, but the best gift was a pair of beautiful wings which had belonged to a large white fly. And they fastened them to Thumbelina's shoulders so that she might fly from flower to flower. Then there was much rejoicing, and the little swallow, who sat above them in his nest, was asked to sing a wedding song, which he did as well as he could. But in his heart he felt sad, for he was very fond of Thumbelina and would have liked never to part from her again.

"You must not be called Thumbelina any more," said the spirit of the flowers to her. "It is an ugly name and you are so very pretty. We will call you Maia."

" Farewell, farewell," said the swallow, with a heavy heart, as he left the warm countries to fly back to Denmark. There he had a nest over the window of a house in which dwelt the writer of fairy tales. The swallow sang, " Tweet, tweet," and from his song came the whole story.

The Emperor's New Clothes

Many years ago there was an Emperor who was so excessively fond of new clothes that he spent all his money on them. He cared nothing about his soldiers, nor for the theatre, nor for driving in the woods except for the sake of showing off his new clothes. He had a costume for every hour in the day. Instead of saying as one does about any other king or emperor, "He is in his council chamber," the people here always said, "The Emperor is in his dressing room."

Life was very gay in the great town where he lived. Hosts of strangers came to visit it every day, and among them one day were two swindlers. They gave themselves out as weavers and said that they knew how to weave the most beautiful fabrics imaginable. Not only were the colors and patterns unusually fine, but the clothes that were made of this cloth had the peculiar quality of becoming invisible to every person who was not fit for the office he held, or who was impossibly dull.

"Those must be splendid clothes," thought the Emperor. "By wearing them I should be able to discover which men in my kingdom are unfitted for their posts. I shall distinguish the wise men from the fools. Yes, I certainly must order some of that stuff to be woven for me."

The Emperor paid the two swindlers a lot of money in advance, so that they might begin their work at once.

They did put up two looms and pretended to weave, but they had nothing whatever upon their shuttles. At the outset they asked for a quantity of the finest silk and the purest gold thread, all of which they put into their own bags while they worked away at the empty looms far into the night.

"I should like to know how those weavers are getting on with their cloth," thought the Emperor, but he felt a little queer when he reflected that anyone who was stupid or unfit for his post would not be able to see it. He certainly thought that he need have no fears for himself, but still he thought he would send somebody else first to see how it was getting on. Everybody in the town knew what wonderful power the stuff possessed, and everyone was anxious to see how stupid his neighbor was.

"I will send my faithful old minister to the weavers," thought the Emperor. "He will be best able to see how the stuff looks, for he is a clever man and no one fulfills his duties better than he does."

So the good old minister went into the room where the two swindlers sat working at the empty loom.

"Heaven help us," thought the old minister, opening his eyes very wide. "Why, I can't see a thing! " But he took care not to say so.

Both the swindlers begged him to be good enough to step a little nearer, and asked if he did not think it a good pattern and beautiful coloring. They pointed to the empty loom. The poor old minister stared as hard as he could, but he could not see anything, for of course there was nothing to see.

"Good heavens," thought he. "Is it possible that I am a fool? I have never thought so, and nobody must know it. Am I not fit for my post? It will never do to say that I cannot see the stuff."

"Well, sir, you don't say anything about the stuff," said the one who was pretending to weave.

"Oh, it is beautiful—quite charming," said the minister, looking through his spectacles. "Such a pattern and such colors! I will certainly tell the Emperor that the stuff pleases me very much."

"We are delighted to hear you say so," said the swindlers, and then they named all the colors and described the peculiar pattern. The old minister paid great attention to what they said, so as to be able to repeat it when he got home to the Emperor.

Then the swindlers went on to demand more money, more silk, and more gold, to be able to proceed with the weaving. But they put it all into their own pockets. Not a single strand was ever put into the loom, but they went on as before, weaving at the empty loom.

The Emperor soon sent another faithful official to see how the stuff was getting on and if it would soon be ready. The same thing happened to him as to the minister. He looked and looked, but as there was only the empty loom, he could see nothing at all.

"Is not this a beautiful piece of stuff?" said both the swindlers, showing and explaining the beautiful pattern and colors which were not there to be seen.

"I know I am no fool," thought the man, "so it must be that I am unfit for my good post. It is very strange, though. However, one must not let it appear." So he praised the stuff he did not see, and assured them of his delight in the beautiful colors and the originality of the design.

"It is absolutely charming," he said to the Emperor. Everybody in the town was talking about this splendid stuff.

Now the Emperor thought he would like to see it while it was still on the loom. So, accompanied by a number of selected courtiers, among whom were the two faithful officials who had already seen the imaginary stuff, he went to visit the crafty impostors, who were working away as hard as ever they could at the empty loom.

"It is magnificent," said both the honest officials. "Only see, Your Majesty, what a design! What colors!" And they pointed to the empty loom, for they each thought no doubt the others could see the stuff.

"What?" thought the Emperor. "I see nothing at all. This is terrible! Am I a fool? Am I not fit to be Emperor? Why, nothing worse could happen to me!"

"Oh, it is beautiful," said the Emperor. "It has my highest approval." And he nodded his satisfaction as he gazed at the empty loom. Nothing would induce him to say that he could not see anything.

The whole suite gazed and gazed, but saw nothing more than all the others. However, they all exclaimed with His Majesty, "It is very beautiful." And they advised him to wear a suit made of this wonderful cloth on the occasion of a great procession which was just about to take place. "Magnificent! Gorgeous! Excellent!" went from mouth to mouth. They were all equally delighted with it. The Emperor gave each of the rogues an order of knighthood to be worn in their buttonholes and the title of "Gentleman Weaver."

The swindlers sat up the whole night before the day on which the procession was to take place, burning sixteen candles, so that people might see how anxious they were to get the Emperor's new clothes ready. They pretended to take the stuff off the loom. They cut it out in the air with a huge pair of scissors, and they stitched away with needles without any thread in them.

At last they said, "Now the Emperor's new clothes are ready."

The Emperor with his grandest courtiers went to them himself, and both swindlers raised one arm in the air, as if they were holding something. They said, "See, these are the trousers. This is the coat. Here is the mantle," and so on.

"It is as light as a spider's web. One might think one had nothing on, but that is the very beauty of it."

"Yes," said all the courtiers, but they could not see anything, for there was nothing to see.

"Will Your Imperial Majesty be graciously pleased to take off your clothes?" said the impostors. "Then we may put on the new ones, along here before the great mirror."

The Emperor took off all his clothes, and the impostors pretended to give him one article of dress after the other of the new ones which they had pretended to make. They pretended to fasten something around his waist and to tie on something. This was the train, and the Emperor turned round and round in front of the mirror.

"How well His Majesty looks in the new clothes! How becoming they are!" cried all the people round. "What a design, and what colors! They are most gorgeous robes."

"The canopy is waiting outside which is to be carried over Your Majesty in the procession," said the master of the ceremonies.

"Well, I am quite ready," said the Emperor. "Don't the clothes fit well?" Then he turned round again in front of the mirror, so that he should seem to be looking at his grand things.

The chamberlains who were to carry the train stooped and pretended to lift it from the ground with both hands, and they walked along with their hands in the air. They dared not let it appear that they could not see anything.

Then the Emperor walked along in the procession under the gorgeous canopy, and everybody in the streets and at the windows exclaimed, "How beautiful the Emperor's new clothes are! What a splendid train! And they fit to perfection!" Nobody would let it appear that he could see nothing, for then he would not be fit for his post, or else he was a fool.

None of the Emperor's clothes had been so successful before.

"But he has got nothing on," said a little child.

"Oh, listen to the innocent," said its father. And one person whispered to the other what the child had said. "He has nothing on—a child says he has nothing on!"

"But he has nothing on!" at last cried all the people.

The Emperor writhed, for he knew it was true. But he thought, "The procession must go on now." So he held himself stiffer than ever, and the chamberlains held up the invisible train.

Ole Shut-Eye (Italy, 11 years old)
(STORY PAGE 129)

The Little Mermaid

Far out in the sea the water is as blue as the petals of the most beautiful cornflower, and as clear as the purest glass. But it is very deep, deeper than any cable will sound; many steeples must be placed one above the other to reach from the ground to the surface of the water. And down there live the sea people.

Now, you must not believe there is nothing down there but the naked sand; no—the strangest trees and plants grow there, so pliable in their stalks and leaves that at the least motion of the water they move just as if they had life. All fishes, great and small, glide among the twigs, just as here the birds do in the trees. In the deepest spot of all lies the sea king's castle: the walls are of coral, and the tall, Gothic windows of the clearest amber; shells form the roof, and they open and shut according as the water flows. It looks lovely, for in each shell lie gleaming pearls, a single one of which would have great value in a queen's diadem.

The sea king below there had been a widower for many years, while his old mother kept house for him. She was a clever woman, but proud of her rank, so she wore twelve oysters on her tail, while the other great people were only allowed to wear six. Beyond this she was deserving of great praise, especially because she was very fond of her grand-daughters, the little sea princesses. These were six pretty children; but the youngest was the most beautiful of all. Her skin was as clear and as fine as a rose leaf; her eyes were as blue as the deepest sea; but, like all the rest, she had no feet, for her body ended in a fishtail.

All day long they could play in the castle, down in the halls, where living flowers grew out of the walls. The great amber windows were opened, and then the fishes swam in to them, just as the swallows fly in to us when we open our windows; but the fishes swam straight up to the Princesses, ate out of their hands, and let themselves be stroked.

Outside the castle was a great garden with bright red and dark blue flowers; the fruit glowed like gold, and the flowers like flames of fire; and they continually kept moving their stalks and leaves. The earth itself was the finest sand, but blue as the flame of brimstone. A peculiar blue radiance lay upon everything down there: one would have thought oneself high in the air, with the canopy of heaven above and around, rather than at the bottom of the deep sea. During a calm the sun could be seen; it appeared like a purple flower, from which all light streamed out.

Each of the little Princesses had her own little place in the garden, where she might dig and plant at her good pleasure. One gave her flower bed the form of a whale; another thought it better to make hers like a little sea woman; but the youngest made hers quite round, like the sun, and had flowers which gleamed red as the sun itself. She was a strange child, quiet and thoughtful; and when the other sisters made a display of the beautiful things they had received out of wrecked ships, she would have nothing beyond the red flowers which resembled the sun, except a pretty marble statue. This was a figure of a charming boy, hewn out of white clear stone, which had sunk down to the bottom of the sea from a wreck. She planted a pink weeping willow beside this statue; the tree grew famously, and hung its fresh branches over the statue towards the blue sandy ground, where the shadow showed violet, and moved like the branches themselves; it seemed as if the ends of the branches and the roots were playing together and wished to kiss each other.

There was no greater pleasure for her than to hear of the world of men above them. The old grandmother had to tell all she knew of ships and towns, of men and animals. It seemed particularly beautiful to her that up on the earth the flowers shed fragrance, for they had none down at the bottom of the sea, and that the trees were green, and that the fishes which one saw there among the trees could sing so loud and clear that it was a pleasure to hear them. What the grandmother called fishes were the little birds; the Princess could not understand them in any other way, for she had never seen a bird.

" When you have reached your fifteenth year," said the grandmother, " you shall have leave to rise up out of the sea, to sit on the rocks in the moonlight, and to see the great ships as they sail by. Then you will see forests and towns! "

In the next year one of the sisters was fifteen years of age, but each of the others was one year younger than the next; so that the youngest had full five years to wait before she could come up from the bottom of the sea, and find how our world looked. But one promised to tell the others what she had seen and what she had thought the most beautiful on the first day of her visit; for their grandmother could not tell them enough—there was so much about which they wanted information.

No one was more anxious about these things than the youngest—just that one who had the longest time to wait, and who was always quiet and thoughtful. Many a night she stood by the open window, and looked up through the dark blue water at the fishes splashing with their fins and tails. Moon and stars she could see; they certainly shone quite faintly, but through the water they looked much larger than they appear in our eyes. When something like a black cloud passed among them, she knew that it was either a whale swimming over her head, or a ship with many people: they certainly did not think that a pretty little mermaid was standing down below stretching up her white hands toward the keel of their ship.

Now the eldest princess was fifteen years old, and might mount up to the surface of the sea.

When she came back, she had a hundred things to tell— but the finest thing, she said, was to lie in the moonshine on a sand bank in the quiet sea, and to look at the neighboring coast, with the large town, where the lights twinkled like a hundred stars, and to hear the music and the noise and clamor of carriages and men, to see the many church steeples, and to hear the sound of the bells. Just because she could not get up to these, she longed for them more than for anything.

O how the youngest sister listened! and afterwards when she stood at the open window and looked up through the dark-blue water, she thought of the great city with all its bustle and noise; and then she thought she could hear the church bells ringing, even down to the depth where she was.

In the following year, the second sister received permission to mount upward through the water and to swim whither she pleased. She rose up just as the sun was setting; and this spectacle, she said, was the most beautiful. The whole sky looked like gold, and as to the clouds, she could not properly describe their beauty. They sailed away over her head, purple and violet-colored, but far quicker than the clouds there flew a flight of wild swans, like a long white veil, over the water toward where the sun stood. She swam toward them; but the sun sank, and the roseate hue faded on the sea and in the clouds.

In the following year the next sister went up. She was the boldest of them all, and therefore she swam up a broad stream that poured its waters into the sea. She saw glorious green hills clothed with vines; palaces and castles shone forth from amid splendid woods; she heard how all the birds sang; and the sun shone so warm that she was often obliged to dive under the water to cool her glowing face. In a little bay she found a whole swarm of little mortals. They were quite naked, and splashed about in the water: she wanted to play with them, but they fled in affright, and a little black animal came—it was a dog, but she had never seen a dog— and it barked at her so terribly that she became frightened, and tried to gain the open sea. But she could never forget the glorious woods, the green hills, and the pretty children, who could swim in the water, though they had not fishtails.

The fourth sister was not so bold: she remained out in the midst of the wild sea, and declared that just there it was most beautiful. One could see for many miles around, and the sky above looked like a bell of glass. She had seen ships, but only in the far distance—they looked like seagulls; and the funny dolphins had thrown somersaults, and the great whales spouted out water from their nostrils, so that it looked like hundreds of fountains all around.

Now came the turn of the fifth sister. Her birthday came in the winter, and so she saw what the others had not seen the first time. The sea looked quite green, and great icebergs were floating about; each one appeared like a pearl, she said, and yet was much taller than the church steeples built by men. They showed themselves in the strangest forms, and shone like diamonds. She had seated herself upon one of the greatest of all, and let the wind play with her long hair; and all the sailing ships tacked about in a very rapid way beyond where she sat: but toward evening the sky became covered with clouds, it thundered and lightened, and the black waves lifted the great ice blocks high up, and let them glow in the red glare. On all the ships the sails were reefed, and there was fear and anguish. But she sat quietly upon her floating iceberg, and saw the forked blue flashes dart into the sea.

Each of the sisters, as she came up for the first time to the surface of the water, was delighted with the new and beautiful sights she saw; but as they now had permission, as grown-up girls, to go whenever they liked, it became indifferent to them. They wished themselves back again, and after a month had elapsed they said it was best of all down below, for there one felt so comfortably at home.

Many an evening hour the five sisters took one another by the arm and rose up in a row over the water. They had splendid voices, more charming than any mortal could have; and when a storm was approaching, so that they could apprehend that ships would go down, they swam on before the ships and sang lovely songs, which told how beautiful it was at the bottom of the sea, and exhorted the sailors not to be afraid to come down. But these could not understand the words, and thought it was the storm sighing; and they did not see the splendors below, for if the ships sank they were drowned, and came as corpses to the sea king's palace.

When the sisters thus rose up, arm in arm, in the evening time, through the water, the little sister stood all alone looking after them; and she felt as if she must weep; but the mermaid has no tears, and for this reason she suffers far more acutely.

"Of if I were only fifteen years old!" said she. "I know I shall love the world up there very much, and the people who live and dwell there."

At last she was really fifteen years old.

"Now, you see, you are grown up," said the grandmother, the old dowager. "Come, let me adorn you like your sisters."

And she put a wreath of white lilies in the little maid's hair, but each flower was half a pearl; and the old lady let eight great oysters attach themselves to the Princess' tail, in token of her high rank.

"But that hurts so!" said the little mermaid.

"Yes, pride must suffer pain," replied the old lady.

O how glad she would have been to shake off all the tokens of rank and lay aside the heavy wreath! Her red flowers in the garden suited her better; but she could not help it. "Farewell!" she said, and then she rose, light and clear as a water bubble, up through the sea.

The sun had just set when she lifted her head above the sea, but all the clouds still shone like roses and gold, and in the pale red sky the evening stars gleamed bright and beautiful. The air was mild and fresh, and the sea quite calm. There lay a great ship with three masts; one single sail only was set, for not a breeze stirred, and around in the shrouds and on the yards sat the sailors. There was music and singing, and as the evening closed in, hundreds of colored lanterns were lighted up, and looked as if the flags of every nation were waving in the air. The little mermaid swam straight to the cabin window, and each time the sea lifted her up, she could look through the panes, which were clear as crystal, and see many people standing within dressed in their best. But the handsomest of all was the young Prince with the great black eyes: he was certainly not much more than sixteen years old; it was his birthday, and that was the cause of all this feasting. The sailors were dancing upon deck, and when the young Prince came out, more than a hundred rockets rose into the air; they shone like day, so that the little mermaid was quite startled, and dived under the water; but soon she put out her head again, and then it seemed just as if all the stars of heaven were falling down upon her. She had never seen such fireworks. Great suns spurted fire all around, glorious fiery fishes flew up into the blue air, and everything was mirrored in the clear blue sea. The ship itself was so brightly lit up that every separate rope could be seen, and the people therefore appeared the more plainly. O how handsome the young Prince was! And he pressed the people's hands and smiled, while the music rang out in the glorious night.

It became late; but the little mermaid could not turn her eyes from the ship and from the beautiful Prince. The colored lanterns were extinguished, rockets ceased to fly into the air, and no more cannons were fired; but there was a murmuring and a buzzing deep down in the sea; and she sat on the water, swaying up and down, so that she could look into the cabin. But as the ship got more way, one sail after another was spread. And now the waves rose higher, great clouds came up, and in the distance there was lightning. O! it was going to be fearful weather, therefore the sailors furled the sails. The great ship flew in swift career over the wild sea: the waters rose up like great black mountains, which wanted to roll over the masts; but like a swan the ship dived into the valleys between these high waves, and then let itself be lifted on high again. To the little mermaid this seemed merry sport, but to the sailors it appeared very differently. The ship groaned and creaked; the thick planks were bent by the heavy blows; the sea broke into the ship; the mainmast snapped in two like a thin reed; and the ship lay over on her side, while the water rushed into the hold. Now the little mermaid saw that the people were in peril; she herself was obliged to take care to avoid the beams and fragments of the ship which were floating about on the waters. One moment it was so pitch dark that not a single object could be described, but when it lightened it became so bright that she could distinguish every one on board. She looked particularly for the young Prince, and when the ship parted she saw him sink into the sea. Then she was very glad, for now he would come down to her. But then she remembered that people could not live in the water, and that when he got down to her father's palace he would certainly be dead. No, he must not die: so she swam about among the beams and planks that strewed the surface, quite forgetting that one of them might have crushed her. Diving down deep under the water, she again rose high up among the waves, and in this way she at last came to the Prince, who could scarcely swim longer in that stormy sea. His arms and legs began to fail him, his beautiful eyes closed, and he would have died had the little mermaid not come. She held his head up over the water, and then allowed the waves to carry her and him whither they listed.

When the morning came the storm had passed by. Of the ship not a fragment was to be seen. The sun came up red and shining out of the water; it was as if its beams brought back the hue of life to the cheeks of the Prince, but his eyes remained closed. The mermaid kissed his high, fair forehead and put back his wet hair, and he seemed to her to be like the marble statue in her little garden: she kissed him again and hoped that he might live.

Now she saw in front of her the dry land—high blue mountains, on whose summits the white snow gleamed as if swans were lying there. Down on the coast were glorious green forests, and a building—she could not tell whether it was a church or a convent—stood there. In its garden grew orange and citron trees, and high palms waved in front of the gate. The sea formed a little bay there; it was quite calm, but very deep. Straight toward the rock where the fine white sand had been cast up, she swam with the handsome Prince, and laid him upon the sand, taking especial care that his head was raised in the warm sunshine.

Now all the bells rang in the great white building, and many young girls came walking through the garden. Then the little mermaid swam farther out between some high stones that stood up out of the water, laid some sea foam upon her hair and neck, so that no one could see her little countenance, and then she watched to see who would come to the poor Prince.

In a short time a young girl went that way. She seemed

to be much startled, but only for a moment; then she brought more people, and the mermaid perceived that the Prince came back to life, and that he smiled at all around him. But he did not cast a smile at her: he did not know that she had saved him. And she felt very sorrowful; and when he was led away into the great building, she dived mournfully under the water and returned to her father's palace.

She had always been gentle and melancholy, but now she became much more so. Her sisters asked her what she had seen the first time she rose up to the surface, but she would tell them nothing.

Many an evening and many a morning she went up to the place where she had left the Prince. She saw how the fruits of the garden grew ripe and were gathered; she saw how the snow melted on the high mountain; but she did not see the Prince, and so she always returned home more sorrowful still. Then her only comfort was to sit in her little garden, and to wind her arm round the beautiful marble statue that resembled the Prince; but she did not tend her flowers; they grew as if in a wilderness over the paths, and trailed their long leaves and stalks up into the branches of trees, so that it became quite dark there.

At last she could endure it no longer, and told all to one of her sisters, and then the others heard of it too; but nobody knew of it beyond these and a few other mermaids, who told the secret to their intimate friends. One of these knew who the Prince was; she too had seen the festival on board the ship; and she announced whence he came and where his kingdom lay.

" Come, little sister! " said the other Princesses; and, linking their arms together, they rose up in a long row out of the sea, at the place where they knew the Prince's palace lay.

This palace was built of a kind of bright yellow stone, with great marble staircases, one of which led directly down into the sea. Over the roof rose splendid gilt cupolas, and between the pillars which surrounded the whole dwelling, stood marble statues which looked as if they were alive. Through the clear glass in the high windows one looked into the glorious halls, where costly silk hangings and tapestries were hung up, and all the walls were decked with splendid pictures, so that it was a perfect delight to see them. In the midst of the greatest of these halls a great fountain plashed; its jets shot high up toward the glass dome in the ceiling, through which the sun shone down upon the water and upon the lovely plants growing in the great basin.

Now she knew where he lived, and many an evening and many a night she spent there on the water. She swam far closer to the land than any of the others would have dared to venture; indeed, she went quite up the narrow channel under the splendid marble balcony, which threw a broad shadow upon the water. Here she sat and watched the young Prince, who thought himself quite alone in the bright moonlight.

Many an evening she saw him sailing, amid the sounds of music, in his costly boat with the waving flags; she peeped up through the green reeds, and when the wind caught her silver-white veil, and any one saw it, he thought it was a white swan spreading out its wings.

Many a night when the fishermen were on the sea with their torches, she heard much good told of the young Prince; and she rejoiced that she had saved his life when he was driven about, half dead, on the wild billows: she thought how quietly his head had reclined on her bosom, and how heartily she had kissed him; but he knew nothing of it, and could not even dream of her.

More and more she began to love mankind, and more and more she wished to be able to wander about among those whose world seemed far larger than her own. For they could fly over the sea in ships, and mount up the high hills far above the clouds, and the lands they possessed stretched out in woods and fields farther than her eyes could reach. There was much she wished to know, but her sisters could not answer all her questions; therefore she applied to the old grandmother; and the old lady knew the upper world, which she rightly called "the countries above the sea," very well.

"If people are not drowned," asked the little mermaid, "can they live forever? Do they not die as we die down here in the sea?"

"Yes," replied the old lady. "They too must die, and their life is even shorter than ours. We can live to be three hundred years old, but when we cease to exist here, we are turned into foam on the surface of the water, and have not even a grave down here among those we love. We have not an immortal soul; we never receive another life; we are like the green seaweed, which, when once cut through, can never bloom again. Men, on the contrary, have a soul which lives forever, which lives on after the body has become dust; it mounts up through the clear air, up to all the shining stars! As we rise up out of the waters and behold all the lands of the earth, so they rise up to unknown glorious places which we can never see."

"Why did we not receive an immortal soul?" asked the little mermaid, sorrowfully. "I would gladly give all the hundreds of years I have to live to be a human being only for one day, and to have a hope of partaking the heavenly kingdom."

"You must not think of that," replied the old lady. "We feel ourselves far more happy and far better than mankind yonder."

"Then I am to die and be cast as foam upon the sea, not hearing the music of the waves, nor seeing the pretty flowers and the red sun? Can I not do anything to win an immortal soul?"

"No!" answered the grandmother. "Only if a man were to love you so that you should be more to him than father

or mother; if he should cling to you with his every thought
and with all his love, and let the priest lay his right hand
in yours with a promise of faithfulness here and in all
eternity, then his soul would be imparted to your body, and
you would receive a share of the happiness of mankind. He
would give a soul to you and yet retain his own. But that
can never come to pass. What is considered beautiful here
in the sea—the fishtail—they would consider ugly on the
earth: they don't understand it; there one must have two
clumsy supports which they call legs, to be called beautiful."

Then the little mermaid sighed and looked mournfully
upon her fishtail.

"Let us be glad!" said the old lady. "Let us dance and
leap in the three hundred years we have to live. That is
certainly long enough; after that we can rest ourselves all
the better. This evening we shall have a court ball."

It was a splendid sight, such as is never seen on earth.
The walls and the ceiling of the great dancing-saloon were
of thick but transparent glass. Several hundreds of huge
shells, pink and grass-green, stood on each side in rows,
filled with a blue fire which lit up the whole hall and shone
through the walls, so that the sea without was quite lit up;
one could see all the innumerable fishes, great and small,
swimming toward the glass walls; of some the scales gleamed
with purple, while in others they shone like silver and gold.
Through the midst of the hall flowed a broad stream, and
on this the sea men and sea women danced to their own
charming songs. Such beautiful voices the people of the
earth have not. The little mermaid sang the most sweetly
of all, and the whole court applauded with hands and tails,
and for a moment she felt gay in her heart, for she
knew she had the loveliest voice of all in the sea or on the
earth. But soon she thought again of the world above her;
she could not forget the charming Prince, or her sorrow at
not having an immortal soul like his. Therefore she crept

out of her father's palace, and while everything within was joy and gladness, she sat melancholy in her little garden. Then she heard the bugle horn sounding through the waters, and thought, "Now he is certainly sailing above, he on whom my wishes hang, and in whose hand I should like to lay my life's happiness. I will dare everything to win him and an immortal soul. While my sisters dance yonder in my father's palace, I will go to the sea witch of whom I have always been so much afraid: perhaps she can counsel and help me."

Now the little mermaid went out of her garden to the foaming whirlpools behind which the sorceress dwelt. She had never traveled that way before. No flowers grew there, no sea grass; only the naked gray sand stretched out toward the whirlpools, where the water rushed round like roaring millwheels and tore down everything it seized into the deep. Through the midst of these rushing whirlpools she was obliged to pass to get into the domain of the witch; and for a long way there was no other road except one which led over warm gushing mud: this the witch called her turf moor. Behind it lay her house in the midst of a singular forest, in which all the trees and bushes were polyps—half-animals, half-plants. They looked like hundred-headed snakes growing up out of the earth. All the branches were long, slimy arms, with fingers like supple worms, and they moved limb by limb from the root to the farthest point; all that they could seize on in the water they held fast and did not let it go. The little mermaid stopped in front of them quite frightened; her heart beat with fear, and she was near turning back; but then she thought of the Prince and the human soul, and her courage came back again. She bound her long, flying hair closely around her head, so that the polyps might not seize it. She put her hands together on her breast, and then shot forward, as a fish shoots through the water, among the ugly polyps, which stretched out their supple arms and fingers after her. She saw that each of them held something it had seized with hundreds of little arms, like strong iron bands. People who had perished at sea, and had sunk deep down, looked forth as white skeletons from among the polyps' arms; ships' oars and chests they also held fast, and skeletons of land animals, and a little sea woman whom they had caught and strangled; and this seemed the most terrible of all to our little Princess.

Now she came to a great marshy place in the wood, where fat water snakes rolled about, showing their ugly cream-colored bodies. In the midst of this marsh was a house built of white bones of shipwrecked men; there sat the sea witch, feeding a toad out of her mouth, just as a person might feed a little canary with sugar. She called the ugly fat water snakes her little chickens, and allowed them to crawl upward and all about her.

" I know what you want," said the sea witch. " It is stupid of you, but you shall have your way, for it will bring you to grief, my pretty Princess. You want to get rid of your fishtail, and to have two supports instead of it, like those the people of the earth walk with, so that the young Prince may fall in love with you, and you may get an immortal soul." And with this the Witch laughed loudly and disagreeably, so that the toad and the water snakes tumbled down to the ground, where they crawled about. "You come just in time," said the Witch: "after tomorrow at sunrise I could not help you until another year had gone by. I will prepare a draught for you, with which you must swim to land tomorrow before the sun rises, and seat yourself there and drink it; then your tail will shrivel up and become what the people of the earth call legs; but it will hurt you—it will seem as if you were cut with a sharp sword. All who see you will declare you to be the prettiest human being they ever beheld. You will keep your graceful walk; no dancer will be able to move so lightly as you; but every step you take will be as if you trod upon sharp knives, and as if your blood must flow. If you will bear all this, I can help you."

"Yes!" said the little mermaid, with a trembling voice; and she thought of the Prince and the immortal soul.

"But remember," said the Witch, "when you have once received a human form, you can never be a mermaid again; you can never return through the water to your sisters, or to your father's palace; and if you do not win the Prince's love, so that he forgets father and mother for your sake, is attached to you heart and soul, and tells the priest to join your hands, you will not receive an immortal soul. On the first morning after he has married another, your heart will break, and you will become foam on the water."

"I will do it," said the little mermaid; but she became as pale as death.

"But you must pay me, too," said the Witch; "and it is not a trifle that I ask. You have the finest voice of all here at the bottom of the water; with that you think to enchant him; but this voice you must give to me. The best thing you possess I will have for my costly draught! I must give you my own blood in it, so that the draught may be sharp as a two-edged sword."

"But if you take away my voice," said the little mermaid, "what will remain to me?"

"Your beautiful form," replied the Witch, "your graceful walk, and your speaking eyes: with those you can take captive a human heart. Well, have you lost your courage? Put out your little tongue, and then I will cut it off for my payment, and then you shall have the strong draught."

"It shall be so," said the little mermaid.

And the Witch put on her pot to brew the draught.

"Cleanliness is a good thing," said she; and she cleaned out the pot with the snakes, which she tied up in a big knot; then she scratched herself, and let her black blood drop into it. The stream rose up in the strangest forms, enough

The Emperor's New Clothes (Guatemala, 15 years old)
(STORY PAGE 59)

to frighten the beholder. Every moment the Witch threw something else into the pot; and when it boiled thoroughly, there was a sound like the weeping of a crocodile. At last the draught was ready. It looked like the purest water.

"There you have it," said the Witch.

And she cut off the little mermaid's tongue, so that now the Princess was dumb, and could neither sing nor speak.

She could see her father's palace. The torches were extinguished in the great hall, and they were certainly sleeping within, but she did not dare to go to them, now that she was dumb and was about to quit them forever. She felt as if her heart would burst with sorrow. She crept into the garden, took a flower from each bed of her sisters, blew a thousand kisses toward the palace, and rose up through the dark blue sea.

The sun had not yet risen when she beheld the Prince's castle, and mounted the splendid marble staircase. The moon shone beautifully clear. The little mermaid drank the burning sharp draught, and it seemed as if a two-edged sword went through her delicate body. She fell down in a swoon, and lay as if she were dead. When the sun shone out over the sea she awoke, and felt a sharp pain; but just before her stood the handsome young Prince. He fixed his coal-black eyes upon her, so that she cast down her own, and then she perceived that her fishtail was gone, and that she had the prettiest pair of white feet a little girl could have. But she had no clothes, so she shrouded herself in her long hair. The Prince asked how she came there; and she looked at him mildly, but very mournfully, with her dark-blue eyes, for she could not speak. Then he took her by the hand, and led her into the castle. Each step she took was, as the Witch had told her, as if she had been treading on pointed needles and knives, but she bore it gladly. At the Prince's right hand she moved on, light as a soap bubble, and he, like all the rest, was astonished at her graceful, swaying movements.

6

She now received splendid clothes of silk and muslin. In the castle she was the most beautiful creature to be seen; but she was dumb, and could neither sing nor speak. Lovely slaves, dressed in silk and gold, stepped forward, and sang before the Prince and his royal parents; one sang more charmingly than all the rest, and the Prince smiled at her and clapped his hands. Then the little mermaid became sad; she knew that she herself had sung far more sweetly, and thought—

" O! that he only knew I had given away my voice forever to be with him! "

Now the slaves danced pretty waving dances to the loveliest music; then the little mermaid lifted her beautiful white arms, stood on the tips of her toes, and glided dancing over the floor as no one had yet danced. At each movement her beauty became more apparent, and her eyes spoke more directly to the heart than the songs of the slaves.

All were delighted, and especially the Prince, who called her his little foundling; and she danced again and again, although every time she touched the earth it seemed as if she were treading upon sharp knives. The Prince said that she should always remain with him, and she received permission to sleep on a velvet cushion before his door.

He had a page's dress made for her, that she might accompany him on horseback. They rode through the blooming woods, where the green boughs swept their shoulders, and the little birds sang in the fresh leaves. She climbed with the Prince up the high mountains, and although her delicate feet bled so that even the others could see it, she laughed at it herself, and followed him until they saw the clouds sailing beneath them, like a flock of birds traveling to distant lands.

At home in the Prince's castle, when the others slept at night, she went out on to the broad marble steps. It cooled her burning feet to stand in the cold sea water, and then she thought of the dear ones in the deep.

Once, in the nighttime, her sisters came, arm in arm. Sadly they sang as they floated above the water; and she beckoned to them, and they recognized her, and told her how she had grieved them all. Then she visited them every night; and once she saw in the distance her old grandmother, who had not been above the surface for many years, and the sea king with his crown upon his head. They stretched out their hands toward her, but did not venture so near the land as her sisters.

Day by day the Prince grew more fond of her. He loved her as one loves a dear, good child, but it never came into his head to make her his wife; and yet she must become his wife, or she would not receive an immortal soul, and would have to become foam on the sea on his marriage morning.

"Do you not love me best of them all?" the eyes of the little mermaid seemed to say, when he took her in his arms and kissed her fair forehead.

"Yes, you are the dearest to me!" said the Prince, "for you have the best heart of them all. You are the most devoted to me, and are like a young girl whom I once saw, but whom I certainly shall not find again. I was on board a ship which was wrecked. The waves threw me ashore near a holy temple, where several young girls performed the service. The youngest of them found me by the shore and saved my life. I only saw her twice: she was the only one in the world I could love; but you chase her picture out of my mind, you are so like her. She belongs to the holy temple, and therefore my good fortune has sent you to me. We will never part!"

"Ah! he does not know that I saved his life," thought the little mermaid. "I carried him over the sea to the wood where the temple stands. I sat there under the foam and looked to see if any one would come. I saw the beautiful girl whom he loves better than me." And the mermaid sighed deeply—she could not weep. "The maiden belongs to the holy temple," she said, "and will never come out into the world—they will meet no more. I am with him and see him every day; I will cherish him, love him, give up my life for him."

But now they said that the Prince was to marry, and that the beautiful daughter of a neighboring King was to be his wife, and that was why such a beautiful ship was being prepared. The story was, that the Prince traveled to visit the land of the neighboring King, but it was done that he might see the King's daughter. A great company was to go with him. The little mermaid shook her head and smiled; she knew the Prince's thoughts far better than any of the others.

"I must travel," he had said to her; "I must see the beautiful Princess: my parents desire it, but they do not wish to compel me to bring her home as my bride. I cannot love her. She is not like the beautiful maiden in the temple whom you resemble. If I were to choose a bride, I would rather choose you, my dear dumb foundling with the speaking eyes."

And he kissed her red lips and played with her long hair, so that she dreamed of happiness and of an immortal soul.

"You are not afraid of the sea, my dumb child?" said he, when they stood on the superb ship which was to carry him to the country of the neighboring King; and he told her of storm and calm, of strange fishes in the deep, and of what the divers had seen there. And she smiled at his tales, for she knew better than any one what happened at the bottom of the sea.

In the moonlight night, when all were asleep, except the steersman who stood by the helm, she sat on the side of the ship gazing down through the clear water. She fancied she saw her father's palace. High on the battlements stood her old grandmother, with the silver crown on her head, and looking through the rushing tide up to the vessel's keel. Then her sisters came forth over the water, and looked mournfully at her and wrung their white hands. She beckoned to them, smiled, and wished to tell them that she was well and happy; but the cabin boy approached her and her sisters dived down, so that he thought the white objects he had seen were foam on the surface of the water.

The next morning the ship sailed into the harbor of the neighboring King's splendid city. All the church bells sounded, and from the high towers the trumpets were blown, while the soldiers stood there with flying colors and flashing bayonets. Each day brought some festivity with it; balls and entertainments followed one another; but the Princess was not yet there. People said she was being educated in a holy temple far away, where she was learning every royal virtue. At last she arrived.

The little mermaid was anxious to see the beauty of the Princess, and was obliged to acknowledge it. A more lovely apparition she had never beheld. The Princess' skin was pure and clear, and behind the long dark eyelashes there smiled a pair of faithful, dark-blue eyes.

"You are the lady who saved me when I lay like a corpse upon the shore!" said the Prince; and he folded his blushing bride to his heart. "O, I am too, too happy!" he cried to the little mermaid. "The best hope I could have is fulfilled. You will rejoice at my happiness, for you are the most devoted to me of them all!"

And the little mermaid kissed his hand; and it seemed already to her as if her heart was broken, for his wedding morning was to bring death to her, and change her into foam on the sea.

All the church bells were ringing, and heralds rode about the streets announcing the betrothal. On every altar fragrant oil was burning in gorgeous lamps of silver. The priests swung their censers, and bride and bridegroom laid hand in hand,

and received the bishop's blessing. The little mermaid was dressed in cloth of gold, and held up the bride's train; but her ears heard nothing of the festive music, her eye marked not the holy ceremony; she thought of the night of her death, and of all that she had lost in this world.

On the same evening the bride and bridegroom went on board the ship. The cannon roared, all the flags waved; in the midst of the ship a costly tent of gold and purple, with the most beautiful cushions, had been set up, and there the married pair were to sleep in the cool, still night.

The sails swelled in the wind, and the ship glided smoothly and lightly over the clear sea. When it grew dark, colored lamps were lighted and the sailors danced merry dances on deck. The little mermaid thought of the first time when she had risen up out of the sea, and beheld a similar scene of splendor and joy; and she joined in the whirling dance, and flitted on as the swallow flits away when he is pursued; and all shouted and admired her, for she had danced so prettily. Her delicate feet were cut as if with knives, but she did not feel it, for her heart was wounded far more painfully. She knew this was the last evening on which she should see him for whom she had left her friends and her home, and had given up her beautiful voice, and had suffered unheard-of pains every day, while he was utterly unconscious of all. It was the last evening she should breathe the same air with him, and behold the starry sky and the deep sea; and everlasting night without thought or dream awaited her, for she had no soul, and could win none. And everything was merriment and gladness on the ship till past midnight, and she laughed and danced with thoughts of death in her heart. The Prince kissed his beautiful bride, and she played with his raven hair, and hand in hand they went to rest in the splendid tent. It became quiet on the ship; only the helmsman stood by the helm, and the little mermaid leaned her white arms upon the bulwark and gazed out toward the east for the morning dawn—the first ray, she knew, would kill her. Then she saw her sisters rising out of the flood; they were pale, like herself; their long, beautiful hair no longer waved in the wind; it had been cut off.

" We have given it to the Witch, that we might bring you help, so that you may not die tonight. She has given us a knife; here it is—look! how sharp! Before the sun rises you must thrust it into the heart of the Prince, and when the warm blood falls upon your feet they will grow together again into a fishtail, and you will become a mermaid again, and come back to us, and live your three hundred years before you become dead salt sea foam. Make haste! He or you must die before the sun rises! Our old grandmother mourns so that her white hair has fallen off, as ours did under the Witch's scissors. Kill the Prince and come back! Make haste! Do you see that red streak in the sky? In a few minutes the sun will rise, and you must die! "

And they gave a very mournful sigh, and vanished beneath the waves. The little mermaid drew back the curtain from the tent, and saw the beautiful bride lying with her head on the Prince's breast; and she bent down and kissed his brow, and gazed up to the sky where the morning red was gleaming brighter and brighter; then she looked at the sharp knife, and again fixed her eyes upon the Prince, who in his sleep murmured his bride's name. She only was in his thoughts, and the knife trembled in the mermaid's hand. But then she flung it far away into the waves—they gleamed red where it fell, and it seemed as if drops of blood spurted up out of the water. Once more she looked with half-extinguished eyes upon the Prince; then she threw herself from the ship into the sea, and felt her frame dissolving into foam.

Now the sun rose up out of the sea. The rays fell mild and warm upon the cold sea foam, and the little mermaid felt nothing of death. She saw the bright sun, and over her head sailed hundreds of glorious ethereal beings—she could see them through the white sails of the ship and the red clouds of the sky; their speech was melody, but of such a spiritual kind that no human ear could hear it, just as no human eye could see them; without wings they floated through the air. The little mermaid found that she had a frame like these, and was rising more and more out of the foam.

" Whither am I going? " she asked; and her voice sounded like that of the other beings, so spiritual, that no earthly music could be compared to it.

"To the daughters of the air! " replied the others. " A mermaid has no immortal soul, and can never gain one, except she win the love of a mortal. Her eternal existence depends upon the power of another. The daughters of the air have likewise no immortal soul, but they can make themselves one through good deeds. We fly to the hot countries, where the close, pestilent air kills men, and there we bring coolness. We disperse the fragrance of the flowers through the air, and spread refreshment and health. After we have striven for three hundred years to accomplish all the good we can bring about, we receive an immortal soul, and take part in the eternal happiness of men. You, poor little mermaid, have striven with your whole heart after the goal we pursue; you have suffered and endured; you have by good works raised yourself to the world of spirits, and can gain an immortal soul after three hundred years."

And the little mermaid lifted her glorified eyes toward God's sun, and for the first time she felt them fill with tears. On the ship there was again life and noise. She saw the Prince and his bride searching for her; then they looked mournfully at the pearly foam, as if they knew that she had thrown herself into the waves. Invisible, she kissed the forehead of the bride, fanned the Prince, and mounted with the other children of the air on the rosy cloud which floated through the ether. After three hundred years we shall thus float into Paradise!

" And we may even get there sooner," whispered a daughter of the air. " Invisibly we float into the houses of men where children are, and for every day on which we find a good child that brings joy to its parents and deserves their love, our time of probation is shortened. The child does not know when we fly through the room; and when we smile with joy at the child's conduct, a year is counted off from the three hundred; but when we see a naughty or a wicked child, we shed tears of grief, and for every tear a day is added to our time of trial."

The Wild Swans

Far away, where the swallows take refuge in winter, lived a King who had eleven sons and one daughter, Elise. The eleven brothers—they were all princes—used to go to school with stars on their breasts and swords at their sides. They wrote upon golden slates with diamond pencils, and could read just as well without a book as with one, so there was no mistake about their being real princes. Their sister Elise sat upon a little footstool of looking glass, and she had a picture book which had cost the half of a kingdom. Oh, these children were very happy, but it was not to last thus forever.

Their father, who was King over all the land, married a wicked Queen who was not at all kind to the poor children. They found that out on the first day. All was festive at the castle, but when the children wanted to play at having company, instead of letting them have all the cakes and baked apples they wanted, she would only let them have some sand in a teacup, and said they must make-believe.

In the following week she sent little Elise into the country to board with some peasants, and it did not take her long to make the King believe so many bad things about the boys that he cared no more about them.

"Fly out into the world and look after yourselves," said the wicked Queen. "You shall fly about like birds without voices."

But she could not make things as bad for them as she would have liked: they turned into eleven beautiful wild swans. They flew out of the palace window with a weird scream, right across the park and the woods.

It was very early in the morning when they came to the place where their sister Elise was sleeping in the peasant's house. They hovered over the roof of the house, turning and twisting their long necks and flapping their wings, but no one either heard or saw them. They had to fly away again, and they soared up towards the clouds, far out into the wide world, and they settled in a big dark wood which stretched down to the shore.

Poor little Elise stood in the peasant's room playing with a green leaf, for she had no other toys. She made a little hole in it which she looked through at the sun, and it seemed to her as if she saw her brothers' bright eyes. Every time the warm sunbeams shone upon her cheek it reminded her of their kisses.

One day passed just like another. When the wind whistled through the rose hedges outside the house, it whispered to the roses, " Who can be prettier than you are? " But the roses shook their heads and answered, " Elise." And when the old woman sat in the doorway reading her psalms, the wind turned over the leaves and said to the book, " Who can be more pious than you? " " Elise," answered the book. Both the roses and the book of psalms spoke only the truth.

She was to go home when she was fifteen, but when the Queen saw how pretty she was, she got very angry and her heart was filled with hatred. She would willingly have turned her into a wild swan like her brothers, but she did not dare to do it at once, because the King wanted to see his daughter.

The Queen always went to the bath in the early morning. It was built of marble and adorned with soft cushions and beautiful carpets.

She took three toads, kissed them, and said to the first,

"Sit upon Elise's head when she comes to the bath, so that she may become sluggish like yourself. Sit upon her forehead," she said to the second, "that she many become ugly like you, and then her father won't know her. Rest upon her heart," she whispered to the third. "Let an evil spirit come over her which may be a burden to her."

Then she put the toads into the clean water and a green tinge immediately came over it. She called Elise, undressed her, and made her go into the bath. When she ducked under the water, one of the toads got among her hair, the other got onto her forehead, and the third onto her bosom. But when she stood up, three scarlet poppies floated on the water! Had the creatures not been poisonous, and been kissed by the sorceress, they would have been changed into crimson roses. Yet they became flowers from merely having rested a moment on her head and her heart. She was far too good and innocent for the sorcery to have any power over her.

When the wicked Queen saw this, she rubbed her over with walnut juice and smeared her face with some evil-smelling salve. She also matted up her beautiful hair. It would have been impossible to recognize pretty Elise. When her father saw her, he was quite horrified and said that she could not be his daughter. Nobody would have anything to say to her, except the yard dog and the swallows, but they were poor dumb animals whose opinion went for nothing.

Poor Elise wept and thought of her eleven brothers who were all lost. She crept sadly out of the palace and wandered about all day, over meadows and marshes and into a big forest. She did not know in the least where she wanted to go, but she felt very sad and longed for her brothers, who, no doubt, like herself had been driven out of the palace.

She made up her mind to go and look for them, but she had only been in the wood for a short time when night fell. She had quite lost her way, so she lay down upon the soft moss, said her evening prayer, and rested her head on a little hillock. It was very still and the air was mild. Hundreds of glowworms shone around her on the grass and in the marsh like green fire. When she gently moved one of the branches over her head, the little shining insects fell over her like a shower of stars.

She dreamt about her brothers all night long. Again they were children playing together. They wrote upon the golden slates with their diamond pencils, and she looked at the picture book which had cost half a kingdom. But they no longer wrote strokes and noughts upon their slates as they used to do. No, they wrote down all their boldest exploits and everything that they had seen and experienced. Everything in the picture book was alive. The birds sang, and the people walked out of the book and spoke to Elise and her brothers. When she turned over a page they skipped back into their places again, so that there should be no confusion among the pictures.

When she woke the sun was already high. It is true she could not see it very well through the thick branches of the lofty forest trees, but the sunbeams cast a golden shimmer around beyond the forest. There was a fresh delicious scent of grass and herbs in the air, and the birds were almost ready to perch upon her shoulders. She could hear the splashing of water, for there were many springs around, which all flowed into a pond with a lovely sandy bottom. It was surrounded with thick bushes but there was one place which the stags had trampled down, and Elise passed through the opening to the waterside. It was so transparent that, had not the branches been moved by the breeze, she must have thought that they were painted on the bottom—so plainly was every leaf reflected, both those on which the sun played and those which were in shade.

When she saw her own face, she was quite frightened to see it so brown and ugly. But when she wet her little hand and rubbed her eyes and forehead, her white skin shone through again. Then she took off all her clothes and went into the fresh water. A more beautiful royal child than she could not be found in all the world.

When she had put on her clothes again and plaited her long hair, she went to a sparkling spring and drank some of the water out of the hollow of her hand. Then she wandered further into the wood, though she had not the least idea where she was going. She thought of her brothers, and she thought of a merciful God who would not forsake her. He lets the wild crab apples grow to feed the hungry, and He showed her a tree the branches of which were bending beneath their weight of fruit. Here she made her midday meal. Then, having put props under the branches, she walked on into the thickest part of the forest. It was so quiet that she heard her own footsteps. She heard every little withered leaf which bent under her feet. Not a bird was to be seen. Not a ray of sunlight pierced the leafy branches, and the tall trunks were so close together that when she looked before her it seemed as if a thick fence of heavy beams hemmed her in on every side. The solitude was such as she had never known before.

It was a very dark night. Not a single glowworm sparkled in the marsh. Sadly she lay down to sleep, and it seemed to her as if the branches above her parted asunder, and that the Saviour looked down upon her with His loving eyes and that little angels' heads peeped out above His head and under His arms.

When she woke in the morning, she was not sure if she had dreamt this or whether it was really true.

She walked a little further when she met an old woman with a basket full of berries, of which she gave her some. Elise asked if she had seen eleven princes ride through the wood.

"No," said the old woman. "But yesterday I saw eleven

swans with golden crowns upon their heads, swimming in
the stream close by there."

She led Elise a little further to a slope, at the foot of
which the stream meandered. The trees on either bank
stretched out their rich leafy branches towards each other.
And where their natural growth did not let them reach each
other, they had torn their roots out of the ground and
leaned over the water in order to interlace their branches.

Elise said good-bye to the old woman and walked along
by the river till it flowed out into the great open sea.

The beautiful open sea lay before the maiden, but not a
sail was to be seen on it, nor a single boat. How was she
ever to get any further? She looked at the numberless little
pebbles on the beach. They were all worn quite round by
the water. Glass, iron, stone—whatever was washed up—had
taken their shapes from the water, which yet was much softer
than her little hand.

" With all its rolling, it is untiring, and everything hard is
smoothed down," she said. " I will be just as untiring. Thank
you for your lesson, you clear rolling waves! Sometime, so
my heart tells me, you will bear me to my beloved brothers."

Eleven white swans' feathers were lying on the seaweed.
She picked them up and made a bunch of them. There were
still drops of water on them, but whether these were dew
or tears no one could tell. It was very lonely there by the
shore, but she did not feel it, for the sea was everchanging.
There were more changes on it in the course of a few hours
than could be seen on an inland fresh-water lake in a year.
If a big black cloud arose, it was just as if the sea wanted
to say, " I can look black too." And then the wind blew up
and the waves showed their white crests. But if the clouds
were red and the wind dropped, the sea looked like a rose
leaf, now white, now green. But however still it was, there
was always a little gentle motion just by the shore. The
water rose and fell softly like the bosom of a sleeping child.

When the sun was about to go down, Elise saw eleven wild swans with golden crowns upon their heads flying towards the shore. They flew in a swaying line one behind the other, like a white ribbon streamer. Elise climbed up onto the bank and hid behind a bush. The swans settled close by her and flapped their great white wings.

As soon as the sun had sunk beneath the water the swans shed their feathers and became eleven handsome princes. They were Elise's brothers. Although they had altered a good deal, she knew them at once. She felt that they must be her brothers and she sprang into their arms, calling them by name. They were delighted when they recognized their little sister who had grown so big and beautiful. They laughed and cried and told each other how wickedly their stepmother had treated them all.

"We brothers," said the eldest, "have to fly about in the guise of swans as long as the sun is above the horizon. When it goes down we regain our human shapes. So we always have to look out for a resting place near sunset, for should we happen to be flying up among the clouds when the sun goes down, we should be hurled to the depths below. We do not live here. There is another land just as beautiful as this, beyond the sea, but the way to it is very long and we have to cross the mighty ocean to get to it. There is not a single island on the way where we can spend the night. Only one solitary little rock rises just above the water midway. It is only just big enough for us to stand upon close together, and if there is a heavy sea the water splashes over us. Yet we thank our God for it. We stay there overnight in our human forms, and without it we could never revisit our beloved fatherland, for our flight takes two of the longest days in the year. We are permitted to visit the home of our father only once a year, and we dare stay for only eleven days. We hover over this big forest from whence we catch a glimpse of the palace where we were born, and where our father lives. Beyond it we can see the high church towers where our mother is buried. We fancy that the trees and bushes here are related to us, and the wild horses gallop over the moors as we used to see them in our childhood. The charcoal burners still sing the old songs we used to dance to when we were children. This is our fatherland. We are drawn towards it and here we have found you again, dear little sister. We may stay here two days longer, and then we must fly away again across the ocean, to a lovely country indeed, but it is not our own dear fatherland. How shall we ever take you with us? We have neither ship nor boat."

"How can I deliver you?" said their sister, and they went on talking to each other nearly all night. They only dozed for a few hours.

Elise was awakened in the morning by the rustling of the swans' wings above her. Her brothers were again transformed and were wheeling round in great circles, till she lost sight of them in the distance. One of them, the youngest, stayed behind. He laid his head against her bosom and she caressed it with her fingers. They remained together all day. Towards evening the others came back, and as soon as the sun went down they took their natural forms.

"Tomorrow we must fly away and we dare not come back for a whole year, but we can't leave you like this. Have you courage to go with us? My wings are strong enough to carry you over the forest, so our united strength ought to be sufficient to bear you across the ocean."

"Oh yes! Take me with you," said Elise.

They spent the whole night in weaving a kind of net of the elastic bark of the willow, bound together with tough rushes. They made it both large and strong. Elise lay down upon it, and when the sun rose and the brothers became swans again, they took up the net in their bills and flew high up among the clouds with their precious sister, who

was fast asleep. As the sunbeams fell straight onto her face,
one of the swans flew over her head so that his broad wings
should shade her.

They were far from land when Elise woke. She thought
she must still be dreaming—it seemed so strange to be carried
through the air so high up above the sea. By her side lay a
branch of beautiful ripe berries and a bundle of savory roots,
which her youngest brother had collected for her and for
which she gave him a grateful smile. She knew it was he
who flew above her head, shading her from the sun. They
were so high up that the first ship they saw looked like a gull
floating on the water. A great cloud came up behind them
like a mountain, and Elise saw the shadow of herself on it,
and those of the eleven swans looking like giants. It was a
more beautiful picture than any she had ever seen before,
but as the sun rose higher, the cloud fell behind and the
shadow picture disappeared.

They flew on and on all day like arrows whizzing through
the air, but they went slower than usual for now they had
their sister to carry. A storm came up, and night was drawing
on. With terror in her heart Elise saw the sun sinking, for
the solitary rock was nowhere to be seen. The swans seemed
to be taking stronger strokes than ever. Alas, she was the
cause of their not being able to get on faster. As soon as the
sun went down they would become men, and they would be
hurled into the sea and drowned. She prayed to God from
the bottom of her heart, but still no rock was to be seen.
Black clouds gathered and strong gusts of wind announced
a storm. The clouds looked like a great threatening leaden
wave, and the flashes of lightning followed each other rapidly.

The sun was now at the edge of the sea. Elise's heart
quaked, when suddenly the swans shot downwards so
suddenly that she thought they were falling. Then they
hovered again. Half of the sun was below the horizon, and
there for the first time she saw the little rock below, which

did not look bigger than the head of a seal above the water. The sun sank very quickly. It was no bigger than a star, but her foot touched solid earth. The sun went out like the last sparks of a bit of burning paper. Her brothers stood arm in arm around her, but there was only just room enough for them. The waves beat upon the rock and washed over them like drenching rain. The heaven shone with continuous fire and the thunder rolled, peal upon peal. But the sister and brothers held each other's hands and sang a psalm which gave them comfort and courage.

The air was pure and still at dawn. As soon as the sun rose, the swans flew off with Elise away from the islet. The sea still ran high. It looked from where they were as if the white foam on the dark green water were millions of swans floating on the waves.

When the sun rose higher, Elise saw before her, half floating in the air, great masses of ice with shining glaciers on the heights. Midway was perched a palace, a mile in length, with one bold colonnade built above another. Below swayed palm trees and gorgeous blossoms as big as mill wheels. She asked if this was the land to which she was going, but the swans shook their heads because what she saw was a mirage. It was the beautiful and ever-changing palace of Fata Morgana. No mortal dared enter it. Elise gazed at it, but as she gazed the palace, gardens, and mountains melted away. And in their place stood twenty proud churches with their high towers and pointed windows. She seemed to hear the notes of the organ, but it was the sea she heard. When she got close to the seeming churches, they changed to a great navy sailing beneath her, but it was only a sea mist floating over the waters.

Yes, she saw constant changes passing before her eyes, but now she saw the real land she was bound to. Beautiful blue mountains rose before her with their cedar woods and palaces. Long before the sun went down, she sat among the hills in front of a big cave covered with delicate green creepers. It looked like a piece of embroidery.

"Now we shall see what you will dream here tonight," said the youngest brother, as he showed her where she was to sleep.

"If only I might dream how I could deliver you!" she said, and this thought filled her mind entirely. She prayed earnestly to God for His help, and even in her sleep she continued her prayer. It seemed to her that she was flying up to Fata Morgana in her castle in the air. The fairy came towards her. She was charming and brilliant, and yet she was very like the old woman who gave her the berries in the wood and told her about the swans with the golden crowns.

"Your brothers can be delivered," she said. "But have you courage and endurance enough for it? The sea is indeed softer than your hands, and it molds the hardest stones, but it does not feel the pain your fingers will feel. It has no heart and does not suffer the pain and anguish you must feel. Do you see the stinging nettle I hold in my hand? Many of this kind grow round the cave where you sleep. Only these and the ones which grow in the churchyards may be used. Mark that! Those you may pluck, although they will burn and blister your hands. Crush the nettles with your feet and you will have flax, and of this you must weave eleven coats of mail with long sleeves. Throw these over the eleven wild swans and the charm is broken. But remember, from the moment you begin this work till it is finished, even if it takes years, you must not utter a word. The first word you say will fall like a murderer's dagger into the hearts of your brothers. Their lives hang on your tongue. Mark this well."

She touched her hand at the same moment. The touch was like burning fire and it woke Elise. It was bright daylight, and close to where she slept lay a nettle like those in her dream. She fell upon her knees with thanks to God and left the cave to begin her work.

She seized the horrid nettles with her delicate hands, and they burnt like fire. Great blisters rose on her hands and arms, but she suffered it willingly if only it would deliver her beloved brothers. She crushed every nettle with her bare feet and twisted it into green flax.

When the sun went down and the brothers came back, they were alarmed at finding her mute. They thought it was some new witchcraft exercised by their wicked stepmother. But when they saw her hands, they understood that it was for their sakes. The youngest brother wept, and wherever his tears fell she felt no more pain and the blisters disappeared.

She spent the whole night at her work, for she could not rest till she had delivered her dear brothers. All the following day, while her brothers were away, she sat solitary, but never had the time flown so fast. One coat of mail was finished and she began the next. Then a hunting horn sounded among the mountains. She was frightened. The sound came nearer and she heard dogs barking. In terror she rushed into the cave and tied the nettles she had collected and woven into a bundle upon which she sat.

At this moment a big dog bounded forward from the thicket, and another and another. They barked loudly and ran backwards and forwards. In a few minutes all the huntsmen were standing outside the cave. The handsomest of them was the King of the country, and he stepped up to Elise. Never had he seen so lovely a girl.

" How came you here, beautiful child? " he said.

Elise shook her head. She dared not speak. The salvation and the lives of her brothers depended upon her silence. She hid her hands under her apron so that the King should not see what she suffered.

" Come with me," he said. " You cannot stay here. If you are as good as you are beautiful, I will dress you in silks and velvets, put a golden crown upon your head, and you shall live with me and have your home in my richest palace." Then he lifted her upon his horse. She wept and wrung her hands, but the King said, " I think only of your happiness. You will thank me one day for what I am doing." Then he darted off across the mountains, holding her before him on his horse, and the huntsmen followed.

When the sun went down, the royal city with churches and cupolas lay before them, and the King led her into the palace. Here great fountains played in the marble halls and the walls and ceilings were adorned with paintings, but she had no eyes for them. She only wept and sorrowed. Passively she allowed the women to dress her in royal robes, to twist pearls into her hair, and to draw gloves onto her blistered hands.

She was dazzlingly lovely as she stood there in all her magnificence. The courtiers bent low before her and the King wooed her as his bride, although the archbishop shook his head and whispered that he feared the beautiful wood maiden was a witch, who had dazzled their eyes and infatuated the King.

The King refused to listen to him. He ordered the music to play, the richest food to be brought, and the loveliest girls to dance before her. She was led through scented gardens into gorgeous apartments, but nothing brought a smile to her lips or into her eyes. Sorrow sat there like a heritage and a possession for all time. Last of all, the King opened the door of a little chamber close by the room where she was to sleep. It was adorned with costly green carpets and made to exactly resemble the cave where he found her. On the floor lay the bundle of flax she had spun from the nettles, and from the ceiling hung the shirt of mail which was already finished. One of the huntsmen had brought all these things away as curiosities.

"Here you may dream that you are back in your former home," said the King. "Here is the work upon which you were engaged. In the midst of your splendor it may amuse you to think of those times."

When Elise saw all these things so dear to her heart, a smile for the first time played upon her lips and the blood rushed back to her cheeks. She thought of the deliverance of her brothers and she kissed the King's hand. He pressed her to his heart and ordered all the church bells to ring marriage peals. The lovely dumb girl from the woods was to be Queen of the country.

The archbishop whispered evil words into the ear of the King, but they did not reach his heart. The wedding was to take place and the archbishop himself had to put the crown upon her head. In his anger he pressed the golden circlet so tightly upon her head that it gave her pain. But a heavier circlet pressed upon her heart, her grief for her brothers, so she thought nothing of the bodily pain. Her lips were sealed. A single word from her mouth would cost her brothers their lives, but her eyes were full of love for the good and handsome King, who did everything he could to please her.

Every day she grew more and more attached to him. She longed to confide in him and tell him her sufferings, but dumb she must remain and in silence must bring her labor to completion. Therefore at night she stole away from his side into her secret chamber, which was decorated like a cave, and here she knitted one shirt after another. When she came to the seventh, all her flax was worked up. She knew that these nettles which she was to use grew in the churchyard, but she had to pluck them herself. How was she to get there?

"Oh, what is the pain of my fingers compared with the anguish of my heart?" she thought. "I must venture out. The good God will not desert me."

With as much terror in her heart as if she were doing some evil deed, she stole down one night into the moonlit garden and through the long alleys out into the silent streets to the churchyard. It was very dark and lonely, but she picked the stinging nettles and hurried back to the palace with them. Only one person saw her but that was the archbishop, who watched while others slept. Surely now all his bad opinions of the Queen were justified. All was not as it should be with her. She must be a witch, and therefore she had bewitched the King and all the people.

He told the King in the confessional what he had seen and what he feared. When those bad words passed his lips, the pictures of the saints shook their heads as if to say, " It is not so. Elise is innocent." The archbishop, however, took it differently. He thought they were bearing witness against her and shaking their heads at her sin.

Two big tears rolled down the King's cheeks, and he went home with doubt in his heart. He pretended to sleep at night, but no quiet sleep came to his eyes. He perceived how Elise got up and went to her private closet. Day by day his face grew darker. Elise saw it but could not imagine what was the cause of it. It alarmed her, and what was she not already suffering in her heart because of her brothers? Her salt tears ran down upon the royal purple velvet and lay there like sparkling diamonds, and all who saw their splendor wished to be Queen.

She had, however, almost reached the end for her labors. Only one shirt of mail was wanting, but again she had no more flax and not a single nettle was left. Once more, for the last time, she must go to the churchyard to pluck a few handfuls. She thought with dread of the solitary walk and the darkness, but her will was as strong as her trust in God.

Elise went, but the King and the archbishop followed her. They saw her disappear within the grated gateway of the churchyard. The King was very sorrowful, because he thought she must surely be a witch.

" The people must judge her," he groaned. And the people judged: " Let her be consumed in the glowing flames."

She was led from her beautiful royal apartments to a dark damp dungeon, where the wind whistled through the grated window. Instead of velvet and silk they gave her the bundle of nettles she had gathered to lay her head upon. The hard burning shirts of mail were to be her covering, but they could have given her nothing more precious.

She set to work again with many prayers to God. Outside her prison the street boys sang derisive songs about her, and not a soul comforted her with a kind word.

Towards evening she heard the rustle of swans' wings close to her window. It was her youngest brother, who at last had found her. He sobbed aloud with joy although he knew that the coming night might be her last. But then her work was almost done and her brothers were there.

The archbishop came to stay with her during her last hours, as he had promised the King. She shook her head at him and by looks and gestures begged him to leave her. She had only this night in which to finish her work, or else all would be wasted—all her pain, her tears and her sleepless nights. The archbishop went away with bitter words against her, but poor Elise knew that she was innocent, and she went on with her work.

The little mice ran about the floor, bringing nettles to her feet so as to give what help they could, and a thrush sat on the grating of the window, where he sang all night as merrily as he could to keep up her courage.

It was still only dawn and the sun would not rise for an hour, when the eleven brothers stood at the gate of the palace, begging to be taken to the King. This could not be done, they were told, for it was still night. The King was asleep and no one dared wake him. All their entreaties and threats were useless. The watch turned out and even the King himself came to see what was the matter. But just then the sun rose, and no more brothers were to be seen—only eleven wild swans hovering over the palace.

The whole populace streamed out of the town gates. They were all anxious to see the witch burnt. A miserable horse drew the cart in which Elise was seated. They had put upon her a smock of green sacking, and all her beautiful long hair hung loose from the lovely head. Her cheeks were deathly pale and her lips moved softly, while her fingers unceasingly twisted the green yarn. Even on the way to her death she could not abandon her unfinished work. Ten shirts lay completed at her feet. She labored away at the eleventh amid the scoffing insults of the populace.

"Look at the witch! How she mutters! She has no book of psalms in her hands. There she sits with her loathsome sorcery. Tear it away from her and into a thousand bits!"

The crowd pressed around her to destroy her work, but just then eleven wild swans flew down and perched upon the cart, flapping their wings. The crowd gave way before them in terror.

"It is a sign from Heaven! She is innocent," they whispered. But they dared not say it aloud.

The executioner seized her by the hand but she hastily threw the eleven shirts over the swans, who were immediately transformed to eleven handsome princes. But the youngest had a swan's wing in place of an arm, for one sleeve was wanting to his shirt of mail. She had not been able to finish it.

"Now I may speak! I am innocent."

The populace who saw what had happened bowed down before her as if she had been a saint, but she sank lifeless in her brother's arms. So great had been the strain, the terror, and the suffering she had endured.

"Yes, innocent she is indeed," said the eldest brother, and he told them all that had happened.

Whilst he spoke a wonderful fragrance spread around, as of millions of roses. Every faggot in the pile had taken root and shot out branches, and a great high hedge of red roses had arisen. At the very top was one pure white blossom. It shone like a star, and the King broke it off and laid it on Elise's bosom, and she woke with joy and peace in her heart.

All the church bells began to ring of their own accord, and the singing birds flocked around them. Surely such a bridal procession went back to the palace as no king had ever seen before!

Great Claus and Little Claus

In a village there once lived two men of the selfsame name. They were both called Claus, but one of them had four horses and the other had only one. So to distinguish them, people called the owner of the four horses "Great Claus," and he who had only one horse was called "Little Claus." Now I shall tell you what happened to them, for this is a true story.

Throughout the week Little Claus was obliged to plow for Great Claus and to lend him his one horse, but once a week—on Sunday—Great Claus lent him all his four horses. How proudly each Sunday Little Claus would smack his whip over all five, for they were as good as his own on that one day.

The sun shone brightly and the church bells rang merrily as the people passed by, dressed in their best and with their prayer books under their arms. They were going to hear the parson preach. They looked at Little Claus plowing with his five horses, and he was so proud that he smacked his whip and said, "Gee-up, my five horses."

"You mustn't say that," said Great Claus, "for only one of them is yours."

But Little Claus soon forgot what he ought not to say, and when anyone passed he would call out, "Gee-up, my five horses."

"I must really beg you not to say that again," said Great Claus. "If you do, I shall hit your horse on the head so that he will drop down dead on the spot. And that will be the end of him."

"I promise you I will not say it again," said the other. But as soon as anybody came by nodding to him and wishing him "Good day," he was so pleased and thought how grand it was to have five horses plowing in his field that he cried out again, "Gee-up, all my horses!"

"I'll gee-up your horses for you," said Great Claus. And seizing the tethering mallet he struck Little Claus's one horse on the head, and it fell down dead.

"Oh, now I have no horse at all," said Little Claus, weeping. But after a while he flayed the dead horse and hung the skin in the wind to dry.

Then he put the dried skin into a bag, hung it over his shoulder, and went off to the next town to sell it. But he had a long way to go and had to pass through a dark and gloomy forest.

Presently a storm arose and he lost his way. And before he discovered the right path, evening was drawing on, and it was still a long way to the town and too far to return home before nightfall.

Near the road stood a large farmhouse. The shutters outside the windows were closed, but lights shone through the crevices and at the top. "They might let me stay here for the night," thought Little Claus, so he went up to the door and knocked.

The farmer's wife opened the door, but when she heard what he wanted she told him to go away. Her husband was not at home and she could not let any strangers in.

"Then I shall have to lie out here," said Little Claus to himself, as the farmer's wife shut the door in his face.

Close to the farmhouse stood a large haystack, and between it and the house there was a small shed with a thatched roof. " I can lie up there," said Little Claus, as he saw the roof. " It will make a famous bed, but I hope the stork won't fly down and bite my legs." A live stork who had his nest on the roof was standing up there.

So Little Claus climbed on to the roof of the shed. And as he turned about to make himself comfortable, he discovered that the wooden shutters did not reach to the top of the windows. He could see into the room, in which a large table was laid out with wine, roast meat, and a splendid fish. The farmer's wife and the sexton were sitting at table together. Nobody else was there. She was filling his glass and helping him plentifully to fish, which appeared to be his favorite dish.

" If only I could have some too," thought Little Claus. Then he stretched out his neck towards the window and spied a beautiful large cake. Indeed, they had a glorious feast before them.

At that moment he heard someone riding down the road towards the farm. It was the farmer coming home.

He was a good man but he had one very strange prejudice—he could not bear the sight of a sexton. If he happened to see one, he would get into a terrible rage. Because of this dislike, the sexton had gone to visit the farmer's wife during her husband's absence from home, and the good woman had put before him the best of everything she had in the house to eat.

When they heard the farmer they were dreadfully frightened, and the woman made the sexton creep into a large chest which stood in a corner. He went at once, for he was well aware of the poor man's aversion to the sight of a sexton. The woman then quickly hid all the nice things and the wine in the oven, because if her husband had seen it he would have asked why it was provided.

" Oh dear," sighed Little Claus, on the roof, when he saw the food disappearing.

"Is there anyone up there?" asked the farmer, peering up at Little Claus. "What are you doing up there? You had better come into the house."

Then Little Claus told him how he had lost his way and asked if he might have shelter for the night.

"Certainly," said the farmer. "But the first thing is to have something to eat."

The woman received them both very kindly, laid the table, and gave them a large bowl of porridge. The farmer was hungry and ate it with a good appetite, but Little Claus could not help thinking of the good roast meat, the fish, and the cake, which he knew were hidden in the oven. He had put his sack with the hide in it under the table by his feet, for as we remember he was on his way to the town to sell it. He did not fancy the porridge, so he trod on the sack and made the dried hide squeak quite loudly.

"Hush!" said Little Claus to his sack, at the same time treading on it again so that it squeaked louder than ever.

"What on earth have you got in your sack?" asked the farmer.

"Oh, it's a goblin," said Little Claus. "He says we needn't eat the porridge, for he has charmed the oven full of roast meat and fish and cake."

"What do you say?" said the farmer, opening the oven door with all speed and seeing the nice things the woman had hidden, but which her husband thought the goblin had produced for their special benefit.

The woman dared not say anything but put the food before them, and then they both made a hearty meal of the fish, the meat, and the cake.

Then Little Claus trod on the skin and made it squeak again.

"What does he say now?" asked the farmer.

"He says," answered Little Claus, "that he has also charmed three bottles of wine into the oven for us."

The Wild Swans (Italy, 8 years old)
(STORY PAGE 91)

So the woman had to bring out the wine too, and the farmer drank it and became very merry. Wouldn't he like to have a goblin for himself, like the one in Little Claus's sack!

"Can he charm out the devil?" asked the farmer. "I shouldn't mind seeing him, now that I am in such a merry mood."

"Oh yes!" said Little Claus. "My goblin can do everything that we ask him. Can't you?" he asked, trampling on the sack till it squeaked louder than ever. "Did you hear him say yes? But the devil is so ugly, you'd better not see him."

"Oh, I'm not a bit frightened. Whatever does he look like?"

"Well, he will show himself in the image of a sexton."

"Oh dear!" said the farmer. "That's bad! I must tell you that I can't bear to see a sexton. However, it doesn't matter. I shall know it's only the devil and then I shan't mind so much. Now my courage is up! But he mustn't come too close."

"I'll ask my goblin about it," said Little Claus, treading on the bag and putting his ear close to it.

"What does he say?"

"He says you can go along and open the chest in the corner, and there you'll see the devil moping in the dark. But hold the lid tight so that he doesn't get out."

"Will you help me to hold it?" asked the farmer, going along to the chest where the woman had hidden the real sexton, who was shivering with fright. The farmer lifted up the lid a wee little bit and peeped in.

"Ha!" he shrieked, and sprang back. "Yes, I saw him and he looked just exactly like our sexton. It was a horrible sight!" They had to have a drink after this, and there they sat drinking till far into the night.

"You must sell me that goblin," said the farmer. "You

8

may ask what you like for him! I'll give you a bushel of money for him."

"No, I can't do that," said Little Claus. "You must remember how useful my goblin is to me."

"Oh, but I should so like to have him," said the farmer and he went on begging for him.

"Well," said Little Claus at last, "as you have been so kind to me I shall have to give him up. You shall have him for a bushel of money, but I must have it full to the brim."

"You shall have it," said the farmer. "But you must take that chest away with you! I won't have it in the house for another hour. I'd never know whether he's there or not."

So Little Claus gave his sack with the dried hide in it to the farmer and received in return a bushel of money, and the measure was full to the brim. The farmer also gave him a large wheelbarrow to take the money and the chest away in.

"Good-bye," said Little Claus, and off he went with his money and the big chest with the sexton in it.

There was a wide and deep river on the other side of the wood. The current was so strong that it was almost impossible to swim against it. A large new bridge had been built across it, and when they got into the very middle of it, Little Claus said quite loud, so that the sexton could hear him, "What am I to do with this stupid old chest? It might be full of paving stones—it's so heavy. I am quite tired of wheeling it along, so I'll just throw it into the river. If it floats down the river to my house, well and good; and if it doesn't, I shan't care."

Then he took hold of the chest and raised it up a bit, as if he were about to throw it into the river.

"No, no! Let it be!" shouted the sexton. "Let me get out!"

"Hullo!" said Little Claus, pretending to be frightened. "Why, he's still inside it! Then I must heave it into the river to drown him."

"Oh no! Oh no!" shouted the sexton. "I'll give you a bushel full of money if you'll let me out!"

"Oh, that's another matter," said Little Claus, opening the chest. The sexton crept out at once and pushed the empty chest into the water, and then went home and gave Little Claus a whole bushel full of money. He had already had one from the farmer, you know, so now his wheelbarrow was quite full of money.

"I got a pretty fair price for that horse, I must admit," said he to himself when he got home to his own room and turned the money out of the wheelbarrow into a heap on the floor. "What a rage Great Claus will be in when he discovers how rich I have become through my one horse. But I won't tell him the truth about it." So he sent a boy to Great Claus to borrow a bushel measure.

"What does he want that for?" thought Great Claus. And he rubbed some tallow on the bottom of the measure, so that a little of whatever was to be measured might stick to it. So it did, for when the measure came back three new silver threepenny bits were sticking to it.

"What's this?" said Great Claus, and he ran straight along to Little Claus. "Where on earth did you get all that money?"

"Oh, that was for my horse's hide which I sold last night."

"That was well paid, indeed!" said Great Claus. And he ran home, took an ax, and hit all his four horses on the head. He then flayed them and went off to the town with the hides.

"Skins! Skins! Who will buy skins?" he shouted up and down the streets.

All the shoemakers and tanners in the town came running up and asked him how much he wanted for them.

"A bushel of money for each," said Great Claus.

"Are you mad?" they all said. "Do you imagine we have money by the bushel?"

" Skins! Skins! Who will buy skins? " he shouted again.

The shoemakers took up their measures and the tanners their leather aprons, and beat Great Claus through the town. "Skins! Skins!" they mocked him. "Yes, we'll give you a raw hide. Out the town with him!" they shouted, and Great Claus had to hurry off as fast as ever he could go. He had never had such a beating in his life.

"Little Claus shall pay for this," he said when he got home. "I'll kill him for it."

Little Claus's old grandmother had just died in his house. She certainly had been very cross and unkind to him, but now that she was dead he felt quite sorry about it. He took the dead woman and put her into his warm bed to see if he could bring her to life again. He meant her to stay there all night, and he would sit on a chair in the corner. He had slept like that before.

As he sat there in the night, the door opened and in came Great Claus with his ax. He knew where Little Claus's bed stood, and he went straight up to it and hit the dead grandmother a blow on the forehead, thinking that it was Little Claus.

"Just see if you'll cheat me again after that," he said. Then he went home again.

"What a bad, wicked man he is," said Little Claus. "He was going to kill me there. What a good thing that poor old granny was dead already, or else he would have killed her."

He now dressed his old grandmother in her best Sunday clothes, borrowed a horse from his neighbor, harnessed it to a cart, and set his grandmother on the back seat so that she could not fall out when the cart moved. Then he started off through the wood. When the sun rose he was just outside a big inn, and Little Claus drew up his horse and went in to get something to eat. The landlord was a very, very rich man and a very good man, but he was fiery-tempered, as if he were made of pepper and tobacco.

" Good morning," said he to Little Claus. " You've got your best clothes on very early this morning! "

" Yes," said Little Claus. " I'm going to town with my old grandmother. She's sitting out there in the cart. I can't get her to come in. Won't you take her out a glass of mead? You'll have to shout at her, for she's very hard of hearing."

" Yes, she shall have it," said the innkeeper, and he poured out a large glass of mead which he took out to the dead grandmother in the cart.

" Here is a glass of mead your son has sent," said the innkeeper, but the dead woman sat quite still and never said a word. " Don't you hear? " shouted the innkeeper as loud as he could. " Here is a glass of mead from your son! "

Again he shouted and then again as loud as ever, but as she did not stir he got angry and threw the glass of mead in her face. The mead ran all over her and she fell backwards out of the cart, for she was only stuck up and not tied in.

" Now," shouted Little Claus, as he rushed out of the inn and seized the landlord by the neck. " You have killed my grandmother! Just look! There's a great hole in her forehead."

" Oh, what a misfortune! " exclaimed the innkeeper, clasping his hands. " That's the consequence of my fiery temper. Good Little Claus, I will give you a bushel of money and bury your grandmother as if she had been my own, if you will only say nothing about it. Otherwise they will chop my head off, and that is so nasty."

So Little Claus had a whole bushel of money, and the innkeeper buried the old grandmother just as if she had been his own.

When Little Claus got home again with his money, he immediately sent his boy over to Great Claus to borrow his measure.

" What? " said Great Claus, " Is he not dead? I shall have

to go and see about it myself." So he took the measure over
to Little Claus himself.

"I say, wherever did you get all that money?" asked he,
his eyes round with amazement at what he saw.

"It was my grandmother you killed instead of me," said
Little Claus. "I have sold her and got a bushel of money
for her."

"That was good pay indeed!" said Great Claus, so he
hurried home, took an ax, and killed his old grandmother.

He then put her in a cart and drove off to town with
her where the apothecary lived, and asked if he would buy
a dead body.

"Who is it, and where did the body come from?" asked
the apothecary.

"It is my grandmother, and I have killed her for a bushel
of money," said Great Claus.

"Heaven preserve us!" said the apothecary. "You are
talking like a madman. Pray don't say such things! You
might lose your head." And he pointed out to him what a
horribly wicked thing he had done and what a bad man he
was, and that he deserved to be punished. Great Claus was
so frightened that he rushed straight out of the shop, jumped
into the cart, whipped up his horse, and galloped home.
The apothecary and everyone else thought he was mad, and
so they let him drive off.

"You shall be paid for this!" said Great Claus, when he
got out on the highroad. "You shall pay for this, Little
Claus!"

As soon as he got home, he took the biggest sack he could
find, went over to Little Claus and said, "You have deceived
me again. First I killed my horses, and then my old grandmother. It's all your fault, but you shan't have the chance of
cheating me again!" Then he took Little Claus by the waist
and put him into the sack, put it on his back, and shouted
to him, "I'm going to drown you now!"

It was a long way to go before he came to the river, and Little Claus was not so light to carry. The road passed close by a church in which the organ was playing, and the people were singing beautifully. Great Claus put down the sack with Little Claus in it close by the church door. He thought he would like to go and hear a psalm before he went any further. As Little Claus could not get out of the bag, and all the people were in the church, Great Claus went in too.

"Oh dear, oh dear!" sighed Little Claus in the sack. He turned and twisted, but it was impossible to undo the cord. Just then an old cattle drover with white hair and a tall stick in his hand came along. He had a whole drove of cows and bulls before him. They ran against the sack Little Claus was in and upset it.

"Oh dear," sighed Little Claus. "I am so young to be going to the Kingdom of Heaven!"

"And I," said the cattle drover, "am so old and cannot get there yet!"

"Open the sack!" shouted Little Claus. "Get in in place of me, and you will get to Heaven directly."

"That will just suit me," said the cattle drover, undoing the sack for Little Claus, who immediately sprang out. "You must look after the cattle now," said the old man as he crept into the sack. Little Claus tied it up and walked off driving the cattle before him.

A little while afterwards Great Claus came out of the church. He took the sack again on his back and he certainly thought it had grown lighter, for the old cattle drover was not more than half the weight of Little Claus.

"How light he seems to have got! That must be because I have been to church and said my prayers." Then he went on to the river, which was both wide and deep, and threw the sack with the old cattle drover in it into the water.

"Now, you won't cheat me again!" he shouted, for he thought it was Little Claus.

Then he went homewards, but when he reached the cross-roads he met Little Claus with his herd of cattle.

" What's the meaning of this? " exclaimed Great Claus. " Didn't I drown you? "

" Yes," said Little Claus. " It's just about half an hour since you threw me into the river."

" But where did you get all those splendid beasts? " asked Great Claus.

" They are sea cattle," said Little Claus. " I will tell you the whole story, and indeed I thank you heartily for drowning me. I'm at the top of the tree now and a very rich man, I can tell you. I was so frightened when I was in the sack! The wind whistled in my ears when you threw me over the bridge into the cold water. I immediately sank to the bottom but I was not hurt, for the grass is beautifully soft down there. The sack was opened at once by a beautiful maiden in snow-white clothes with a green wreath on her wet hair. She took my hand and said, ' Are you there, Little Claus? Here are some cattle for you, and a mile further up the road you will come upon another herd which I will give you too! ' Then I saw that the river was a great highway for the sea folk. Down at the bottom of it they walked and drove about, from the sea right up to the end of the river. The flowers were lovely and the grass was so fresh! The fishes which swam about glided close to me just like birds in the air. How nice the people were, and what a lot of cattle strolled about in the ditches! "

" But why did you come straight up here again then? " asked Great Claus. " I shouldn't have done that if it was so fine down there."

" Oh," said Little Claus, " that's just my cunning. You remember I told you the mermaid said that a mile further up the road—and by the road she means the river, for she can't go anywhere else—I should find another herd of cattle waiting for me. Well, I know how many bends there are

The Swineherd
(Denmark, 15 years old)
(STORY PAGE 147)

in the river and what a roundabout way it would be. It's ever so much shorter if you can come up on dry land and take the short cuts. You save a couple of miles by it and can get the cattle much sooner."

"Oh, you *are* a fortunate man," said Great Claus. "Do you think I should get some sea cattle if I were to go down to the bottom of the river?"

"I'm sure you would," said Little Claus. "But I can't carry you in the sack to the river. You're too heavy for me. If you'd like to walk there and then get into the sack, I'll throw you into the river with the greatest pleasure in the world."

"Thank you," said Great Claus. "But if I don't get any sea cattle when I get down there, see if I don't give you a sound thrashing."

"Oh, don't be so hard on me!" said Little Claus.

Then they walked off to the river. As soon as the cattle saw the water they rushed down to drink, for they were very thirsty. "See what a hurry they're in," said Little Claus. "They want to get down to the bottom again."

"Now, help me first," said Great Claus, "or else I'll thrash you." He then crept into a big sack which had been lying across the back of one of the cows. "Put a big stone in, or I'm afraid I shan't sink," said Great Claus.

"Oh, have no fear of that," said Little Claus, and he put a big stone into the sack and gave it a push. Plump went the sack and Great Claus was in the river, where he sank to the bottom at once.

"I'm afraid he won't find any cattle," said Little Claus, as he drove his herd home.

The Steadfast Tin Soldier

There were once five and twenty tin soldiers, all brothers, for they were the offspring of the same old tin spoon. Each man shouldered his gun, kept his eyes well to the front, and wore the smartest red and blue uniform imaginable. The first thing they heard in their new world, when the lid was taken off the box, was a little boy clapping his hands and crying, " Soldiers, soldiers! "

It was his birthday and they had just been given to him, so he lost no time in setting them up on the table. All the soldiers were exactly alike with one exception, and he differed from the rest in having only one leg. For he was made last, and there was not quite enough tin left to finish him. However, he stood just as well on his one leg as the others did on two. In fact he was the very one who became famous.

On the table where they were being set up were many other toys, but the chief thing which caught the eye was a delightful paper castle. You could see through the tiny windows right into the rooms. Outside there were some little trees surrounding a small mirror, representing a lake, whose surface reflected the waxen swans which were swimming about on it. It was altogether charming, but the prettiest thing of all was a little maiden standing at the open door of the castle.

She too was cut out of paper, but she wore a dress of the

lightest gauze, with a dainty little blue ribbon over her shoulders, by way of a scarf, set off by a brilliant spangle as big as her whole face. The little maid was stretching out both arms, for she was a dancer. And in the dance one of her legs was raised so high into the air that the tin soldier could see absolutely nothing of it, and supposed that she like himself had but one leg.

"That would be the very wife for me!" he thought, "but she is much too grand. She lives in a palace, while I only have a box, and then there are five and twenty of us to share it. No, that would be no place for her. But I must try to make her acquaintance!" Then he lay down full length behind a snuffbox which stood on the table. From that point he could have a good look at the lady, who continued to stand on one leg without losing her balance.

Late in the evening the other soldiers were put into their box, and the people of the house went to bed. Now was the time for the toys to play. They amused themselves with paying visits, fighting battles, and giving balls. The tin soldiers rustled about in their box for they wanted to join the games, but they could not get the lid off. The nutcrackers turned somersaults and the pencil scribbled nonsense on the slate. There was such a noise that the canary woke up and joined in, but his remarks were in verse. The only two who did not move were the tin soldier and the little dancer. She stood as stiff as ever on tiptoe, with her arms spread out. He was equally firm on his one leg, and he did not take his eyes off her for a moment.

Then the clock struck twelve, when pop! up flew the lid of the snuffbox, but there was no snuff in it. No! There was a little black goblin, a sort of jack-in-the-box.

"Tin soldier," said the goblin, "have the goodness to keep your eyes to yourself." But the tin soldier feigned not to hear.

"Ah! you just wait till tomorrow," said the goblin.

In the morning when the children got up, they put the

tin soldier on the window frame, and whether it was caused
by the goblin or by a puff of wind, I do not know, but all
at once the window burst open and the soldier fell head
foremost from the third story.

It was a terrific descent, and he landed at last with his
leg in the air and resting on his cap, with his bayonet fixed
between two paving stones. The maidservant and the little
boy ran down at once to look for him, but although they
almost trod on him they could not see him. Had the soldier
called out, "Here I am!" they would have found him. But
he did not think it proper to shout when he was in uniform.

Presently it began to rain, and the drops fell faster and
faster till there was a regular torrent. When it was over, two
street boys came along. "Look out!" said one. "There is a
tin soldier. He shall go for a sail."

So they made a boat out of a newspaper and put the soldier
into the middle of it, and he sailed away down the gutter.
Both boys ran alongside clapping their hands. Good heavens!
what waves there were in the gutter, and what a current,
but then it certainly had rained cats and dogs. The paper
boat danced up and down, and now and then whirled round
and round. A shudder ran through the tin soldier, but he
remained undaunted and did not move a muscle. He only
looked straight before him with his gun shouldered. All at
once the boat drifted under a long wooden tunnel, and it
became as dark as it was in his box.

"Where on earth am I going now?" thought he. "Well,
well, it is all the fault of that goblin! Oh, if only the little
maiden were with me in the boat, it might be twice as dark
for all I should care."

At this moment a big water rat, who lived in the tunnel,
came up.

"Have you a pass?" asked the rat. "Hand up your pass."

The tin soldier did not speak, but clung still tighter to his
gun. The boat rushed on, the rat close behind. Phew, how

he gnashed his teeth and shouted to the bits of stick and straw, " Stop him! Stop him! He hasn't paid his toll. He hasn't shown his pass."

But the current grew stronger and stronger. The tin soldier could already see daylight before him at the end of the tunnel, but he also heard a roaring sound, fit to strike terror to the bravest heart. Just imagine: where the tunnel ended, the stream rushed straight into the big canal. That would be just as dangerous for him as it would be for us to shoot a great rapid.

He was so near the end now that it was impossible to stop. The boat dashed out. The poor tin soldier held himself as stiff as he could. No one should say of him that he even winced!

The boat swirled round three or four times and filled with water to the edge; it must sink. The tin soldier stood up to his neck in water, and the boat sank deeper and deeper. The paper became limper and limper, and at last the water went over his head. Then he thought of the pretty little dancer whom he was never to see again, and this refrain rang in his ears:

> " Onward! Onward! Soldier!
> For death thou canst not shun."

At last the paper gave way entirely and the soldier fell through, but at the same moment he was swallowed by a big fish.

Oh, how dark it was inside the fish! It was worse even than being in the tunnel. And then it was so narrow! But the tin soldier was as dauntless as ever and lay full length, shouldering his gun.

The fish rushed about and made the most frantic movements. At last it became quite quiet, and after a time a flash like lightning pierced it. The soldier was once more in the broad daylight, and someone called out loudly, " A tin soldier! " The fish had been caught, taken to market, sold, and brought into the kitchen, where the cook cut it open with a large knife. She took the soldier up by the waist with two fingers and carried him into the parlor, where everyone wanted to see the wonderful man who had traveled about in the stomach of a fish. But the tin soldier was not at all proud. They set him up on the table, and—wonder of wonders! he found himself in the very same room that he had been in before. He saw the very same children, and the toys were still standing on the table, as well as the beautiful castle with the pretty little dancer.

She still stood on one leg and held the other up in the air. You see, she also was unbending. The soldier was so much moved that he was ready to shed tears of tin, but that would not have been fitting. He looked at her and she looked at him, but they said never a word. At this moment one of the little boys took up the tin soldier, and without rhyme or reason threw him into the fire. No doubt the little goblin in the snuffbox was to blame for that. The tin soldier stood there, lighted up by the flame and in the most horrible heat, but whether it was the heat of the real fire, or the warmth of his feelings, he did not know. He had lost all his gay color. It might have been from his perilous journey, or it might have been from grief. Who can tell?

He looked at the little maiden and she looked at him, and he felt that he was melting away, but he still managed to keep himself erect, shouldering his gun bravely.

A door was suddenly opened. The draught caught the little dancer and she fluttered like a sylph, straight into the fire, to the soldier, blazed up and was gone!

By this time the soldier was reduced to a mere lump, and when the maid took away the ashes next morning she found him in the shape of a small tin heart. All that was left of the dancer was her spangle, and that was burned as black as a coal.

The Nightingale (France, 6 years old)
(STORY PAGE 163)

Ole Shut-Eye

In the whole world there is nobody who knows so many
stories as Ole Shut-Eye; he can tell capital ones!

As evening comes on, when the children still sit nicely at
table or on their stools, then comes Ole Shut-Eye. He comes
up the stairs quite softly, for he walks in his stocking feet;
he opens the door noiselessly, and st! he squirts sweet milk
in the children's eyes, a small, small stream, but enough to
prevent them from keeping their eyes open; and thus they
cannot see him. He creeps just among them, and blows softly
upon their necks, and this makes their heads heavy. O yes,
but it doesn't hurt them, for Ole Shut-Eye is very fond of
the children; he only wants them to be quiet, and that they
are not until they are taken to bed: they are to be quiet
that he may tell them stories.

When the children sleep, Ole Shut-Eye sits down upon
their bed. He is well dressed: his coat is of silk, but it is
impossible to say of what color, for it shines red, green, and
blue, according as he turns. Under each arm he carries an
umbrella: the one with pictures on it he spreads over the
good children, and then they dream all night the most
glorious stories; but on his other umbrella nothing at all is
painted, and this he spreads over the naughty children, and
these sleep in a dull way, and when they awake in the
morning they have not dreamed of anything.

9

Now we shall hear how Ole Shut-Eye, every evening through one whole week, came to a little boy named Hjalmar, and what he told him. There are seven stories, for there are seven days in the week.

MONDAY

" Listen," said Ole Shut-Eye in the evening, when he had put Hjalmar to bed; " now I'll clear up."

And all the flowers in the flowerpots became great trees, stretching out their long branches under the ceiling of the room and along the walls, so that the whole room looked like a lovely bower; and all the twigs were covered with flowers, and each flower was more beautiful than a rose, and smelt so sweet that one wanted to eat it; it was sweeter than jam. The fruit gleamed like gold, and there were cakes bursting with raisins. It was splendid. But at the same time a terrible wail sounded from the table drawer, where Hjalmar's schoolbook lay.

" Whatever can that be? " said Ole Shut-Eye; and he went to the table, and opened the drawer. It was the slate which was suffering from convulsions, for a wrong number had got into the sum, so that it was nearly falling in pieces; the slate pencil tugged and jumped at its string, as if it had been a little dog who wanted to help the sum; but he could not. And thus there was a great lamentation in Hjalmar's copybook; it was quite terrible to hear. On each page the great letters stood in a row, one underneath the other, and each with a little one at its side; that was the copy; and next to these were a few more letters which thought they looked just like the first; and these Hjalmar had written; but they lay down just as if they had tumbled over the pencil lines on which they were to stand.

"See, this is how you should hold yourselves," said the Copy. "Look, sloping in this way, with a powerful swing!"

"O, we should be very glad to do that," replied Hjalmar's Letters, "but we cannot; we are too weakly."

"Then you must take medicine," said Ole Shut-Eye.

"O no," cried they; and they immediately stood up so gracefully that it was beautiful to behold.

"Yes, now we cannot tell any stories," said Ole Shut-Eye; "now I must exercise them. One, two; one, two!" and thus he exercised the Letters; and they stood quite slender, and as beautiful as any copy can be. But when Ole Shut-Eye went away, and Hjalmar looked at them next morning, they were as weak and miserable as ever.

TUESDAY

As soon as Hjalmar was in bed, Ole Shut-Eye touched all the articles of furniture in the room with his little magic gun, and they immediately began to talk together, and each one spoke of itself, with the exception of the spittoon, which stood silent, and was vexed that they should be so vain as to speak only of themselves, and think only of themselves, without any regard for him who stood so modestly in the corner for every one's use.

Over the chest of drawers hung a great picture in a gilt frame—it was a landscape. One saw therein large old trees, flowers in the grass, and a broad river which flowed round about a forest, past many castles, and far out into the wide ocean.

Ole Shut-Eye touched the painting with his magic gun, and the birds began to sing, the branches of the trees stirred, and the clouds began to move across it; one could see their shadows glide over the landscape.

Now Ole Shut-Eye lifted little Hjalmar up to the frame,

and put the boy's feet into the picture, just in the high grass; and there he stood; and the sun shone upon him through the branches of the trees. He ran to the water, and seated himself in a little boat which lay there; it was painted red and white, the sails gleamed like silver, and six swans, each with a gold circlet round its neck, and a bright blue star on its forehead, drew the boat past the great wood, where the trees tell of robbers and witches, and the flowers tell of the graceful little elves, and of what the butterflies have told them.

Gorgeous fishes, with scales like silver and gold, swam after their boat; sometimes they gave a spring, so that it splashed in the water; and birds, blue and red, little and great, flew after them in two long rows; the gnats danced, and the cockchafers said, "Boom! boom! " They all wanted to follow Hjalmar, and each one had a story to tell.

That was a pleasure voyage. Sometimes the forest was thick and dark, sometimes like a glorious garden full of sunlight and flowers; and there were great palaces of glass and of marble; on the balconies stood princesses, and these were all little girls whom Hjalmar knew well; he had already played with them. Each one stretched forth her hand, and held out the prettiest sugar heart which ever a cake-woman could sell; and Hjalmar took hold of each sugar heart as he passed by, and the Princess held fast, so that each of them got a piece—she the smaller share, and Hjalmar the larger. At each palace little princes stood sentry. They shouldered golden swords, and caused raisins and tin soldiers to shower down: one could see that they were real princes. Sometimes Hjalmar sailed through forests, sometimes through great halls, or through the midst of a town. He also came to the town where his nurse lived, who had carried him in her arms when he was quite a little boy, and who had always been so kind to him; and she nodded and beckoned, and

sang the pretty verse she had made herself and had sent
to Hjalmar—

> *I think of you, so oft, so oft,*
> > *My own Hjalmar, ever dear;*
> *I've kissed your little lips so soft,*
> > *Your forehead and your cheeks so clear.*
> *I heard you utter your first word,*
> > *Then was I forced to say farewell;*
> *Now will I trust you to our Lord,*
> > *A good boy here, an angel there to dwell.*

And all the birds sang too, the flowers danced on their
stalks, and the old trees nodded, just as if Ole Shut-Eye had
been telling stories to *them*.

WEDNESDAY

How the rain was streaming down without! Hjalmar could
hear it in his sleep; and when Ole Shut-Eye opened a window,
the water stood quite up to the window sill: there was
quite a lake outside, and a noble ship lay close by the house.

" If thou wilt sail with me, little Hjalmar," said Ole Shut-
Eye, "thou canst voyage tonight to foreign climes, and be
back again tomorrow."

And Hjalmar suddenly stood in his Sunday clothes upon
the glorious ship, and immediately the weather became fine,
and they sailed through the streets and steered round by the
church; and now everything was one great wild ocean. They
sailed on until land was no longer to be seen, and they saw
a number of storks, who also came from their home, and
were traveling towards the hot countries: these storks flew
in a row, one behind the other, and they had already flown
far—far! one of them was so weary that his wings would
scarcely carry him farther: he was the very last in the row,
and soon remained a great way behind the rest; at last he

sank, with outspread wings, deeper and deeper; he gave a
few more strokes with his pinions, but it was of no use; now
he touched the rigging of the ship with his feet, then he
glided down from the sail, and—bump!—he stood upon the
deck.

Now the cabin boy took him and put him into the hen
coop with the fowls, ducks, and the turkeys; and the poor
stork stood among them quite embarrassed.

"Just look at the fellow!" said all the fowls.

And the turkey cock swelled himself up as much as ever
he could, and asked the stork who he was; and the ducks
walked backward and quacked to each other, "Quackery!
quackery!"

And the stork told them of hot Africa, of the pyramids,
and of the ostrich, which runs like a wild horse through the
desert; but the ducks did not understand what he said, and
they said to one another—

"We're all of the same opinion, namely, that he's stupid."

"Yes, certainly he's stupid," said the turkey cock; and he
gobbled.

Then the stork was quite silent, and thought of his Africa.

"Those are wonderful thin legs of yours," said the turkey
cock. "Pray, how much do they cost a yard?"

"Quack! quack! quack!" grinned all the ducks; but the
stork pretended not to hear it at all.

"You may just as well laugh too," said the turkey cock to
him, "for that was very wittily said. Or was it, perhaps, too
high for you? Yes, yes, he isn't very penetrating. Let us
continue to be interesting among ourselves."

And then he gobbled, and the ducks quacked, "Gick! gack!
gick! gack!" It was terrible how they made fun among
themselves.

But Hjalmar went to the hen coop, opened the back door,
and called to the stork; and the stork hopped out to him on
to the deck. Now he had rested, and it seemed as if he nodded

to Hjalmar, to thank him; then he spead his wings, and flew away to the warm countries; but the fowls clucked, and the ducks quacked, and the turkey cock became fiery red in the face.

"Tomorrow we shall make songs of you," said Hjalmar; and so saying he awoke, and was lying in his linen bed. It was a wonderful journey that Ole Shut-Eye had caused him to take that night.

THURSDAY

"I tell you what," said Ole Shut-Eye, "you must not be frightened. Here you shall see a little mouse," and he held out his hand with the pretty little creature in it. "It has come to invite you to a wedding. There are two little mice here who are going to enter into the marriage state tonight. They live under the floor of your mother's store closet: that is said to be a charming dwelling place!"

"But how can I get through the little mouse-hole in the ffoor?" asked Hjalmar.

"Let me manage that," said Ole Shut-Eye. "I will make you small."

And he touched Hjalmar with his magic gun, and the boy began to shrink and shrink, until he was not so long as a finger.

"Now you may borrow the uniform of a tin soldier: I think it would fit you, and it looks well to wear a uniform when one is in society."

"Yes, certainly," said Hjalmar.

And in a moment he was dressed like the smartest of tin soldiers.

"Will your honor not be kind enough to take a seat in your mamma's thimble?" asked the mouse. "Then I shall have the honor of drawing you."

" Will the young lady really take so much trouble? " cried Hjalmar.

And thus they drove to the mouse's wedding. First they came into a long passage beneath the boards, which was only just so high that they could drive through it in the thimble; and the whole passage was lit up with rotten wood.

" Is there not a delicious smell here? " observed the mouse. " The entire road has been greased with bacon rinds, and there can be nothing more exquisite."

Now they came into the festive hall. On the right hand stood all the little lady mice; and they whispered and giggled as if they were making fun of each other; on the left stood all the gentlemen mice, stroking their whiskers with their fore paws; and in the center of the hall the bridegroom and bride might be seen standing in a hollow cheese rind, and kissing each other terribly before all the guests; for this was the betrothal, and the marriage was to follow immediately.

More and more strangers kept flocking in. One mouse nearly trod another to death; and the happy couple had stationed themselves just in the doorway, so that one could neither come in nor go out. Like the passage, the room had been greased with bacon rinds, and that was the entire banquet; but for the dessert a pea was produced, in which a mouse belonging to the family had bitten the name of the betrothed pair—that is to say, the first letter of the name: that was something quite out of the common way.

All the mice said it was a beautiful wedding, and that the entertainment had been very agreeable. And then Hjalmar drove home again: he had really been in grand company; but he had been obliged to crawl, to make himself little, and to put on a tin soldier's uniform.

" It is wonderful how many grown-up people there are who would be glad to have me! " said Ole Shut-Eye; " especially those who have done something wrong. ' Good little Ole,' they say to me, 'we cannot close our eyes, and so we lie all night and see our evil deeds, which sit on the bedstead like ugly little goblins, and throw hot water over us; will you not come and drive them away, so that we may have a good sleep?' and then they sigh deeply—'We would really be glad to pay for it. Good-night, Ole: the money lies on the window sill.' But I do nothing for money," said Ole Shut-Eye.

" What shall we do this evening? " asked Hjalmar.

" I don't know if you care to go to another wedding tonight. It is of a different kind from that of yesterday. Your sister's great doll, that looks like a man, and is called Hermann, is going to marry the doll Bertha. Moreover, it is the doll's birthday, and therefore they will receive very many presents."

" Yes, I know that," replied Hjalmar. " Whenever the dolls want new clothes, my sister lets them either keep their birthday or celebrate a wedding; that has certainly happened a hundred times already."

" Yes, but tonight is the hundred and first wedding; and when number one hundred and one is past, it is all over; and that is why it will be so splendid. Only look! "

And Hjalmar looked at the table. There stood the little cardboard house with the windows illuminated, and in front of it all the tin soldiers were presenting arms. The bride and bridegroom sat quite thoughtful, and with good reason, on the floor, leaning against a leg of the table. And Ole Shut-Eye, dressed up in the grandmother's black gown, married them to each other. When the ceremony was over, all the pieces of furniture struck up the following beautiful song, which the

Pencil had written for them. It was sung to the melody of the soldiers' tattoo—

> *Let the song swell like the rushing wind,*
> *In honor of those who this day are joined,*
> *Although they stand here stiff and blind,*
> *Because they are both of a leathery kind.*
> *Hurrah! hurrah! though they're deaf and blind,*
> *Let the song swell like the rushing wind.*

And now they received presents—but they had declined to accept provisions of any kind, for they intended to live on love.

"Shall we now go into a summer lodging, or start on a journey?" asked the bridegroom.

And the swallow, who was a great traveler, and the old yard Hen, who had brought up five broods of chickens, were consulted on the subject. And the swallow told of the beautiful warm climes, where the grapes hung in ripe, heavy clusters, where the air is mild, and the mountains glow with colors unknown here.

"But you have not our brown cole there!" objected the Hen. "I was once in the country, with my children, in one summer that lasted five weeks. There was a sand pit, in which we could walk about and scratch; and we had the *entrée* to a garden where brown cole grew: it was so hot there that one could scarcely breathe; and then we have not all the poisonous animals that infest these warm countries of yours, and we are free from robbers. He is a villain who does not consider our country the most beautiful—he certainly does not deserve to be here!" And then the Hen wept, and went on: "I have also traveled. I rode in a coop above twelve miles; and there is no pleasure at all in traveling!"

"Yes, the Hen is a sensible woman!" said the doll Bertha. "I don't think anything of traveling among mountains, for you only have to go up, and then down again. No, we will go into the sand pit beyond the gate, and walk about in the cabbage garden."

And so it was settled.

"Am I to hear some stories now?" asked little Hjalmar, as soon as Ole Shut-Eye had sent him to sleep.

"This evening we have no time for that," replied Ole Shut-Eye; and he spread his finest umbrella over the lad. "Only look at these Chinese!"

And the whole umbrella looked like a great china dish, with blue trees and pointed bridges, with little Chinese upon them, who stood there nodding their heads.

"We must have the whole world prettily decked out for tomorrow morning," said Ole Shut-Eye, "for that will be a holiday—it will be Sunday. I will go to the church steeples to see that the little church goblins are polishing the bells, that they may sound sweetly. I will go out into the field, and see if the breezes are blowing the dust from the grass and leaves; and, what is the greatest work of all, I will bring down all the stars, to polish them. I take them in my apron; but first each one must be numbered, and the holes in which they are placed up there must be numbered likewise, so that they may be placed in the same grooves again; otherwise they would not sit fast, and we should have too many shooting stars, for one after another would fall down."

"Hark ye! Do you know, Mr. Ole Shut-Eye," said an old Portrait which hung on the wall where Hjalmar slept, "I am Hjalmar's great-grandfather? I thank you for telling the boy stories; but you must not confuse his ideas. The stars cannot come down and be polished! The stars are world-orbs, just like our own earth, and that is just the good thing about them."

"I thank you, old great-grandfather," said Ole Shut-Eye, "I thank you! You are then the head of the family. You are the ancestral head; but I am older than you! I am an old heathen: the Romans and Greeks called me the Dream God! I have been in the noblest houses, and am admitted there still! I know how to act with great people and with small! Now you may tell your own story!" and Ole Shut-Eye took his umbrella, and went away.

"Well, well! May one not even give an opinion nowadays?" grumbled the old Portrait. And Hjalmar awoke.

SUNDAY

"Good evening!" said Ole Shut-Eye; and Hjalmar nodded, and then ran and turned his great-grandfather's Portrait against the wall, that it might not interrupt them, as it had done yesterday.

"Now you must tell me stories; about the five green peas that lived in one shell, and about the cock's foot that paid court to the hen's foot, and of the darning needle who gave herself such airs because she thought herself a working needle."

"There may be too much of a good thing!" said Ole Shut-Eye. "You know that I prefer showing you something. I will show you my own brother. His name, like mine, is Ole Shut-Eye, but he never comes to any one more than once; and he takes him to whom he comes upon his horse, and tells him stories. He only knows two. One of these is so exceedingly beautiful that no one in the world can imagine it, and the other so horrible that it cannot be described."

And then Ole Shut-Eye lifted little Hjalmar up to the window, and said—

"There you will see my brother, the other Ole Shut-Eye. They also call him Death! Do you see, he does not look so terrible as they make him in the picture books, where he is only a skeleton. No, that is silver embroidery that he has on his coat; that is a splendid hussar's uniform; a mantle of black velvet flies behind him over the horse. See how he gallops along!"

And Hjalmar saw how this Ole Shut-Eye rode away, and took young people as well as old upon his horse. Some of them he put before him, and some behind: but he always asked first, "How stands it with the mark book?" "Well," they all replied. "Yes, let me see it myself," he said. And then each one had to show him the book; and those who had "very well" and "remarkably well" written in their books, were placed in front of his horse, and a lovely story was told to them; while those who had "middling" or "tolerably well," had to sit up behind, and hear a very terrible story indeed. They trembled and wept, and wanted to jump off the horse, but this they could not do, for they had all, as it were, grown fast to it.

"But Death is a most splendid Ole Shut-Eye," said Hjalmar. "I am not afraid of him!"

"Nor need you be," replied Ole Shut-Eye; "but see that you have a good mark book!"

"Yes, that is improving!" muttered the great-grandfather's Picture. "It is of some use giving one's opinion." And now he was satisfied.

You see, that is the story of Ole Shut-Eye; and now he may tell you more himself, this evening!

The Wicked Prince

A LEGEND

Once upon a time, there was a wicked and haughty prince, whose thoughts constantly dwelt on how he might conquer all the nations of the earth, and make his name a terror to all men. He ravaged with fire and sword; his soldiers trod down the grain in the fields; they put the torch to the peasant's cottage, so that the red flame licked the very leaves from the trees, and the fruit hung roasted from the black and singed limbs. Many a poor mother, with her naked babe, hid away behind the smoking ruins, and the soldiers sought her, and found her and the child, and then began their devilish sport: the demons of the pit could do no worse; but the Prince found it all to his liking; day by day he grew mightier, his name was feared by everybody, and good fortune came upon him to his heart's content. From the conquered cities he carried away gold and great treasure, and amassed in his capital such riches as were never before found together in one place. Then he built superb palaces, temples, and arches; and whoever saw his magnificence, exclaimed, "What a great Prince!"—never thinking of the desolation he had brought over many lands, nor listening to the groans and wailings that arose from the cities which fire had laid waste.

The Prince looked upon his gold, looked upon his superb buildings, and thought, as folks did, " What a great Prince! " " But I wish to have more, much more! No power is there that can equal, much less surpass, mine! " And so he went to war with his neighbors and subdued them all. The vanquished kings he chained to his chariot with golden chains, when he drove through the streets; and when he sat down to his table, they were made to lie at his and his courtiers' feet, and eat the morsels that might be thrown to them.

Now the Prince caused his image to be set up in the market places and in the royal palaces; he would even have set it up in the temples before the altar of the Lord; but the priests said, " Prince, thou art great, but God is greater: we dare not do it."

" Well," said the wicked Prince, " then I shall conquer Him likewise! " and in his heart's pride and folly, he built an artfully contrived ship, in which he could sail through the air; it was decked with peacocks' feathers, and seemed spangled with a thousand eyes; but each eye was a gun's mouth, and the Prince sat in the midst of the ship, and, upon his touching a certain spring, a thousand bullets would dart forth, and the guns would at once be loaded afresh. Hundreds of strong eagles were harnessed to the ship, and so it flew away, up towards the sun. The earth lay far beneath; at first it appeared, with its mountains and forests, like a plowed meadow, with a tuft of green here and there peeping out from under the upturned sod; then it resembled an unrolled map; and presently it was wholly hid in mists and clouds. Higher and higher the eagles flew; when God sent forth a single one of his countless angels, at whom the wicked Prince immediately let fly a thousand bullets; but the bullets dropped like hail from the angel's shining wings, and one drop of blood—but one—dripped from one of the white pinions, and fell on the ship wherein sat the Prince; it burned itself fast there, and weighed with a weight of a thousand hundredweight, and with thundering speed tore the ship down back to the earth. The eagles' strong wings were broken, the winds roared about the Prince's head; and the clouds round about, which had sprung from the smoke of the burned cities, formed themselves into terrific shapes—anon like mile-long crab-fish, reaching out their huge claws after him—anon like rolling boulders or like fiery dragons: half dead he lay in his ship, when it finally was caught in the tangled branches of a dense forest.

"I *will* conquer God!" said he; "I have vowed it, and my will shall be done!" and during seven years he builded artfully contrived vessels, in which to sail through the air, and caused thunderbolts to be forged from the hardest of steel, wherewith to batter down heaven's battlements. From all countries, he assembled vast armies, which covered many miles of ground in length and breadth, when formed in battle array. They embarked in the artfully built vessels, and already the King himself approached his; when God sent forth a swarm of gnats—one little swarm—which buzzed about the King, and stung his face and hands. In anger he drew his sword; but he beat the void air only: the gnats he could not strike. Whereupon he commanded that costly cloths be brought, and wrapped about him, so that no gnat might reach him with its sting. It was done as he had commanded; but one little gnat had lodged itself in the folds of the inmost cloth, and crept into the King's ear and stung him; the sting smarted as fire, the poison flew up into his head; he tore himself loose, flung the cloths far away, rent his garments asunder, and danced naked before the rough and savage soldiers, who now mocked the mad Prince that had set out to besiege God, and had been himself undone by one tiny gnat.

The Swineherd

There was once a poor prince who had only a tiny kingdom, but it was big enough to allow him to marry, and he was bent upon marrying.

Now it certainly was rather bold of him to say to the Emperor's daughter, "Will you have me?" He did, however, venture to say so, for his name was known far and wide. And there were hundreds of princesses who would have said "Yes," and "Thank you, kindly," but see if *she* would!

Let us hear about it.

A rose tree grew on the grave of the Prince's father. It was such a beautiful rose tree. But it bloomed only every fifth year, and then bore only one blossom. What a rose that was! By merely smelling it one forgot all of one's cares and sorrows.

Then he had a nightingale which sang as if every lovely melody in the world dwelt in her little throat. This rose and this nightingale were to be given to the Princess, so they were put into great silver caskets and sent to her.

The Emperor had them carried before him into the great hall where the Princess was playing at "visiting" with her ladies-in-waiting—they had nothing else to do. When she saw the caskets with the gifts, she clapped her hands with delight.

"If it were only a little pussy cat!" said she. But there was the lovely rose.

"Oh, how exquisitely it is made!" said all the ladies-in-waiting.

"It is more than beautiful," said the Emperor. "It is neatly made." But the Princess touched it, and then she was ready to cry.

"Fie, papa!" she said. "It is not made. It is a real one."

"Fie," said all the ladies-in-waiting. "It is a real one."

"Well, let us see what there is in the other casket, before we get angry," said the Emperor, and out came the nightingale. It sang so beautifully that at first no one could find anything to say against it.

"*Superbe! charmant!*" said the ladies-in-waiting, for they all had a smattering of French; one spoke it worse than the other.

"How that bird reminds me of our lamented Empress' musical box," said an old courtier. "Ah yes, they are the same tunes and the same beautiful execution."

"So they are," said the Emperor, crying like a little child.

"I should hardly think it could be a real one," said the Princess.

"Yes, it is a real one," said those who had brought it.

"Oh, let that bird fly away then," said the Princess, and she would not hear of allowing the Prince to come. But he was not to be crushed. He stained his face brown and black and, pressing his cap over his eyes, he knocked at the door.

"Good morning, Emperor," said he. "Can I be taken into service in the palace?"

"Well, there are so many wishing to do that," said the Emperor. "But let me see. Yes, I need somebody to look after the pigs. We have so many of them."

So the Prince was made imperial swineherd. A horrid little room was given him near the pigsties, and here he had to live. He sat busily at work all day, and by the evening he had made a beautiful little cooking pot. It had bells all round it, and when the pot boiled, they tinkled delightfully and played the old tune:

> "*Ach du lieber Augustin,*
> *Alles ist weg, weg, weg!*" °

But the greatest of all its charms was that by holding one's finger in the steam, one could immediately smell all the dinners that were being cooked at every stove in the town. Now this was a very different matter from a rose.

The Princess came walking along with all her ladies-in-waiting, and when she heard the tune she stopped and looked pleased, for she could play "Ach du lieber Augustin" herself. It was her only tune, and she could only play it with one finger.

"Why, that is my tune," she said. "This must be a cultivated swineherd. Ask him what the instrument costs."

So one of the ladies-in-waiting had to go into his room, but before she entered she put on wooden clog-shoes.

"How much do you want for the pot?" she asked.

"I must have ten kisses from the Princess," said the swineherd.

"Heaven preserve us!" said the lady.

"I won't take less," said the swineherd.

"Well, what does he say?" asked the Princess.

"I really cannot tell you," said the lady-in-waiting. "It is so shocking."

"Then you must whisper it." And she whispered it.

"He is a wretch!" said the Princess and went away at once. But she had only gone a little way when she heard the bells tinkling beautifully:

> "*Ach du lieber Augustin.*"

° Alas, dear Augustin,
  All is lost, lost, lost!

"Go and ask him if he will take ten kisses from the ladies-in-waiting."

"No, thank you," said the swineherd. "Ten kisses from the Princess, or I keep my pot."

"How tiresome it is," said the Princess. "Then you will have to stand round me, so that no one may see."

So the ladies-in-waiting stood round her and spread out their skirts while the swineherd took his ten kisses, and then the pot was hers.

What a delight it was to them! The pot was kept on the boil day and night. They knew what was cooking on every stove in the town, from the chamberlain's to the shoemaker's. The ladies-in-waiting danced about and clapped their hands.

"We know who has sweet soup and pancakes for dinner, and who has cutlets. How amusing it is."

"Highly interesting," said the mistress of the robes.

"Yes, but hold your tongues, for I am the Emperor's daughter."

"Heaven preserve us!" they all said.

The swineherd—that is to say, the Prince, only nobody knew that he was not a real swineherd—did not let the day pass in idleness, and he now constructed a rattle. When it was swung round it played all the waltzes, galops and jig tunes ever heard since the creation of the world.

"But this is *superbe!*" said the Princess, as she walked by. "I have never heard finer compositions. Go and ask him what the instrument costs, but let us have no more kissing."

"He wants a hundred kisses from the Princess," said the lady-in-waiting.

"I think he is mad!" said the Princess, and she went away, but she had not gone far when she stopped.

"One must encourage art," she said. "I am the Emperor's daughter. Tell him he can have ten kisses, the same as yesterday, and he can take the others from the ladies-in-waiting."

"But we don't like that at all," said the ladies.

"Oh, nonsense! If I can kiss him you can do the same. Remember that I pay you wages as well as give you board and lodging." So the lady-in-waiting had to go again.

"A hundred kisses from the Princess, or let each keep his own."

"Stand in front of me," said she, and all the ladies stood round while he kissed her.

"Whatever is the meaning of that crowd round the pigsties?" said the Emperor as he stepped out on to the veranda. He rubbed his eyes and put on his spectacles. "Why, it is the ladies-in-waiting. What game are they up to? I must go and see!" So he pulled up the heels of his slippers for they were shoes which he had trodden down.

Bless us, what a hurry he was in! When he got into the yard he walked very softly, and the ladies were so busy counting the kisses, so that there should be fair play, and neither too few nor too many kisses, that they never heard the Emperor. He stood on tiptoe.

"What is all this?" he said when he saw what was going on, and he hit them on the head with his slipper just as the swineherd was taking his eighty-sixth kiss.

"Out you go!" said the Emperor. He was very furious, and he put both the Princess and the Prince out of his realm.

There she stood crying, and the swineherd scolded, and the rain poured down in torrents.

"Oh, miserable creature that I am!" said the Princess. "If only I had accepted the handsome Prince. Oh, how unhappy I am!"

The swineherd went behind a tree, wiped the black and brown stain from his face, and threw away his ugly clothes. When he stepped out dressed as a prince, he was so handsome that the Princess could not help curtseying to him.

"I am come to despise thee," he said. "Thou wouldst not have an honorable prince. Thou couldst not prize the rose

or the nightingale. But thou wouldst kiss the swineherd for
a trumpery musical box! As thou hast made thy bed, so must
thou lie upon it."

Then he went back into his own little kingdom and shut
and locked the door. So she had to stand outside and sing
in earnest:

> *" Ach du lieber Augustin,*
> *Alles ist weg, weg, weg! "*

Hans Clodhopper

There was once an old mansion in the country in which lived an old squire with his two sons, and these two sons were too clever by half. They had made up their minds to propose to the King's daughter. And they ventured to do so because she had made it known that she would take any man for a husband who had most to say for himself.

These two took a week over their preparations. It was all the time they had for it, but it was quite enough with all their accomplishments, which were most useful. One of them knew the Latin dictionary by heart, as well as the town newspapers for three years, either forwards or backwards. The second one had made himself acquainted with all the statutes of the Corporations and what every alderman had to know, so he thought he was competent to talk about affairs of state. And he also knew how to embroider harnesses, for he was clever with his fingers.

"I shall win the King's daughter," they both said, and their father gave each of them a beautiful horse. The one who could repeat the dictionary and the newspapers had a coal-black horse, while the one who was learned in guilds and embroideries had a milk-white one. Then they smeared the corners of their mouths with oil to make them more flexible. All the servants were assembled in the courtyards to see them mount, but just then the third brother came up—for there were three. Only nobody made any account of this one, Hans Clodhopper, as he had no accomplishments like his brothers.

"Where are you going in your fine clothes?" he asked.

"To court, to talk ourselves into favor with the Princess. Haven't you heard the news which is being drummed all over the country?" And then they told him the news.

"Preserve us! Then I must go too," said Hans Clodhopper. But his brothers laughed and rode away.

"Father, give me a horse. I want to get married too. If she takes me she takes me, and if she doesn't take me, I shall take her all the same."

"Stuff and nonsense!" said his father. "I will give no horse to you. Why, you have got nothing to say for yourself, but your brothers are fine fellows."

"If I mayn't have a horse," said Hans Clodhopper, "I'll take the billy goat. He is my own and he can carry me very well!" And he seated himself astride the billy goat, dug his heels into its sides, and galloped off down the highroad. Whew! what a pace they went at.

"Here I come," shouted Hans Clodhopper, and he sang till the air rang.

The brothers rode on in silence. They did not say a word to each other, for they had to store up every good idea which they wanted to produce later on, and their speeches had to be very carefully thought out.

"Hallo!" shouted Hans Clodhopper. "Here I come. See what I've found on the road!" And he showed them a dead crow.

"What on earth will you do with that, Clodhopper?" said they.

"I will give it to the King's daughter."

"Yes, I would do that," said they, and they rode on laughing.

"Hallo, here I come! See what I have found! One doesn't

find such a thing as this every day on the road." The brothers
turned round to see what it was.

"Clodhopper," said they, "it's nothing but an old wooden
shoe with the upper part broken off. Is the Princess to have
that too?"

"Yes indeed she is," said Hans, and the brothers again
rode on laughing.

"Hallo, hallo, here I am!" shouted Hans Clodhopper.
"Now this is something wonderful!"

"What have you found this time?" asked the brothers.

"Won't the Princess be delighted!"

"Why," said the brothers, "it's only sand picked up out
of the ditch!"

"Yes, that it is," said Hans Clodhopper, "and the finest
kind of sand, too. You can hardly hold it." And he filled his
pockets with it. His brothers rode on as fast as they could,
and arrived at the town gates a whole hour before him. At
the gate suitors received tickets in the order of their arrival,
and they were arranged in rows, six in each file and so
close together that they could not move their arms. This was
a very good thing, or they would have torn each other's
garments off, merely because one stood in front of the other.
All the other inhabitants of the town stood round the castle,
peeping in at the windows to see the King's daughter receive
the suitors. And as each one of them came into the room
he lost the power of speech.

"No good," said the Princess. "Away with him!"

Now came the brother who could repeat the dictionary,
but he had entirely forgotten it while standing in the ranks.
The floor creaked and the ceiling was made of looking glass,
so that he saw himself standing on his head. And at every
window sat three clerks and an alderman, who wrote down
all that was said, so that it might be sent to the papers at
once and sold for a halfpenny at the street corners. It was

terrible, and the stoves had been heated to such a degree that they got red-hot at the top.

"It is terribly hot in here," said the suitor.

"That is because my father is roasting cockerels today," said the Princess.

Bah! There he stood like a fool. He had not expected a conversation of this kind, and he could not think of a word to say, just when he wanted to be specially witty.

"No good," said the King's daughter. "Away with him!" And he had to go.

Then came the second brother. "There's a fearful heat here," said he.

"Yes, we are roasting cockerels today," said the King's daughter.

"What did—what?" said he. And all the reporters duly wrote, "What did—what."

"No good," said the King's daughter. "Away with him!"

Then came Hans Clodhopper. He rode the billy goat right into the room.

"What a burning heat you have here," said he.

"That is because I am roasting cockerels," said the King's daughter.

"That is very convenient," said Hans Clodhopper. "Then I suppose I can get a crow roasted too."

"Yes, very well," said the King's daughter. "But have you anything to roast it in? I have neither pot nor pan."

"But I have," said Hans Clodhopper. "Here is a cooking pot." And he brought out the wooden shoe and put the crow into it.

"Why you have enough for a whole meal," said the King's daughter. "But where shall we get any dripping to baste it with?"

"Oh, I have some in my pocket," said Hans Clodhopper. "I have enough and to spare." And he poured a little of the sand out of his pocket.

"Now I like that," said the Princess. "You have an answer for everything, and you have something to say for yourself. I will have you for a husband. But do you know that every word we have said will be in the paper tomorrow? For at every window sit three clerks and an alderman, and the alderman is the worst, for he doesn't understand." She said this to frighten him. All the clerks sniggered and made blots of ink on the floor.

"Oh, those are the gentry!" said Hans Clodhopper. "Then I must give the alderman the best thing I have." And he turned out his pockets and threw the sand in his face.

"That was cleverly done," said the Princess. "I couldn't have done it, but I will try to learn."

So Hans Clodhopper became King, gained a wife and a crown, and sat upon the throne. We have this straight out of the alderman's newspaper, but it is not to be depended upon.

The Love Affair of the Top and the Ball

A Top and a little Ball were together in a drawer among some other toys; and the Top said to the Ball—

"Shall we not be lovers, as we live together in the same box?"

But the Ball, which had a coat of morocco leather, and was just as conceited as any fine lady, would make no answer to such a proposal. The next day came the little boy to whom the toys belonged: he painted the Top red and yellow, and hammered a brass nail into it; and it looked splendid when the Top turned round.

"Look at me!" he cried to the little Ball. "What do you say now? Shall we not be engaged to each other? We suit one another so well! You jump and I dance! No one could be happier than we two should be."

"Indeed! Do you think so?" replied the little Ball. "Perhaps you do not know that my papa and my mamma were morocco slippers, and that I have a Spanish cork inside me?"

"Yes, but I am made of mahogany," said the Top; "and the mayor himself turned me. He has a turning lathe of his own, and it amuses him greatly."

"Can I depend on that?" asked the little Ball.

"May I never be whipped again if it is not true!" replied the Top.

"You can speak well for yourself," observed the Ball,

"but I cannot grant your request. I am as good as engaged to a swallow: every time I leap up into the air he puts his head out of the nest and says, 'Will you?' And now I have silently said 'Yes,' and that is as good as half engaged; but I promise I will never forget you."

"Yes, that will be much good!" said the Top.

And they spoke no more to each other.

Next day the Ball was taken out by the boy. The Top saw how she flew high into air, like a bird; at last one could no longer see her. Each time she came back again, but gave a high leap when she touched the earth, and that was done either from her longing to mount up again, or because she had a Spanish cork in her body. But the ninth time the little Ball remained absent, and did not come back again; and the boy sought and sought, but she was gone.

"I know very well where she is!" sighed the Top. "She is in the Swallow's nest, and has married the Swallow!"

The more the Top thought of this, the more it longed for the Ball. Just because it could not get the Ball, its love increased; and the fact that the Ball had chosen another formed a peculiar feature in the case. So the Top danced round and hummed, but always thought of the little Ball, which became more and more beautiful in his fancy. Thus several years went by, and now it was an old love.

And the Top was no longer young! But one day he was gilt all over; never had he looked so handsome; he was now a golden Top, and sprang till he hummed again. Yes, that was something worth seeing! But all at once he sprang too high, and—he was gone!

They looked and looked, even in the cellar, but he was not to be found. Where could he be?

He had jumped into the dust box, where all kinds of things were lying: cabbage stalks, sweepings, and dust that had fallen down from the roof.

The Love Affair of the Top and the Ball (Cuba, 14 years old)
(STORY PAGE 159)

"Here's a nice place to lie in! The gilding will soon leave me here. Among what a rabble have I alighted!"

And then he looked sideways at a long leafless cabbage stump, and at a curious round thing like an old apple; but it was not an apple—it was an old Ball, which had lain for years in the roof gutter and was quite saturated with water.

"Thank goodness, here comes one of us, with whom one can talk!" said the little Ball, and looked at the gilt Top. "I am really morocco, worked by maidens' hands, and have a Spanish cork within me; but no one would think it, to look at me. I was very near marrying a swallow, but I fell into the gutter on the roof, and have lain there full five years, and become quite wet through. You may believe me, that's a long time for a young girl."

But the Top said nothing. He thought of his old love; and the more he heard, the clearer it became to him that this was she. Then came the servant girl, and wanted to turn out the dust box. "Aha! there's a gilt top!" she cried. And so the Top was brought again to notice and honor, but nothing was heard of the little Ball. And the Top spoke no more of his old love; for that dies away when the beloved object has lain for five years in a roof gutter and got wet through; yes, one does not know her again when one meets her in the dust box.

11

The Nightingale

In China, as you know, the Emperor is a Chinese and all the people around him are Chinese too. It is many years since the story I am going to tell you happened, but that is all the more reason for telling it, lest it should be forgotten.

The Emperor's palace was the most beautiful thing in the world. It was made entirely of finest porcelain, which was very costly, and so fragile that it could be touched only with the very greatest of care. The most extraordinary flowers were to be seen in the garden. The most beautiful ones had little silver bells tied to them which tinkled perpetually, so that no one could pass the flowers without looking at them. Every little detail in the garden had been most carefully thought out, and it was so big that even the gardener himself did not know where it ended.

If one went on walking, one came to beautiful woods with lofty trees and deep lakes. The woods extended to the sea, which was deep and blue, deep enough for large ships to sail up right under the branches of the trees. Among these trees lived a nightingale, which sang so deliciously that even the poor fisherman, who had plenty of other things to do, lay still to listen to it when he was out at night drawing in his nets.

"Heavens, how beautiful it is," he said, but then he had to attend to his business and forgot it. The next night when he heard it again he would again exclaim, " Heavens, how beautiful it is."

Travelers came to the Emperor's capital from every country in the world. They admired everything very much, especially the palace and the gardens, but when they heard the nightingale they all said, " This is better than anything."

When they got home they described it, and learned men wrote many books about the town, the palace, and the garden. But nobody forgot the nightingale—it was always put above everything else. Those among them who were poets wrote the most beautiful poems, all about the nightingale in the woods by the deep blue sea. These books went all over the world, and in course of time some of them reached the Emperor. He sat in his golden chair reading and reading, and nodding his head, well pleased to hear such beautiful descriptions of the town, the palace, and the garden. " But the nightingale is the best of all," he read.

" What is this? " said the Emperor. " The nightingale? Why, I know nothing about it. Is there such a bird in my kingdom, and in my own garden, and I have never heard of it? Imagine my having to discover this from a book."

Then he called his gentleman-in-waiting, who was so grand that when anyone of a lower rank dared to speak to him or to ask him a question, he would only answer, " P," which means nothing at all.

" There is said to be a very wonderful bird called a nightingale here," said the Emperor. " They say that it is better than anything else in all my great kingdom. Why have I never been told anything about it? "

" I have never heard it mentioned," said the gentleman-in-waiting. " It has never been presented at court."

" I wish it to appear here this evening to sing to me," said the Emperor. " The whole world knows what I am possessed of, and I know nothing about it! "

" I have never heard it mentioned before," said the

gentleman-in-waiting. "I will seek it, and I will find it." But where was it to be found? The gentleman-in-waiting ran upstairs and downstairs and in and out of all the rooms and corridors. No one of all those he met had ever heard anything about the nightingale. So the gentleman-in-waiting ran back to the Emperor and said that it must be a myth, invented by the writers of the books. "Your Imperial Majesty must not believe everything that is written! Books are often mere inventions, even if they do not belong to what we call the black art."

"But the book in which I read it was sent to me by the powerful Emperor of Japan. Therefore it can't be untrue. I will hear this nightingale. I insist upon its being here tonight. I extend my most gracious protection to it, and if it is not forthcoming, I will have the whole court trampled upon after supper."

"Tsing-pe!" said the gentleman-in-waiting, and away he ran again, up and down all the stairs, in and out of all the rooms and corridors. Half the court ran with him, for none of them wished to be trampled on. There was much questioning about this nightingale, which was known to all the outside world but to no one at court.

At last they found a poor little maid in the kitchen, who said, "Oh heavens! The nightingale? I know it very well. Yes indeed, it can sing. Every evening I am allowed to take broken meat to my poor sick mother who lives down by the shore. On my way back, when I am tired I rest awhile in the wood, and then I hear the nightingale. Its song brings the tears into my eyes. I feel as if my mother were kissing me."

"Little kitchen maid," said the gentleman-in-waiting, "I will procure you a permanent position in the kitchen and permission to see the Emperor dining, if you will take us to the nightingale. It is commanded to appear at court tonight."

Then they all went out into the woods where the nightingale usually sang. Half the court was there. As they were going along at their best pace, a cow began to bellow.

"Oh," said a young courtier, "there we have it. What wonderful power for such a little creature. I have certainly heard it before."

"No, those are the cows bellowing. We are a long way from the place." Then frogs began to croak in the marsh.

"How beautiful!" said the Chinese chaplain. "It is just like the tinkling of church bells."

"No, those are the frogs," said the little kitchen maid. "But I think we shall soon hear it now."

Then the nightingale began to sing.

"Listen, listen! There it sits," said the little girl. And she pointed to a little gray bird up among the branches.

"Is it possible?" said the gentleman-in-waiting. "I should never have thought it was like that. How common it looks. Seeing so many grand people must have frightened all its colors away."

"Little nightingale," called the kitchen maid quite loud, "Our Gracious Emperor wishes you to sing to him."

"With the greatest pleasure," said the nightingale, warbling away in the most delightful fashion.

"It is just like crystal bells," said the gentleman-in-waiting. "Look at its little throat, how active it is. It is extraordinary that we have never heard it before. I am sure it will be a great success at court."

"Shall I sing again to the Emperor?" said the nightingale, who thought he was present.

"My precious little nightingale," said the gentleman-in-waiting, "I have the honor to command your attendance at a court festival tonight, where you will charm His Gracious Majesty the Emperor with your fascinating singing."

"It sounds best among the trees," said the nightingale, but it went with them willingly when it heard that the Emperor wished it.

The palace had been brightened up for the occasion. The walls and the floors, which were all of china, shone by the light of many thousand golden lamps. The most beautiful flowers, all of the tinkling kind, were arranged in the corridors. There was hurrying to and fro, and a great draught, but this was just what made the bells ring. One's ears were full of the tinkling. In the middle of the large reception room where the Emperor sat, a golden rod had been fixed, on which the nightingale was to perch. The whole court was assembled, and the little kitchen maid had been permitted to stand behind the door, as she now had the actual title of Cook. They were all dressed in their best. Everybody's eyes were turned towards the little gray bird at which the Emperor was nodding.

The nightingale sang delightfully, and the tears came into the Emperor's eyes and rolled down his cheeks. And when the nightingale sang more beautifully than ever, its notes melted all hearts. The Emperor was so charmed that he said the nightingale should have his gold slipper to wear round its neck. But the nightingale declined with thanks—it had already been sufficiently rewarded.

"I have seen tears in the eyes of the Emperor," he said. "That is my richest reward. The tears of the Emperor have a wonderful power. God knows I am sufficiently recompensed." And it again burst into its sweet heavenly song.

"That is the most delightful coquetting I have ever seen!" said the ladies. And they took some water into their mouths to try and make the same gurgling, when anyone spoke to them, thinking so to equal the nightingale. Even the lackeys and the chambermaids announced that they were satisfied, and that is saying a great deal. They are always the most difficult people to please. Yes indeed, the nightingale had made a sensation. It was to stay at court now, and have its own cage, as well as liberty to walk out twice a day and once in the night. It always had twelve footmen, with each one holding a ribbon which was tied round its leg. There was not much pleasure in an outing of that sort.

The whole town talked about the marvelous bird. If two people met, one said to the other "Night," and the other answered "Gale." And then they sighed, perfectly understanding each other. Eleven cheesemongers' children were named after it, but not one among them could sing anything.

One day a large parcel came for the Emperor. Outside was written the word "Nightingale."

"Here we have another new book about this celebrated bird," said the Emperor. But it was not a book. It was a little work of art in a box, an artificial nightingale exactly like the living one, except that it was studded all over with diamonds, rubies, and sapphires.

When the artificial bird was wound up, it could sing one of the songs the real one sang, and it wagged its tail, which glittered with silver and gold. A ribbon was tied round its neck on which was written, "The Emperor of Japan's nightingale is very poor compared to the Emperor of China's."

Everybody said, "Oh, how beautiful!" And the person who brought the artificial bird immediately received the title of Imperial Nightingale-Carrier-in-Chief.

"Now, they must sing together. What a duet that will be!"

Then they had to sing together, but they did not get on very well, for the real nightingale sang in its own way and the artificial one could only sing waltzes.

"There is no fault in that," said the music master, "It is perfectly in time and correct in every way."

Then the artificial bird had to sing alone. It was just as great a success as the real one, and it was much prettier to look at, because it glittered like bracelets and breastpins.

It sang the same tune three and thirty times over, and yet it was not tired. People would willingly have heard it from the beginning again, but the Emperor said that the real one must have a turn now. But where was it? No one had noticed that it had flown out of the open window, back to its own green woods.

"What is the meaning of this?" said the Emperor.

All the courtiers railed at it and said it was a most ungrateful bird.

"We have got the best bird though," said they, and then the artificial bird had to sing again. This was the thirty-fourth time that they had heard the same tune, but they did not know it thoroughly even yet because it was so difficult.

The music master praised the bird tremendously and insisted that it was better than the real nightingale, not only on the outside with all its diamonds, but inside too.

"You see, my ladies and gentlemen, and the Emperor before all, in the real nightingale you never know what you will hear, but in the artificial one everything is decided beforehand. So it is, and so it must remain. It can't be otherwise. You can account for things: you can open it and show the human ingenuity in arranging how the waltzes go, and how one note follows upon another."

"Those are exactly my opinions," they all said, and the music master got leave to show the bird to the public next Sunday. They were also to hear it sing, said the Emperor. So they heard it, and all became as enthusiastic over it as if they had drunk themselves merry on tea, because that is a thoroughly Chinese habit.

Then they all said, "Oh!" and stuck their forefingers in the air and nodded their heads. But the poor fisherman who had heard the real nightingale said, "It sounds very nice, and it is very nearly like the real one, but there is something wanting. I don't know what." The real nightingale was banished from the kingdom.

The artificial bird had its place on a silken cushion, close to the Emperor's bed. All the presents it had received of gold and precious jewels were scattered round it. Its title had risen to be Chief Imperial Singer-of-the-Bed-Chamber. In rank it

stood number one on the left side, for the Emperor reckoned
that side where the heart was seated was the important one.
And even an Emperor's heart is on the left side.

The music master wrote five and twenty volumes about
the artificial bird. The treatise was very long, and was
written in all the most difficult Chinese characters. Everybody said they had read and understood it, for otherwise
they would have been reckoned stupid, and then their bodies
would have been trampled upon.

Things went on in this way for a whole year. The Emperor,
the court, and all the other Chinese knew every little gurgle
in the song of the artificial bird by heart. But they liked it
all the better for this, and they could all join in the song
themselves. Even the street boys sang "Zizizi! cluck, cluck,
cluck!" And the Emperor sang it too.

But one evening, when the bird was singing its best and
the Emperor was lying in bed listening to it, something
gave way inside the bird with a "whizz." "Whirr!" went
all the wheels, and the music stopped.

The Emperor jumped out of bed and sent for his private
physicians, but what good could they do? Then they sent for
the watchmaker, who after a good deal of talk and examination got the works to go again somehow. But he said the bird
would have to be spared as much as possible, because it
was so worn out, and that he could not renew the works
so as to be sure of the tune. This was a great blow! They
now dared to let the artificial bird sing only once a year, and
hardly that. But then the music master made a little speech
using all the most difficult Chinese words. He said it was
just as good as ever, and his saying it made it so.

Five years passed, and then a great grief came upon the
nation. They were all very fond of their Emperor, and now
he was ill and could not live, it was said. A new Emperor
was already chosen, and people stood about in the street

and asked the gentleman-in-waiting how the Emperor was getting on.

"P," answered he, shaking his head.

The Emperor lay pale and cold in his gorgeous bed. The courtiers thought he was dead, and they all went off to pay their respects to their new Emperor. The lackeys ran off to talk matters over, and the chambermaids gave a great coffee party. Cloth had been laid down in all the rooms and corridors so as to deaden the sounds of footsteps, so it was very, very quiet. But the Emperor was not dead yet. He lay stiff and pale in the gorgeous bed with velvet hangings and heavy golden tassels. There was an open window high above him, and the moon streamed in upon the Emperor and the artificial bird beside him.

The poor Emperor could hardly breathe. He seemed to have a weight on his chest. He opened his eyes and then he saw that it was Death sitting upon his chest, wearing his golden crown. In one hand he held the Emperor's golden sword, and in the other his Imperial banner. From among the folds of the velvet hangings peered many curious faces. Some were hideous, others gentle and pleasant. They were all the Emperor's good and bad deeds, which now looked him in the face when Death was weighing him down.

"Do you remember that?" whispered one after the other. "Do you remember this?" And they told him so many things that the perspiration poured down his face.

"I never knew that," said the Emperor. "Music, music! Sound the great Chinese drums," he cried, "that I may not hear what they are saying." But they went on and on, and Death sat nodding his head like a Chinese at everything that was said. "Music, music!" shrieked the Emperor. "You precious little golden bird, sing, sing! I have loaded you with precious stones, and even hung my own golden slipper round your neck. Sing, I tell you, sing!"

But the bird stood silent. There was nobody to wind it

up, so of course it could not go. Death continued to fix the great empty sockets of its eyes upon him, and all was silent, terribly silent.

Suddenly, close to the window there was a burst of lovely song. It was the living nightingale, perched on a branch outside. It had heard of the Emperor's need and had come to bring comfort and hope to him. As it sang, the faces round became fainter, and the blood coursed with fresh vigor in the Emperor's veins and through his feeble limbs. Even Death himself listened to the song and said, " Go on, little nightingale, go on! "

" Yes, if you give me the gorgeous golden sword. Yes, if you give me the Imperial banner. Yes, if you give me the Emperor's crown."

And Death gave back each of these treasures for a song, and the nightingale went on singing. It sang about the quiet churchyard where the roses bloom, where the elder flowers scent the air, and where the fresh grass is ever moistened anew by the tears of the mourners. This song brought to Death a longing for his own garden, and like a cold gray mist he passed out of the window.

" Thanks, thanks! " said the Emperor. " You heavenly little bird, I know you. I banished you from my kingdom, and yet you have charmed the evil visions away from my bed by your song, and even Death away from my heart. How can I ever repay you? "

" You have rewarded me," said the nightingale. " I brought tears to your eyes the very first time I ever sang to you, and I shall never forget it. Those are the jewels which gladden the heart of a singer. But sleep now, and wake up fresh and strong. I will sing to you."

Then it sang again, and the Emperor fell into a sweet refreshing sleep. The sun shone in at his window, and he awoke refreshed and well. None of his attendants had yet come back to him, for they thought he was dead, but the nightingale still sat there singing.

"You must always stay with me," said the Emperor. "You shall sing only when you like, and I will break the artificial bird into a thousand pieces."

"Don't do that," said the nightingale. "It did all the good it could. Keep it as you have always done. I can't build my nest and live in this palace, but let me come whenever I like. Then I will sit on the branch in the evening and sing to you. I will sing to cheer you and to make you thoughtful too. I will sing to you of the happy ones and of those that suffer. I will sing about the good and the evil, which are kept hidden from you. The little singing bird flies far and wide, to the poor fisherman and to the peasant's home, to numbers who are far from you and your court. I love your heart more than your crown, and yet there is an odor of sanctity round the crown too! I will come, and I will sing to you. But you must promise me one thing."

"Everything!" said the Emperor, who stood there in his imperial robes which he had just put on, and he held the sword heavy with gold upon his heart.

"Only one thing I ask you. Tell no one that you have a little bird who tells you everything. It will be better so."

Then the nightingale flew away. The attendants came in to look after their dead Emperor—and there he stood, bidding them "Good morning!"

The Ugly Duckling

It was so glorious out in the country; it was summer; the cornfields were yellow, the oats were green, the hay had been put up in stacks in the green meadows, and the stork went about on his long red legs and chattered Egyptian, for this was the language he had learned from his good mother. All around the fields and meadows were great forests, and in the midst of these forests lay deep lakes. Yes, it was right glorious out in the country. In the midst of the sunshine there lay an old farm, with deep canals about it, and from the wall down to the water grew great burdocks, so high that little children could stand upright under the loftiest of them. It was just as wild there as in the deepest wood, and here sat a Duck upon her nest; she had to hatch her ducklings; but she was almost tired out before the little ones came; and then she so seldom had visitors. The other ducks liked better to swim about in the canals than to run up to sit down under a burdock, and cackle with her.

At last one eggshell after another burst open. " Piep! piep! " it cried, and in all the eggs there were little creatures that stuck out their heads.

" Quack! quack! " they said; and they all came quacking out as fast as they could, looking all round them under the green leaves; and the mother let them look as much as they chose, for green is good for the eye.

" How wide the world is! " said all the young ones, for they certainly had much more room now than when they were in the eggs.

" D'ye think this is all the world? " said the mother. " That stretches far across the other side of the garden, quite into the parson's field; but I have never been there yet. I hope you are all together," and she stood up. " No, I have not all. The largest egg still lies there. How long is that to last? I am really tired of it." And she sat down again.

" Well, how goes it? " asked an old Duck who had come to pay her a visit.

" It lasts a long time with that one egg," said the Duck who sat there. " It will not burst. Now, only look at the others; are they not the prettiest little ducks one could possibly see? They are all like their father: the rogue, he never comes to see me."

" Let me see the egg which will not burst," said the old visitor. " You may be sure it is a turkey's egg. I was once cheated in that way, and had much anxiety and trouble with the young ones, for they are afraid of the water. Must I say it to you, I could not get them to venture in. I quacked and I clacked, but it was no use. Let me see the egg. Yes, that's a turkey's egg. Let it lie there, and teach the other children to swim."

" I think I will sit on it a little longer," said the Duck. " I've sat so long now that I can sit a few days more."

" Just as you please," said the old Duck; and she went away.

At last the great egg burst. " Piep! piep! " said the little one, and crept forth. It was very large and very ugly. The Duck looked at it.

" It's a very large duckling," said she; " none of the others look like that: can it really be a turkey chick? Well, we shall soon find out. It must go into the water, even if I have to thrust it in myself."

The Tinder Box (United States, 9 years old)
(STORY PAGE 3)

The next day, it was bright, beautiful weather; the sun shone on all the green trees. The Mother Duck went down to the canal with all her family. Splash! she jumped into the water. "Quack! quack!" she said, and one duckling after another plunged in. The water closed over their heads, but they came up in an instant, and swam capitally; their legs went of themselves, and were all in the water. The ugly gray Duckling swam with them.

"No, it's not a turkey," said she; "look how well it can use its legs, and how straight it holds itself. It is my own child! On the whole it's quite pretty, if one looks at it rightly. Quack! quack! come with me, and I'll lead you out into the great world, and present you in the duck yard; but keep close to me, so that no one may tread on you, and take care of the cats!"

And so they came into the duck yard. There was a terrible riot going on in there, for two families were quarreling about an eel's head, and the cat got it after all.

"See, that's how it goes in the world!" said the Mother Duck; and she whetted her beak, for she too wanted the eel's head. "Only use your legs," she said. "See that you can bustle about, and bow your heads before the old Duck yonder. She's the grandest of all here; she's of Spanish blood—that's why she's so fat; and d'ye see? she has a red rag round her leg; that's something particularly fine, and the greatest distinction a duck can enjoy: it signifies that one does not want to lose her, and that she's to be known by the animals and by men too. Shake yourselves—don't turn in your toes; a well-brought-up duck turns its toes quite out, just like father and mother—so! Now bend your necks and say 'Quack!'"

And they did so: but the other ducks round about looked at them, and said quite boldly—

"Look there! now we're to have these hanging on, as if there were not enough of us already! And—fie!—how that

Duckling yonder looks; we won't stand that! " And one Duck
flew up at it, and bit it in the neck.

" Let it alone," said the mother; " it does no harm to anyone."

" Yes, but it's too large and peculiar," said the Duck who
had bitten it; " and therefore it must be put down."

" Those are pretty children that the mother has there," said
the old Duck with the rag round her leg. " They're all pretty
but that one; that was rather unlucky. I wish she could bear
it over again."

" That cannot be done, my lady," replied the Mother Duck.
" It is not pretty, but it has a really good disposition, and
swims as well as any other; yes. I may even say it swims
better. I think it will grow up pretty, and become smaller
in time; it has lain too long in the egg, and therefore is not
properly shaped." And then she pinched it in the neck, and
smoothed its feathers. " Moreover it is a drake," she said,
" and therefore it is not so much consequence. I think he will
be very strong: he makes his way already."

" The other ducklings are graceful enough," said the old
Duck. " Make yourself at home; and if you find an eel's
head, you may bring it to me."

And now they were at home. But the poor Duckling which
had crept last out of the egg, and looked so ugly, was bitten
and pushed and jeered, as much by the ducks as by the
chickens.

" It is too big! " they all said. And the turkey cock, who
had been born with spurs, and therefore thought himself an
emperor, blew himself up like a ship in full sail, and bore
straight down upon it; then he gobbled and grew quite red
in the face. The poor Duckling did not know where it
should stand or walk; it was quite melancholy because it
looked ugly, and was the butt of the whole duck yard.

So it went on the first day; and afterwards it became worse
and worse. The poor Duckling was hunted about by every
one; even its brothers and sisters were quite angry with it,

and said, "If the cat would only catch you, you ugly creature!" And the mother said, "If you were only far away!" And the ducks bit it, and the chickens beat it, and the girl who had to feed the poultry kicked at it with her foot.

Then it ran and flew over the fence, and the little birds in the bushes flew up in fear.

"That is because I am so ugly!" thought the Duckling; and it shut its eyes, but flew on further; and so it came out into the great moor, where the wild ducks lived. Here it lay the whole night long; and it was weary and downcast.

Towards morning the wild ducks flew up, and looked at their new companion.

"What sort of a one are you?" they asked; and the Duckling turned in every direction, and bowed as well as it could. "You are remarkably ugly!" said the wild ducks. "But that is nothing to us, so long as you do not marry into our family."

Poor thing! it certainly did not think of marrying, and only hoped to obtain leave to lie among the reeds and drink some of the swamp water.

Thus it lay two whole days; then came thither two wild geese, or, properly speaking, two wild ganders. It was not long since each had crept out of an egg, and that's why they were so saucy.

"Listen, comrade," said one of them. "You're so ugly that I like you. Will you go with us, and become a bird of passage? Near here, in another moor, there are a few sweet lovely wild geese, all unmarried, and all able to say 'Rap!' you've a chance of making your fortune, ugly as you are."

"Piff! paff!" resounded through the air; and the two ganders fell down dead in the swamp, and the water became blood red. "Piff! paff!" it sounded again, and the whole flock of wild geese rose up from the reeds. And then there was another report. A great hunt was going on. The sportsmen were lying in wait all round the moor, and some were even sitting up in the branches of the trees, which spread far over the reeds. The blue smoke rose up like clouds among the dark trees, and was wafted far away across the water; and the hunting dogs came—splash, splash!—into the swamp, and the rushes and the reeds bent down on every side. That was a fright for the poor Duckling! It turned its head, and put it under its wing; but at that moment a frightful great dog stood close by the Duckling. His tongue hung far out of his mouth, and his eyes gleamed horrible and ugly; he thrust out his nose close against the Duckling, showed his sharp teeth, and—splash, splash!—on he went, without seizing it.

" O, Heaven be thanked! " sighed the Duckling. " I am so ugly, that even the dog does not like to bite me! "

And so it lay quite quiet, while the shots rattled through the reeds and gun after gun was fired. At last, late in the day, all was still; but the poor Duckling did not dare to rise up; it waited several hours before it looked round, and then hastened away out of the moor as fast as it could. It ran on over field and meadow; there was such a storm raging that it was difficult to get from one place to another.

Towards evening the Duckling came to a little miserable peasant's hut. This hut was so dilapidated that it did not itself know on which side it should fall; and that's why it remained standing. The storm whistled round the Duckling in such a way that the poor creature was obliged to sit down, to stand against it; and the wind blew worse and worse. Then the Duckling noticed that one of the hinges of the door had given way, and the door hung so slanting that the Duckling could slip through the crack into the room; and that is what it did.

Here lived a woman, with her Cat and her Hen. And the Cat, whom she called Sonnie, could arch his back and purr, he could even give out sparks; but for that one had to stroke his fur the wrong way. The Hen had quite little short legs, and therefore she was called Chickabiddy Shortshanks; she laid good eggs, and the woman loved her as her own child.

In the morning the strange Duckling was at once noticed, and the Cat began to purr and the Hen to cluck.

"What's this?" said the woman, and looked all round; but she could not see well, and therefore she thought the Duckling was a fat duck that had strayed. "This is a rare prize!" she said. "Now I shall have duck's eggs. I hope it is not a drake. We must try that."

And so the Duckling was admitted on trial for three weeks; but no eggs came. And the Cat was master of the house, and the Hen was the lady, and always said "We and the world!" for she thought they were half the world, and by far the better half. The Duckling thought one might have a different opinion, but the Hen would not allow it.

"Can you lay eggs?" she asked.

"No."

"Then will you hold your tongue!"

And the Cat said, "Can you curve your back, and purr, and give out sparks?"

"No."

"Then you will please have no opinion of your own when sensible folks are speaking."

And the Duckling sat in a corner and was melancholy; then the fresh air and the sunshine streamed in; and it was seized with such a strange longing to swim on the water, that it could not help telling the Hen of it.

"What are you thinking of?" cried the Hen. "You have nothing to do, that's why you have these fancies. Lay eggs, or purr, and they will pass over."

"But it is so charming to swim on the water!" said the Duckling, "so refreshing to let it close above one's head, and to dive down to the bottom."

"Yes, that must be a mighty pleasure, truly," quoth the

Hen. " I fancy you must have gone crazy. Ask the Cat about it—he's the cleverest animal I know—ask him if he likes to swim on the water, or to dive down: I won't speak about myself. Ask our mistress, the old woman; no one in the world is cleverer than she. Do you think she has any desire to swim, and to let the water close above her head? "

" You don't understand me," said the Duckling.

" We don't understand you? Then pray who is to understand you? You surely don't pretend to be cleverer than the Cat and the woman—I won't say anything of myself. Don't be conceited, child, and thank your Maker for all the kindness you have received. Did you not get into a warm room, and have you not fallen into company from which you may learn something? But you are a chatterer, and it is not pleasant to associate with you. You may believe me, I speak for your good. I tell you disagreeable things, and by that one may always know one's true friends! Only take care that you learn to lay eggs, or to purr, and give out sparks! "

" I think I will go out into the wide world," said the Duckling.

" Yes, do go," replied the Hen.

And so the Duckling went away. It swam on the water, and dived, but it was slighted by every creature because of its ugliness.

Now came the autumn. The leaves in the forest turned yellow and brown; the wind caught them so that they danced about, and up in the air it was very cold. The clouds hung low, heavy with hail and snowflakes, and on the fence stood the raven, crying, " Croak! croak! " for mere cold; yes, it was enough to make one feel cold to think of this. The poor little Duckling certainly had not a good time. One evening— the sun was just setting in his beauty—there came a whole flock of great, handsome birds out of the bushes; they were dazzlingly white, with long, flexible necks; they were swans.

They uttered a very peculiar cry, spread forth their glorious great wings, and flew away from that cold region to warmer lands, to fair open lakes. They mounted so high, so high! and the ugly Duckling felt quite strangely as it watched them. It turned round and round in the water like a wheel, stretched out its neck towards them, and uttered such a strange, loud cry as frightened itself. O! it could not forget those beautiful, happy birds; and so soon as it could see them no longer, it dived down to the very bottom, and when it came up again, it was quite beside itself. It knew not the name of those birds, and knew not whither they were flying; but it loved them more than it had ever loved any one. It was not at all envious of them. How could it think of wishing to possess such loveliness as they had? It would have been glad if only the ducks would have endured its company—the poor, ugly creature!

And the winter grew cold, very cold! The Duckling was forced to swim about in the water, to prevent the surface from freezing entirely; but every night the hole in which it swam about became smaller and smaller. It froze so hard that the icy covering cracked again; and the Duckling was obliged to use it continually to prevent the hole from freezing up. At last it became exhausted, and lay quite still, and thus froze fast into the ice.

Early in the morning a peasant came by, and when he saw what had happened, he took his wooden shoe, broke the ice-crust to pieces, and carried the Duckling home to his wife. Then it came to itself again. The children wanted to play with it; but the Duckling thought they wanted to hurt it, and in its terror fluttered up into the milk pan, so that the milk spurted down into the room. The woman clasped her hands, at which the Duckling flew down into the butter tub, and then into the meal barrel and out again. How it looked then! The woman screamed, and struck at it with the fire tongs; the children tumbled over one another in their efforts

to catch the Duckling; and they laughed and they screamed!
—well it was that the door stood open, and the poor creature
was able to slip out between the shrubs into the newly-fallen
snow—there it lay quite exhausted.

But it would be too melancholy if I were to tell all the
misery and care which the Duckling had to endure in the
hard winter. It lay out on the moor among the reeds, when
the sun began to shine again and the larks to sing: it was
a beautiful spring.

Then all at once the Duckling could flap its wings: they
beat the air more strongly than before, and bore it strongly
away; and before it well knew how all this happened, it
found itself in a great garden, where the elder trees smelled
sweet, and bent their long green branches down to the canal
that wound through the region. O, here it was so beautiful,
such a gladness of spring! and from the thicket came three
glorious white swans; they rustled their wings, and swam
lightly on the water. The Duckling knew the splendid
creatures, and felt oppressed by a peculiar sadness.

"I will fly away to them, to the royal birds! and they will
beat me, because I, that am so ugly, dare to come near them.
But it is all the same. Better to be killed by *them* than to be
pursued by ducks, and beaten by fowls, and pushed about
by the girl who takes care of the poultry yard, and to suffer
hunger in winter!" And it flew out into the water, and swam
towards the beautiful swans: these looked at it, and came
sailing down upon it with outspread wings. "Kill me!" said
the poor creature, and bent its head down upon the water,
expecting nothing but death. But what was this that it saw
in the clear water? It beheld its own image; and, lo! it was
no longer a clumsy dark-gray bird, ugly and hateful to look
at, but a—swan!

It matters nothing if one is born in a duck yard, if one
has only lain in a swan's egg.

It felt quite glad at all the need and misfortune it had

suffered, now it realized its happiness in all the splendor that surrounded it. And the great swans swam round it, and stroked it with their beaks.

Into the garden came little children, who threw bread and corn into the water; and the youngest cried, "There is a new one!" and the other children shouted joyously, "Yes, a new one has arrived!" And they clapped their hands and danced about, and ran to their father and mother; and bread and cake were thrown into the water; and they all said, "The new one is the most beautiful of all! so young and handsome!" and the old swans bowed their heads before him.

Then he felt quite ashamed, and hid his head under his wings, for he did not know what to do; he was so happy, and yet not at all proud. He thought how he had been persecuted and despised; and now he heard them saying that he was the most beautiful of all birds. Even the elder tree bent its branches straight down into the water before him, and the sun shone warm and mild. Then his wings rustled, he lifted his slender neck, and cried rejoicingly from the depths of his heart—

"I never dreamed of so much happiness when I was the Ugly Duckling!"

The Little Match Girl

It was terribly cold; it snowed and was already almost dark, and evening came on, the last evening of the year. In the cold and gloom a poor little girl, bareheaded and barefoot, was walking through the streets. When she left her own house she certainly had had slippers on; but of what use were they? They were very big slippers, and her mother had used them till then, so big were they. The little maid lost them as she slipped across the road, where two carriages were rattling by terribly fast. One slipper was not to be found again, and a boy had seized the other, and run away with it. He thought he could use it very well as a cradle, some day when he had children of his own. So now the little girl went with her little naked feet, which were quite red and blue with the cold. In an old apron she carried a number of matches, and a bundle of them in her hand. No one had bought anything of her all day, and no one had given her a farthing.

Shivering with cold and hunger she crept along, a picture of misery, poor little girl! The snowflakes covered her long fair hair, which fell in pretty curls over her neck; but she did not think of that now. In all the windows lights were shining, and there was a glorious smell of roast goose, for it was New Year's Eve. Yes, she thought of that!

In a corner formed by two houses, one of which projected

beyond the other, she sat down, cowering. She had drawn up her little feet, but she was still colder, and she did not dare to go home, for she had sold no matches, and did not bring a farthing of money. From her father she would certainly receive a beating, and besides, it was cold at home, for they had nothing over them but a roof through which the wind whistled, though the largest rents had been stopped with straw and rags.

Her little hands were almost numb with the cold. Ah! a match might do her good, if she could only draw one from the bundle, and rub it against the wall, and warm her hands at it. She drew one out. R-r-atch! how it sputtered and burned! It was a warm bright flame, like a little candle, when she held her hands over it; it was a wonderful little light! It really seemed to the little girl as if she sat before a great polished stove, with bright brass feet and a brass cover. How the fire burned! how comfortable it was! but the little flame went out, the stove vanished, and she had only the remains of the burned match in her hand.

A second was rubbed against the wall. It burned up, and when the light fell upon the wall it became transparent like a thin veil, and she could see through it into the room. On the table a snow-white cloth was spread; upon it stood a shining dinner service; the roast goose smoked gloriously, stuffed with apples and dried plums. And what was still more splendid to behold, the goose hopped down from the dish, and waddled along the floor, with a knife and fork in its breast, to the little girl. Then the match went out, and only the thick, damp, cold wall was before her. She lighted another match. Then she was sitting under a beautiful Christmas tree; it was greater and more ornamented than the one she had seen through the glass door at the rich merchant's. Thousands of candles burned upon the green branches, and colored pictures like those in the print shops looked down upon them. The little girl stretched forth her hand toward them; then the match went out. The Christmas lights mounted higher. She saw them now as stars in the sky: one of them fell down, forming a long line of fire.

"Now some one is dying," thought the little girl, for her old grandmother, the only person who had loved her, and who was now dead, had told her that when a star fell down a soul mounted up to God.

She rubbed another match against the wall; it became bright again, and in the brightness the old grandmother stood clear and shining, mild and lovely.

"Grandmother!" cried the child. "O! take me with you! I know you will go when the match is burned out. You will vanish like the warm fire, the warm food, and the great, glorious Christmas tree!"

And she hastily rubbed the whole bundle of matches, for she wished to hold her grandmother fast. And the matches burned with such a glow that it became brighter than in the middle of the day; grandmother had never been so large or so beautiful. She took the little girl in her arms, and both flew in brightness and joy above the earth, very, very high, and up there was neither cold, nor hunger, nor care—they were with God.

But in the corner, leaning against the wall, sat the poor girl with red cheeks and smiling mouth, frozen to death on the last evening of the Old Year. The New Year's sun rose upon a little corpse! The child sat there, stiff and cold, with the matches, of which one bundle was burned. "She wanted to warm herself," the people said. No one imagined what a beautiful thing she had seen, and in what glory she had gone in with her grandmother to the New Year's Day.

The Rags

At the door of a paper mill stood heaps of dust and rubbish, piled up into stacks; they had been gathered far and wide, and every rag in them had a tale to tell, and told it too; but we cannot listen to them all. Some of the rags were native, others came from foreign lands. Here now was a Danish rag, lying close to a rag from Norway; rank Danish was the one, and rank Norse the other; and there was likely to be some fun between the two, as any experienced Dane or Norseman could tell you.

They understood each other well enough, though the two languages were as different—so the Norwegian said—as French and Hebrew. "We go to the hillside for ours, and get it fresh from the fountainhead, while the Dane cooks up a mawkish, wishy-washy sort of a lingo."

The rags talked, and rags are rags all the world over; they are thought nothing of except in the dust heap.

"I am Norse," said the Norwegian; "and when I have said I am Norse, I guess I have said enough. I am firm of fiber, like the granite rocks of old Norway. The land there has a constitution, just like free America. It sets my fibers tickling to think of what I am, and to ring out my thoughts in words of the real old grit."

"But we have a complete literature," said the Danish rag; "do you understand what that is?"

" Understand! " repeated the Norwegian: " O this flatland creature! shall I give him a hoist uphill, and a Northern Light or two, clout as he is? When the Norway sun has thawed the ice, then come lubberly Danish hulks, bringing us butter and cheese, a right noble cargo; and they bring, too, by way of ballast, the Danish literature. We don't want it. One can do without stale beer in a land of sparkling springs, and up yonder is a natural well that was never bored; no, nor yet puffed into European notice by news-mongers, confederate jobbers, and bookmaking tourists in foreign parts. I speak free from the bottom of my lungs, and the Dane must get used to free sound; and so he will some day, in his Scandinavian clamber up our proud mountain land—that primary knob of the universe! "

" A Danish rag could never talk like that; no! " said the Dane. " It is not our nature: I know myself: and all our rags are like me. We are so good-natured, so unassuming. We only think too little of ourselves. Not that we gain much by our modesty: but I do like it; I consider it quite charming. Still I am perfectly aware of my own good qualities, I assure you, but I don't talk about them: nobody shall ever bring such a charge against me. I am gentle and complaisant; bear everything patiently, spite nobody, and speak good of all men—though there is not much good to be said of other people; but that is their business. I can afford to smile at it, I feel myself so much superior."

" Have done with this flatland drivel; it turns me sick," said the Norwegian, caught a puff of wind, and fluttered away from his own heap on to another.

Paper they both became, and, as chance would have it, the Norwegian rag became a sheet on which a Norseman wrote a true-love letter to a Danish girl; and the Danish rag became the manuscript for a Danish ode in honor of Norway's strength and beauty.

The Ugly Duckling (Finland, 7 years old)
(STORY PAGE 175)

Something good there may come even of rags, when they are once out of the dust heap, and the change has been made in favor of truth and beauty; they keep up a good understanding between us, and in that there is a blessing.

The story is done. It is rather pretty, and offensive to nobody except to rags.

The Red Shoes

There was once a little girl. She was a tiny delicate little thing, but she always had to go about barefoot in summer, because she was very poor. In winter she had only a pair of heavy wooden shoes, and her ankles were terribly chafed.

An old mother shoemaker lived in the middle of the village, and she made a pair of little shoes out of some strips of red cloth. They were very clumsy, but they were made with the best intention, for the little girl was to have them. Her name was Karen.

These shoes were given to her, and she wore them for the first time on the day her mother was buried. They were certainly not mourning shoes, but she had no others, and so she walked barelegged in them behind the poor pine coffin.

Just then a big old carriage drove by, and a big old lady was seated in it. She looked at the little girl and felt very, very sorry for her, and said to the parson, " Give the little girl to me and I will look after her and be kind to her." Karen thought it was all because of the red shoes, but the old lady said they were hideous, and they were burnt. Karen was well and neatly dressed, and had to learn reading and sewing. People said she was pretty, but her mirror said, " You are more than pretty. You are lovely! "

At this time the Queen was taking a journey through the country, and she had her little daughter the Princess with her. The people, and among them Karen, crowded round the palace where they were staying, to see them. The little Princess stood at a window to show herself. She wore neither a train nor a golden crown, but she was dressed all in white with a beautiful pair of red morocco shoes. They were indeed a contrast to those the poor old mother shoemaker had made for Karen. Nothing in the world could be compared to these red shoes.

The time came when Karen was old enough to be confirmed. She had new clothes and she was also to have a pair of new shoes. The rich shoemaker in the town was to take the measure of her little foot. His shop was full of glass cases of the most charming shoes and shiny leather boots. They looked beautiful but the old lady could not see very well, so it gave her no pleasure to look at them. Among all the other shoes there was one pair of red shoes like those worn by the Princess. Oh, how pretty they were! The shoemaker told them that they had been made for an earl's daughter, but they had not fitted. "I suppose they are patent leather," said the old lady. "They are so shiny."

"Yes, they do shine," said Karen, who tried them on. They fitted and were bought, but the old lady had not the least idea that they were red, or she would never have allowed Karen to wear them for her confirmation. This she did however.

Everybody looked at her feet, and when she walked up the church to the chancel she thought that even the old pictures, those portraits of dead and gone priests and their wives, with stiff collars and long black clothes, fixed their eyes upon her shoes. She thought of nothing else when the minister laid his hand upon her head and spoke to her of holy baptism, the covenant of God, and said that henceforth she was to be a responsible Christian person. The solemn notes of the organ resounded, the children sang with their sweet voices, and the old precentor sang, but Karen thought only about her red shoes.

By the afternoon the old lady had been told on all sides that the shoes were red, and she said it was very naughty and most improper. For the future, whenever Karen went to the church she was to wear black shoes, even if they were old. Next Sunday there was holy communion, and Karen was to receive it for the first time. She looked at the black shoes and then at the red ones. Then she looked again at the red—and at last put them on.

It was beautiful sunny weather. Karen and the old lady went by the path through the cornfield, and it was rather dusty. By the church door stood an old soldier with a crutch. He had a curious long beard; it was more red than white—in fact it was almost red. He bent down to the ground and asked the old lady if he might dust her shoes. Karen put out her little foot too. " See what beautiful dancing shoes! " said the soldier. " Mind you stick fast when you dance." And as he spoke he struck the soles with his hand. The old lady gave the soldier a copper and went into the church with Karen. All the people in the church looked at Karen's red shoes, and all the portraits looked too. When Karen knelt at the altar rails and the chalice was put to her lips, she thought only of the red shoes. She seemed to see them floating before her eyes. She forgot to join in the hymn of praise, and she forgot to say the Lord's Prayer.

Now everybody left the church, and the old lady got into her carriage. Karen lifted her foot to get in after her, but just then the old soldier, who was still standing there, said, " See what pretty dancing shoes! " Karen couldn't help it: she took a few dancing steps, and when she began her feet continued to dance. It was just as if the shoes had a power over them. She danced right round the church. She couldn't stop. The coachman had to run after her, take hold of her, and lift her into the carriage; but her feet continued to dance, so that she kicked the poor lady horribly. At last they got the shoes off and her feet had a little rest.

When they got home the shoes were put away in a cupboard, but Karen could not help going to look at them.

The old lady became very ill. They said she could not live. She had to be carefully nursed and tended, and no one was nearer than Karen to do this. But there was to be a grand ball in the town and Karen was invited. She looked at the old lady, who after all could not live. Then she looked at the red shoes—she thought there was no harm in doing so. She put on the red shoes—that much she thought she might do—and then she went to the ball and began to dance. The shoes would not let her do what she liked: when she wanted to go to the right, they danced to the left. When she wanted to dance up the room, the shoes danced down the room, and then down the stairs, through the streets and out of the town gate. Away she danced, and away she had to dance, right away into the dark forest. Something shone up above the trees and she thought it was the moon, for it was a face, but it was the old soldier with the red beard. He nodded and said, " See what pretty dancing shoes! "

This frightened her terribly and she wanted to throw off the red shoes, but they stuck fast. She tore off her stockings, but the shoes had grown fast to her feet. So off she danced, and off she had to dance, over fields and meadows, in rain and sunshine, by day and by night, but at night it was fearful.

She danced into the open churchyard, but the dead did not join her dance; they had something much better to do. She wanted to sit down on a pauper's grave where the bitter wormwood grew, but there was no rest nor repose for her. When she danced towards the open church door, she saw an angel standing there in long white robes and wings which reached from his shoulders to the ground. His face was grave and stern, and in his hand he held a broad and shining sword.

" Dance you shall! " said he. " You shall dance in your red

shoes till you are pale and cold. Till your skin shrivels up and you are a skeleton! You shall dance from door to door, and wherever you find proud vain children, you must knock at the door so that they may see you and fear you. Yea, you shall dance— "

" Mercy! " shrieked Karen, but she did not hear the angel's answer, for the shoes bore her through the gate into the fields, and over roadways and paths. Ever and ever she was forced to dance.

One morning she danced past a door she knew well. She heard the sound of a hymn from within, and a coffin covered with flowers was being carried out. Then she knew that the old lady was dead, and it seemed to her that she was forsaken by all the world and cursed by the holy angels of God.

On and ever on she danced. Dance she must, even through the dark nights. The shoes bore her away over briars and stubble till her feet were torn and bleeding. She danced away over the heath till she came to a little lonely house. She knew the executioner lived here, and she tapped with her fingers on the window pane and said, " Come out! Come out! I can't come in for I am dancing! "

The executioner said, " Don't you know who I am? I chop the bad people's heads off, and I see that my ax is quivering."

" Don't chop my head off," said Karen, " for then I can never repent of my sins. But pray, pray chop off my feet with the red shoes! "

Then she confessed all her sins and the executioner chopped off her feet with the red shoes, but the shoes danced right away with the little feet into the depths of the forest.

Then he made her a pair of wooden feet and crutches, and he taught her a psalm, the one penitents always sing. And she kissed the hand which had wielded the ax and went away over the heath.

" I have suffered enough for those red shoes! " said she. " I will go to church now, so that they may see me." And she went as fast as she could to the church door. When she got there, the red shoes danced right up in front of her, and she was frightened and went home again.

She was very sad all the week and shed many bitter tears, but when Sunday came she said, "Now then, I have suffered long enough. I should think I am quite as good as many who sit holding their heads so high in church."

She went along quite boldly, but she did not get further than the gate before she saw the red shoes dancing in front of her. She was more frightened than ever and turned back, this time with real repentance in her heart. Then she went to the parson's house and begged to be taken into service. She would be very industrious and work as hard as she could. She didn't care what wages they gave her, if only she might have a roof over her head and live among kind people. The parson's wife was sorry for her, and took her into her service. She proved to be very industrious and thoughtful. She sat very still and listened most attentively in the evening when the parson read the Bible. All the little ones were very fond of her, but when they chattered about finery and dress and about being as beautiful as a queen, she would shake her head.

Next Sunday they all went to church and they asked her if she would go with them, but she looked sadly, with tears in her eyes, at her crutches. And they went without her to hear the word of God, while she sat in her little room alone. It was only big enough for a bed and a chair. She sat there with her prayer book in her hand, and as she read it with a humble mind she heard the notes of the organ, borne from the church by the wind. She raised her tear-stained face and said, "Oh, God help me!"

Then the sun shone brightly round her, and the angel in the white robes whom she had seen that night at the church door stood before her. He no longer held the sharp sword in his hand, but a beautiful green branch covered with roses.

He touched the ceiling with it and it rose to a great height, and wherever he touched it a golden star appeared. Then he touched the walls and they spread themselves out, and she saw and heard the organ. She saw the pictures of the old parsons and their wives. The congregation were all sitting in their seats singing aloud—for the church itself had come home to the poor girl in her narrow little chamber, or else she had been taken to it. She found herself on the bench with the other people from the parsonage. And when the hymn had come to an end, they looked up and nodded to her and said, " It was a good thing you came after all, little Karen! "

" It was through God's mercy! " she said. The organ sounded and the children's voices echoed so sweetly through the choir. The warm sunshine streamed brightly in through the window, right up to the bench where Karen sat. Her heart was so overfilled with the sunshine, with peace, and with joy, that it broke. Her soul flew with the sunshine to heaven, and no one there asked about the red shoes.

A Picture from the Castle Ramparts

It is autumn; we stand on the Castle Ramparts and look out across the sea with its many ships to the Swedish coast rising beyond, bright in the evening sunshine. Behind us the rampart descends abruptly; magnificent trees, whose yellow leaves are falling fast, grow below, and behind them are certain close-built, dull-looking houses with wooden palisades; a dreary walk has the sentinel who paces to and fro among them, but still drearier and darker must it be within those grated windows, for there dwell convict slaves, the worst of criminals.

A beam from the setting sun strays into the bare chamber, for the sun shines alike on the evil and on the good. The sullen, savage felon gazes gloomily on the cold sunbeam. A little bird flies upon the grating; his song, too, is for the evil as for the good. "Quirrevit!" his song is a brief one, but he remains perched on the grating; he flaps his wings, plumes his feathers, one tiny feather falls off, the others he ruffles up round his neck. And the chained criminal looks on, and a softer expression passes over his hard, coarse features, a feeling he is scarcely conscious of springs up within his heart, a feeling in some way akin to the sunbeam that has darted through the trellis, and the fragrance of the violets that in the spring cluster so abundantly outside his prison. But now sounds the horn of some home-bound huntsman;

clear, strong, and lively are the notes. Away from the grating flies the bird, from the bare wall fades away the sunbeam, and all is dark again within the chamber, dark again in the convict's heart. But, thank Heaven! the sun has shone therein, the bird's song has been heard, though but for one minute.

Die not away so soon, ye sweet, clear tones from the huntsman's horn! The evening is mild, the sea calm and smooth as a mirror.

A Vision of the Last Day

Of all the days of our life the greatest and most solemn is the day on which we die. Hast thou ever tried to realize that most sure, most portentous hour, the last hour we shall spend on earth?

There was a certain man, an upholder of truth and justice, a Christian man and orthodox, so the world esteemed him. And, in sooth, it may be that some good thing was found in him, since in sleep, amid the visions of the night, it pleased the Father of spirits to reveal him to himself, making manifest to him what he was in truth, namely, one of those who trust in themselves that they are righteous and despise others.

He went to rest, secure that his accounts were right with all men, that he had paid his dues and wrought good works that day; of the secret pride of his heart, of the harsh words that had passed his lips, he took no account at all. And so he slept, and in his sleep Death stood by his bedside, a glorious Angel, strong, spotless, beautiful, but unlike every other angel, stern, unsmiling, pitiless of aspect.

"Thine hour is come, and thou must follow me!" spake Death. And Death's cold finger touched the man's feet, whereupon they became like ice, then touched his forehead, then his heart. And the chain that bound the immortal soul to clay was riven asunder, and the soul was free to follow the Angel of Death.

But during those brief seconds, while yet that awful touch thrilled through feet, and head, and heart, there passed over the dying man, as in great, heaving ocean waves, the recollection of all that he had wrought and felt in his whole life; just as one shuddering glance into a whirlpool suffices to reveal in thought rapid as lightning, the entire unfathomable depth! just as in one momentary glance at the starry heavens we can conceive the infinite multitude of that glorious host of unknown orbs.

In such a retrospect the terrified sinner shrinks back into himself, and finding there no stay by which to cling, must feel shrinking into infinite nothingness; while the devout soul raises its thoughts to the Almighty, yielding itself up to Him in childlike trust, and praying, " Thy will be done in me! "

But this man had not the childlike mind, neither did he tremble like the sinner; his thoughts were still the self-praising thoughts in which he had fallen asleep. His path, he believed, must lead straight heavenward, and Mercy, the promised Mercy, would open to him the gates.

And, in his dream, the Soul followed the Angel of Death, though not without first casting one wistful glance at the couch where lay, in its white shroud, the lifeless image of clay, still, as it were, bearing the impress of the soul's own individuality. And now they hovered through the air, now glided along the ground. Was it a vast, decorated hall they were passing through, or a forest? It seemed hard to tell; Nature, it appeared, was formally set out for show, as in the artificial old French gardens, and amid its strange, carefully arranged scenes, passed and repassed troops of men and women, all clad as for a masquerade.

" Such is human life! " said the Angel of Death.

The figures seemed more or less disguised; those who swept by in the glories of velvet and gold were not all among the noblest or most dignified looking, neither were all those who wore the garb of poverty insignificant or vulgar. It was a strange masquerade! But most strange it was to see how one and all carefully concealed under their clothing something they would not have others perceive, but in vain, for each was bent upon discovering his neighbor's secret, and they tore and snatched at one another till, now here, now there, some part of an animal was revealed. In one was found the grinning head of an ape, in another the cloven foot of a goat, in a third the poison fang of a snake, in a fourth the clammy fin of a fish.

All had in them some token of the animal—the animal which is fast rooted in human nature, and which here was seen struggling to burst forth. And, however closely a man might hold his garment over it, the others would never rest till they had rent the hiding veil, and all kept crying out, "Look here! look now! here he is! there she is! "—and every one mockingly laid bare his fellow's shame.

"And what was the animal in me? " inquired the disembodied Soul; and the Angel of Death pointed to a haughty form, around whose head shone a bright, wide-spread glory of rainbow-colored rays, but at whose heart might be seen lurking, half hidden, the feet of the peacock; the glory was, in fact, merely the peacock's gaudy tail.

And as they passed on, large, foul-looking birds shrieked out from the boughs of the trees; with clear, intelligible, though harsh, human voices they shrieked, "Thou that walkest with Death, dost remember me? " All the evil thoughts and desires that had nestled within him from his birth until his death now called after him, "Rememberest thou me? "

And the Soul shuddered, recognizing the voices; it could not deny knowledge of the evil thoughts and desires that were now rising up in witness against it.

"In our flesh, in our evil nature, dwelleth no good thing," cried the Soul; "but, at least, thoughts never with me ripened into actions; the world has not seen the evil fruit." And the

Soul hurried on to get free from the accusing voices; but the great black fowls swept in circles round, and screamed out their scandalous words louder and louder, as though they would be heard all over the world. And the Soul fled from them like the hunted stag, and at every step stumbled against sharp flint stones that lay in the path. "How came these sharp stones here? They look like mere withered leaves lying on the ground."

"Every stone is for some incautious word thou hast spoken, which lay as a stumbling block in thy neighbor's path, which wounded thy neighbor's heart far more sorely and deeply than these sharp flints now wound thy feet."

"Alas! I never once thought of that," sighed the Soul.

And those words of the Gospel rang through the air, "Judge not, that ye be not judged."

"We have all sinned," said the Soul, recovering from its momentary self-abasement. "I have kept the Law and the Gospel, I have done what I could, I am not as others are!"

And in his dream this man now stood at the gates of heaven, and the Angel who guarded the entrance inquired, "Who art thou? Tell me thy faith, and show it to me in thy works."

"I have faithfully kept the Commandments, I have humbled myself in the eyes of the world, I have preserved myself free from the pollution of intercourse with sinners, I have hated and persecuted evil, and those who practice it, and I would do so still, yea, with fire and sword, had I the power."

"Then thou art one of Mohammed's followers?" said the Angel.

"I? a Mohammedan?—never!"

"'He who strikes with the sword shall perish by the sword,' thus spake the Son; His religion thou knowest not. It may be that thou art one of the children of Israel, whose maxim is, 'An eye for an eye, a tooth for a tooth,'—art thou such?"

Thumbelina (Chile, 6 years old)
(STORY PAGE 45)

" I am a Christian."

" I see it not in thy faith or in thine actions. The law of Christ is the law of forgiveness, love, and mercy."

" Mercy! " The gracious echo of that sweet word thrilled through infinite space, the gates of heaven opened, and the Soul hovered toward the realms of endless bliss.

But the flood of light that streamed forth from within was so dazzlingly bright, so transcendently white and pure, that the Soul shrank back as from a two-edged sword, and the hymns and harp tones of Angels mingled in such exquisite celestial harmony as the earthly mind has not power either to conceive or to endure. And the Soul trembled and bowed itself deeper and deeper, and the heavenly light penetrated it through and through, and it felt to the quick, as it had never truly felt before, the burden of its own pride, cruelty, and sin.

" What I have done of good in the world, that did I because I could not otherwise, but the evil that I did—that was of myself! "

This confession was wrung from him; more and more the man felt dazzled and overpowered by the pure light of heaven; he seemed falling into a measureless abyss, the abyss of his own nakedness and unworthiness. Shrunk into himself, humbled, cast out, unripe for the kingdom of heaven, shuddering at the thought of the just and holy God—hardly dared he to gasp out, " Mercy! "

And the face of the Angel at the portal was turned toward him in softening pity. " Mercy is for them who implore it, not claim it; there is Mercy also for thee. Turn thee, child of man, turn thee back the way thou camest to thy clayey tabernacle; in pity is it given thee to dwell in dust yet a little while. Be no longer righteous in thine own eyes, copy Him who with patience endured the contradiction of sinners, strive and pray that thou mayest become poor in spirit, and so mayest thou yet inherit the Kingdom."

14

"Holy, loving, glorious forever shalt thou be, O, erring human spirit!"—thus rang the chorus of Angels. And again overpowered by those transcendent melodies, dazzled and blinded by that excess of purest light, the Soul again shrank back into itself. It seemed to be falling an infinite depth; the celestial music grew fainter and fainter, till common earthly sights and sounds dispelled the vision. The rays of the early morning sun falling full on his face, the cheerful crow of the vigilant cock, called the sleeper up to pray.

Inexpressibly humbled, yet thankful, he arose and knelt beside his bed. "Thou, who hast shown me to myself, help me now, that I may not only do justly, but love mercy, and walk humbly with my God. Thou, who hast convicted me of sin, now purify me, strengthen me, that, though ever unworthy of Thy presence, I may yet, supported by Thy love, dare to ascend into Thine everlasting light!"

The Vision was his; be the lesson, the prayer, also ours.

The Greenies

A rose tree stood in the window. Only a short time ago it was green and fresh, and now it looked sickly—no doubt it was in poor health. A whole regiment was quartered on it and was eating it up; but notwithstanding this greediness, the regiment was a very decent and respectable one. It wore bright green uniforms. I spoke to one of the " Greenies "; he was but three days old, and yet he was already a grandfather. Do you know what he said? It is all true—he spoke of himself and of the rest of the regiment. Listen!

" We are the most wonderful creatures in the world. We are engaged at a very early age, and immediately have the wedding. When the cold weather comes, we lay our eggs; the little ones lie snug and warm. The wisest of creatures, the ant (we have the greatest respect for him!) understands us. He appreciates us, you may be sure. He does not eat us up at once; he takes our eggs, lays them in the family ant hill, on the ground floor—lays them, labeled and numbered, side by side, layer on layer, so that each day a new one may creep out of the egg. Then he puts us in a stable, pinches our hind legs, and milks us till we die. He has given us the prettiest name—'Little milch-cow!'

" All creatures, who, like the ant, are gifted with common sense, call us so: it is only human beings who do not; they give us another name, and that we feel to be a great affront—

great enough to embitter our whole life. Could you not write a protest against it for us? could you not rouse these human beings to a sense of the wrong they do us? They look at us so stupidly, at times with such envious eyes, just because we eat a rose leaf, while they eat every created thing, all that is green and grows. O, they give us the most humiliating name! I will not even mention it. Ugh! I feel it in my stomach; I cannot even pronounce it—at least not when I have my uniform on, and I always wear that.

"I was born on a rose leaf. And the whole regiment live on the rose tree. We live off it, in fact; but then it lives again in us, who belong to the higher order of created beings. The human beings do not like us; they come and murder us with soapsuds—it is a horrid drink! I seem to smell it even now; it is dreadful to be washed when one was not made to be washed. Man! you who look at us with your severe soapsud eyes, think what our place in nature is: we are born on roses, we die in roses—our whole life is a poem. Do not give us the name which you yourself think most despicable, the name that I cannot bear to pronounce; call us the ants' milch-cows—the rose-tree regiment—the little green things."

And I—the man—stood looking at the tree, and at the little greenies—whose name I shall not mention, for I should not like to wound the feelings of one of the citizens of the rose tree, a large family with eggs and young ones—and at the soapsuds that I was going to wash them in, for I had come with soap and water, and murderous intentions; but now I will use it for soap bubbles. Look! how beautiful! perhaps there lies a fairy tale in each, and the bubble grows so large and radiant, and it looks as if there were a pearl lying inside of it!

The bubble swayed and swung, and flew to the door and then burst; but the door opened wide, and there stood Dame Fairy Tale herself! and now she will tell you better than

I can about—I won't say the name—the little green things.

"Tree-lice!" said Dame Fairy Tale. "One must call things by their right names; and if one may not do so always, one must at least have the privilege of doing so in fairy tales!"

What One Can Invent!

There was once a young man who wanted to become a poet. He wanted to be a poet by the next Easter, that he might marry and live by poetizing, and that, he knew, consisted merely in a knack of inventing, but then he never could invent! He was quite sure that he had been born too late; every subject had been taken before he came into the world, and there was nothing left for him to write about!

"What happy mortals were those who were born a thousand years ago," he sighed, "for then it was an easy matter to become immortal! Even those who were born but a hundred years ago were enviable; even at that time there was still something left to poetize about. But now all subjects are worn threadbare, and there is no use in my trying to write the nap on again!"

He thought and thought about it, till he grew quite thin and forlorn, poor fellow. No doctor could help him; there was but one who would be able to find the right remedy for him, and that was that wonderfully clever little old woman who lived in the little hut by the turnpike gate, that she opened and shut for all who passed that way. But she was wise and learned, and could open far more than the gate; she was much wiser than the doctor who drives in his carriage, and pays title taxes.

"I must go to her," said the young man. Her home was

small and tidy, but tiresome to look at—not a tree, not a flower, grew anywhere near it. There was a beehive at the door—very useful! There was a little potato field—very useful! and a ditch with a blackthorn bush that had flowered, and was bearing fruit—berries that draw your mouth together if you eat of them before the frost has nipped them.

"What a picture all this is of our unpoetic time," thought the young man. At least here was a thought, a grain of gold dust that he found at the door of the little old woman's cottage.

"Write that thought down," she said. "Crumbs are bread, too. I know why you have come here; you cannot invent, and yet you want to be a poet by next Easter!"

"Everything has been written about," he sighed; "our time is not as the olden time."

"No, it is not," said the old woman. "In the olden time such as I, who knew many weighty secrets, and how to cure by the help of wonderful herbs, were burned alive; and in the olden time, the poets went about with empty stomachs and out at elbows. Ours is a very good time, the very best, much better than the olden time; but your want of invention all lies in your having no eyes to see with, and no ears to hear, and you do not say your prayers of an evening. There are any amount of things all around you that one might poetize and write about, when one knows *how* to write stories. You can find it in the earth where it grows and sprouts; you can dip into the running or the stagnant water, and you will find it there; but first of all, you must understand the way of doing it—must know how to catch a ray of sunshine. Now, just try my spectacles, put my ear trumpet to your ear, say your prayers, and do, for once, leave off thinking of yourself."

That last request was almost more than he could fulfill—more than even such a wonderful old woman ought to ask.

He got the spectacles and the ear trumpet, and was put

The Little Match Girl (Morocco, 10 years old)
(STORY PAGE 187)

out into the middle of the potato field; then she gave him a huge potato in his hand; presently he seemed to hear sounds in the potato, then came a song with words, a "story of everyday life," in ten volumes—but ten hills will do as well.

What was it the potato sang? It sang about itself and its ancestors, the arrival of the potato in Europe, and all it had had to suffer from suspicion and ill will before its value was recognized—before it was felt to be a much greater blessing than would be a lump of gold.

"We were distributed, by order of the King, at the court-house in every town; and there was issued a circular, setting forth our value and great merits, but no one believed it; they had not even the slightest idea how to plant us. One man dug a hole and threw his whole bushel of potatoes into it; another stuck them into the ground, one here, another there, and then waited for them to grow, and expected them to shoot up like trees that would bear potatoes, just as apple trees bear apples. There came buds, and stems, and flowers, and watery fruit, but it all withered away, and no one thought of the real blessing, the potato, that lay hidden under it all, in the ground. Yes, we have suffered much and been tried—that is, our forefathers have, but it all comes right in the end. Now you know our story."

"That's enough," said the old woman; "now look at the blackthorn."

"We, too," said the blackthorn, "have many relations in the land where the potatoes came from. A party of bold Norwegians from Norway steered their course westward through storm and fog till they came to an unknown country, where, under the ice and snow, they found herbs and grass, and bushes with blue-black berries of the vine—the black-thorn it was, whose berries ripen with the frost, and so do we. And that country they call 'Vineland,' and 'Greenland,' and 'Blackthorn Land.'"

"Why, that is quite a romantic story," said the young man.

"Now just follow me," said the little old woman, as she led him to the beehive. What life and movement there was! Then he looked in; there were bees standing in all the corridors, moving their wings like fans, so that there might be plenty of fresh air all through that large honey factory; that was their department. Then there were bees coming in from outside, from the sunshine and the flowers; they had been born with baskets on their legs; they brought the dust of the flowers and emptied it out of their little leg baskets; then it was sorted and worked up into honey and wax. Some came, some went; the queen of the hive wanted to fly, but when she flies, then all the others must fly too, and the right time for that had not yet come; but fly she would, and then to prevent her doing so, they bit her majesty's wings off—so that she was obliged to stay where she was.

"Now get up on the side of the ditch, where you can see all the town folk going past," said the little old woman.

"Goodness! what an endless number of people," said the young man. "One story after another! I seem to hear such buzzing and singing, and now it all grows quite confused! I feel quite dizzy—I shall fall!"

"No, don't," said the old woman—"don't fall backward; just go forward, right into the crowd of people; have eyes for all you see there, ears for all you hear, and above all, have a heart in it all! and before long you will be able to *invent*, and have thoughts for writing down—but before you go you must give me back my spectacles and my ear trumpet," and then she took both.

"Now I see nothing more," said the young man. "I do not even hear anything."

"In that case, it is quite impossible for you to be a poet by next Easter," said the old woman.

"But *when* shall I be a poet?" asked he.

"Neither by Easter nor by Whitsuntide! You have no knack at inventing," said she.

"But how then must I do, to get my living as by poetizing?"

"That I will tell you: write about those who have written. To hit their writings is to hit them. Don't let yourself be frightened; the more you do of such writing, the more you will earn, and you and your wife will be able to eat cake every day."

"What a trick *she* has at inventing," thought the young man, when he had thanked the old woman and bidden her good-bye. And he did as she had told him. Finding he could not be a poet himself, invent, and have bright ideas that people would talk of, he took to handling—and rather roughly—all those that were poets.

All this the little old woman has told me; she knows what one can invent!

It's Perfectly True!

"That's a terrible thing!" said a Hen; and she said it in a quarter of the town where the occurrence had not happened. "That's a terrible affair in the poultry house. I cannot sleep alone tonight! It is quite fortunate that there are many of us on the roost together!" And she told a tale, at which the feathers of the other birds stood on end, and the cock's comb fell down flat. It's perfectly true!

But we will begin at the beginning; and the beginning begins in a poultry house in another part of the town. The sun went down, and the fowls jumped up on their perch to roost. There was a Hen, with white feathers and short legs, who laid her right number of eggs, and was a respectable hen in every way; as she flew up on to the roost she pecked herself with her beak, and a little feather fell out.

"There it goes!" said she; "the more I peck myself the handsomer I grow!" And she said it quite merrily, for she was a joker among the hens, though, as I have said, she was very respectable; and then she went to sleep.

It was dark all around; hen sat by hen, but the one that sat next to the merry Hen did not sleep: she heard and she didn't hear, as one should do in this world if one wishes to live in quiet; but she could not refrain from telling it to her next neighbor.

"Did you hear what was said here just now? I name no

names; but here is a hen who wants to peck her feathers
out to look well. If I were a cock I should despise her."

And just above the hens sat the Owl, with her husband
and her little owlets; the family had sharp ears, and they
all heard every word that the neighboring Hen had spoken,
and they rolled their eyes, and the Mother-Owl clapped her
wings and said.

"Don't listen to it! But I suppose you heard what was
said there? I heard it with my own ears, and one must hear
much before one's ears fall off. There is one among the fowls
who has so completely forgotten what is becoming conduct
in a hen that she pulls out all her feathers, and then lets the
cock see her."

"*Prenez garde aux enfants,*" said the Father-Owl. "That's
not fit for the children to hear."

"I'll tell it to the neighbor owl; she's a very proper owl
to associate with." And she flew away.

"Hoo! hoo! to-whoo!" they both screeched in front of the
neighbor's dovecot to the doves within. "Have you heard it?
Have you heard it? Hoo! hoo! there's a hen who has pulled
out all her feathers for the sake of the cock. She'll die with
cold, if she's not dead already."

"Coo! coo! Where, where?" cried the Pigeons.

"In the neighbor's poultry yard. I've as good as seen it
myself. It's hardly proper to repeat the story, but it's quite
true!"

"Believe it! believe every single word of it!" cooed the
Pigeons, and they cooed down into their own poultry yard.
"There's a hen, and some say that there are two of them
that have plucked out all their feathers, that they may not
look like the rest, and that they may attract the cock's attention. That's a bold game, for one may catch cold and die
of a fever, and they are both dead."

"Wake up! Wake up!" crowed the Cock, and he flew
up on to the plank; his eyes were still very heavy with

sleep, but yet he crowed. "Three hens have died of an unfortunate attachment to a cock. They have plucked out all their feathers. That's a terrible story. I won't keep it to myself; let it travel farther."

"Let it travel farther!" piped the bats; and the fowls clucked and the cocks crowed, "Let it go farther! let it go farther!" And so the story traveled from poultry yard to poultry yard, and at last came back to the place from which it had gone forth.

"Five fowls," it was told, "have plucked out all their feathers to show which of them had become thinnest out of love to the cock; and then they have pecked each other, and fallen down dead, to the shame and disgrace of their families, and to the great loss of the proprietor."

And the Hen who had lost the little loose feather, of course did not know her own story again; and as she was a very respectable Hen, she said—

"I despise those fowls; but there are many of that sort. One ought not to hush up such a thing, and I shall do what I can that the story may get into the papers, and then it will be spread over all the country, and that will serve those fowls right, and their families too."

It was printed in the newspaper; and it's perfectly true— one little feather can easily become five hens.

There's a Difference

It was in the month of May; the wind was still cold, but trees and bushes, fields, and meadows, all proclaimed that spring was come. Flowers sprang forth everywhere, even the hedges were full of them, alive with them, one might say: it seemed as though they were the language wherein Spring announced herself, every single bright blossom a gladsome word of greeting. But the loveliest thing in the hedge was a little apple tree, and in that tree there was one bough especially fresh and blooming, completely weighed down by its wealth of delicate rosy buds, just ready to open. This bough was so lovely, it could not help knowing it, and therefore it was not one bit surprised when a grand carriage, passing along the road, stopped in front of it, and a young countess sitting in the carriage declared that of all the sweet, bright things of spring, that apple bough was the sweetest and brightest of all. And the apple bough was broken off, and the young countess held it in her own dainty hand, shading it from the sun with her silk parasol; and then they drove on to her home, a stately castle, full of lofty walls and decorated salons; where gauzy white curtains fluttered at the open windows, and transparent vases stood full of beautiful flowers, and in one of these, which was carved as it were out of new-fallen snow, the apple bough was placed, among fresh, light-green beech leaves, and a pretty sight it was!

And so it came to pass that the apple bough grew proud, quite like a human being.

All sorts of people passed through the rooms, and expressed their admiration diversely; some said too much, some said too little, some said nothing at all; and the apple bough began to understand that there is a difference between human beings as between vegetables. "Some are for use, some are for ornament, and some could be dispensed with altogether," thought the apple bough. And as his position at the open window commanded a view over gardens and meadows below, he could look down upon all sorts of flowers and plants, consider, and draw distinctions between them. They stood beneath him all, some rich, some poor, some too poor.

"Miserable, rejected herbs!" snorted the apple bough. "It is right and just that a distinction should be made—and yet how unhappy they must feel, if indeed that sort of creature is capable of feeling, like me and my equals; there is indeed a difference, but it must be made, else all would be treated as though they were alike." And the apple bough looked down with especial compassion upon one kind of flowers that grew in great multitudes upon the meadows and ditches; no one gathered them for bouquets—they were too common, they could be found springing up even between the paving stones, they shot up everywhere, the rankest, most worthless of weeds: they were dandelions, but the lower classes in Denmark have given them the name of "Milk-pails."

"Poor despised outcasts!" went on the apple bough; "you cannot help being what you are, so common! and with such a vulgar name! But it is with vegetables as with men, there must be a difference."

"A difference?" repeated the Sunbeam, as it kissed the blossoming apple bough, and then flew on to kiss also the golden "Milk-pails" out in the fields. And the Sunbeam's sisters all did the same, kissing all the flowers equally, poor as well as rich.

Now the apple bough had never thought about our Lord's infinite love for all that lives and moves in Him, had never thought how much that is good and beautiful can lie hidden, but not forgotten. The apple bough had lived with human beings, and grown like them in this.

But the glorious Sunbeam knew better. "You are neither clear nor farsighted! What is this outcast herb that you are pitying so much?"

"The Milk-pails down there," replied the apple bough; "they are never tied up in bouquets, they are trodden under foot, there are too many of them; and when they run to seed they fly about in small bits of wool, and hang upon people's clothes. Weeds! weeds! but they must be as they are. I am really and truly grateful that I am not as one of them."

And now a whole troop of children roamed over the meadow, the youngest of them so tiny that he had to be carried by the others; and as he was now set down in the grass among the golden blossoms, he laughed for joy, kicked about with his short legs, rolled over and over, and plucked none but the yellow dandelions, which he kissed in his innocent delight. The bigger children busied themselves in breaking the flowers of the dandelions off from their hollow stalks, and joining these stalks into chains, first one for a necklace, then a longer chain to hang across the shoulders and round the waist, and last, a third for a circlet round the head; very soon they stood arrayed in splendid green chains. But the biggest of all the children carefully gathered the stalks bearing crowns of seed—that loose, aerial, woolly blossom, that wonderfully perfect ball of dainty white plumes; they held the white ball to their lips, trying to blow away all the white feathers with one puff of breath; whoever could do that would get new clothes before the year was out—so granny had told them. The poor despised herb was held as a prophet by this generation.

"Do you see now?" asked the Sunbeam; "don't you see its beauty and its power?"

"Yes, for children," replied the apple bough.

Presently came into the meadow an old woman. She stooped down and began digging for the dandelion roots with a blunt knife that had lost its handle. Some of the roots she would roast instead of coffee berries, others she would sell to the apothecary, who valued them as drugs.

"But beauty is something higher," protested the apple bough. "Only the chosen few can be admitted into the kingdom of the beautiful; there is a difference among plants as among men."

Then the Sunbeam spoke of the infinite love of the Creator for all His creatures, for all that has life, and His providence watching equally over all.

"Well, that is your opinion," replied the apple bough.

Some people now came into the room, among them the young countess who had placed the apple bough in the white vase by the window, and she carried in her hand something that was concealed by three or four large leaves held round it, lest a draught of air should injure it. Was it a flower? it was carried so carefully, more tenderly than the apple bough had been, when brought to the castle. Very gently the large leaves were removed, and behold the delicate globe of starry seeds borne by the despised dandelion plant! This it was which she had plucked so cautiously, carried so tenderly, lest one only of the dainty feathered arrows that help to round its globe-like form and sit so lightly, should be blown away. But it was quite perfect, not one seed was lost, and she admired so much the beautiful form, the airy lightness, the wondrous mechanism of a thing destined to be so soon scattered by the wind.

"Only see how wonderfully beautiful our Lord has made

it! " she said. "I will put it in a picture together with the apple bough: that is very lovely too; but this poor little weed is equally lovely, only in another way. Very different are they, and yet both are children in the kingdom of the beautiful."

And the Sunbeam kissed the poor weed, and then kissed the blossoming apple bough, whose delicate petal seemed to blush into a brighter red.

The Swan's Nest

Between the Baltic and the North Sea lies an old Swans' Nest—it is called Denmark; in it have been born, and will be born hereafter, Swans whose names shall never die.

In the olden time, a flock of Swans flew thence over the Alps to Milan's lovely green plains. There they lighted down and dwelt, for right pleasant was it there to dwell. These Swans were called Lombards.

Another flock, with bright shining plumage, and clear, truthful eyes, lighted down at Byzantium, nestled round the Emperor's throne, and spread out their broad white wings as shields to protect him. These were known as Varangians.

From the coasts of France arose a cry of anguish and terror—terror at the bloody Swans who, with fire under their wings, flew thither from the North. Loud was the prayer of village and town, "God save us from the wild Normans!"

On England's fresh meadow turf, near the shore, wearing a triple crown on his kingly head, his golden scepter stretching far over the land, stood the royal Swan, Canute the Dane.

And on Pomerania's shores the heathens bowed the knee, for thither, too, with drawn swords, and bearing the standard of the cross, had flown the Danish Swans.

"But this was in the days of old."

In times nearer our own, then, have mighty Swans been seen to fly out from the Nest. A flash of lightning cleft the air—lightning that shone over all Europe—for a Swan had flapped his strong wings and scattered the twilight mist, and the starry heavens became more visible—were brought, as it were, nearer the earth. The Swan's name was Tycho Brahe.

" Yes, just that once," it will be said; " but now, in our own generation? "

Well, in our own generation we have beheld Swans soaring in a high and glorious flight.

One we saw gently sweep his wings over the golden chords of the harp, whereupon sweet music thrilled through the northern lands, the wild Norwegian mountains lifted their proud crests higher in the full sunlight of the olden time, pine and birch bowed their heads and rustled their leaves, the " Gods of the North "—the heroes and noble women of Scandinavian history—lived and breathed again, their tall, stately figures standing out from the dark background of deep forests.

A second Swan we saw strike his pinions upon the hard marble rock till it cleft asunder, and new forms of beauty, hitherto shut up in the stone, were revealed to the light of day, and the nations of Europe gazed in wonder and admiration at the glorious statuary.

A third Swan we have seen weaving threads of thoughts that spun and spread around the earth, so that words can fly with lightning speed from land to land.

Dear to the protecting heavens above is the old Swans' Nest between the Baltic and the North Sea. Let mighty birds of prey, if they will, speed thither to tear it down. It shall not be! Even the unfledged, unplumed young ones will press forward to the margin of the Nest—we have seen it—will fight desperately with beak and claw, will offer their bleeding breast in defense of their home.

The Steadfast Tin Soldier (Sweden, 7 years old)
(STORY PAGE 123)

Centuries will pass away, and Swans will still fly forth from the Nest, and make themselves seen and heard far over the world; long will it be before the time shall come when in sad truth it may be said, "Behold the last Swan! Listen to the last sweet song from the Swans' Nest!"

The Comet

Now the comet came with its shining nucleus and its nebulous tail. At the great castle they gazed at it, and from the poor shanty; the crowd in the street stared at it, and the solitary man, that went his way over the pathless heath. Every one had his own thoughts. "Come and look at the vault of heaven; come out and look at the wonderful sight," they cried, and all hastened to look. But inside the room there sat yet a little boy and his mother. The tallow candle was burning, and the mother thought that there was a moth in the light; the tallow formed in ragged edges around the candle, and ran down the sides; this, she believed, betokened that her son should die very soon—the shining little moth was turning toward him.

This was an old superstition in which she believed. The little boy was destined to live many years here on earth, and, indeed, lived to see the comet again, when it returned sixty years after.

The boy did not see the candlemoth in the light, and thought not of the comet, which then, for the first time in his life, looked brightly down from the skies. He sat quietly with an earthen dish before him; the dish being filled with soap water, in which he dipped the head of a clay pipe, and then put the stem in his mouth, and made soap bubbles, big and small. They quivered and fluttered in their beautiful colors; they changed from yellow to red, from red to purple and blue; then they colored green, like leaves when the sun is shining through them. "May God give thee many years to live here on earth, as many as the bubbles thou art blowing."

"So many, so many!" cried the little fellow. "I can never blow all the soap water into bubbles. There flies one year, there flies another!" exclaimed he, when a new bubble broke loose from the pipe and flew off. Some of them flew into his eyes: they burned and smarted, and caused tears to flow. In every bubble he saw a picture of the future, glimmering and glittering.

"This is the time to see the comet!" exclaimed the neighbors; "come out of doors, and don't sit in the room."

And the mother took the boy by the hand; he had to lay the clay pipe aside, and leave his play with the soap bubbles; the comet was there.

And the boy saw the brilliant fireball, and the shining tail. Some said it was three yards long, others insisted it was several millions of yards long—only a slight difference.

Most of the people who had said that, were dead and gone when the comet came again; but the little fellow, toward whom the candlemoth had been turned, of whom the mother thought, "He will die soon," he still lived, had become old and white-haired. "White hairs are the flower of old age," says the proverb; and he had a good many of such flowers. He was now an old schoolmaster. The schoolchildren said that he was very wise, and knew so very much; he knew history, and geography, and all that was known about heaven and its stars.

"Everything comes again," said he; "only pay attention to persons and events, and you will learn that they always return; there may be a hundred years between, or many hundred years, but then we shall have the same persons again, only in another coat, and in another country." And the schoolmaster told them about William Tell, who was compelled to shoot an apple from his son's head; but before he shot the arrow, he hid another one in his bosom, to shoot into the breast of the wicked Gesler. This took place in Switzerland. But many years before that happened, the same event occurred in Denmark with Walraloke; he was also obliged to shoot an apple from his son's head, and he also hid an arrow in his bosom, to avenge the cruelty. And several thousand years before that, the same story was written down in Egypt. This is a story, and a true one; it came again, and will come again, like the comet, that returns, "flies away through space, stays away, but returns." And he spoke of the comet that was expected, the same comet that he had seen when yet a boy.

The schoolmaster knew what took place in the skies, but he did not therefore forget history and geography. His garden was laid out in the shape of a map of Denmark. Here were herbs and flowers, which belong to different parts of the land.

"Fetch me herbs," said he, and they went to the bed that represented Laaland; "fetch me buckwheat," and they went to Langeland. The beautiful blue gentian was found in Skagen. The shining Christthorn, at Silkeborg. Towns and cities were marked with images. Here stood St. Knud, with the dragon, which meant Odense; Absalon, with the Bishop's staff, meant Sorö. The old boat with the oars was a sign that there stood Aarhuus. From the schoolmaster's garden you could learn the geography of Denmark; but one had to be instructed by him first, and that was a great pleasure.

Now the comet was expected again, and of that he spoke; and he related what people had said in the olden times, when it appeared last; they had said that a comet year was a good wine year, and that one could mix water with that wine, without its being detected. Therefore the merchants thought so much of a comet year.

The sky was overcast for two weeks, they could not see the comet, and yet it was there. The old schoolmaster sat in his little chamber adjoining the schoolroom. The old Bornholm clock of his grandfather's time stood in the corner; the heavy lead weights did neither ascend nor descend, the pendulum did not move. The little cuckoo, that used to come forward in past times to cuckoo the passing hours, had for many years ceased to do his duty. Everything was dumb and silent; the clock was out of order.

But the old clavichord near by, made in his father's time, had yet a spark of life left. The strings could yet ring; true, they were a little hoarse, but they could ring the melodies of a whole lifetime. With these, the old man remembered so much, both joyful and sorrowful, that had happened in the long series of years that had passed by since he, a little boy, saw the comet; and now, when that comet had come again, he remembered what his mother had said about the moth in the light; he remembered the beautiful soap bubbles that he blew, each of them representing a year of his life, as he had said, shining and sparkling in wonderful hues. He saw in them all his pleasures and sorrows, everything beautiful and sorrowful. He saw the child and its plays, the youth and his fancies, the whole world, in wavy brightness, opening before his gazing eyes; and in that sunlight he saw his future grow. These were the bubbles of coming time; now, an old man, he heard from the clavichord's strings the melodies of passing time, mind's bubbles, with memory's variegated colors. And he heard his nurse's knitting song—

For sure no Amazone
Did ever stocking knit.

And then the strings sang the song the old papa of the house was wont to sing to him, when a child—

> *In truth full many dangers*
> *Will grow up here below,*
> *For him, that yet is young,*
> *And doth not fully know.*

Now the melodies of the first ball were ringing the minuet and molinasky; then the melancholy notes of the flute passed by: bubble after bubble they hurried on, very much like those that he blew with soap water, when a little boy.

His eyes were turned toward the window: a cloud in the sky was gliding by, and, as it passed, revealed the comet to his gaze, the sparkling nucleus, the shining tail.

It seemed as if it had been only the evening of yesterday that he had seen that comet, and yet a whole eventful lifetime lay between that evening and this. Then he was a child, and looked through the bubbles into the future; now the bubbles pointed back in the past.

Once more he had a child's feeling and a child's trust; his eyes sparkled, and his hands sank down upon the keys. There came a sound as of the breaking of a string.

"Come out and see!" shouted the neighbors; "the comet is here, and the sky is so clear; come out and look!"

The old schoolmaster answered not; he had gone where he should see more clearly: his soul was upon a journey far greater than the comet's, and into a wider space than the comet has to fly through.

And the comet was again seen from the rich castle, and from the poor shanty; the crowd in the street gazed at it, and the solitary man that walked through the pathless heath. But the schoolmaster's soul was seen by God, and the dear ones that had preceded, and whom he so much longed for.

The Little Match Girl (Switzerland, 12 years old)
(STORY PAGE 187)

"Good-for-Nothing"

The sheriff stood at the open window; he wore ruffles, and a dainty breastpin decorated the front of his shirt; he was neatly shaven, and a tiny little strip of sticking plaster covered the little cut he had given himself during the process. "Well, my little man?" quoth he.

The "little man" was no other than the laundress' son, who respectfully took off his cap in passing. His cap was broken in the rim, and adapted to be put into the pocket on occasion; his clothes were poor, but clean, and very neatly mended, and he wore heavy wooden shoes. He stood still when the sheriff spoke, as respectfully as though he stood before the king.

"Ah, you're a good boy, a well-behaved boy!" said the sheriff. "And so your mother is washing down at the river; *she* isn't good for much. And you're going to her, I see. Ah, poor child!—well, you may go."

And the boy passed on, still holding his cap in his hand, while the wind tossed to and fro his waves of yellow hair. He went through the street, down a little alley to the brook, where his mother stood in the water, at her washing stool, beating the heavy linen. The water mill's sluices were opened, and the current was strong; the washing stool was nearly carried away by it, and the laundress had hard work to strive against it.

" I am very near taking a voyage," she said, " and it is so cold out in the water; for six hours have I been standing here. Have you anything for me? "—and the boy drew forth a phial, which his mother put to her lips. " Ah, that is as good as warm meat, and it is not so dear. O, the water is so cold— but if my strength will but last me out to bring you up honestly, my sweet child! "

At that moment approached an elderly woman, poorly clad, blind of one eye, lame on one leg, and with her hair brushed into one large curl to hide the blind eye—but in vain, the defect was only the more conspicuous. This was " Lame Maren," as the neighbors called her, a friend of the washerwoman's. " Poor thing, slaving and toiling away in the cold water! it is hard that you should be called names " —for Maren had overheard the sheriff speaking to the child about his own mother—" hard that your boy should be told you are good-for-nothing."

" What! did the sheriff really say so, child? " said the laundress, and her lips quivered. " So you have a mother who is good-for-nothing! Perhaps he is right, only he should not say so to the child—but I must not complain, for good things have come to me from that house."

" Why yes, you were in service there once, when the sheriff's parents were alive, many years since. There is a grand dinner at the sheriff's today," went on Maren; " it would have been put off, though, had not everything been prepared. I heard it from the porter. News came in a letter, an hour ago, that the sheriff's younger brother, at Copenhagen, is dead."

" Dead! " repeated the laundress, and she turned as white as a corpse.

" What do you care about it? " said Maren. " To be sure, you must have known him, since you served in the house."

" Is he dead? he was the best, the kindest of creatures! indeed, there are not many like him," and the tears rolled down her cheeks. "O, the world is turning round, I feel so ill!" and she clung to the washing stool for support.

"You are ill, indeed!" cried Maren. "Take care, the stool will overturn. I had better get you home at once."

"But the linen?"

"I will look after that—only lean on me. The boy can stay here and watch it till I come back and wash what is left; it is not much."

The poor laundress' limbs trembled under her. "I have stood too long in the cold water; I have had no food since yesterday. O, my poor child!" and she wept.

The boy cried too, as he sat alone beside the brook, watching the wet linen. Slowly the two women made their way up the little alley and through the street, past the sheriff's house. Just as she reached her humble home, the laundress fell down on the paving stones, fainting. She was carried upstairs and put to bed. Kind Maren hastened to prepare a cup of warm ale—that was the best medicine in this case, she thought— and then went back to the brook and did the best she could with the linen.

In the evening she was again in the laundress' miserable room. She had begged from the sheriff's cook a few roasted potatoes and a little bit of bacon, for the sick woman. Maren and the boy feasted upon these, but the patient was satisfied with the smell of them—that, she declared, was very nourishing.

Supper over, the boy went to bed, lying crosswise at his mother's feet, with a coverlet made of old carpet ends, blue and red, sewed together.

The laundress now felt a little better; the warm ale had strengthened her, the smell of the meat done her good.

"Now, you good soul," said she to Maren, "I will tell you all about it, while the boy is asleep. That he is already; look at him, how sweetly he looks with his eyes closed; he little thinks how his mother has suffered. May he never feel the like! Well, I was in service with the sheriff's parents when their youngest son, the student, came home; I was a wild young thing then, but honest—that I must say for myself. And the student was so pleasant and merry, a better youth never lived. He was a son of the house, I only a servant, but we became sweethearts—all in honor and honesty—and he told his mother that he loved me; she was like an angel in his eyes, so wise, kind, and loving! And he went away, but his gold ring of betrothal was on my finger. When he was really gone, my mistress called me in to speak to her; so grave, yet so kind she looked, so wisely she spoke, like an angel, indeed. She showed me what a gulf of difference in tastes, habits, and mind lay between her son and me. 'He sees you now to be good-hearted and pretty, but will you always be the same in his eyes? You have not been educated as he has been; intellectually you cannot rise to his level. I honor the poor,' she continued, 'and I know that in the kingdom of heaven many a poor man will sit in a higher seat than the rich; but that is no reason for breaking the ranks in this world, and you two, left to yourselves, would drive your carriage full tilt against all obstacles till it toppled over with you both. I know that a good honest handicraftsman, Erik, the glovemaker, has been your suitor; he is a widower without children, he is well off; think whether you cannot be content with him.' Every word my mistress spoke went like a knife through my heart, but I knew she was right; I kissed her hand, and shed such bitter tears! But bitterer tears still came when I went into my chamber and lay upon my bed. O, the long, dreary night that followed! Our Lord alone knows what I suffered. Not till I went to church on Sunday did a light break upon my darkness. It seemed providential that as I came out of church I met Erik the glovemaker. There were no more doubts in my mind; he was a good man, and of my own rank. I went straight to him, took his hand, and asked, 'Are you still in the same

mind toward me?'—'Yes, and I shall never be otherwise
minded,' he replied. ' Do you care to have a girl who likes
and honors you, but does not love you?'—'I believe love
will come,' he said, and so he took my hand. I went home
to my mistress; the gold ring that her son had given me, that
I wore all day next to my heart, and on my finger at night in
bed, I now drew forth; I kissed it till my mouth bled, I gave
it to my mistress, and said that next week the banns would
be read for me and the glovemaker. My mistress took me
in her arms and kissed me; she did not tell me I was good-
for-nothing; I was good for something then, it seems, before
I had known so much trouble. The wedding was at Candle-
mastide, and our first year all went well, my husband had
apprentices, and you, Maren, helped me in the housework."

" O, and you were such a good mistress! " exclaimed Maren.
" Never shall I forget how kind you and your husband were
to me."

" Ah, you were with us during our good times! We had no
children then. The student I never saw again—yes, once I
saw him, but he did not see me. He came to his mother's
funeral; I saw him standing by her grave, looking so sad,
so ashy pale—but all for his mother's sake. When afterward
his father died, he was abroad and did not come to the
funeral. Nor has he been here since; he is a lawyer, that I
know, and he has never married. But he thought no more
of me, and had he seen me, he would certainly have never
recognized me, so ugly as I am now. And it is right it should
be so."

Then she went on to speak of the bitter days of adversity,
when troubles had come upon them in a flood. They had
five hundred rix-dollars, and as in their street a house could
be bought for two hundred, it was considered a good
investment to buy it, take it down, and build it anew. The
house was bought; masons and carpenters made an estimate
that one thousand and twenty rix-dollars more would be

required. Erik arranged to borrow this sum from Copenhagen, but the ship that was to bring him the money was lost, and the money with it. "It was just then that my sweet boy, who lies sleeping here, was born. Then his father fell sick; for three quarters of a year I had to dress and undress him every day. We went on borrowing and borrowing; all our things had to be sold, one by one; at last Erik died. Since then I have toiled and moiled for the boy's sake, have gone out cleaning and washing, done coarse work or fine, whichever I could get; but I do everything worse and worse; my strength will never return any more; it is our Lord's will! He will take me away, and find better provision for my boy."

She fell asleep. In the morning she seemed better, and fancied she was strong enough to go to her work again. But no sooner did she feel the cold water than a shivering seized her, she felt about convulsively with her hands, tried to step forward, and fell down. Her head lay on the dry bank, but her feet were in the water of the brook, her wooden shoes were carried away by the stream. Here she was found by Maren.

A message had been taken to her lodging that the sheriff wanted her, had something to say to her. It was too late; the poor washerwoman was dead. The letter that had brought the sheriff news of his brother's death also gave an abstract of his will; among other bequests he had left six hundred rix-dollars to the glovemaker's widow, who had formerly served his parents. "There was some love nonsense between my brother and her," quoth the sheriff. "It is all as well she is out of the way; now it will all come to the boy, and I shall apprentice him to honest folk who will make him a good workman." For whatever the sheriff might do, were it ever so kind an action, he always spoke harshly and unkindly. So he now called the boy to him, promised to provide for him, and told him it was a good thing his mother was dead; she was good-for-nothing!

She was buried in the paupers' churchyard. Maren planted a little rose tree over the grave; the boy stood by her side the while.

" My darling mother! " he sighed, as the tears streamed down from his eyes. " It was not true that she was good-for-nothing! "

" No, indeed! " cried her old friend, looking up to heaven. " Let the world say she was good-for-nothing; our Lord in his heavenly kingdom will not say so."

The Windmill

A windmill stood upon the hill, proud to look at, and it was proud too.

"I am not proud at all," it said, "but I am very much enlightened without and within. I have sun and moon for my outward use, and for inward use too; and into the bargain I have tallow candles, train-oil lamps, and wax candles; I may well say that I'm enlightened. I am a thinking being, and so well constructed that it's quite delightful. I have a good windpipe in my chest, and I have four wings that are placed outside my head, just beneath my hat; the birds have only two wings, and are obliged to carry them on their backs. I am a Dutchman by birth—that may be seen by my figure— a flying Dutchman. They are considered supernatural beings, I know, and yet I am quite natural. I have a gallery round my chest, and house room beneath it; that's where my thoughts dwell. My strongest thought, who rules and reigns, is called by the others 'The Man in the Mill.' He knows what he wants, and is lord over the meal and the bran; but he has his companion too, and she calls herself 'Mother.' She is the very heart of me. She does not run about stupidly and awkwardly, for she knows what she wants, she knows what she can do; she's as soft as a zephyr and as strong as a storm; she knows how to begin a thing carefully, and to have her own way. She is my soft temper, and the father is my hard one: they are two, and yet one; they each call the other ' My half.' These two have some little boys, young thoughts, that can grow. The little ones keep everything in order. When, lately, in my wisdom, I let the father and the boys examine my throat and the hole in my chest, to see what was going on there—for something in me was out of order, and it's well to examine oneself—the little ones made a tremendous noise. The youngest jumped up into my hat, and shouted so there that it tickled me. The little thoughts may grow; I know that very well; and out in the world thoughts come too, and not only of my kind, for as far as I can see I cannot discern anything like myself; but the wingless houses, whose throats make no noise, have thoughts too, and these come to my thoughts, and make love to them, as it is called. It's wonderful enough—yes, there are many wonderful things. Something has come over me, or into me —something has changed in the millwork: it seems as if the one half, the father, had altered, and had received a better temper and a more affectionate helpmate—so young and good, and yet the same, only more gentle and good through the course of time. What was bitter has passed away, and the whole is much more comfortable.

"The days go on, and the days come nearer and nearer to clearness and to joy; and then a day will come when it will be over with me; but not over altogether. I must be pulled down that I may be built up again; I shall cease, but yet shall live on. To become quite a different being, and yet remain the same! That's difficult for me to understand, however enlightened I may be with sun, moon, stearine, train-oil, and tallow. My old woodwork and my old brick-work will rise again from the dust!

"I will hope that I may keep my old thoughts, the father in the mill, and the mother, great ones and little ones—the family; for I call them all, great and little, the *company of thoughts*, because I must, and cannot refrain from it.

" And I must also remain 'myself,' with my throat in my chest, my wings on my head, the gallery round my body; else I should not know myself, nor could the others know me, and say, ' There's the Mill on the hill, proud to look at, and yet not proud at all.' "

That is what the Mill said. Indeed, it said much more, but that is the most important part.

And the days came, and the days went, and yesterday was the last day.

Then the mill caught fire. The flames rose up high, and beat out and in, and bit at the beams and planks, and ate them up. The mill fell, and nothing remained of it but a heap of ashes. The smoke drove across the scene of the conflagration, and the wind carried it away.

Whatever had been alive in the mill remained, and what had been gained by it has nothing to do with this story.

The miller's family—one soul, many thoughts, and yet only one—built a new, a splendid mill, which answered its purpose. It was quite like the old one, and people said, " Why, yonder is the mill on the hill, proud to look at! " But this mill was better arranged, more according to the time than the last, so that progress might be made. The old beams had become worm-eaten and spongy—they lay in dust and ashes. The body of the mill did not rise out of the dust as they had believed it would do: they had taken it literally, and all things are *not* to be taken literally.

The Neck of a Bottle

In a narrow, crooked street, among many shabby dwellings, stood one very narrow, very tall house. None but poor folk lived here, but poorest of all looked the attic, where, outside the little window, hung in the sunshine an old bird cage, that could not even boast of a proper bird glass; it had instead the neck of a bottle, placed upside down, with a cork stopping up the mouth. At the open window stood an old maid; she had just been adorning the cage with chickweed; the little canary who lived a prisoner within it hopped from perch to perch, and sang with all his might.

"Ah! you may well sing!" said the broken bottle. Truly it could not speak aloud as we speak, but it had its own thoughts within for all that. "Ah! it is easy for you to sing! —you, with your limbs whole. You should just try what it is to have lost one's lower half—to have only a neck and a mouth left, and then a cork stuffed into one. I should like to hear you sing then! But it is well somebody is pleased. I have no cause to sing, neither can I, but I could sing, once, when I was a whole bottle—I was called a lark then. Did not I sing that day in the wood when the furrier's daughter was betrothed? I remember it as though it had happened yesterday. I have lived through many things—I have been through fire and water—down in the black earth and higher up than most. And now I hover amid air and sunshine

outside the cage. It might be worth while to listen to my
history, but I am not going to proclaim it aloud, for one
good reason—I can't! "

And so it told, or rather thought over, its own history to
itself in silence, and the little bird sang merrily the while,
and the people down below drove, or rode, or walked through
the street, each thinking of his own affairs, just as the broken
bottle did.

It remembered the fiery furnace in the factory, where it
had been blown into being; it remembered how warm it was
at first—how it had looked into the wild furnace, the home
of its birth, and longed to leap into it again. But then, little
by little, as it cooled, it found itself well off where it was,
standing in a row with a whole regiment of brothers and
sisters, all born from the same furnace, but some blown into
champagne bottles, others into bottles for ale—and this makes
a difference. Certainly, in the course of time and events, an
ale flask may possibly embrace the costliest Lachryma Christi,
and a champagne bottle may be basely filled with blacking;
but what each was born for will still be apparent through
the form of each, and not even blacking can efface that
patent of nobility.

All the bottles were soon packed up, and packed off, our
bottle among them. Little at that time did it think of ending
thus serving as a bird glass. No matter, it is an honorable
life that is thus useful to the last. It first saw daylight again,
after it had been unpacked, together with its comrades, in
a wine merchant's cellar, and was then, for the first time,
rinsed out—which was a ridiculous performance, it thought.
The bottle now lay empty and corkless—felt itself wonderfully dull, as though wanting something—it knew not what.
But now it was filled with good, glorious wine, received a
cork, and was sealed up, with a label pasted on it, " Best
Quality." It felt it was now a first-class bottle; the wine was
good, and the bottle was good. Something within it seemed

to be singing of things it knew nothing whatever about. The green sunlit mountains, where grows the vine, and where fair girls and merry youths sing and dance together. Ah! there it is right pleasant to live! Something seemed singing about this inside the bottle, as within the hearts of young poets, who yet know no more about the matter than the bottle knew.

One morning it was bought. The furrier's boy was sent to fetch a bottle of the best wine, and thus it became transported into a large basket, together with ham, cheese, and sausages, the best butter, and the whitest bread. The furrier's daughter herself packed the basket. She was very young and very pretty; she had laughing brown eyes, and smiling lips, almost as expressive as the eyes; her hands were small, soft, and white, but not so white as her forehead and her throat. She was one of the prettiest girls in the town, and not yet betrothed.

And the basket lay in her lap while the party drove out into the wood. The neck of the bottle peeped forth between the folds of the white tablecloth; there was red sealing wax on the cork, and this sealing wax looked right into the young girl's face, and into the face of the young man who sat next to her; he had been her companion from childhood; he was a portrait-painter's son, who had lately passed with honorable mention through his examination for the naval service. On the morrow he was to go with his ship to foreign lands; there was some talk about his voyage, and just while this was talked about it was not quite so pleasant to look at the eyes and lips of the furrier's pretty daughter.

The two young people took a walk in the green forest, talking—what did they talk about? The bottle could not hear that—it was left in the basket. It was very, very long before the basket was unpacked, but then? Why certainly some pleasant things must have happened meanwhile, for all eyes were laughing, even those of the furrier's daughter, though she talked less than before, and her cheeks blushed like two red roses.

The furrier took up the bottle, took up the corkscrew. O! what a strange sensation was that when, for the first time, the cork was drawn! The bottle had never been able to forget that solemn moment; and then the gurgling noise wherewith the wine flowed out into the glasses!

"The health of the betrothed!" cried the father, and every glass was emptied, and the young man kissed his pretty bride. Then he refilled the glasses, exclaiming: "To our joyful wedding this day next year!" And when the glasses had been emptied the second time, he took the bottle and raised it high in the air, saying: "You have served us here on the brightest day of my life, you shall never be profaned by any meaner service!"

And he flung it high into the air. But it came down again —it fell softly among the thick reeds fringing the little woodland lake. The broken bottle remembered perfectly well how it had lain there, thinking: "I gave them wine, they gave me muddly water; no matter, it was well meant!" It could see no more of the happy couple and the pleased parents, but it could hear them talking and singing in the distance. And presently two peasant boys came that way; they peeped in among the reeds, spied out the bottle, and took it away. Now it was provided for.

At their home in the little woodland hut, where they dwelt, they had, the day before, parted from their elder brother, who was a sailor, and had been to say farewell before going out on a long voyage. The mother was now packing up a few things which the father was to take to him in the town that evening—he would see him once more before his departure. A little flask full of spiced brandy had been placed in the parcel, but now the boys showed the larger and stronger bottle which they had found—it could hold more than the little one. So it was filled now, not with red wine as before,

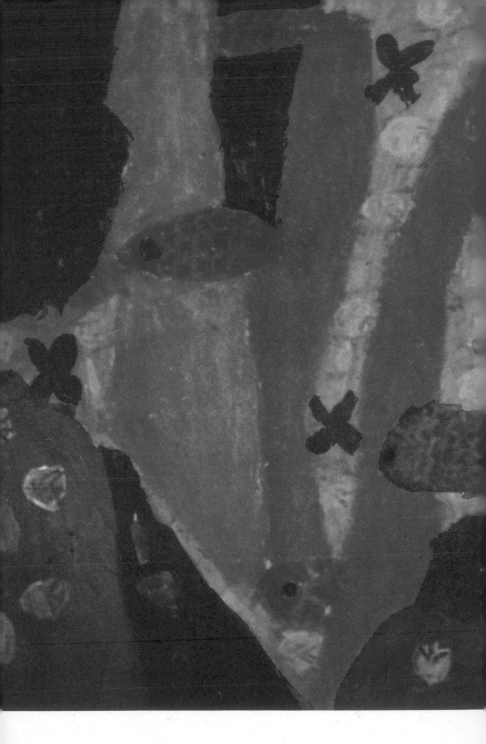

The Little Mermaid (Japan, 9 years old)
(STORY PAGE 65)

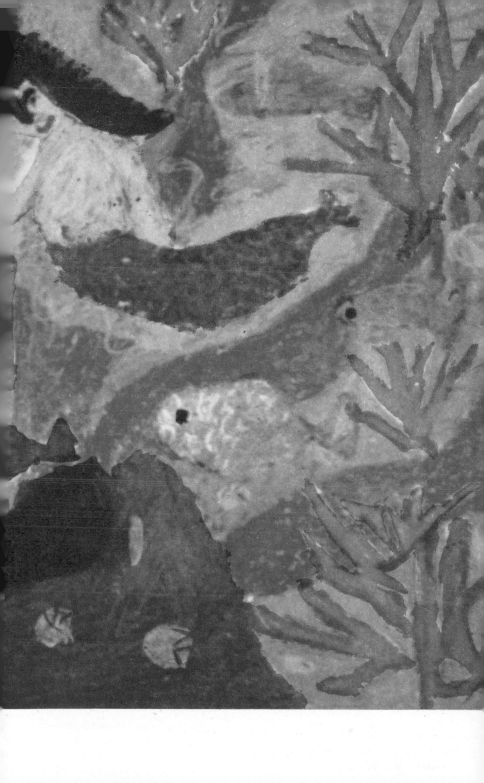

but with bitter, wholesome drops, good for the stomach. The new-found bottle was to go, the little one to stay at home. So now the bottle went forth on its travels; it went on board to be Peter Jensen's property, on board the very same ship by which went the young mate who had been betrothed that morning. He never looked at the bottle, or if he had, it would never have occurred to him to think, " This is the same bottle from which our health was drunk."

And now it contained not wine indeed, but something as good as wine. When Peter Jensen took it out, his comrades always called it " The apothecary "; it gave right good medicine, they thought, and it helped them as long as a drop was left in it. It was a pleasant time, and the bottle sang after its fashion; and thus it came to be nicknamed, " The great lark," " Peter Jensen's lark."

A long time had passed away, and it had long stood empty in a corner, when—the bottle knew not whether it was on its way out, or on the way home, it had not been ashore—a mighty storm arose. It was night, and pitch dark; great heavy black waves surged and tossed the vessel to and fro; the mast broke, the planks flew out, the pumps were of no avail. The ship was sinking; but in the last minute the young sailor wrote on a fragment of paper: " Lord Jesu, have mercy on us! we perish! " He added his bride's name, his own, and that of the ship, rolled the note into an empty bottle that came to his hand, pressed the cork down tight, and flung the bottle far into the stormy sea. Little thought he that this was the same bottle that had given him wine on the day of his happiness and hope. Now it rocked and tossed upon the billows, bearing its message, its greeting from the dead to the living.

The ship sank, the crew perished, but the bottle flew on like a bird—it bore a love letter. And the sun rose up and the sun went down—that reminded the bottle of the hour of its birth, in the red glowing furnace; it longed to fly into

17

his embrace. It encountered new storms; still it was neither
swallowed up by sharks nor dashed against rocks. For more
than a year and a day it drifted about, now northward, now
southward, as it was carried by the tide. Certainly it was
its own master; but one may get tired of that.

The letter, the last farewell from bridegroom to bride,
would bring only sorrow, if it ever fell into the right hands.
But where were those hands? the hands that gleamed so white
when they spread the tablecloth over the fresh grass in the
green wood, on the day of betrothal? Where was the furrier's
daughter? Where, indeed; What land was nearest now? The
bottle could not answer these questions; it drifted and drifted,
and was at last so weary of drifting—for which it had never
been intended; but it drifted on all the same, till at last it
was cast ashore on a foreign land. It understood not a word
of what was spoken here; it was not the language it had
always heard before, and one loses much in a country where
one does not understand the language.

The bottle was picked up and examined, the letter inside
was noticed, taken out, turned and twisted about, but not a
word of what was written thereon could the folk make out.
They understood, of course, that the bottle had been flung
overboard, and that something was written on the paper,
but that " something " was a complete mystery. And so the
note was rolled up and put into the bottle again, and the
bottle was placed in a large cabinet, in a large room, in a
large house. Every time strangers came to the house the
note was taken out, unrolled, turned and twisted about, until
the writing—it was only pencil writing—became more and
more illegible: at last the letters could hardly be traced at
all. For a year the bottle remained in the cabinet, then it
was sent up into an attic, where it got smothered up with
dust and spider webs; there it lurked and thought of its
better days, when it poured out red wine in the fresh wood;

when it was rocked by the billows and had had a secret, a letter, a sigh of farewell, intrusted to its safe keeping.

It was left among old lumber for twenty years; it would have been left there longer still, had not the house been rebuilt. The roof was taken off, the bottle was descried, remarks were made upon it, but it could not understand. One learns nothing, banished to a lumber room—not even in twenty years. "Had I only spent that time in the parlor downstairs!" sighed the bottle, "how much I should have learned!"

It was now washed and rinsed out; in truth, it needed washing. It felt itself quite clear and transparent; it had renewed its youth in its old age, but the note, the precious note, was lost in the process. It was now filled with seed-corn, corked up tight, and well packed—it knew not where, but it could see neither lamp nor candle, not to speak of sun or moon; and "it is a pity to see nothing when one is traveling," thought the bottle. It saw nothing, but it did something—that was more important; it traveled, and arrived at the place for which it was destined. It was unpacked.

"What a deal of trouble those outlandish folk have taken about it!" Those were the first words it heard, and it understood them well; they were spoken in the language the bottle had heard from the first, at the factory, at the wine merchant's, in the wood, and on shipboard; the only right, good old language, made to be understood! The bottle had come home to its own country! it nearly sprang out of the hands that held it, in its joy. It was emptied of its contents, and sent down into the cellar to be out of the way; no matter! home is home, even in the cellar! There it never thought how long it lay unnoticed, it lay comfortably; and, after a long interval, one day people came in, took this bottle and others, and went out.

The garden of the house was decked out in great magnificence; bright-colored lamps were hung in wreaths, and paper lanterns shone like large bright tulips. It was a lovely evening; the air was still and mild, the stars glittered brilliantly, and as for the new moon, why, people with good eyesight could see the whole, like a round, grayish globe, with one corner tinged with gold.

In the sidewalks there were a few illuminations too, though not so many as in the center of the garden; a row of bottles, each with a candle in it, was set up along the hedges. The bottle that we know was among these; it felt perfectly in a state of rapture; it was now in a garden, as formerly it had been in the wood; again it heard festive sounds, song and music, the hum and buzz of passers-by, especially from the garden side, where the lamps were burning, and the paper lanterns displayed their varied colors. For its own part, it stood in a sidewalk—that even supplied matter for thought; the bottle stood bearing its light—stood there for use and for ornament both, and that was just right. In such an hour one forgets twenty years spent in a lumber room—and it is good to forget when memory is sadness.

Close by passed a pair, arm in arm, like the bridal pair out in the wood, like the mate and the furrier's daughter; the bottle could have believed it had lived it all over again. A tide of guests passed to and fro in the gardens, and among them an old maid, not friendless, indeed—far from it! but one who had survived all her relatives; and she was thinking of the same day years ago that the bottle thought of—she thought of the green wood and the young pair of betrothed lovers. Well might she think of them! for of those two she had been one; she was the survivor! that had been the happiest hour of her life—an hour never to be forgotten, however old an old maid may be. But she did not recognize the bottle, neither did the bottle recognize her; and thus folk pass one another by in this world. But they are sure to meet again, sooner or later, as did these two, who were now denizens of the same town.

The bottle's fate took it from the garden to the wine-merchant's; there it was again filled with wine, and then sold to the aeronaut, who took it with him on his next ascent in his balloon. A crowd of people came to look on, a band of musicians had been engaged, and many other preparations made; the bottle witnessed all these from a basket, wherein he lay in company with a live rabbit, who was wretchedly low-spirited, because he knew he went up only to come down again with the parachute. The bottle, on the contrary, knew nothing about the matter; it saw how the balloon swelled out larger and larger, and when larger could not be, it began to lift itself higher and higher, to roll uneasily; then the ropes that held it down were cut, and up it flew with aeronaut, basket, rabbit, and bottle; the musicians struck up, and the people all cried, " Hurra! "

" This is a new style of navigation," thought the bottle. " There's one good point about it; one can hardly run upon rocks this way."

And the eyes of several thousands of people looked after the balloon, and the old maid watched it too; she was standing at her open attic window, where hung the cage with the little canary, who at that time did not possess a glass for his water, but was obliged to content himself with a cup. In the window stood a flowering myrtle; the old maid had thrust it on one side while she leaned forward to look out; she could see into the balloon; she saw how the aeronaut let the rabbit fall with the parachute; how he drank to the health of the crowd down below, and then flung the bottle high into the air. But she little thought that she had seen this identical bottle flying in the air once before, on her day of happiness in the green wood, in the time of her youth.

The bottle had no time to think at all, so unexpectedly had he attained the highest point of his life. Towers and roofs

lay far below; men were so tiny, they could hardy be seen
at all.

And now it sank, quite after a different fashion from the
rabbit's. The bottle made somersaults in the air, felt itself
so young, so wild! it was half filled with wine at first, but
not for long. What an air voyage! The sun shone on the
bottle, the eyes of all men followed it; the balloon was already
far away. Soon the bottle fell upon one of the roofs and
dashed in two, but such a spirit seemed to animate the fragments, they could not be still! They leaped and they rolled,
ever downward, downward, till they reached the courtyard,
where they broke into smaller fragments. Only the neck of
the bottle was left whole; it looked as if it had been cut off
with a diamond.

"It is still good for a bird glass," said the man who lived
in the cellar; but he himself possessed neither bird nor cage,
and it would have been hardly worth while to procure these
only because a fragment of a bottle that might be used as a
glass had fallen into his hands. But it might be useful to the
old maid in the attic, he thought; and thus the broken bottle
was taken upstairs, a cork was put in, the part that had formerly been uppermost was set lowest, as often happens in
changes, fresh water was poured in, and it was hung on the
side of the cage for the use of the little bird who sang so
merrily.

"Ah, it is easy for you to sing!" quoth the bird glass. It
was a remarkable bird glass, certainly; it had been up in a
balloon; that, at least, was known of its history. Now, in its
place by the cage, it could hear the hum and buzz of the
people in the street below, could hear the old maid chatting
in her chamber: she had a visitor just now, a friend of her
own age, and they were talking, not about the bird glass,
but about the myrtle at the window.

"Indeed, I will not let you throw away two rix-dollars for
your daughter's bridal bouquet," said the old maid. "You

shall have a charming one, full of flowers! Just look at my beautiful myrtle! It is only an offshoot from the myrtle you gave me the day after my betrothal—don't you remember? I was to have made my bridal bouquet from it, when the year was up. But my wedding day never came! Those eyes closed to this world that were to have been my light and joy through life; down, down, low beneath the waves he sleeps sweetly, my own darling! And the myrtle and I grew old together; and when the myrtle withered, I took the last fresh bough, and set it in the mold, and now the bough is a tree, and shall serve at last at a wedding feast—shall supply your daughter's bridal bouquet! "

And there were tears in the old maid's eyes, as she remembered her betrothal in the wood, her lover's bright face, his caressing words, his first kiss—but she said no more; she was an old maid now. She thought of so many things; but she never thought at all that just outside her window was a memorial of that time, even the neck of the bottle whence had gushed the wine from which her own and her lover's health had been drunk. Neither did the old bottle recognize her, for it did not listen to a single word she said, partly and chiefly because it thought only of itself.

Golden Treasure

The drummer's wife went to church; she saw the new altar, the pictures on the walls, the angel faces carved on the arches. Beautiful were the figures in the pictures, dressed in bright colors, and with a glory round their heads; beautiful were the carved cherubs too, painted and gilded both, their hair shining like gold, like sunshine. But the sunshine itself was still more beautiful, the sunshine that God, not man, had made; ever brighter and redder it glowed between the dark trees, as the sun went down. And she gazed upon the red setting sun, and had her own thoughts about it and many other things, but most of all about the little child that the stork would bring her; and the drummer's wife felt so happy while she gazed, and she wished most fervently that her child might be a creature bright as a sunbeam, or at least as one of the shining angels in the church.

And when she actually held her little one in her arms, and lifted it up to show her husband, it seemed to her that her infant really had some resemblance to the cherubs; it had hair like gold, hair that had caught the reflection of the setting sun.

"My sunshine, my wealth, my golden treasure!" cried the mother, kissing the bright locks; and all was gladness, music, and song in the drummer's home. The drummer himself beat a whirlwind on his drum, and the drum seemed to cry,

" Red hair! the young one has red hair! listen, believe the drum and not thy mother; drum-a-drum, drum! "

And the town agreed with the drum.

The boy was taken to church and christened; he was named Peter. All the town called him " Peter, the drummer's red-haired boy "; but his mother kissed his red hair and called him " Golden Treasure."

In the hollow way, in the soft clay, had a multitude of folk scratched their names with a penknife. " That is fame," quoth the drummer; " every one likes to be remembered "; and he too scratched his name and that of his little son there. But in spring came the swallows; during their travels they had seen all manner of characters in the rockside, or within the temple walls of India, chronicling great deeds of mighty kings, immortal names, so old that no one could spell them out. Such is fame! And the swallows built their nests in the clay, and the mold crumbled, and the rain came down, washing away all traces of the names, the drummer's and his little son's among them. " At any rate, Peter's name was there for a year and a half," quoth his father.

" Fool! " thought the drum; but it could only say, " Drum-a-drum-drum! Drum-a-drum-drum! "

A boy full of life and spirit was " the drummer's red-haired son." A lovely voice he had, and he sang like the birds in the wood—all melody, and yet no tune. " He must be a choirboy," said his mother; " he must sing in the church, standing under the pretty gilded cherubs, whom he is so like."

" Choirboy? " repeated the wits of the town. " Say rather fireboy "; and the drum heard it.

" Don't go home, Peter," cried the boys in the street. " If they send you to sleep in the attic, your hair will set the thatch on fire."

" Beware of the drumsticks! " returned Peter, clinching his

little fists; and tiny fellow as he was, his neighbors learned to keep out of his way.

The town musician was stiff and proud, a great gentleman in his way; he thought well of Peter, took him home with him, and gave him a lesson on the violin; he fancied there was something in the boy's fingers that showed him born to become more than a drummer.

" I will be a soldier! " declared Peter, who considered it the finest thing in the world to wear a uniform, shoulder a gun, and march, " Left, right! left, right! "

" Ah, thou shalt learn to obey the drumskin, drum-a-drum-drum! " quoth the drum.

" It is all very well being a soldier when there's a war," said Peter's father, " so that one may march home a general."

" God save us from a war! " cried his mother.

" Why, we have nothing to lose," rejoined the drummer.

" Yes, we have my boy," she replied.

" But just think, if he were to come home a general? " asked the father.

" Without arms and legs! No, thank you; I would rather keep my Golden Treasure entire."

Drum, drum-a-drum-drum! War came, in real earnest; the soldiers marched forth, and the drummer's red-haired boy with them. The mother wept for her " Golden Treasure "; the father saw him in imagination return home " famous "; the town musician thought he had better have stayed at home and studied music.

" Red-tuft! " cried the soldiers, and Peter only laughed; but when some called him " Foxy," he bit his lips and looked another way; that was a jest he did not relish. But the boy was brisk, merry, and good-humored, and thus soon became a favorite. Amid rain and mist, wet through to the skin, he had to sleep many a night under the open sky; but his good humor did not fail him, and he was up again briskly and sounded with his drumsticks, "Drum-a-drum-drum! up every man!" Certainly he was a born drummer boy.

It was a day of battle: the sun was not yet risen, but it was morning; the air was cold, the struggle hot, the morning was misty, but still more mist came from the gunpowder. Bullets and grenades flew overhead; still "Forward." One after another the men sank down, their temples bleeding, their cheeks white as ashes. But the little drummer boy's color was still fresh; not a whit hurt, he looked with beaming eyes at the dog belonging to the regiment as it ran by his side; the whole seemed more like a game to him, the child to whom the balls might have been playthings.

"March, forward, march!" were the words of command given to the drummers; but orders may have to be reversed —and with good reason too—and now the word was "Backward!" But still the little drummer boy sounded "March, forward," not understanding that the order was reversed; and the soldiers obeyed the drum, and still advanced. It was well they did so, the blunder gave them a victory.

But victory is dearly bought. The grenades tear off the flesh in bleeding morsels, set fire to the heap of straw whither the poor wounded wretch had dragged himself, thinking to lie safe for many hours, though perhaps only to die forgotten and forsaken. These are ill things to think upon, yet think on them one must even in the peaceful town far off. How often did not Peter's father and mother think of them while he was in the war!

It was the day of battle; the sun had not yet risen, but it was morning. The drummer and his wife had fallen into a slumber after a wakeful night, spent in talking about their boy. But he, wherever he was, God's hand was over him they knew. And his father now dreamt that the war ended, that the soldiers came home, and that Peter wore a silver cross on his breast; but his mother dreamt that she was in church gazing on the pictures and the carved angels with gilded hair, and that her own boy—her heart's Golden Treasure—stood in white robes amid the angels, and sang so sweetly, as only angels can sing, and was lifted up into the sunshine with them, nodding a kindly greeting to his mother.

"My Golden Treasure!" she exclaimed, and she awoke. "Now I know that our Lord has taken him," said she, and she clasped her hands, leant her head against the bed curtains, and wept. "Where has he found his rest? in the wide grave they dig for so many of the brave dead, or in the waters of the marsh? No one will know his grave, no holy words will be read over it." And the Lord's Prayer passed mutely through her mind, her head drooped in weariness, and she fell asleep.

Days slip away, now in waking hours, now in dreams.

It was evening; a rainbow arched over the field of battle, touching the skirt of the wood and the deep moor. There is a popular saying, "Where the rainbow touches the earth a treasure lies buried—a golden treasure"; so it was here; no one thought of the little drummer boy as his mother thought, and therefore had she thus dreamt of him. But not a hair of his head was lost, not a single golden hair. "Drum-a-drum-drum; see him come, see him come!" For with song and shout, and decked with the green leaves of victory, the regiment marched home; the war was ended, peace was proclaimed. The dog belonging to the regiment jumped and ran, making many wide circuits, as though to make the journey three times longer.

Days and weeks slipped away, and, behold, Peter entered his parents' room: he was as brown as a wild man of the woods, his eyes so bright, his face beaming as the sunshine. And his mother clasped him in her arms, kissed his lips, his eyes, his red hair. She had her boy again: there was no silver cross on his breast, as his father had dreamt, but he had his whole bones, which his mother had not dreamt. What

joy! all three laughed and wept by turns, and Peter embraced
the old drum in the corner: "Here it stands still, the old
thing!" and his father beat a tattoo upon it, "as much fuss as
though there were a fire in the town," quoth the old drum
to itself.

And now what next? Ask the town musician. "Peter grows
too big to be a drummer boy," said he; "Peter will be a
bigger man than I," which was true enough, for all that he
had taken a lifetime to learn, Peter learned in half a year.
And he took such delight in learning, he enjoyed everything,
his eyes sparkled and his hair shone, as could not be denied.
   "He should dye his hair," said their next-door neighbor.
"The police chief's daughter did, and how well it answered;
she was betrothed immediately."
   "But her hair soon afterward grew as green as duckweed,
and she has had to dye it again, ever so many times."
   "Well, she can afford it, and so can Peter. Does not he
go into the best houses, even to the mayor's, to teach Miss
Lotty the harpsichord!" Ah! Peter knew how to play, to
play right out of his heart charming pieces that had never
been noted down on music paper. Through moonlight nights
and stormy nights he played alike—played till his thoughts
grew strong and soaring, and great plans for the future
hovered before him. And he sat beside the mayor's daughter,
Miss Lotty, at the harpsichord, and her delicate fingers
danced lightly over chords that vibrated right into Peter's
heart; it seemed as though it were growing too big for his
body to hold it, and this happened not once only, but many
times, and so it chanced that one day he seized the delicate
fingers and the daintily formed hand and kissed it, and looked
right into her large brown eyes. There's no telling what he
said, but we may guess it. And Lotty colored crimson, face
and neck, and not a word did she answer, and just then
strangers came into the room, among them the councilor's

son, with his high smooth forehead. But Peter stayed on, and Lotty's kindest glances were given to him.

That evening at home he talked of going abroad, and of the golden treasure that his violin was for him. "Drum-a-drum-drum," thought the old drum in the corner. "So Peter has gone mad; the house is on fire, methinks."

Next day the mother went to market. "Have you heard the news, Peter?" began she on her return. "Charming news! The mayor's daughter, Miss Lotty, was betrothed to the councilor's son yesterday evening!"

"No!" cried Peter, springing up from his chair. But his mother insisted "Yes"; she had it from the barber's wife, and the barber had it from the mayor's own lips. And Peter grew pale as death, and sat down again in his chair.

"What is the matter with you?" cried his mother.

"All right! let me alone!" said he, but the tears rolled down his cheeks.

"My sweet child! my Golden Treasure!" muttered the mother; and she wept, while the old drum in the corner sang to itself: "Lotty is dead! Lotty is dead! and now the song is ended!"

But no, the song was not ended; many verses, and some of the best, had yet to be sung. "What a fuss she makes!" quoth the next-door neighbor of Peter's mother. "All the world must read the letters she gets from her Golden Treasure, and hear what the newspapers say about him and his violin. He sends her money too, and he had need, now she is a widow."

"He plays before kings and emperors," said the town musician. "That never fell to my lot, but he is at least my pupil, and will not forget his old master."

"My husband dreamed," said his mother, "that Peter came home from the war with a silver cross on his breast; he does wear a cross now, though not one earned in the war;

he bears an order of knighthood. His father should have lived
to see it! "

" He is famous! " quoth the old drum, and everybody in his
native town said the same. Peter, the drummer's red-haired
boy—Peter, whom they had seen in wooden shoes, a little
drummer boy—was now famous.

" He played to us before he played to the king," said the
mayor's wife. " Once upon a time he was mad about our
Lotty—how my husband laughed when he was told of it!
Ah! that boy must be always looking so high! "

Yes, a golden treasure lay hidden in the heart and soul
of the drummer's boy, who had formerly sounded " Forward! " to troops ready to retreat—a golden treasure, the
gift of music. In his violin seemed sometimes to dwell the
power and volume of an organ; while at other times all the
elves of Midsummer Eve seemed dancing as he touched the
strings, and the throstle's song and the human voice were
heard between; and thus all hearts were moved when he
played, and his name was borne throughout all lands. " And
then he is so handsome! " said some of the ladies, old as well
as young; and one lady who had set up an album for the
locks of celebrated characters, begged for a tress from the
young violinist's abundance of hair, " red," or " golden," as
you liked to call it.

And now once more to the drummer's lowly dwelling
returned the son, handsome as a prince, happier than a king,
his eyes sparkling, his face like sunshine. And he held his
mother in his arms, and she kissed him, and wept for joy;
and he greeted as old friends every piece of worn-out furniture the room possessed, even to the chest of drawers, with
the teacups and flower-glass upon it, and the little cot where
he had slept when a child. But the old drum he dragged
forward into the middle of the room, saying: " Father would
have sounded a welcome upon thee today, but now I must
do it instead." And he thundered so upon the drum! a regular

Thumbelina (Sweden, 11 years old)
(STORY PAGE 45)

tempest it was, and the old drum felt honored thereby. But somehow it chanced that the drumskin burst.

"Well! he *has* a fist! " quoth the old drum to itself. "Now I shall always keep a souvenir of him! I expect that mother, too, will burst for joy over her Golden Treasure! "

This is the history of Golden Treasure.

The Old Bachelor's Nightcap

There is in Copenhagen a street known by the strange name of Hysken Street. Why is it so named? what can "Hysken" mean? The name was originally German; "Häuschen," it ought to be called, meaning "small houses." For the houses in this street at the time it received its name were very much like the wooden booths we still see set up in the markets—a little bigger perhaps, and provided with windows; but then these windows were made only of horn or stretched bladder, for at that time glass windows were too dear to be common. And the time referred to is so very long ago, that my great-great-grandfather, when he spoke of it, always called it "the days of old." It was, in fact, several hundred years ago.

The rich merchants of Bremen and Lübeck used then to trade in Copenhagen, not in their own persons, but sending thither their clerks, who dwelt in the wooden booths in the Street of Small Houses, and there sold their ales and spicery; good German ales of different kinds, and all manner of spices, saffron, anise, ginger, and especially pepper. And from this very pepper which they sold, these petty German traders in Denmark came to be called "Pebersvende," or "Pepper-boys." And as it formed part of the engagement they entered into before they left home that they were not to marry in Denmark, and as many of them sojourned in Copenhagen till they were quite old men, living alone, cooking and doing everything for themselves, they often grew such odd old fellows, with such peculiar whims and ways—and from them the name of " Pebersvend " has come to be given to all single men who have attained old age. So much by way of introduction.

Up in the Street of Small Houses, in the old times, there was no pavement; folk tumbled into hole after hole, and very narrow was it; the booths were such near neighbors that in summertime a rope was often suspended across the street from one booth to the opposite one. And everywhere was such an aromatic odor of pepper, saffron, and ginger. Behind the counters stood not young lads, no, but old fellows clad after old fashions. It is a pity it never occurred to one of them to have his portrait painted, for it would be worth while now to possess a picture of any one of them, as he stood behind the counter or walked to church on holidays. The hat was broad-brimmed and high-crowned, with perhaps a feather in it, if the wearer were not very old; the woollen shirt was concealed by a smooth linen collar; the jacket was neatly buttoned up, the cape hung loosely over it, and the breeches reached down to the square-toed shoes; stockings they wore not. In the belt were fastened a spoon and knife, to be used at meals, nay, also a larger knife, or dagger, for self-defense, as was often needed in those days. Clad after this fashion, on festival days, was old Anthony, one of the oldest traders of the Small Houses, with this addition, that under his hat he wore a knitted cap, a regular nightcap. He was accustomed to it, and wore it always; he possessed two exactly alike; he was just the old fellow for a picture: long and lean as a lath, wrinkled about the lips and eyes; he had long bony fingers and gray bushy eyebrows. Over his left eye hung a perfect tuft; it was not handsome, certainly, but it made him a man easily recognized. It was said of him that he came from Bremen: this was a mistake;

his mother lived there, but he himself came from Thuringia, from the town of Eisenach, close under Wartburg. Of these places old Anthony spoke but little, but he thought the more.

The old fellows in the Small Houses rarely met together; each sojourned in his own booth, which was shut up early in the evening, and then looked dark enough, with only a faint ray of light piercing through the little horn window-pane on the roof. Within, perhaps, the solitary foreigner was sitting on his bed, chanting his evening psalm out of his old German hymnbook, or was poking about over his house-hold matters. A merry life it was not by any means; a bitter lot is that of the stranger in a strange land.

A miserable place indeed was the Street of Small Houses on a dark, stormy night, amid wind and rain. Not a light could be seen save the one very small lamp hanging just at the end of the street under the picture of the Blessed Virgin which was painted on the wall, and the water was heard splashing, splashing ceaselessly against the woodwork. Such evenings must be long and lonesome, and would be worse still were people unoccupied. To pack and unpack, polish one's scales, etc., cannot be necessary every day, but then one generally finds something else to be done. So at least always did old Anthony; he had his clothes to patch, his shoes to mend. And when at last he got into bed, and drew his nightcap closer over his face, he was pretty sure to draw it up again to see if his light were properly extinguished. He would feel about, draw down the wick, turn round on the other side, and lie down again, but then would come the thought, " I wonder whether every coal has really burnt out in the little fire; one spark might kindle up into mischief," and with this idea he would creep out of bed, grope his way down the steps—staircase it could not be called—and yet when he got down there was sure to be not a single spark left in the little firepot. Yet before he had got halfway back

to bed, he would feel uncertain whether he had drawn the
iron bolt over his door. His lean limbs shivered, and his teeth
chattered with cold before he got safe into bed again; then
he would draw the coverlet closer, his nightcap closer over
his eyes, and turn his thoughts right away from the burden
and labor of the day; but hardly was this to his comfort.
For old memories came then and drew their curtains round,
and O! there lurk sharp needles in them; when we touch
them they pierce the tender skin, draw blood, burn within
us, bring tears to our eyes! So at least was it with old Anthony; oftentimes hot tears like the brightest pearls rolled
down over the coverlet or on the floor; his eyes seemed to
burn with them or their light seemed turned into darkness,
but still a vivid picture seemed before his sight. Then he
would wipe his eyes with his nightcap, and both tears and
pictures vanished; but the source of both remained, it lay
deep in his heart. The pictures came not in regular order,
as they had followed one another in his past life, and the
most painful ones came oftenest; but these even had a
brightness and glory of their own, only they cast the deepest
shadows.

"How beautiful are the beech woods of Denmark!" people
are wont to exclaim. But more beautiful to Anthony were the
beech woods near Wartburg; mightier, and more venerable
than any Danish trees were the old oaks up by the proud
baronial castle, where creeping plants trailed over the hard
blocks of stone; sweeter far was the fragrance of the apple-
blossoms there than in the Danish land. He felt this strongly,
bitterly; a large bright tear trickled forth; by its light he
seemed to see two children at play, a boy and a girl. The
boy had red cheeks, curling yellow hair, and honest blue
eyes; he was little Anthony, the rich trader's son, himself, in
fact. The little girl had brown eyes and black hair, and the
expression of her face was both bold and clever; she was
the burgomaster's daughter, Maddalena. The two children

were playing with an apple, shaking it and listening to the pips rattling inside; then they cut it in half, and between them ate it up all but one kernel, which the little girl proposed to put into the ground. "Then you will see what will come of it! something you would never fancy, only not directly. A whole apple tree! think of that." And they planted it in a flower pot, both very zealous in the work, the boy hollowing out a bed for it in the mold with his fingers, the little girl laying it in, and then both together smoothed the earth over it. "You must not take it up again tomorrow to see if it has taken root," she said. "One must never do that! I did so with my flowers, but only twice; I wanted to see if they were growing, I did not know any better, and the flowers died."

The flower pot was left with Anthony, and he looked at it every morning all through the winter, but still saw nothing but the black mold. Spring came, the sun shone warmly, and now two tiny green leaves peeped forth. "One for me, and one for Maddalena," thought Anthony; "that is charming!" Soon appeared a third leaf—who was that for? Another followed, and another; every week, every day, it grew bigger and bigger; the plant became a tree.

And all this was seen reflected as it were in that single bright tear that flowed forth and vanished so soon; but more tears like this could gush forth from the fountain, even old Anthony's heart.

Near Eisenach stretches a chain of rocky mountains; one of these has a peculiar round form, and is completely bare of trees, bushes, or grass; it is called the Venus Mountain, for within it dwells Lady Venus, a woman-goddess of heathen times. Every child in Eisenach knows that Lady Venus, or Lady Holle—for she is known by both of these names— dwells here, and that once she allured into her abode that noble knight Tannhäuser, a "minnesinger" belonging to the minstrel band at Wartburg.

Anthony and little Maddalena often played near this

mountain, and once she said to him, "Anthony, darest thou knock at the mountain and say, 'Lady Venus, Lady Venus, open! Tannhäuser is here!'" No, Anthony dared not; Maddalena dared. But only the first few words, "Lady Venus, Lady Venus!" did she speak out boldly and loud, the rest seemed to die away on her lips, and Anthony was sure she had not really spoken them out. And yet she had her bold look, just as she had when sometimes she and other little girls met him in the garden and they all wanted to kiss him, because they knew he did not like to be kissed. "I will," she would say, and Anthony never objected to anything she chose to do. She was so pretty, as well as clever and bold. But there are different kinds of beauty. Lady Venus in the mountain was beautiful, folks said, but it was a wild alluring beauty given by the evil spirit; a very different beauty was that of the holy Elizabeth, the pious Thuringian princess, whose deeds of love and mercy were still remembered by the peasantry around. Her picture hung in the chapel, lighted by silver lamps; she was the protecting saint of the country. But Maddalena was not like her.

The apple tree that the children had planted grew year by year, so that soon it had to be transplanted into the garden; there the dew fell on it, the sun shone warmly on it, and gave it strength to endure the winter. And when winter was past, and spring had returned, it seemed as though it put forth its blossoms purely from joy, because the cold season was gone. And when autumn came, it bore two apples, one for Maddalena, one for Anthony.

And Maddalena grew up quickly, like the apple tree, and her face was as bright and fresh as its blossoms; but not much longer might Anthony enjoy the sight of his fairest flower. Changes came; Maddalena and her father left their old home for a new one. In our time, by the help of steam, the journey might be made in a few hours, but then it took more than a whole day and night to get from Eisenach to the

The Ugly Duckling (Japan, 10 years old)
(STORY PAGE 175)

town which is still called Weimar. When they parted, Maddalena wept as well as Anthony, and she declared she loved him better than all the splendors of Weimar.

One year passed away—two, three years passed away; and in the course of those three years two letters came from her; the first was brought by the carrier, the second by a traveler; the way was long and tedious, with many windings, past different towns.

Often had Anthony and Maddalena listened to the old story of "Tristram and Isolde," and always, when he heard it, had Anthony fancied himself and Maddalena in their case. Only the name of Tristram, meaning "one born in sorrow," suited not him, he thought, neither would he ever be like Tristram in imagining that she whom he loved had forgotten him. That was so unjust! for Isolde never did forget Tristram, and when both were dead, and buried on opposite sides of the church, the lime trees that sprang from their graves would meet over the church roof, entwining their boughs in flowers and sweet odors. That story was so pretty, yet so sad, Anthony thought; but sad should not be his and Maddalena's history, and then he would whistle a song by Walter von der Vogelweide, the minnesinger. "Under the lime tree on the heath," it began, and the burden was so pretty.

> "*Out in the wood, in the quiet dale,*
> *Tandaradai!*
> *Sang so sweetly the nightingale.*"

This was his favorite song, and O! how he sang and whistled it all through the bright moonlight night as he rode along through the deep hollow way, on the road to Weimar, to pay a visit to Maddalena. He had not been invited; he chose to take her by surprise.

He was welcomed with good cheer and good wine, pleasant company, a comfortable room and warm bed—and yet it was not as he had pictured it. He understood neither himself nor his friends; but we can understand it easily! One can so often stay in a family without taking root in it; one talks, as one talks in a post chaise; knows the people, as one can know them on a steamboat; mutual annoyance increases, one wishes either one's self or one's good neighbor right away. Something of this felt Anthony.

"I am an honest girl," said Maddalena to him, "and I will tell thee the truth. Many things have changed since the time when we were together, a couple of children—changed both within us and without us. We cannot make our hearts keep the same; it is impossible. Anthony! I don't want to make thee my enemy—but soon I shall be far away from here. Believe me, I like thee well enough, but love thee, in the way I now know I can love another, that I cannot—I never have loved thee thus! Thou wilt get reconciled to it. Farewell, Anthony!"

And Anthony bade her farewell—he took his leave without a tear. The red-hot bar of iron and the frozen bar of iron alike bite the skin off our lips, if we kiss it; Anthony felt wild with hate now, as before with love.

It did not take Anthony anything like the four-and-twenty hours to ride home to Eisenach, but the poor horse he rode was ruined by his fierce haste. "What matter?" said he; "I am ruined, and I will ruin everything that can remind me of her: Lady Venus, the false heathen! As for the apple tree, I will tear it up by the roots; never shall it bloom or bear fruit again!"

But the apple tree was not laid low; he was himself laid low—brought to his bed by fever. How should he ever be raised up again? A medicine was sent him, the bitterest that could be found, but with power to brace the sick body and shrinking spirit. For Anthony's father was now no longer the rich merchant. Heavy days of trial stood waiting at the door; misfortune rushed in; like a flood it streamed upon the once rich house. The father was now a poor man; sorrow and anxiety palsied him, and Anthony had soon other things to think of besides love, sorrow and wrath against Maddalena. He had to be father and mother both in the house, to arrange, help, work for his bread.

He went to Bremen, and there endured many dreary days of hunger and bitterness, and these either harden or soften the heart. How different was the world of real men and women from the world he had imagined in his childhood! What now to him were the strains of the minnesingers? Mere moonshine! So he felt sometimes, but sometimes also the old songs he had been wont to love seemed to echo in his soul and did him good, made him gentler and more submissive. "God's will is best," he would then say within himself. "Good was it that our Lord would not suffer Maddalena's heart to cling to me, for where would it have ended, now that fortune has turned against me? I am glad she gave me up before she had heard of this change. Our Lord has been merciful toward me; all has been for the best, all things are ordered wisely. And she could not help herself; I was unjust to feel so bitter and wrathful!"

Years went on; Anthony's father was dead, and strangers now dwelt in the old house where he was born. Yet Anthony was to see his home once more, for his rich master sent him on a journey that obliged him to pass through Eisenach. Old Wartburg stood unchanged on the rock; the great oak trees kept their places, the Venus Mountain gleamed gray in its barrenness, as of old. These words sprang to Anthony's lips: "Lady Venus! Lady Venus! open the mountain and take me in! then I shall at least stay in my own land!"

It was a sinful thought, and he hastily crossed himself. A little bird was singing from a bush close by; it reminded him of the old song—

Far in the wood, in the quiet dale,
Tandaradai!
How sweetly sang the nightingale.

It was through a veil of tears that he now again saw the home of his childhood. The house stood exactly as before, but the garden had been laid out afresh, and a road now cut across a corner of the old garden ground, so that the apple tree, which he had never destroyed, now stood outside the inclosure. The sun shone on it, and the dew fell on it, as formerly; it bore rich fruit, and bowed its branches almost to the earth. " It thrives! " quoth he; " that's well." But on closer inspection, he saw that rude hands had broken off one of the largest boughs; the tree stood too near the high-road. " They tear off the blossoms, without one word of thanks; they steal the fruit and break off the branches; one might repeat concerning this tree, as concerning many a human being—

> *" At this tree's cradle who could say*
> *That such would be its fate one day?*

Its history began so prettily, and now it is forsaken and forgotten, a garden tree by the highroad! quite out of place, and ill-treated thus! Well, it will not pine away and die, but every year the blossoms will be fewer, and of fruit there will soon be none—no matter, the history will not be a long one! "

Such were Anthony's musings under the apple tree, and very similar were his nightly thoughts in the tiny, lonesome chamber in the Street of Small Houses, in the foreign Danish land, whither his rich master, a merchant of Bremen, had sent him, under condition that he was not to marry. " Marry, indeed! ho, ho! " and he laughed a strange inward laugh.

The winter came early one year, a sharp frost set in, and a violent snowstorm kept every one indoors who was not obliged to go out. Thus it happened that Anthony's neighbors took no note of his booth having been shut up for two whole days. During those two days old Anthony had never left his bed; he had not the strength, and the intense cold had benumbed his limbs. All forsaken lay the old bachelor; he could not help himself, he could only just reach the water pitcher beside his bed, and now the last drop had been exhausted. It was not fever, it was not sickness; it was old age that had prostrated him thus. It was almost continual night around him, for the days were dark and gray, and his window was not like a glass window. A little spider, unseen, unknown to him, spun contentedly and diligently her web over him, as though to prepare a little fine new crape for mourning, in case the old man's eyes should close in death.

Long and dreary were the hours; tears had he none, neither had he pain. Maddalena was no longer in his thoughts; he felt that the tumult of the world was past for him, that he lay somewhere beyond it, that no one thought of him. For a while he seemed to feel hunger and thirst—O! that was painful! but no one came to help him—no one would come. He thought of others who had suffered the like; he remembered the patron saint of his birthplace, the gentle St. Elizabeth, who, when her people were pining because of the famine, went about bringing help and refreshment to the sick. He remembered the pious words of hope and trust in God that she had been wont to speak to those poor sufferers; how she had bathed their wounds and brought food to the hungry, although her stern husband forbade her with angry words. He remembered the legend, how as she glided along with a basket well packed with bread and meat, her husband, who was watching her footsteps, suddenly stepped forward and asked in wrath, "what it was she carried in her baskets?" And she replied in terror: "These are roses I have gathered in the garden"; whereupon he tore back the cloth laid over the basket, and lo! a miracle! for bread and meat were changed into the loveliest roses!

Thus lived the gentle Duchess of Thuringia in old Anthony's thoughts, thus she stood vividly before his failing eyesight, beside his bed in the miserable wooden booth in the strangers' land. He uncovered his head, looked into her kind eyes, and all around him sprang up a bower of sweet roses, so fair to look on, and so fragrant! And now he was conscious of another, a different perfume; a flowering apple tree stood before him, the same that he and little Maddalena had planted.

And the tree drooped its fragrant petals upon his hot forehead, and their touch cooled it; they fell upon his thirsting lips, and seemed to strengthen him like wine; they drooped upon his breast, and he felt so much easier.

"Now I shall fall asleep," said he to himself. "Sleep will do me so much good, I shall get up tomorrow all right again. O, how beautiful! The apple tree planted in love! I see it now in glory!" And he fell asleep.

The next day—it was the third day that his booth had been shut up—the snow ceased, and old Anthony's opposite neighbor came to look after him. There he lay, stretched out dead, holding his old nightcap between his clasped hands. But another was found laid by, white and clean, ready for him to wear in his coffin.

And where were now the tears he had shed! where were the pearls? They were left in his nightcap—the genuine ones do not get lost in the washing—with the cap they remained; the old thoughts, the old dreams, all were left in the old bachelor's nightcap. Never wish such a one for thyself! it will make thy forehead too hot, thy pulse to beat too fast, will bring dreams as vivid as reality. This was experienced by the burgomaster, who, fifty years after old Anthony's death, chanced to put his nightcap on; he was a comfortable, well-to-do man, with a wife and eleven children; nevertheless, he dreamt straightway of unrequited love, bankruptcy, and hard fare.

"Ugh! how hot this nightcap makes one!" he exclaimed, and tore it off. One pearl after another trickled down and glittered before his eyes. "I must be ill!" declared the burgomaster; "my eyes feel quite dazzled! Can this be gout, I wonder?"

He knew not that what he saw were tears, shed half a hundred years ago—shed by old Anthony of Eisenach.

As for the visions and dreams of those several unhappy ones who have worn the nightcap since, we will leave others to tell the tale, or rather the tales, for there must be many of them; we have now told the first, and with these words we conclude: Never wish for thyself the old bachelor's nightcap.

" Something "

" I will be Something," declared the eldest of five brothers; " I will be of use in the world; be it ever so humble a position that I may hold, let me be but useful, and that will be Something. I will make bricks; folk cannot do without them, so I shall at least do Something."

" Something very little, though," replied the second brother. " Why, it is as good as nothing! it is work that might be done by a machine. Better be a mason, as I intend to be. Then one belongs to a guild, becomes a citizen, has a banner of one's own. Nay, if all things go well, I may become a master, and have apprentices and workmen under me. That will be Something! "

" It will be nothing at all then, I can tell you that! " rejoined the third. " Think how many different ranks there are in a town far above that of a master mason. You may be an honest sort of a man, but you will never be a gentleman; gentle and simple; those are the two grand divisions, and you will always be one of the ' simple.' Well, I know better than that. I will be an architect; I will be one of the thinkers, the artists; I will raise myself to the aristocracy of intellect. I may have to begin from the very lowest grade; I may begin as a carpenter's boy, and run about with a paper cap on my head, to fetch ale for the workmen; I may not enjoy it, but I shall try to imagine it is only a masquerade. ' Tomorrow,'

I shall say, 'I will go my own way, and others shall not come near me.' Yes, I shall go to the Academy, learn to draw, and be called an architect. That will be Something! I may get a title, perhaps; and I shall build and build, as others before me have done. Yes, that will be Something!"

"But it is Something that I care nothing about," said the fourth. "I should not care to go on, on, in the beaten track, to be a mere copyist; I will be a genius, cleverer than all of you put together; I will create a new style, provide ideas for buildings suited to the climate and materials of our country, suited to our national character, and the requirements of the age."

"But supposing the climate and the materials don't agree?" suggested the fifth, "how will you get on then, if they won't co-operate? As for our national character, to be following out that in architecture will be sheer affectation, and the requirements of modern civilization will drive you perfectly mad. I see you will none of you ever be anything, though of course you won't believe me. But do as you please, I shall not be like you. I shall reason over what you execute; there is something ridiculous in everything; I shall find it out, show you your faults—that will be Something!"

And he kept his word; and folk said of this fifth brother, "There is something in him, certainly; he has plenty of brains! but he does nothing." But he was content, he was Something.

But what became of the five brothers? We will hear the whole.

The eldest brother, the brickmaker, found that every brick he turned out whole yielded him a tiny copper coin—only copper—but a great many of these small coins, added together, could be converted into a bright silver dollar, and through the power of this, wherever he knocked, whether at baker's, butcher's, or tailor's, the door flew open, and he received what he wanted. Such was the virtue of his bricks; some, of course, got broken before they were finished, but a use was found even for these. For up by the trench would poor Mother Margaret fain build herself a little house, if she might; she took all the broken bricks, aye, and she got a few whole ones besides, for a good heart had the eldest brother, though only a brickmaker. The poor thing built her house with her own hands; it was very narrow, its one window was all on one side, the door was too low, and the thatch on the roof might have been laid on better, but it gave her shelter and a home, and could be seen far over the sea, which sometimes burst over the trench in its might, and sprinkled a salt shower over the little house, which kept its place there years after he who made the bricks was dead and gone.

As for the second brother, he learned to build after another fashion, as he had resolved. When he was out of his apprenticeship, he buckled on his knapsack, and started, singing as he went, on his travels. He came home again, and became a master in his native town; he built, house after house, a whole street of houses; there they stood, looked well, and were a credit to the town; and these houses soon built him a little house for himself. How? Ask the houses, and they will give you no answer; but the people will answer you and say, " Why, of course, the street built him his house! " It was small enough, and had only a clay floor, but when he and his bride danced over it, the floor grew as smooth as if it had been polished, and from every stone in the wall sprung a flower, that looked as gay as the costliest tapestry. It was a pretty house and a happy wedded pair. The banner of the Masons' Guid waved outside, and workmen and apprentices shouted " Hurra! " Yes, that was Something! and at last he died—that, too, was Something!

Next comes the architect, the third brother. He began as a carpenter's apprentice, and ran about the town on errands, wearing a paper cap; but he studied industriously at the Academy, and rose steadily upward. If the street full of houses had built a house for his brother the mason, the street took its name from the architect; the handsomest house in the whole street was his—that was Something, and he was Something! His children were gentlemen, and could boast of their "birth"; and when he died, his widow was a widow of condition—that is Something—and his name stood on the corner of the street, and was in everybody's lips—that is Something, too!

Now for the genius, the fourth brother, who wanted to invent something new, something original. Somehow, the ground gave way beneath his feet; he fell and broke his neck. But he had a splendid funeral, with music and banners, and flowery paragraphs in the newspapers; and three eulogiums were pronounced over him, each longer than the last, and this would have pleased him mightily, for he loved speechifying of all things. A monument was erected over his grave, only one story high—but that is Something!

So now he was dead, as well as his three elder brothers; the youngest, the critic, outlived them all, and that was as it should be, for thus he had the last word, which to him was a matter of the greatest importance. "He had plenty of brains," folk said. Now his hour had struck, he died, and his soul sought the gates of heaven. There it stood side by side with another soul—old Mother Margaret from the trenches.

"It is for the sake of contrast, I suppose, that I and this miserable soul should wait here together," thought the critic. "Well now, who are you, my good woman?" he inquired.

And the old woman replied, with as much respect as though St. Peter himself were addressing her—in fact, she took him for St. Peter, he gave himself such grand airs—"I am a poor old soul, I have no family, I am only old Margaret from the house near the trenches."

"Well, and what have you done down below?"

"I have done as good as nothing in the world! nothing

whatever! It will be mercy, indeed, if such as I am suffered
to pass through this gate."

" And how did you leave the world? " inquired the critic,
carelessly. He must talk about something; it wearied him to
stand there, waiting.

" Well, I can hardly tell how I left it; I have been sickly
enough during these last few years, and could not well bear
to creep out of bed at all during the cold weather. It has
been a severe winter, but now that is all past. For a few
days, as your highness must know, the wind was quite still,
but it was bitterly cold; the ice lay over the water as far as
one could see. All the people in the town were out on the
ice; there was dancing, and music, and feasting, and sled
racing, I fancy; I could hear something of it all as I lay in
my poor little chamber. And when it was getting toward
evening, the moon was up, but was not yet very bright;
I looked from my bed through the window, and I saw how
there rose up over the sea a strange white cloud; I lay and
watched it, watched the black dot in it, which grew bigger
and bigger, and then I knew what it foreboded; that sign
is not often seen, but I am old and experienced. I knew it,
and I shivered with horror! Twice before in my life have
I seen that sign, and I knew that there would be a terrible
storm and a spring flood; it would burst over the poor things
on the ice, who were drinking, and dancing, and merry-
making. Young and old, the whole town was out on the ice;
who was to warn them, if no one saw it, or no one knew
what I knew? I felt so terrified, I felt all alive, as I had not
felt for years! I got out of bed, forced the window open;
I could see the folk running and dancing over the ice; I
could see the gay-colored flags. I could hear the boys shout
'Hurra!' and the girls and lads a-singing. All were so merry;
and all the time the white cloud with its black speck rose
higher and higher! I screamed as loud as I could; but no one
heard me, I was too far off. Soon would the storm break loose,

the ice would break in pieces, and all that crowd would sink and drown. Hear me they could not; get out to them I could not; what was to be done ? Then our Lord sent me a good thought; I could set fire to my bed; better let my house be burnt to the ground, than that so many should miserably perish. So I kindled a light; I saw the red flame mount up; I got out at the door, but then I fell down; I lay there, I could not get up again. But the flames burst out through the window and over the roof; they saw it down below, and they all ran as fast as they could to help me; the poor old crone they believed would be burnt; there was not one who did not come to help me. I heard them come, and I heard, too, such a rustling in the air, and then a thundering as of heavy cannon shots, for the spring flood was loosening the ice, and it all broke up. But the folk were all come off it to the trenches, where the sparks were flying about me; I had them all safe. But I could not bear the cold and the fright, and that is how I have come up here. Can the gates of heaven be opened to such a poor old creature as I? I have no house now at the trenches; where can I go, if they refuse me here? "

Then the gates opened, and the Angel bade poor Margaret enter. As she passed the threshold, she dropped a blade of straw—straw from her bed—that bed which she had set alight to save the people on the ice, and lo! it had changed into gold! dazzling gold! yet flexible withal, and twisting into various forms.

" Look, that was what yonder poor woman brought," said the Angel. "But what dost thou bring? Truly, I know well that thou hast done nothing, not even made bricks. It is a pity thou canst not go back again to fetch at least one brick—not that it is good for anything when it is made, no, but because anything, the very least, done with a good will, is Something. But thou mayst not go back, and I can do nothing for thee."

Then poor Margaret pleaded for him thus: " His brother

gave me all the bricks and broken bits wherewith I built my poor little house—that was a great kindness toward a poor old soul like me! May not all those bits and fragments, put together, be reckoned as one brick for him? It will be an act of mercy; he needs it, and this the home of mercy."

"To thy brother, whom thou didst despise," said the Angel, "to him whose calling, in respect of worldly honor, was the lowest, shalt thou owe this mite of heavenly coin. Thou shalt not be sent away; thou shalt have leave to stand here without, and think over thy manner of life down below. But within thou canst not enter, until thou hast done something that is good—Something!"

"I fancy I could have expressed that better," thought the critic; but he did not say it aloud, and that was already—Something!

The Nightingale (Turkey, 14 years old)
(STORY PAGE 163)

The Thorny Path of Honor

There is an old romance called " The Thorny Path of Honor, that was trodden by a huntsman named Bryde, who came to great honor and dignity, but not till after manifold adversities, and much peril of life." Many a one of us has heard the tale in childhood, and perchance read it in later years, and thought of his own unrecorded " thorny path " and " manifold adversities." Romance and reality are so much alike, but romance has its happy ending here on earth, whilst reality more often delays it, and refers us to time and eternity.

The world's history is a magic lantern, throwing pictures of light on the dark backgrounds of the ages; to show us how the benefactors of mankind, the martyrs of progress, have trodden " The Thorny Path of Honor."

From all times, from all lands, stand out these dazzling pictures; each picture a moment only, yet a whole life, a lifetime with its struggles and triumphs. Let us glance here and there at a few in the martyr ranks; these ranks that will never be filled till the earth melts away.

Behold a crowded theatre: the *Clouds* of Aristophanes are sending streams of mirth and mockery for the populace; the stage of Athens makes a laughingstock, both body and mind, of her foremost man, who stood between the people and the Thirty Tyrants—he who in the battle fray rescued Alcibiades and Xenophon, he whose spirit soared above the old

world deities, is here himself in person. He has risen among
the spectators, and stands forward from the benches, that
the laughing Athenians may see whether he and the stage
caricature of him are like each other; there he stands erect
before them, and in spirit high above them.

O green, juicy, poisonous hemlock! be thou, and not the
olive tree, the shadowy background of this Athens.

Seven cities claimed to be Homer's birthplace, that is to
say, when he was dead. See him in his lifetime! he wanders
through these very cities, reciting his verses for his liveli-
hood. Thought for the morrow grizzles his hair. He, the
mightiest of seers, is blind and lonely; the sharp thorn rends
the mantle of the poet king.

His songs live still; and in them alone live the gods and
heroes of old.

Picture upon picture billows forth from the morning land
and the evening land, far removed by time and space, and
yet all from the same thorny path, where the thistle never
bears flowers till it can only serve to deck the grave.

From under the palm trees come camels, laden with indigo
and other precious things; they are sent by the lord of the
land to him whose lays are the people's delight, the country's
pride. He whom spite and slander drove into exile, is found
again. The caravan draws near the little town where he has
taken refuge. A poor corpse is being brought out of the
gate: this stops the caravan. The dead is the very man they
seek, Firdusi—ended is "The Thorny Path of Honor."

Yonder sits an African, snub-nosed, blubber-lipped, and
woolly haired, on the marble steps of the palace in Portugal's
capital, and begs; that is the faithful slave of Camöens. If
it were not for him, and the coppers that are thrown him,
his master, the singer of the "Lusiad," might have starved
to death. Now there stands a costly monument on the grave
of Camöens.

Yet another picture. Behind iron bars may be seen a man

with long and matted beard. " I have made an invention,"
he cries, " the greatest for centuries; and they have kept me
for more than twenty years caged up here." " Who is he? "
" A lunatic," says the keeper. What craze may not befall a
man? he thinks that people could get along by steam! It is
Solomon de Caus, the discoverer of steam power. His
prescient words have not been clear enough for a Richelieu,
and he dies imprisoned in a madhouse.

Here stands Columbus, whom once the street boys pursued
and hooted, because he would discover a new world. He has
discovered it. The bells of jubilee ring at his triumphant
return; but soon the bells of envy sound louder still. The
world discoverer, he who raised the American gold land
above ocean, and gave it to his king, is rewarded with iron
chains; he desires them to be laid in his coffin, to mark how
a man is valued by his own age.

Picture throngs upon picture; rich is the Thorny Path of
Honor.

Here in murky gloom sits he who measured the heights
of the moon mountains; he who burst his way forth into space,
among planets and stars; Galileo, the mighty one, who could
see and hear the earth beneath him turning round. Blind
and deaf he sits now, in his old age, suffering tortures of pain
and privation, hardly able to lift his foot—that foot which
once in mental agony, when the words of truth were blotted
out, he stamped on the earth, crying, " Still it moves! "

Here stands a woman with a childlike heart, a creature of
impulse and faith. She bears the banner before the warrior
host, and brings victory and freedom to her fatherland. The
jubilee sounds; the bale fire kindles; Joan of Arc, the witch,
is burned at the stake. Yea, the coming age will spit upon
the white lily; Voltaire, wit's own satyr, will sing of *La
Pucelle*.

At the Viborg-Thing the Danish nobles are burning the
king's laws. They burst into flames that light up both age

and lawgiver, and send a flash of glory into yon dark donjon-tower. Yonder he sits, gray-haired, bent double, furrowing the stone table with his fingers; he once ruled over three kingdoms, the popular chief, the burghers' and peasants' friend, Christian the Second; he of the hard will in the hard age. Enemies wrote his history. Seven-and-twenty years of prison, let us remember, whenever we are reminded of his blood-guiltiness.

There sails a ship from Denmark; there stands a man by the tall mast; he looks upon Hoen for the last time; Tycho Brahe, who raised Denmark's name to the stars, and was repaid with scathe and scorn, is setting forth on his way to a foreign land. "Heaven is everywhere, what want I more?" such are his words; and away he sails, our most famous man sure in foreign lands of being honored and free.

"Free! ah, if only free from the intolerable pains of this body!" sighs a voice of the bygone age to us. What a picture! Griffenfeldt, the Danish Prometheus, fettered to Mumkholm's rocky isle.

We are in America, by one of the large rivers; crowds of people have gathered, a ship is to sail against wind and tide, to be a power against the elements. Robert Fulton is the name of him who thinks he can do this. The ship begins its course, suddenly it stops; the crowd laughs, whistles, and whoops, his own father whoops with them. "Presumption! madness! he has got his deserts; lock him up, the wiseacre!" Then clicks a small nail, which for a moment had stopped the machinery; the wheels work the paddles round, break the opposition of the waves—the ship sails.

Steam's weaver-shuttle turns hours into minutes between the lands of the world.

Mankind, canst thou realize the bliss of such a moment of assurance, when the sorest wounds from the Thorny Path of Honor—though one's own fault may have caused them— are healed, are forgotten in spiritual health, and strength, and freedom. When all discords melt into harmony; and men acknowledge a revelation of God's grace, vouchsafed to one alone, and by him made known to all.

Then the Thorny Path of Honor shines like a glory round the earth. Happy he who is chosen to be a pilgrim thereon, and without any merit of his own, to be made one of the master builders of the bridge between God and man.

The Genius of History wings his mighty way throughout the ages, and gives us comfort and good cheer, and thoughtful calm of mind, by showing, in sunbright pictures upon murky backgrounds, the Thorny Path of Honor: not a path that ends, like a fairy tale, in gladness and glitter here on earth, but one that points onward, and upward, far away into time and eternity.

The Days of the Week

"We will also have a good time for once," said the Days of the Week; "we will come together and have a feast." But every one of the seven Days was so much occupied all the year round, that they had not a free moment left for enjoyment. They wanted to have a whole day to themselves, and such a day they get every four years in the intercalary day; this day is placed at the end of February, for the purpose of bringing order in the account of time.

And on this inserted day they decided to meet together, and hold their feast. February being the month of carnivals, they agreed to come together in a carnival fashion, every one dressed according to his profession and destination; have the best things to eat, and drink the best wines, make speeches, and tell each other the most agreeable and most disagreeable things in unrestrained fellowship. The Norse heroes had a custom, in the good old times, of shying the bones, which they had cleared of all the meat, at each other's head; but the weekdays thought of throwing bombshells at each other with their mouths, in the form of scorching witticisms, such as might be in keeping with innocent carnival amusements.

And the twenty-ninth of February came in due time; with it they assembled.

Sunday, foreman of the weekdays, came first, dressed in a

black silk cloak. The pious people mistook the cloak for a minister's gown. The worldly minded, however, saw that he was dressed in domino for a frolic, and the full-blown carnation, which he wore in his buttonhole, was nothing but a little red theatre lantern, which said, "No more tickets: standing room only; hope you will enjoy yourself."

Monday, a young mechanic, a distant relative of Sunday, and much given to pleasures, came next. No sooner did he hear the military music of the parade, than he rushed out, saying, "I must go and hear Offenbach's music; it does not go to my head, neither to the heart: but it itches in the muscles of my legs. I must dance, and have a swing with the girls, get me a blue eye, and then sleep upon it; the next day I go to work with new vigor: did you see the new moon of the week?"

Tuesday is Tyr's day, the day of strength. "Yes, that I am," said Tuesday. "I take hold of the work, fasten Mercury's wings to the merchant's boots, look after the factory, and see that the wheels are oiled, and turn easily. I also see to it that the tailor sits upon his table, and the street paver is by his paving stones. I hold everybody to his business, and have an eye upon them all, and therefore I appear among you in a policeman's uniform, and my name is 'Politics day.' If this is a bad joke, then you may think of a better one, every one of you."

"And now come I," said Wednesday. "I stand in the middle of the week; the Germans call me Mr. Midweek. I stand like a young clerk in a store, like a flower among the other honored days of the week. If we march up in file, then have I three days in front of me, and three days behind; they are my bodyguard: and I may with propriety say that I am the most prominent of all the days of the week."

And now Thursday came in, dressed up like a coppersmith, with a hammer and a copper kettle—token of his aristocratic descent. "I am of very high birth," said he. "In

Thumbelina (France, 15 years old)
(STORY PAGE 45)

the northern countries I am named after Thor, the god of thunder; and in the south, after Jupiter, the god of lightning; these two understood how to thunder and lighten, and that has remained in the family."

And then he beat his copper kettle, and thus proved his high descent.

Friday was dressed up like a young girl, who called herself Freia, the goddess of beauty of the North; for variety's sake she called herself Venus; that depended altogether on the language of the country in which she appeared. She was of a quiet, cheerful character, she said; but this was the odd day of the leap year, which gives liberty to woman, that she may, according to an old custom, propose to the man she likes, without waiting for him to propose to her.

Last came Saturday, waddling along like an old house-keeper, with broom, dustpan, and other cleansing articles. Her favorite dish was beer soup, but she was not particularly anxious to have it put on the table on that festive occasion.

And thus the weekdays held a banquet, as I have described them; here they are, ready for family use as tableaux. Of course you may improve upon them; we give them only as vignettes for February, the only month that receives a day in addition.

The Storm Moves the Signboards

In olden times, when Grandfather was quite a little boy
and wore red trousers and a red jacket, with a sash round
his waist, and a feather in his cap—for thus in his childhood
little boys were dressed when they were very smart—so many
things were different from what they are now. There were
often pageants in the street—such ones as we do not see
nowadays, for these things are abolished: they became so
old-fashioned; but pleasant it is to hear Grandfather tell of
them.

It must indeed have been a show when the shoemakers
moved signboards, when they changed Corporation Hall.
On their waving silk banner were painted a large boot and a
two-headed eagle; the younger journeymen, with red and
white ribbons fluttering down from their shirt sleeves, carried
the welcome cup and the box; the older ones wore drawn
swords with lemons on the points. There was a full band,
but the finest of all the instruments was "the Bird," as
Grandfather called the long pole with the half-moon, with
all its ringing, tingling, and dangling things—real Turkish
music. It was lifted and swung, and it almost hurt the eyes
to look at it when the sun shone upon all that gold, silver,
and brass.

Before the procession ran Harlequin, in clothes made of
patches of every possible color, and with black face, and

bells on his head just like a sleigh horse; and he beat the people with his wand, that smacked without hurting, and they squeezed each other to get onward; little boys and girls fell over their own legs straight down into the gutters; while old dames elbowed their way, looking cross and scolding. Some laughed, others chatted; there were people on the steps and in the windows—nay, even on the roofs. The sun shone; now and then, indeed, a little rain fell, but that was a good thing for the farmer; and even if enough fell to make the people wringing wet, why, that was a true blessing to the land.

Ah! what things Grandfather could tell! He had, when a little boy seen all that grand show in its fullest splendor. The oldest journeyman of the Corporation delivered a speech from the scaffold where the signboard was hung out; the speech ran in verses just like a piece of poetry, which, indeed, it was; there had been three about it, and before making it, they had drunk a whole bowl of punch, so that it might be really good. And the people gave cheers for the speech, but still more cheers for the Harlequin when he appeared on the scaffold and mimicked the speaker. The fool did his foolery so capitally, and drank beer from drug-measuring glasses, which he then flung out among the people, who grasped them in the air. Grandfather had one of them, which the mortar mixer had caught and given him. It was fun indeed. And the signboard hung, with flowers and wreaths, on the new Corporation Hall.

Such a sight, one never forgets, however old one becomes, Grandfather said; and he, indeed, never forgot it, though afterward he saw much show and grandeur and knew how to tell about it; but funniest of all it was, when he told of the moving of the signboards in the great city.

Grandfather had been there with his parents while he was a little boy; and that was the first time he saw the largest town of the country.

Such a number of people were in the streets, that he thought the "Moving of the Signboards" was just then going on; and there were many signboards to be moved: one might have filled hundreds of rooms with these pictures if they had been hung up inside instead of outdoors. Thus, there were all kinds of garments painted where the tailors lived; they could change people till they became genteel instead of vulgar. There were tobacconists' signboards with the most charming little boys, smoking cigars, just as they do in reality; there were signboards with butter and red herrings, clergymen's ruffs, and coffins; and besides there were other signboards with inscriptions and announcements. Indeed, one might go for a whole day up and down the streets and be gratified by looking at pictures; and then at the same time one learned what people those were who lived inside: they had themselves hung their signs outside; and this is a very good thing, Grandfather said: in a large town it is so instructive to know what is indoors.

Well, then, that funny affair with the signboards happened just as Grandfather came to town; he said so himself, and he was not then thinking of any mischief, as mother used to say he was when he wanted to make a fool of me—he looked quite trustworthy.

The first night after he had come to the great town, there was as awful weather as has ever been told about in the papers—such weather as there had not been within the memory of man. All the air was filled with tiles; old wooden fences were overturned; nay, there was a wheelbarrow that ran by itself along the street to save its life. There was a howling in the air, and a wailing and shaking; it was, indeed, a terrible storm. The water in the canal ran quite over the banks, not knowing where it dared be. The Storm went swooping over the town, taking the chimneys with him; more than one grand old church spire had to bend, and has never been quite right since.

There stood a sentry box before the house of the honest old captain of the firemen—he who was always the last with his engine; the Storm grudged him that little box, and it was flung down the steps, and rolled along the street; and then—strange to say—it arose and remained standing before the house where lived the poor carpenter's apprentice who saved the lives of three persons the last time there was a fire; but the sentry box did not mean anything by this. The barber's signboard—a large brazen dish—was pulled down and moved straight into the councilor's window recess; and this seemed almost like malice, said all the neighbors, who, with the most intimate lady friends of the family, called the mistress "the Razor"—she was so sharp, and knew more about people than they knew themselves.

A signboard with a rough-drawn dry stockfish flew straight on till it stood over the door of a house where lived a man who edited a newspaper. That was a poor joke of the Stormwind; he did not remember, I dare say, that a man who edits newspapers is not at all a person to be joked with: he is a king in his own paper and in his own opinion.

The Weathercock flew over to the roof of the opposite neighbor's house, and stayed there—in the blackest malice, the other neighbors said.

The barrel maker's cask got hung just under the sign for " Ladies' outfits."

The restaurant's bill of fare, which hung near the door in a heavy frame, was placed by the Storm just over the entrance to the theatre, where people never went; it was a funny bill: "Horseradish Soup and Farced Cabbage"; but then people came.

The furrier's foxskin, which is his honest sign, was removed to the bellwire of the young man who always went to the early morning service, looking like an umbrella let down, followed the truth, and was "a pattern," his aunt said.

The inscription, "Establishment for Higher Education,"

was removed to the billiard club; and the establishment itself got the board inscribed, "Babies brought up by hand here": this was not at all witty—only naughty; but the Storm did it, and him we cannot control.

It was a terrible night; and—only think—in the morning almost all the signboards in the town were moved; and in some cases it was done with so much malice, that Grandfather would not talk about them; but he laughed inwardly—that, I well saw, and perhaps he had then some mischievous thought.

The poor folks in the large town—especially those that were strangers—were quite puzzled to know "who was who"; and it could not be otherwise when they judged according to the signboards. Some folks who thought they were coming into a very grave meeting of elders, assembled to discuss the most important matters, came instead into a school, full of noisy boys, nearly jumping upon the desks.

There were folks who mistook the church for the theatre; and that is indeed deadful!

Such a Storm has never blown in our time; it is only Grandfather who lived to witness it, and then he was quite a little one; such a Storm, perhaps, never will come in our time, but in our grandchildren's; and then we must indeed hope and pray that they may keep quiet while "the Storm moves the Signboards."

The Porter's Son

The general's family lived on the drawing-room floor, the Porter's lived in the cellar. There was a great distance between the two families—the whole ground floor and the grades of society; but both lived under the same roof, and their windows looked out upon the street and the same yard. In this yard there was a blooming acacia—whenever it did bloom; and the smart nurse used to sit under it with the still smarter child, the General's "Little Emily." The Porter's little boy, with his large brown eyes and dark hair, used to dance bare-legged before them; and the child would laugh at him, and stretch her tiny hands to him; and if the General saw this from his window, he would nod down at them, and say, "*Charmant!*" The General's lady, who was so young that she might almost have been her husband's daughter by an early marriage, never herself looked out of the window into the yard; but she had given orders that the cellar-people's boy might play about near her own child, but never touch it. The nurse kept strictly to her ladyship's orders.

And the sun shone in upon those on the drawing-room floor, and upon those in the cellar. The acacia put forth its blossoms; they fell off, and new ones came again next year. The tree bloomed, and the Porter's little boy bloomed; he looked quite like a fresh tulip.

The General's little daughter grew a delicate child, like
the faint rosy leaf of the acacia blossom. She seldom came
now under the tree; the fresh air she took in a carriage.
She went with mamma for her drives and she always nodded
to the Porter's George; aye, and kissed her fingers at him, till
her mother told her that she was now grown too big for that.

One morning he had to go up to the General's floor with
the letters and newspapers which had been left at the Porter's
lodge in the morning. When he had mounted the staircase,
and was passing the door of the sand bin, he heard something
wailing inside it. He thought it was a stray chicken chirping
to get out; and lo! it was the General's little daughter in
muslin and lace!

"Don't tell papa and mamma; they will be so angry!"

"What is the matter, little lady?" asked George.

"It's burning all over!" said she; "it's burning and
blazing!"

George opened the door to the little nursery; the window-
curtain was nearly burned: the curtain rod had caught fire,
and stood in flames. George sprang up, pulled it down, and
called for help; without him there would have been a house
on fire.

The General and her ladyship examined little Emily.

"I only just took one match," said she, "and that lighted
up, and then the curtain lighted up. I spit all I could, but it
was no good, and so I came out and hid myself, for papa
and mamma would be so angry."

"Spit!" said the General; "what sort of word is that?
When did you ever hear papa or mamma talk of spitting?
That you have learned downstairs."

But little George got a penny. It did not go to the candy
store, but into the saving box; and there were soon so many
pennies that he could buy himself a paint box, and put color
to his drawings; and of these he had many: they seemed to

come out of his pencil and his finger ends. The first colored pictures were presented to little Emily.

"*Charmant!*" said the General. Her ladyship herself admitted that one could see clearly enough what the little one meant in his pictures. "There's genius in him!"

Such were the words which the Porter's wife brought down into the cellar.

The General and his lady were people of rank: they had two armorial shields on their carriage, one for each of them. Her ladyship had arms worked on every bit of clothing inside and out, on her nightcap, and on her night bag. This, her own shield, was a costly one, bought by her father for shining dollars; for he had not been born with it, no, nor she either; she had come into the world prematurely, seven years before the shield of arms; a fact that was remembered by most people, though not by the family. The General's shield was old and large; one's back might well creak with the dignity of this alone, to say nothing of two shields; and there was a creaking in the back of her ladyship, when stiff and stately she drove to the court ball.

The General was old and gray, but sat well on horseback; he was quite aware of it, and rode out every day, with a groom at a respectful distance behind him. When he came to a party, it was just as if he came riding in on his high horse, and he wore orders enough to bewilder one; but that was not by any means *his* fault. As a very young man he had performed military duties, by taking a part in the great autumnal reviews, which used to be held in the piping days of peace. Of that time he had an anecdote to tell, the only one he had. His lieutenant cut off and took prisoner one of the princes; and the Prince with his little troop of soldiers, prisoners like himself, had to ride back to town behind the General. It was an event never to be forgotten, and the General told and retold it, year after year, always ending with the remarkable words which he had spoken when he returned the Prince's saber to him: "Only my lieutenant could have made your Royal Highness a prisoner, I myself—never!" and the Prince had answered: "Monsieur, you are incomparable!"

In active service the General had never been; for when the war went through his native land, he went on the diplomatic road, through three foreign countries. He talked the French language till he almost forgot his own; he danced well, he rode well, orders grew on his coat in indescribable profusion, the sentinels presented arms to him, one of the prettiest of girls presented herself to him—and she became the General's lady; and they had a pretty babe that seemed to have fallen from the sky, it was so pretty; and the Porter's son danced in the yard before it as soon as it could take notice, and gave it all his colored drawings; and it looked at them, and was delighted with them, and tore them to pieces. She was such a dear sweet little thing!

"My rose leaf!" said the General's lady, "thou art born to be a prince's bride!"

The Prince was already standing outside the door, though nobody knew of it. People cannot see much further than the doorstep.

"T'other day our George shared his bread and butter with her, that he did!" said the Porter's wife. "There was no cheese, nor yet meat with it; yet she relished it every bit as well as roast beef. There'd have been a fine to-do if some folks had seen the little feast; but they didn't see it."

George had shared bread and butter with little Emily; gladly would he have shared his heart with her. He was a good boy, clever and sprightly; and he now went to the evening school at the Academy in order to learn drawing thoroughly. Little Emily, too, made some progress in learning: she talked French with her "Bonne," and had a dancing-master.

" George is to be confirmed at Easter," said the Porter's wife. So far advanced now was George.

" It wouldn't be amiss either to have him 'prenticed," said the father, " to something tidy, of course; and so we shall get him out in the world."

" He would come home, though, to sleep at nights," said the mother. " It wouldn't be easy to find a master with a spare room. Clothes, too, we should have to give him: the bit of food he now eats is easily come at, he can make himself happy with a couple of baked potatoes; and he has his teaching free. Just let him go his own way, and he'll turn out a blessing to us, you may be sure! Didn't the Professor say so? "

The confirmation clothes were ready. Mother herself did the sewing, but they had been cut out by the jobber, and he knew how to cut them: if he'd only been better placed, and could have opened a shop and taken 'prentices, said the Porter's wife, the man might have become court tailor.

The clothes were ready, and the candidate was ready. On the confirmation day George received a great imitation-gold watch from his godfather, the flax dealer's old shopman, the richest of George's godfathers. The watch was old and well tried: it always went too fast, but that is better than going too slow. This was a splendid present; and from the General's came a hymnbook bound in morocco, sent by the little lady to whom George had presented his pictures. On the flyleaf stood his name and her name, and " his gracious well wisher." This was written after the dictation of the General's lady, and the General had read it through, and said, " *Charmant!* "

" That was really a great attention from such grand gentlefolk," said the Porter's wife; and George had to go upstairs in his confirmation clothes, and with his hymnbook, to show himself and return thanks.

Her ladyship sat in a number of wrappings, and she had one of her bad headaches, which always came when she felt *ennui.* She looked kindly at George, and wished him everything that was good, and none of her headache. The General was in his dressing gown, and wore a tasseled cap, and boots with tops of red russia. He paced up and down the floor three times, in thoughts and remembrances of his own, stopped still, and said—

" Little George, then, is now a Christian man! Let him be likewise an honest man, and pay due respect to his superiors! This sentence, some day, when you are old, you can say that the General taught you."

This was a longer speech than the General was accustomed to make; and he fell back into meditation, and looked imposing. But of all that George heard or saw up there, nothing remained fixed in his memory so clearly as little Miss Emily. How winning she looked, how soft, how fluttering, how fragile! If her portrait was to be painted, it must be in a soap bubble. There was a fragrance about her clothes and her curly yellow hair as if she were a fresh-blossomed rose tree. And with her he had once shared bread and butter; and she had eaten it with a sharp appetite, and nodded to him at every mouthful. Could she possibly recollect it still? Surely yes; it was " in remembrance " of this that she had given him the handsome hymnbook. And so, next year, as soon as the New Year's new moon was shining, he went out of doors with a loaf and a shilling in his hand, and opened the book to see what hymn he should turn up. It was a hymn of praise and thanksgiving. And he opened it again to see what would turn up for little Emily. He was mightily careful not to dip into one part of the book—the place of the funeral hymns; and yet, for all his care, he *did* dip in between death and the grave. This was not the sort of thing to believe in; not a bit of it! and yet frightened he was, when soon afterwards the dainty little girl was laid up in bed, and when the hall door was visited daily by the doctor's carriage.

"They'll not keep her," said the Porter's wife; "our Lord knows right well whom He will take to himself."

But they did keep her, and George drew pictures to send her. He drew the castle of the Czar, the old Kremlin at Moscow, exactly as it stood, with turrets and cupolas: they looked like gigantic green and gilt cucumbers—at least, they looked so in George's drawing. It pleased little Emily so much, that in the course of the week George sent some more pictures, all of them buildings; for then she would have plenty to think about, wondering what was inside the door and the windows.

He drew a Chinese house, with bells hanging to all the sixteen stories. He drew two Greek temples, with slender marble pillars and steps round them. He drew a Norwegian church; one could see it was entirely built of timbers, deeply carved and quaintly set up; every story looked as if it had cradle rockers. But most beautiful of all was one design, a castle, which he called "Little Emily's." This was to be her dwelling place, and so George had imagined it all himself, and picked out for it whatever seemed prettiest in each of the other buildings. It had carved beams, like the Norwegian church; marble pillars, like the Greek temples; a peal of bells on every story; and at the top of all, cupolas, green and gilded, like those upon the Kremlin of the Czar. It was a true child's palace! And under every window was written what the hall or chamber was intended for: "Here Emily sleeps": "Here Emily dances": and "Here she is to play at 'visitors coming.' " It was amusing to look at, and looked at it was, you may be sure.

"*Charmant!*" said the General.

But the old Count—for there was an old Count, who was even grander than the General, and had a castle and mansion of his own—said nothing He had been told that this had been imagined and drawn by the Porter's little son. Not that the boy was so very little now; indeed, he was confirmed.

The old Count looked at the pictures, and had his own quiet thoughts about them.

One morning, when the weather was downright gray, damp and dismal, it proved one of the brightest and best of days for little George. The Professor at the Art Academy called him into his private room.

"Listen, my lad," said he; "let us have a little talk together. Our Lord has favored you with good abilities; he is now favoring you with good friends. The old Count at the corner house has spoken to me about you. I have seen your pictures also; between ourselves, we may cross them out, they require so much correction. But henceforward you may come twice a week to my drawing school, and so learn in time to do better. I believe there is more stuff in you to make an architect than a painter. This you will have time to consider; but go up at once to the old Count at the corner house, and give thanks to our Lord for such a friend."

It was a fine mansion, that corner house: round the windows were carved figures, both elephants and dromedaries, all of the olden time; but the old Count was fondest of the modern time, and whatever good it brought, whether out of drawing room, or the cellar, or the garret.

"I do think," said the Porter's wife, "that the more folks are really grand, the less they are stuck up. You should see the old Count, ever so sweet and affable! and he can talk, bless you, just like you and me—you won't find that at the General's. There was George yesterday, clean upside down with delight, the Count treated him so graciously; and I am much the same today, after getting a talk with the great man. Wasn't it lucky now, that we didn't prentice George to a trade? The boy has good parts in him."

"But they must have help from outside," said the father.

"Well, and now he has got help," said the mother. "The Count spoke out, plain and straightforward, that he did."

"It was at the General's thought, that it was all set going," said the father: "they must have their turn of thanks, too."

"They may have it, and welcome," said the mother; "yet there's not overmuch to thank them for, I reckon. I'll thank our Lord above all, and thank Him all the more, now that little Emily is coming round again."

Emily kept getting on, and George kept getting on; in the course of the year he won, first the small silver medal, and then the great one.

"It would have been better, after all, to have 'prenticed him!" said the Porter's wife, in tears; "we should have kept him here, then. What does he want in Rome? Never more shall I set eyes on him, even if he ever comes home again; and that he won't do, poor dear child!"

"But it's for his own good and glory," said the father.

"Ah! it's all very fine talking, husband," said the mother, "but you don't mean what you say. You are just as down-hearted as I am."

And it was all true, both as to the grief and the going away. It was a grand piece of luck for the young man, said the neighbors.

And there was a round of leave-taking, including the General's. Her ladyship did not appear; she had her bad headache. The General at parting related his only anecdote—what he had said to the Prince, and how the Prince had said to him, "Monsieur, you are incomparable!" and then he gave George his hand—his slack old hand.

Emily, too, gave George her hand, and looked almost dismal; but there was no one so dismal as George.

Time goes on. Whether one is busy or idle. Time is equally long, though not equally profitable. To George it was profitable, and never seemed long, except when he thought of those at home: how were they getting on, upstairs and downstairs? Well, tidings were sent of them: and so much may be wrapped up in a letter—both the bright sunshine and the gloomy shade. The shade of death lay in the letter, that told him his mother was left a lonesome widow. Emily had been an angel of comfort: "she had come down below, she had," wrote mother. As for herself, she added, she had got leave to take father's post at the Porter's lodge.

The General's lady kept a diary: every ball was entered in it, every party she had been to, and every visit she had received. The volume was illustrated with cards of diplomatists, and other grandees. She was proud of her diary; it increased in growth, season after season, during many great headaches, but also during many bright nights—that is to say, court balls.

Emily had now been to her first court ball. The mother was in pink, with black lace—Spanish; the daughter was in white, so clear, so fine! green ribbons fluttered, like bulrush-leaves, in her curly yellow locks, and she was crowned with a wreath of white water lilies. With her sparkling blue eyes, and soft, rosy lips, she resembled a little mermaid, as beautiful as one could imagine. Three princes danced with her, one after another. Her ladyship had no headache for a whole week.

But the first ball was not the last. It was getting too much for Emily; and so it was well that summer came, with rest and change of air. The family was invited to the castle of the old Count.

This castle had a garden worth seeing. One part of it was quite in the old style, with stiff, green alleys, where one seemed to be walking between tall green screens, pierced with peeping holes; box trees and yew trees stood clipped into stars and pyramids; water sprang from great grottoes, set with cockelshells; stone figures stood all round about, of the very heaviest stone, as one could plainly perceive by the faces and draperies; every flower bed had its own device— such as a fish, a heraldic shield, or a monogram: this was the

French part of the garden. From this part one came out, as it were, into the fresh wildwood, where the trees could grow as they pleased, and were therefore great and splendid. There was a green turf, inviting one's feet to tread on it, well mown, well rolled, and well kept altogether. This was the English part of the garden.

"Olden times and modern times!" said the Count: "here they meet with loving embraces. In about two years the house itself will assume its proper importance. It will undergo a perfect change into something handsomer and better. I will show you the plans, and I will show you the architect; he is coming here to dinner."

"*Charmant!*" said the General.

"This garden is paradisiacal!" said her ladyship; "and yonder you have a baronial castle."

"That is my hen house," said the Count; "the pigeons live in the tower, the turkeys on the first floor, but in the parlor reigns old Dame Else. She has spare rooms on all sides; this for the sitting hen, that for the hen and chickens, while the ducks have their own outlet to the water."

"*Charmant!*" repeated the General, and they all went to see the fine show.

Old Else stood in the middle of the parlor, and beside her stood the architect—George! He and little Emily met—after so many years—met in the hen house.

Aye, there he stood a comely figure to look at: his countenance open and determined, his hair black and glossy, and his mouth with a smile that said, "There is a little rogue behind my ear, that knows you outside and inside!" Old Else had taken off her wooden shoes and stood in her stockings, out of respect for her illustrious visitors. The hens clucked, the cock crowed, and the ducks waddled along, rap, rap. But the pale slender girl, the friend of his childhood, the General's daughter, stood before him; her pale cheeks flushing with the rose, her eyes opening eagerly, and her mouth speaking without uttering a syllable. Such was the greeting he received; the prettiest that any young man could desire from a young lady; unless, indeed, they were of the same family, or had often danced together; but these two had never danced together.

The Count grasped his hand and presented him, saying, "Not a complete stranger, our young friend, Mr. George."

Her ladyship curtsied; her daughter was about to give him her hand, but she did not give it him.

"Our little Mr. George!" said the General. "Old house-friends: *charmant!*"

"You have grown quite an Italian," said her ladyship; "and you speak the language, no doubt, like a native."

Her ladyship could sing Italian, but not speak it, added the General.

At the dinner table George sat at the right hand of Emily. The General had led her in; and the Count had led in her ladyship.

George talked, and told anecdotes, and he could tell them well. He was the life and soul of the party; though the old Count could have been so too, if it had suited him. Emily sat silent; her ears listened, her eyes shone, but she said nothing.

They stood, she and George, among the flowers in the veranda behind a screen of roses. It was left to George again to begin speaking.

"Thanks for your kindness to my mother," said he; "I know that, on the night of my father's death, you went down and stayed with her, till his eyes were closed. Thanks!" He raised Emily's hand, and kissed it; he might fairly do so on that occasion. She grew blushing red; but pressed his hand in return, and looked at him with her tender blue eyes.

"Your mother was a loving soul; how fond she was of you! All your letters she brought me to read, so I seem almost to know you. I remember too when I was little, how kind you were to me. You gave me pictures "—

" Which you tore in pieces," said George.

" Nay, I have still my own castle left—that drawing of it."

" And now I must build it in reality! " said George, and grew quite hot himself as he said it.

The General and his lady, in their own rooms, talked about the Porter's son. Why, he could express himself with knowledge, with refinement! " He is fit to be engaged as a tutor," said the General.

" Genius! " said her ladyship; and that was all she said.

Again and again, in those fine summer days, did George come to the castle of the Count. He was missed when he did not come.

" How much more God has given to you than to us ordinary mortals! " said Emily to him. " Are you grateful for that now? "

It flattered George, that this fair young girl should look up to him, and he thought she had rare powers of appreciation.

And the General felt more and more convinced that Mr. George could hardly be a genuine child of the cellar. " Otherwise, the mother was a right honest woman," said he; " that sentence I owe to her epitaph! "

Summer went; winter came; and there was more to tell about Mr. George. He had received notice and favor in the highest of high places. The General had met him at the court ball.

And now there was to be a ball at home, for little Emily. Could Mr. George be invited?

" Whom the King invites, the General can invite! " said the General, and drew himself up a good inch higher.

Mr. George was invited, and he came. And princes and counts came, and each danced better than the other. But Emily danced only the first dance, for in the course of it she sprained her ankle, not dangerously, but enough to give her pain; and so she had to be prudent, and stop dancing, and look on at the others. And there she sat, looking on, while the architect stood by her side.

"You are giving her the whole of St. Peter's at Rome," said the General, as he passed, smiling like benevolence itself.

With the same smile of benevolence he received Mr. George a few days afterward. The young man came to thank him for the ball, of course. Was there anything else to say? Yes, indeed, astounding—amazing—raving madness, that was all! The General could scarcely believe his own ears. A "pyramidal declamation!" an unheard-of proposition! Mr. George asked for little Emily as his wife!

"Man!" said the General, and he began to boil, "I cannot understand you! What is it you say? What is it you want? I don't know you. Sir! Fellow! you choose to come and break into my house! am I to stay here, or am I not?" And he backed out into his bedroom, and locked the door. George stood alone for a few moments, and then turned on his heel. In the corridor he met Emily.

"My father answered?"—she asked, with a trembling voice.

George pressed her hand. "He ran away from me—a better time will come."

There were tears in Emily's eyes: in those of the young man were courage and confidence; and the sun shone in upon them both and blessed them.

In his bedroom sat the General, boiling more and more; boiling over, and sputtering out "Lunacy! Porter-madness!"

Before an hour was past, the General's lady learned it all from the General's own mouth, and she called for Emily, and sat alone with her.

"Poor girl," she said; "to think of his insulting you so, insulting us all! You have tears in your eyes, I see: they are quite becoming to you. You look charming in tears. You remind me of myself on my wedding day. Go on crying, little Emily."

" That I must, indeed! " said Emily, " unless you and papa say 'Yes!'"

" Child," cried her ladyship, " you are ill! you are delirious! and I am getting my dreadful headache! O, the miseries that are coming down upon our house! Do not let your mother die, Emily; then you will have no mother."

And her ladyship's eyes were wet: she could not bear to think of her own death.

Among other announcements in the *Gazette* might be seen: " Mr. George, appointed Professor, 5th class, No. 8."

" What a pity his father and mother are in the grave, and can't read it! " said the new porter folks, who now lived in the cellar under the General. They knew that the Professor had been born and bred within the four walls.

" Now he'll come in for the title tax! " said the man.

" Well, it's no such mighty matter for a poor child! " said the wife.

" Eighteen rix-dollars a years! " said the man. " *I* call it a good round sum."

" No, no; it's the title *I'm* talking of! " said the wife. " You don't suppose he'll be bothered by having the tax to pay? He can earn as much over and over again, and a rich wife into the bargain. If we had little ones, husband, a child of ours, too, would some day be architect and professor."

Thus George was well mentioned in the cellar, and he was well mentioned on the drawing-room floor: the old Count took good care of that.

It was the old set of childish picture drawings that introduced his name. But how came these to be mentioned? Why, the talk turned upon Russia, upon Moscow: and thus one was led right up to the Kremlin, of which our friend George made a drawing once, when he was little, for the

little Miss Emily. What a number of pictures he used to draw!
one the Count especially remembered—"Little Emily's
Castle," with scrolls showing where she slept, where she
danced, and where she played at "Visitors coming." The
Professor had great ability. He might live to be an old veteran
privy counselor—that was not at all improbable: aye, and
build a real castle for the young lady before he died—why
not?

"That was a strange burst of vivacity," remarked the
General's lady, when the Count was gone. The General
nodded his head, thoughtfully, and went out riding, with his
groom at a respectful distance behind him, and he sat prouder
than ever on his high horse.

Little Emily's birthday came, bringing cards and notes,
books and flowers. The General kissed her on the brow, and
her ladyship kissed her on the lips. They were patterns of
parental affection; and they were all three honored with high
visitors—two of the princes. Then there was talk about balls
and theatres, about diplomatic embassies, and the govern-
ment of kingdoms and empires. There was talk about rising
men, about native talent; and this brought up the name of
the young professor, Mr. George, the architect.

"He is building for immortality!" it was said; "meanwhile
he is building himself into one of the first families."

"One of the first families!" repeated the General, when
he was left alone with her ladyship: "which one of our first
families?"

"I can guess which was alluded to," said her ladyship;
"but I don't choose to speak, nor even think of it. God may
ordain it so, but I shall be quite astounded!"

"Astounded!" echoed the General. "Look at me; I haven't
a single idea in my head!" and he sank into a reverie, waiting
for thoughts to come.

There is an unspeakable power bestowed on a many by
a few dewdrops of grace—grace from above—whether the

grace of kings, or the grace of God; and both of these combined in favor of little George.

But we are forgetting the birthday.

Emily's chamber was fragrant with flowers, sent by her friends and playmates: on her table lay fine presents, tokens of greeting and remembrance; but not one from George. Gifts from him would not have reached her, but they were not needed; the whole house was a remembrance of him. From the very sand bin under the stairs peeped a memorial flower, even as Emily had peeped, when the curtain was in flames, and George rushed up as first fireman. One glance out of the window, and the acacia tree reminded her of the days of childhood. Blossoms and leaves were gone, but the tree stood in hoarfrost, like a vast branch of coral; and full and clear between the branches shone the moon, unchanged though ever changing, the same as when boy George shared his bread and butter with baby Emily.

She opened a drawer and took out the pictures—the Kremlin of the Czar, and her own castle—keepsakes from George. They were looked on and mused upon, and thought after thought kept rising. She remembered the day when, unmarked by father or mother, she stole down to where the Porter's wife lay breathing her last; she sat by her side, held her hand, and heard her dying words, "Blessing— George!" The mother was thinking of her son. But now, to Emily, the words seemed to bear a deeper meaning. In good truth, George was with her on her birthday.

The next day, as it happened, was another birthday, the General's own, for he had been born the day after his daughter—naturally earlier, many years earlier. Again there came presents; and among the rest a saddle of a peculiar make, and comfortable and costly; there was only one of the princes who had the fellow to it. From whom could it have come? The General was in ecstasy. It bore a little ticket. Now, if this had said, "Thanks for yesterday," any of us could have guessed whom it came from, but the ticket said, "From one whom the General does not know."

"Who in the world is there I do not know?" said the General. "I know everybody," and his thoughts went paying visits in the great world. He knew them all there, one and all. "It comes from my wife!" he said, at last. "She is making fun of me! *Charmant!*"

But she was not making fun of him; that time was gone by.

Once more there was a feast; but not at the General's. It was a fancy ball given by one of the princes: masking was allowed there.

The General went as Rubens, in a Spanish dress with a small ruff, upright as his rapier. Her ladyship was Madame Rubens, in black velvet, a high bodice, terribly warm, and her neck in a millstone, that is to say, in a large ruff. She looked the image of a Dutch painting of the General's, the hands in which were especially admired, and were thought exactly like those of her ladyship.

Emily was Psyche, in muslin and lace. She was a floating tuft of swan's-down; she was in no need of wings, and only wore them as the Psyche badge.

It was a scene of pomp and splendor, lights and flowers, magnificence and taste. One had hardly time to pay attention to Madame Rubens and her beautiful hands.

A black Domino, with an acacia flower in his hood, danced with Psyche.

"Who is he?" asked the General's lady.

"His Royal Highness," said the General. "I am quite sure of that. I knew him at once by his hand-salute."

Her ladyship doubted.

General Rubens did not doubt. He drew near the black Domino, and wrote royal initials on the palm of his hand. They were not acknowledged; but a certain hint was given in return: the motto of the saddle!—" One whom the General does not know! "

"Yet something I do know of you," said the General; "it was you who sent me the saddle."

The Domino waved his hand, and disappeared among the others.

"Who is the black Domino you have been dancing with, Emily? " asked her mother.

"I did not ask his name," she answered.

"Because you knew it! It is the Professor. Your protégé, Count, is there," she continued, turning to the Count, who stood close by; "the black Domino with the acacia flower."

"Very likely, your ladyship," he replied; "but still, there is one of the princes in the same costume."

"I know that hand-salute," said the General. "From the Prince I received the saddle! I feel so sure of my man, that I would ask him to dinner."

"Do so," said the Count; "if it's the Prince he will be sure to come."

"And if it is the other he will not come," said the General; and made his way to the black Domino, who stood talking with the King. The General offered him a most respectful invitation, together with hopes of better acquaintance. The General smiled in full confidence, he knew so well whom he was inviting, and he spoke aloud and distinctly.

The Domino lifted his mask; it was George!

"Does the General repeat his invitation? " he asked.

The General drew himself an inch higher, assumed a stiffer bearing, took two steps backward, and one step forward, as if dancing a minuet; and all the gravity and expression he could muster—*all the General*, in short—stood in his fine features.

"I never retract my offers—the Professor is invited! " and he bowed, with a sidelong glance at the King, who might certainly have heard the whole of it.

And thus the General gave a dinner, at which his only guests were the old Count and his protégé.

" My foot under the table! " thought George; " the foundation stone is laid." And so it was indeed; and it was laid with great solemnity on the part of the General and her ladyship.

The man had come and gone; and, as the General was quite ready to confess, had behaved like a member of good society, and had been vastly agreeable; the General had often found himself repeating his " *Charmant.*" Her ladyship also talked of her dinner; talked of it to one of the highest and most highly gifted of the court ladies, and the latter begged an invitation for herself, next time the Professor came. So he must needs be reinvited. And invited he was, and came, and again he was " *Charmant* "; he could even play at chess!

" He is not from the cellar," said the General. " Most undoubtedly he is some scion of nobility—there are many such noble scions—and that is not any fault of the young man's! "

Mr. Professor could enter the King's house, and so might very well enter the General's; but strike root there—no! Who could talk of such a thing?—Why, the whole town, that was all.

He did strike root, and he grew. The dew of grace fell from above.

There was nobody, therefore, astonished that, when the Professor became State Counselor, Emily became *State Counseloress.* " Life is tragedy or comedy," said the General: " in tragedy they die; in comedy they win each other."

Here they won each other. And they won three sturdy boys, though not all at once.

The sweet children rode on sticks from room to room, whenever they came to see grandfather and grandmother. And the General rode on a stick behind them, " as groom for the small State Counselors! "

Her ladyship sat on the sofa and smiled, even if she had got her bad headache.

So far did George get on in the world, and much farther too; or else it would not have been worth my while to tell the story of " The Porter's Son."

Aunty

You should have known Aunty. She was so charming. Yes; that is to say, not at all charming in the usual sense of charming, but sweet and quaint, and funny in her own way; just the thing, in short, to chat about, when one feels in the mood for gossiping and laughing. She was fit to be put in a play; and that simply and solely because she herself lived for the theatre, and all that goes on in it. She was far above any scandal; and even Commercial Agent Bigg (or Pig, as Aunty called him) could only say she was stage struck.

"The theatre is my schoolroom," said she; "my fountain of knowledge. There I have rubbed up my old Bible history; take ' Moses,' for instance, or ' Joseph and his Brethren '; they are operas now. It is there that I have studied my General History, my Geography, and foreign Manners and Customs. From French pieces I have learned Paris life— rather naughty, but highly interesting. How I have cried over the ' Riguebourg Family '; to think that the husband must drink himself to death, and all to let his wife get her young sweetheart. Aye, many and many's the tear I've shed, all those fifty years of playgoing."

Aunty knew every piece, every bit of scenery, every actor that came on, or ever had come on. She could hardly be said to live, except in the nine theatrical months. A summer without a summer spectacle was enough to age her; while a play night that lasted till morning was a prolongation of life. She did not say like other people, "We shall soon have spring: the stork is come!" or "There is news in the paper of the early strawberries!" No; the autumn was what she announced, thus: "Have you seen the box office is open; they'll soon begin the performances."

She reckoned the worth of a house and its situation by its distance from the theatre. It was grief to her to leave the narrow court behind the theatre, and flit to the wide street a little further off, and live there without any opposite neighbors.

"At home my windows should be my theatre box. One can't sit there in the dumps, never seeing a soul. But where I live now I seem to be clean out in the country; not a living creature in sight unless I go into the back kitchen, and clamber up on the sink; that's the only way of getting at my neighbors. Now, in that old court of mine, I could look right into the flax dealer's; and then I had only three hundred steps to take to the theatre; now it takes me three thousand steps, and trooper's steps too."

Aunty might sometimes be out of sorts; but, well or ill, she never neglected the theatre. Her doctor ordered her, one evening, to put her feet in poultices; she did as he told her; but rode off to the theatre, and sat there with her feet in poultices. If she had died there, she would have been contented. Thorwaldsen died in the theatre; this she called "a blessed death."

She could not form any notion of heaven if there was to be no theatre there. It was not exactly promised us: but only think of all the great actors and actresses who had gone before; surely they must find some fresh scene of action.

Aunty had her own electric wire from the theatre to her room; the telegram came every Sunday to coffee. Her electric wire was "Mr. Sivertsen of the stage machinery department."

The Steadfast Tin Soldier (Monaco, 5 years old)
(STORY PAGE 123)

It was he who gave the signals for up or down, on or off, with the curtain and scenery.

From him she received a brief and businesslike report of the coming pieces. Shakespeare's *Tempest* he called "wretched stuff! there is so much to set up! why, it begins with water to back-scene No. 1." That was to say, that so far backward stretched the rolling billows. On the other hand, if a piece could get through five acts without a single change of decorations, he pronounced it sensible and well constructed; a steady-going piece that could play itself, without any pushing or pulling.

Aunty used to talk about "a goodish time back," meaning some thirty and odd years, when she and Mr. Sivertsen were both younger; how he was then already in the machinery department, and how he became her "benefactor." In those days it was the custom, at the great and only theatre of the town, to admit spectators into the cockloft; every carpenter could dispose of one or two places. It was soon chockfull; and the company was very select; the wives of generals and aldermen had been there, it was said; it was so interesting to look down behind the scenes, and observe how the performers stood and moved, when the curtain was down.

Aunty had many times been there; especially to tragedies and ballets: for the pieces that required the largest *personale* were the most interesting to see from the cockloft. One sat up there in darkness pretty nearly. Most people brought their suppers with them. Once three apples, a slice of bread and butter, and a sausage roll came straight down into the prison where *Ugolino* and his sons were about to die of hunger. This sausage roll produced a great effect. It was cheered by the public; but it determined the managing committee to shut up the cockloft.

"But still, I have been there seven-and-thirty times," said Aunty; "and that I shall always remember of Mr. Sivertsen."

On the very last evening that the cockloft was open to the

public, the *Judgment of Solomon* was played; Aunty could remember it so well. From her benefactor, Mr. Sivertsen, she had obtained a ticket for Agent Bigg. Not that he deserved one; he was always flouting and fleering at the theatre, and quizzing her about it; still she did get him a place in the cockloft. He wanted to look at the playhouse articles wrong side uppermost: "these were his very words, and just like him," said Aunty.

So he saw the *Judgment of Solomon* from above, and fell asleep. It was easy to guess that he had been dining out and joining in several toasts. He slept till he was locked in, and sat the whole dark night in the theatre loft. He had a story to tell of his waking up; but Aunty did not believe a bit of it. The play was played out, the lamps and lights were all out, all the people were out, above and beneath; but then began the after-piece, the genuine comedy, the best of all, said the agent. There came life into the properties; it was not *Solomon's Judgment* that was given now, but *Judgment Day at the Theatre*. And all this did Agent Bigg, in his impudence, try to cram into Aunty; that was her thanks for getting him into the cockloft.

What the agent went on to tell might be comical enough, but there was mockery and spite at the bottom of it.

"It was dark up there," said the agent; "but then began the demon-show, the grand spectacle, *Judgment Day at the Theatre*. Check takers stood at the doors, and every spectator had to show his spiritual testimonial, to settle whether he was to enter freehanded or handcuffed, and with or without a gag in his mouth. Fine gentlefolk, who came too late, when the performance had already begun, and young fellows given to losing their time, were tethered outside. There they were shod with felt, so as to creep in gently before the next act, besides being gagged. And so began *Judgment Day at the Theatre*."

The Little Match Girl (Egypt, 11 years old)
(STORY PAGE 187)

" Mere spite," said Aunty; " which our Lord knows nothing of."

The scene painter, if he wished to get into heaven, had to clamber up some stairs which he had painted himself, but which were too high for the longest pair of legs. That, to be sure, was only a sin against perspective. All the trees, flowers, and buildings, which the machinist had taken such pains to plant in lands quite foreign to them, the poor wretch had to transplant into their proper homes, and all before cockcrow, if he looked for any chance of heaven. Mr. Bigg had better mind his own chances of getting there! And then to hear what he told of the performers, both in tragedy and comedy, in song and in dance—why, it was shameful of Mr. Bigg! Mr. *Pig* indeed! he never deserved his place in the cockloft. Aunty would not believe him on his oath. It was all written out, he said; and he swore (the pig!) it should be printed when he was dead and buried—not before, he had no wish to be flayed alive.

Aunty had once been in terror and anguish in her own temple of happiness, the theatre. It was a winter day; one of those days when we have just two hours of foggy daylight. It was bleak and snowy; but Aunty was bound for the theatre. They were to give *Herman von Unna* besides a little opera and a great ballet, a prologue and an epilogue: it would last over the night. Aunty must needs be off: her lodger had lent her a pair of winter boots, shaggy both outside and inside; they reached the whole way up the legs.

She came to the theatre and into her box; the boots were warm, so she kept them on. Suddenly there arose a cry of " Fire! " Smoke came from one of the wings, smoke came from the cockloft; there was a frightful uproar. People stormed out. Aunty sat furthest from the door. " Second tier, lefthand side; the decorations tell best there," she used to say; " they are always arranged to look prettiest from the king's side of the house." Aunty now wished to get out of it, but

those before her, in their blundering excitement, slammed
the door fast. There stood Aunty; there was no way out, and
no way in, for the next box had too high a partition. She
called; nobody heard her. She looked over at the tier
underneath; it was empty; the balustrade was low; there was
not far to drop. In her fright she felt young and active. She
prepared for a jump. She got one foot on the bench, the other
over the balustrade; and there she sat astride, well draped
in her flowered skirt, with a long leg dangling below it,
displaying an enormous boot. That was a sight to see! Seen
it was, and Aunty heard at last; and she easily saved, for
there was no fire to speak of.

That was the most memorable evening in her life, she used
to say; and she thanked Heaven she did not see herself, or
she would have died of shame.

Her benefactor in the machinery department, Mr. Sivertsen,
came to her regularly every Sunday. But it was a long time
from Sunday to Sunday. Latterly, therefore, in the middle
of the week, a small child came up for " the leavings "; that
is to say, to make a supper off the remains of Aunty's dinner.

This child was a young member of the ballet, only too
happy to get a meal. She used to tread the boards as a page
or a fairy. Her hardest part was that of hindlegs for the lion
in Mozart's *Magic Flute*. She grew up in time to be forelegs;
for this she was only paid three marks, though she had been
paid a rix-dollar when she was hindlegs; but then she had
had to creep about stooping, and panting for want of fresh
air. This was very interesting to know, observed Aunty.

If every one got his deserts, Aunty would have lasted as
long as the theatre. But she could not hold out so long.
Neither did she die in it, but quietly and decently in her
own bed. Meanwhile her dying words were full of meaning;
she asked, " What are they going to play tomorrow? "

She left behind her about five hundred rix-dollars—so at
least we conclude from the yearly income, which amounts

to twenty dollars. The money was left as a legacy to some one or other deserving old spinster, living alone in the world. It was to be used for taking a place on the second tier, left side, every Saturday; for on that day they gave the best pieces. Only one condition was imposed on the legatee. As she sat in the theatre, every Saturday, she was to think of Aunty who lay in her grave.

This was Aunty's Religious Foundation.

The Drop of Water

Surely you know what a microscope is—that wonderful glass which makes everything appear a hundred times larger than it really is. If you look through a microscope at a single drop of ditch water, you will perceive more than a thousand strange-shaped creatures, such as you never could imagine dwelling in the water. It looks not unlike a plateful of shrimps, all jumping and crowding upon each other; and so ferocious are these little creatures, and they will tear off each other's arms and legs without mercy; and yet they are happy and merry after their fashion.

Now there was once an old man, whom all his neighbors called Cribbley Crabbey—a curious name to be sure! He always liked to make the best of everything, and, when he could not manage it otherwise, he tried magic.

So one day he sat with his microscope held up to his eye, looking at a drop of ditch water. O, what a strange sight was that! All the thousand little imps in the water were jumping and springing about, and devouring each other, or pulling each other to pieces.

"Upon my word, this is too horrible!" cried old Cribbley Crabbey; "there must surely be some means of making them live in peace and quiet." And he thought and thought, but still could not hit on the right expedient. "I must give them a color," he said at last; "then I shall be able to see them

more distinctly." And accordingly he let fall into the water
a tiny drop of something that looked like red wine, but in
reality it was witches' blood; whereupon all the strange little
creatures immediately became red all over, not unlike the
Red Indians; the drop of water now seemed a whole townful
of naked wild men.

"What have you there?" inquired another old magician,
who had no name at all, which made him more remarkable
even than Cribbley Crabbey.

"Well, if you can guess what it is," replied Cribbley
Crabbey, "I will give it you; but I warn you, you'll not
find it out so easily."

And the magician without a name looked through the
microscope. The scene now revealed to his eyes actually
resembled a town where all the inhabitants were running
about without clothing; it was a horrible sight! But still more
horrible was it to see how they kicked and cuffed, struggled
and fought, pulled and bit each other. All those that were
lowest must needs strive to get uppermost, and all those
that were highest must be thrust down. "Look, look!" they
seemed to be crying out, "his leg is longer than mine; pah!
off with it! And there is one who has a little lump behind
his ear—an innocent little lump enough, but it pains him,
and it shall pain him more!" And they hacked at it, and
seized hold of him, and devoured him, merely because of this
little lump. Only one of the creatures was quiet, very quiet,
and still; it sat by itself, like a little modest girl, wishing
for nothing but peace and rest. But the others would not
have it so; they pulled the little girl forward, cuffed her, cut
at her, and ate her.

"This is most uncommonly amusing," remarked the
nameless magician.

"Do you think so? Well, but what is it?" asked Cribbley
Crabbey. "Can you guess, or can you not? That's the
question."

"To be sure I can guess," was the reply of the nameless magician, "easy enough. It is either Copenhagen or some other large city; I don't know which, for they are all alike. It is some large city."

"It is a drop of ditch water!" said Cribbley Crabbey.

The Rose Elf

In the midst of the garden grew a rosebush, which was quite covered with roses; and in one of them, the most beautiful of all, there dwelt an Elf. He was so tiny that no human eye could see him. Behind every leaf in the rose he had a bedroom. He was as well formed and beautiful as any child could be, and had wings that reached from his shoulders to his feet. O, what a fragrance there was in his rooms! and how clear and bright were the walls! They were made of the pale pink rose leaves.

The whole day he rejoiced in the warm sunshine, flew from flower to flower, danced on the wings of the flying butterfly, and measured how many steps he would have to take to pass along all the roads and crossroads that are marked out on a single hidden leaf. What we call veins on the leaf were to him highroads and crossroads. Yes, those were long roads for him! Before he had finished his journey the sun went down, for he had begun his work too late!

It became very cold, the dew fell, and the wind blew: now the best thing to be done was to come home. He made what haste he could, but the rose had shut itself up, and he could not get in; not a single rose stood open. The poor little Elf was very much frightened. He had never been out at night before; he had always slumbered sweetly and comfortably behind the warm rose leaves. O, it certainly would be the death of him.

At the other end of the garden there was, he knew, an arbor of fine honeysuckle. The flowers looked like great painted horns, and he wished to go down into one of them to sleep till the next day.

He flew thither. Silence! two people were in there—a handsome young man and a young girl. They sat side by side, and wished that they need never part. They loved each other better than a good child loves its father and mother.

"Yet we must part!" said the young man. "Your brother does not like us, therefore he sends me away on an errand so far over mountains and seas. Farewell, my sweet bride, for that you shall be!"

And they kissed each other, and the young girl wept, and gave him a rose. But, before she gave it him, she impressed a kiss so firmly and closely upon it that the flower opened. Then the little Elf flew into it, and leaned his head against the delicate fragrant walls. Here he could plainly hear them say "Farewell! farewell!" and he felt that the rose was placed on the young man's heart. O, how that heart beat! the little Elf could not go to sleep, it thumped so.

But not long did the rose rest undisturbed on that breast. The man took it out, and as he went lonely through the wood, he kissed the flower so often and so fervently that the little Elf was almost crushed. He could feel through the leaf how the man's lips burned, and the rose itself had opened, as if under the hottest noonday sun.

Then came another man, gloomy and wicked; he was the bad brother of the pretty maiden. He drew out a sharp knife, and while the other kissed the rose the bad man stabbed him to death, and then, cutting off his head buried both head and body in the soft earth under the linden tree.

"Now he's forgotten and gone!" thought the wicked brother; "he will never come back again. He was to have

The Ugly Duckling (United States, 4 years old)
(STORY PAGE 175)

taken a long journey over mountains and seas. One can easily lose one's life, and he has lost his. He cannot come back again, and my sister dare not ask news of him from me."

Then with his feet he shuffled dry leaves over the loose earth, and went home in the dark night. But he did not go alone, as he thought; the little Elf accompanied him. The Elf sat in a dry, rolled-up linden leaf that had fallen on the wicked man's hair as he dug. The hat was now placed over the leaf, and it was very dark in the hat, and the Elf trembled with fear and with anger at the evil deed.

In the morning hour the bad man got home; he took off his hat, and went into his sister's bedroom. There lay the beautiful blooming girl, dreaming of him whom she loved from her heart, and of whom she now believed that he was going across the mountains and through the forests. And the wicked brother bent over her and laughed hideously, as only a fiend can laugh. Then the dry leaf fell out of his hair upon the coverlet; but he did not remark it, and he went out to sleep a little himself in the morning hour. But the Elf slipped forth from the withered leaf, placed himself in the ear of the sleeping girl, and told her, as in a dream, the dreadful history of the murder; described to her the place where her brother had slain her lover and buried his corpse; told her of the blooming linden tree close by it, and said—

"That you may not think it is only a dream that I have told you, you will find on your bed a withered leaf."

And she found it when she awoke. O, what bitter tears she wept! The window stood open the whole day: the little Elf could easily get out to the roses and all the other flowers, but he could not find it in his heart to quit the afflicted maiden. In the window stood a plant, a monthly rosebush: he seated himself in one of the flowers, and looked at the poor girl. Her brother often came into the room, and, in spite of his wicked deed, he always seemed cheerful, but she dared not say a word of the grief that was in her heart.

As soon as the night came, she crept out of the house, went to the wood, to the place where the linden tree stood, removed the leaves from the ground, turned up the earth, and immediately found him who had been slain. O, how she wept, and prayed that she might die also!

Gladly would she have taken the corpse home with her, but that she could not do. Then she took the pale head with the closed eyes, kissed the cold mouth, and shook the earth out of the beautiful hair. "That I will keep," she said. And when she had laid earth upon the dead body, she took the head, and a little sprig of the jasmine that bloomed in the wood where he was buried, home with her.

As soon as she came into her room, she brought the greatest flowerpot she could find: in this she laid the dead man's head, strewed earth upon it, and then planted the jasmine twig in the pot.

"Farewell! farewell!" whispered the little Elf: he could endure it no longer to see all this pain, and therefore flew out to his rose in the garden. But the rose was faded; only a few pale leaves clung to the wild bush.

"Alas! how soon everything good and beautiful passes away!" sighed the Elf.

At last he found another rose, and this became his house; behind its delicate fragrant leaves he could hide himself and dwell.

Every morning he flew to the window of the poor girl, and she was always standing weeping by the flowerpot. The bitter tears fell upon the jasmine spray, and every day, as the girl became paler and paler, the twig stood there fresher and greener, and one shoot after another sprouted forth, little white buds burst out, and these she kissed. But the bad brother scolded his sister, and asked if she had gone mad. He could not bear it, and could not imagine why she was always weeping over the flowerpot. He did not know what closed eyes were there, what red lips had there faded into earth. And she bowed her head upon the flowerpot, and the little Elf of the rose bush found her slumbering there. Then he seated himself in her ear, told her of the evening in the arbor, of the fragrance of the rose, and the love of the elves. And she dreamed a marvelously sweet dream, and while she dreamed her life passed away. She had died a quiet death, and she was in heaven, with him whom she loved.

And the jasmine opened its great white bells. They smelled quite peculiarly sweet; it could not weep in any other way over the dead one.

But the wicked brother looked at the beautiful blooming plant, and took it for himself as an inheritance, and put it in his bedroom, close by his bed, for it was glorious to look upon, and its fragrance was sweet and lovely. The little Rose Elf followed, and went from flower to flower—for in each dwelt a little soul—and told of the murdered young man, whose head was now earth beneath the earth, and told of the evil brother and of the poor sister.

"We know it!" said each soul in the flowers; "we know it: have we not sprung from the eyes and lips of the murdered man? We know it! we know it!"

And then they nodded in a strange fashion with their heads.

The Rose Elf could not at all understand how they could be so quiet, and he flew out to the bees that were gathering honey, and told them the story of the wicked brother. And the bees told it to their Queen, and the Queen commanded that they should all kill the murderer next morning. But in the night—it was the first night that followed upon the sister's death—when the brother was sleeping in his bed, close to the fragrant jasmine, each flower opened, and invisible, but armed with poisonous spears, the flower-souls came out and seated themselves in his ear, and told him bad dreams, and then flew across his lips and pricked his tongue with the poisonous spears.

"Now we have avenged the dead man!" they said, and flew back into the jasmine's white bells.

When the morning came and the windows of the bedchamber were opened, the Rose Elf and the Queen Bee and the whole swarm of bees rushed in to kill him.

But he was dead already. People stood around his bed, and said, "The scent of the jasmine has killed him!" Then the Rose Elf understood the revenge of the flowers, and told it to the Queen and to the bees, and the Queen hummed with the whole swarm around the flowerpot. The bees were not to be driven away. Then a man carried away the flowerpot, and one of the bees stung in the hand, so that he let the pot fall, and it broke in pieces.

Then they beheld the whitened skull, and knew that the dead man on the bed was a murderer.

And the Queen Bee hummed in the air, and sang of the revenge of the bees, and of the Rose Elf, and said that behind the smallest leaf there dwells One who can bring the evil to light, and repay it.

The Wild Swans (Mexico, 10 years old)
(STORY PAGE 91)

The Leapfrog

A flea, a grasshopper, and a leapfrog once wanted to see
which could jump highest; and they invited the whole world,
and everybody else besides who chose to come, to see the
festival. Three famous jumpers were they, as every one would
say, when they all met together in the room.

"I will give my daughter to him who jumps highest,"
exclaimed the King; "for it is not so amusing where there
is no prize to jump for."

The flea was the first to step forward. He had exquisite
manners, and bowed to the company on all sides; for he
had noble blood, and was, moreover, accustomed to the
society of man alone; and that makes a great difference.

Then came the grasshopper. He was considerably heavier,
but he was well-mannered, and wore a green uniform, which
he had by right of birth; he said, moreover, that he belonged
to a very ancient Egyptian family, and that in the house
where he then was he was thought much of. The fact was,
he had been just brought out of the fields, and put in a
pasteboard house, three stories high, all made of court cards
with the colored side inwards; and doors and windows cut
out of the body of the Queen of Hearts. "I sing so well," said
he, "that sixteen native grasshoppers who have chirped from
infancy, and yet had no house built of cards to live in, grew

thinner than they were before for sheer vexation when they heard me."

It was thus that the flea and the grasshopper gave an account of themselves, and thought they were quite good enough to marry a princess.

The leapfrog said nothing; but people gave it as their opinion that he therefore thought the more; and when the house dog snuffed at him with his nose, he confessed the leapfrog was of good family. The old councilor, who had had three orders given him to make him hold his tongue, asserted that the leapfrog was a prophet; for that one could see on his back if there would be a severe or mild winter, and that was what one could not see even on the back of the man who writes the almanac.

"I say nothing, it is true," exclaimed the King; "but I have my own opinion notwithstanding."

Now the trial was to take place. The flea jumped so high that nobody could see where he went to; so they all asserted he had not jumped at all; and that was dishonorable.

The grasshopper jumped only half as high; but he leaped into the King's face, who said that was ill-mannered.

The leapfrog stood still for a long time lost in thought; it was believed at last he would not jump at all.

"I only hope he is not unwell," said the house dog; when, pop! he made a jump all on one side into the lap of the Princess, who was sitting on a little golden stool close by.

Hereupon the King said, "There is nothing above my daugther; therefore to bound up to her is the highest jump that can be made: but for this, one must possess understanding, and the leapfrog has shown that he *has* understanding. He is brave and intellectual."

And so he won the Princess.

"It's all the same to me," said the flea; "she may have the old leapfrog, for all I care. I jumped the highest; but in this world merit seldom meets its reward. A fine exterior is what people look at nowadays."

The flea then went into foreign service, where, it is said, he was killed.

The grasshopper sat without on a green bank, and reflected on wordly things; and he said too, "Yes, a fine exterior is everything—a fine exterior is what people care about." And then he began chirping his peculiar melancholy song, from which we have taken this history; and which may, very possibly, be all untrue, although it does stand here printed in black and white.